HARD LESSONS

Christopher G. Nuttall

Printed in the United States of America.

ISBN: 1523432896
ISBN 13: 9781523432899

http://www.chrishanger.net
http://chrishanger.wordpress.com/
http://www.facebook.com/ChristopherGNuttall

All Comments Welcome!

HISTORIAN'S NOTE

Hard Lessons picks up the story fifty years after the founding of the Solar Union, which was described in *A Learning Experience*.

PROLOGUE

From: *The First Fifty Years:A History of the Solar Union*

People ask, as people do, why the Tokomak – the unquestioned rulers of the largest galactic empire known to exist – never squashed the Solar Union in its early years. A single battle squadron from their navy could have smashed Earth's primitive, makeshift defences with ease. In hindsight, it seems absurd the Tokomak left the human race alone long enough for the Solar Union to grow into a genuine threat.

The answer is quite simple. Earth was *tiny*. As far as the Tokomak were concerned, Earth was a single world, home to a mere seven billion intelligent beings, each one utterly unaware of the giant civilisation that existed beyond the edges of the Solar System. To the Tokomak, Earth was good for nothing more than supplying DNA for cybersoldiers, a practice that required nothing more than kidnapping a few hundred humans from isolated locations around the planet. There was no reason to assume that Earth would become a threat. Indeed, when the Tokomak thought about it – if they ever bothered to do so – they almost certainly believed that humanity would become a client state. The idea that Earth would serve as the birthplace of the next great galactic empire would have seemed laughable, on a par with Micronesia growing to dominate the world.

Earth's isolation from galactic affairs, however, was precisely what prevented the destruction of the human race. There was no formal attempt to make contact with the human race, nor was there any large-scale attempt to take humans into the galactic mainstream (although rumours of alien abduction were prevalent on Earth, for reasons unknown). Instead, the last alien race to visit Earth was the Horde – a group of barbaric aliens who had obtained ships from a more advanced race, ships they simply didn't know how to operate properly. When they abducted a number of humans, all former military personnel, those humans broke free and took control of the Horde starship. Humanity's first steps into interstellar space had begun.

Those humans, sceptical of their governments, chose to establish their own government in the Solar System and invite others to join them. Within months, combining Galactic technology with human ingenuity, the Solar Union had set up colonies on Luna, Mars and various asteroids. In addition, the introduction of some alien technology on Earth helped to solve the ongoing military, political and financial crisis threatening the planet's stability.

Most significantly of all, however, was human involvement in the ongoing border war between a coalition of alien races and the Tokomak-backed Varnar (who had been responsible for abducting a number of humans from Earth). By the time the Tokomak finally noticed that the war was not going in their favour, humanity had some powerful allies and friends among the Galactics.

They were going to need them.

ONE

...Based upon reports from operatives and private news agencies, we are looking at the collapse of North America within twenty years. By then, Europe will have fallen into chaos too...

—Solar Union Intelligence Report, Year 51

"That's the bus, young man."

Martin Luther Douglas jerked awake, then rubbed his eyes as the bus came into view, moving brazenly down a street that even armed policemen feared to tread. It looked absurdly civilian, nothing more than a yellow school-bus, but the sigil on the front warned gangsters and drug lords – to say nothing of ethnic rights groups – to stay well away from the bus, its passengers and those who would join them. No one fucked with the Solar Union.

He rose to his feet and nodded to the elderly man who'd been sweeping the street, as if it was a habit he could not break. He'd been there when Martin had arrived, nodded to him once and then simply ignored the younger man while he waited for the bus. It had been hard to tell if the man was too old to be nervous around a young man from the derelict parts of Detroit or if he'd been beaten down by the system, like so many others. Martin rather hoped it was the former, but he suspected it was the latter. In the end, white or black, the system screwed them all.

"Thank you," he said, trying hard to speak without the ghetto accent. Young men and women had been taunted for 'acting white' until the ghetto accent had almost become a separate accent in its own right. "I..."

The roar of the bus's engines drowned out his words as it pulled up to the marker and stopped, the door hissing open a moment later. Martin reached for his ID card as he climbed up the steps – it was impossible to do anything in America without an ID card now – but the driver merely waved him into the vehicle. He put the card back in his pocket, feeling oddly exposed as he made his way down the aisle, looking for an empty seat. There was only one, next to a teenage girl who seemed to be a mixture of White American and Asian, with long black hair and very pale skin. The girl, her attention held by the handheld player in her lap, barely paid him any attention as he sat down. Moments later, the bus lurched to life and started back down the road.

Martin sat back in his seat and stared out at the surrounding buildings. They were rotting away, slowly collapsing into rubble. No one, whatever the politicians said, was interested in investing in Detroit, not when the gangs controlled much of the city. There was no point in spending money when it would be wasted, not when what little capital remained in the United States was heading to orbit. And besides, he had to admit, who would *want* to help the residents? They were either members of the gangs or their victims.

He must have fallen asleep, for the next thing he knew was the bus shuddering to a halt. Opening his eyes, he looked out of the window and saw a large fence, blocking the bus's way. A large sign, displayed prominently on the gate, warned the passengers that the territory beyond the fence was governed by the rules and laws of the Solar Union. Below it, there was a second sign informing drivers that they could abandon their vehicles to the left. Martin looked and saw a colossal car park, crammed with rusting cars. They'd simply been taken to the complex and abandoned. He couldn't help wondering why no one was trying to take the cars and put them back into service. It wasn't as though the original owners wanted them any longer.

The gate opened, revealing a handful of buildings set within a garden. One large building, rather like a school, was right in front of the bus; behind it, a number of smaller buildings lay, surrounded by people, stalls and several teleoperated machines. It reminded him of the one and only bake sale he'd attended at school, before they'd been banned. The sight brought an odd pang to his heart, even though he would have sworn he would never look back on his school days with anything approaching nostalgia.

"If I could have your attention, please," the driver said, as he parked the bus. "Go into the main building for the orientation talk, then follow instructions. Make sure you take all your personal possessions with you. Anything you leave on the bus will be discarded and either recycled or junked, depending. There will be no chance to recover anything after you leave the bus."

Martin shrugged. All he had was a holdall containing a change of clothes, some money he'd been able to scrounge up from the remains of his home and a picture of his family, in the days before they'd fallen apart. There was no point in keeping it, really; whatever happened, he was privately resolved never to go back to Detroit. Beside him, the girl unplugged the earbuds from her ears and placed her handheld terminal in a small bag. She didn't seem to have much else, not even clothes.

"Yolanda," she said, holding out a hand. "Pleased to meet you."

"Martin," Martin said. The girl's face, so exotic compared to the girls he knew from home, left him feeling tongue-tied. "Are you planning to leave too?"

"Nothing to stay for," Yolanda said. She followed him out of the seat, then down towards the ground. "What about yourself? Any family?"

"Not any longer," Martin said, feeling a fresh pang of grief and rage. Life was cheap in the ghetto – only a handful of families enjoyed both a mother and a father – but it shouldn't be that way. "I'm trying to get away from the memories."

Yolanda nodded, then looked past him towards a large bin. A handful of their fellow travellers were dropping cards into the bin. It puzzled

Martin until they reached the bin and looked inside. It held ID cards, Ethnic Entitlement Cards and Social Security cards. He reached into his pocket, recalling the dire warnings about what happened to anyone who happened to lose his or her card, then dropped the ID card in the bin. It wouldn't be needed any longer.

His Ethnic Entitlement Card glowed faintly as he dragged it out of his wallet. A line of coding seemed to shimmer under his touch, informing all and sundry that he was descended from Africans who had been abducted from their homeland by white slave traders, granting him specific rights of recompense for past wrongs. His face glowered up at him. He'd been going through a rebellious phase at the time and he'd insisted on scowling into the camera, when his picture had been taken. In hindsight, it hadn't been a very good move. It might explain why he'd never been able to get a proper job after leaving school at fifteen.

Yolanda's card was more detailed than his, he noted, as she dropped it in the bin. He wondered, as he dropped his own card after hers, just what sort of benefits a mixed-race child drew from the society security bureaucrats. But it was never enough, he knew, recalling his mother's endless struggle with the social workers. No level of resources provided could get the family through increasingly troubled times. He'd grown up angry and resentful. It had taken him far too long to realise that society itself, in the name of helping him, was keeping him in the ghetto. Discarding the cards left him feeling free.

"This way," a man called. "Hurry!"

Martin smiled, then strode next to Yolanda as they entered the building and walked into a large auditorium. Warning signs were everywhere, some simple and easy to understand, others complex and puzzling. The walls were decorated with large portraits of men and women, looking larger than life, wearing the black and gold uniforms of the Solar Navy. He had to admit they looked impressive. And, unlike so many others, proud to wear their uniforms.

"Be seated," a thin-faced white man said, standing on the tiny stage. His voice echoed around the chamber, even though he didn't seem to be wearing a microphone. "Welcome to the Solar Union. My name is Horace Bradley, Director of this Immigration Centre. This is a very small talk to get you orientated, then you can proceed to the next step. I suggest you listen carefully and save your questions until after I have finished.

"The good news is that you don't have to worry about much bureaucracy here" – there were a handful of cheers, swiftly muted – "but the bad news is that there are few people charged with helping you. We believe that immigrants succeed or fail by their own devices. There are opportunities galore for all of you, no matter where you come from, but you have to take them for yourselves. None of us will give you a kick in the ass to get you started."

He paused, then continued. "There are no real government handouts in the Solar Union. We will give you a basic immigrant's pack, which contains a terminal, a basic guide to the Solar Union and a bank chip loaded with five hundred solar dollars. The terminal comes preloaded with email and other facilities you can use, if you wish, to find a job and a place to stay. It also contains a set of guidelines, an introduction to society and other pieces of information you need to know. None of us will make you read the documents, but remember; ignorance of the law is not an excuse."

Martin frowned, then understood. At school, they'd been drilled extensively to recall pieces of pointless knowledge, which they'd then cheerfully forgotten after passing the exams. The teachers had been considered liable for not teaching their charges everything and so they'd struggled to stuff information into unwilling brains. But the Solar Union, it seemed, wanted them to have the motivation to learn on their own. There would be no one forcing them to learn – or to succeed.

"There are fifty-seven stalls in this complex," Bradley concluded. "Those of you who have contracts with established companies and suchlike can make your way directly to their stalls, where you will be escorted to your final destination. Everyone else, unless you want to join the military, can visit the different booths and choose your destination. Military recruits are advised to go to the barracks, where the next introductory talk is starting in one hour. I advise you to check the paperwork carefully before you sign anything. Good luck."

He nodded to them, then turned and walked out, without waiting for questions. Martin watched him go, then looked at Yolanda. The girl was eying her handheld processor wistfully, as if she wished she were listening to it now. Martin hesitated, then asked the question that had been nagging at his mind since Bradley's speech.

"Where are you going?"

"The military," Yolanda said. "I've been practicing with navigational sims and I think the military is the best place to get spacer qualifications."

Martin gaped at her. "The military? You?"

Yolanda smirked. "Don't you think I can hack it?"

"I don't know," Martin confessed. "I was planning to try out for the military myself."

"Then we go together," Yolanda said. She rose to her feet, then started to walk towards the door, where a pair of young men were handing out the promised terminals. "Come on."

The barracks didn't *look* like a barracks, Martin decided, although his only experience of barracks came from semi-forbidden movies showing the military life. He experimented with his new terminal as he joined a line, which slowly moved into the building and past a grim-faced man with a facemask covering half of his skull. No, Martin saw as they came closer, it wasn't a mask. He'd chopped away part of his face and replaced it with a cyborg attachment that seemed to defy logic or common sense. Martin couldn't help staring at him as he took the sheet of paper, then checked it quickly. It was nothing more than a standard recruitment form.

"You can fill it out on your terminal, if you like," the man grunted. Even his *voice* was vaguely electronic. "Then just upload it into the datanet."

"I don't know how," Martin confessed.

"I'll show you," Yolanda said. "The operating system will be as simple as possible..."

"I want to make a complaint," a girl said, pushing her way up to the guard. "I should be first in line and…"

The guard cut her off. "This isn't the socialist states of America," he said. "We don't care what entitlements you might have from anywhere outside the wire. Wait your turn in the line."

Martin stared. It was rare – vanishingly rare – for *anyone* to stand up to a claim of entitlement from anyone. Anything that could be used to screw an advantage out of the system, be it race, religion, gender, sexual orientation or anything else *would* be used. It had pleased him, at first, to know that his skin colour gave him precedence over others, until he'd realised that the system was nonsensical. *He'd* never been a slave, nor had his great-grandparents. *And* he certainly didn't have any Native American blood running through his veins.

The girl stared at the cyborg for a long moment, then – when he seemed utterly unmoved – turned and stamped back to the rear of the line, muttering just loudly enough to be heard about how the guard should check his privilege. Her words were almost drowned out by snickers and an overwhelming sense of relief that seemed to spin through the air. Martin smiled to himself, then followed Yolanda into another large chamber. A holographic image of a giant starship floated in front of them, and then shifted into a man wearing a massive suit of powered combat armour. The gun he was carrying in one hand looked larger than he was.

Yolanda giggled as they sat down. "He must be compensating for something," she said. "Do you think he's a defender or a mercenary?"

"I have no idea," Martin confessed. He opened his terminal and started to fill out the form, cursing his poor reading skills. Each question was simple, yet he needed to read through them twice to be sure he was saying the right things. Thankfully, none of the questions actually required him to *lie*. "But I'd be either, if it meant getting out of here."

The holographic image faded away, leaving the room dark and bare. Martin felt another pang, then sat upright as a man wearing a black uniform that matched the colour of his skin strode out onto the stage. He looked too muscular to be real, Martin thought; it didn't seem possible that any human could have so many muscles. And yet, from the ease he carried himself, it was impossible to think otherwise. Martin was impressed. He'd met too many thugs, gangbangers and snobbish social workers in his life, but this was the first real *man*.

Maybe my father was like him, he thought, suddenly. *But would he have left if he was?*

"Good afternoon," the man said. His voice was sharp, oddly accented. He spoke in a manner that demanded their full attention. "I am Drill Instructor Denver. You are here because you are interested in joining the Solar Navy or associated forces. If you wish to be anywhere else, piss off now and save me some time."

There was a pause. No one left.

"Good," Denver said. "You will know, I think, that the Solar Union is a very loose society, almost anarchistic. There are relatively few laws to follow and you can do whatever the hell you like, assuming you don't harm others. That is not true of the military. Depending on which branch of the service you join, you will have to serve a five, ten, fifteen or twenty year term. During that time, we will own your asses. You will have very limited choice in assignments and, unless you earn a medical discharge, you will not be allowed to leave without fucking up your future. If you're not committed, like I said, piss off now and save me some time.

"The Solar Navy is charged with defending the human race against the Galactics," he continued, without a break. "You may not like Earth as it is now, but it would be a great deal worse if the Galactics took over. We cannot afford to fuck around like the politically-correct" – he pronounced the words as if they were curses – "officers who have ruined the western militaries over the past seventy years. The Solar Navy is all that stands between us and alien rule.

"There will be a three-month period at Boot Camp for all of you," he concluded. "This is to get you used to life in the Solar Union and, also, to give us a chance to evaluate you. After that, you will be assigned to separate training streams, where your talents can be shaped to suit our needs. At that point, you will be committed."

He paused. "Any questions?"

"Yeah," a young man said. "When can we quit?"

Denver eyed him darkly. "You can quit up to one week in Boot Camp without penalty," he said. "At that point, you will receive your implants. Should you quit after that, you will be charged the full price for the implants, which have to be tailor-made for you personally. And then, when you are steered into your training streams, you will be committed. The military life is not for everyone."

That, Martin knew, was true. But it was also his only hope of leaving Earth behind. He had no educational qualifications that meant a damn in the Solar Union, no hope of obtaining them…it was the military or grunt labour, which offered no prospect of advancement. If he'd wanted that, he would have gone to work for McDonalds-Taco Bell, if there had been a place available. Most fast-food takeouts were purely robotic these days.

"The choice is yours," Denver said. "If you're still interested, walk through the doors at the rear of this chamber. There will be a brief medical exam, then a shuttle flight to Sparta Training Base. Good luck."

Martin and Yolanda exchanged glances as Denver walked out of the room, then, without hesitation, rose and walked through the door.

TWO

Fighting was reported today in Paris between footsoldiers of the French Nationalist Brigade and the Algerian Jihad. French news agencies claim the battle was a minor clash between rival gangs; sources on the ground assert that tanks and soldiers from nearby French Army bases assisted on both sides…

—Solar News Network, Year 51

It was an odd contradiction, Kevin Stuart had often considered, that a government based on openness and universal political participation required a secret council. Indeed, very few citizens of the Solar Union had even *heard* of the Special Security Council and the Government took pains to keep it that way. Open awareness of the council could do nothing, but make it impossible for the council to do its work. As always, secrecy, security and the Solar Constitution were uneasy bedfellows.

He stepped into the council chamber and looked around, marvelling – as always – at just how unadorned the chamber was, compared to conference rooms on Earth. There was nothing in the room, save for a large portrait of Steve Stuart, a table, a number of chairs and a drinks dispenser. But it was rare for Councillors, even the highest-ranking officials in the Solar Union, to meet in person. It was far more convenient for them to meet over the secure datanet, while remaining on their home asteroids and tending to their constituents.

We didn't want them to grow into bad habits, like those assholes in Washington, Kevin thought, as he poured himself a cup of coffee – no servants here, not in the secure compartment – and sat down at the table. *They need to remember that they are the servants of the people, not their masters.*

He looked up as the door hissed open again, revealing Councillor Marie Jackson and Councillor Richard Bute. The former had frozen her age at roughly thirty, combining a certain degree of red-haired attractiveness with a maturity that had allowed her to score a victory in the notoriously rough-and-tumble politics of the Solar Union. Behind her, Councillor Bute looked older, roughly fifty years old. Studies had shown that voters preferred older leaders, after all, even though nanotechnology could make a ninety-year-old man look like a teenager. Kevin had wondered, more than once, just what the long-term effects of frozen aging would be.

"Councillors," he said. "Thank you for coming."

"We were informed we had no choice," Bute said, gravely. "I hadn't even *heard* of this council until I received the notification."

"Not many people have," Kevin said. "You were selected to serve on it at random."

"Your brother would not have approved," Councillor Jackson said, stiffly. She nodded towards the portrait on the wall. "I think he would have refused to serve, if asked."

Kevin shrugged. Steve Stuart – the founder of the Solar Union and Kevin's older brother – might well have refused to approve of the council. But Steve had never really been able to cope with the clashes between his libertarian dreams and cold hard reality. It was why, in the end, he had taken a starship and set out as an interstellar trader, accompanied only by his wife. Kevin and Mongo had remained behind to ensure the Solar Union didn't lose sight of its original purpose.

Speak of the devil, he thought, as the hatch opened again. This time, it revealed Mongo Stuart, Kevin's other brother. He nodded to Mongo – the

Stuart Family had never been one for enthusiastic greetings – then waved him to the drinks dispenser. Behind him, Admiral Keith Glass stepped into the compartment and sat down next to Kevin.

The President of the Solar Union – Allen Ross – followed them into the compartment, accompanied by three other Councillors. Kevin rose to his feet and nodded to the President – Mongo and Glass saluted – and then watched as the President sat down at the head of the table. It was informal, compared to meetings on Earth, but it helped make everyone comfortable. Given what they were going to be discussing, Kevin knew, the more comfortable they were, the better.

"Mr. President," Bute said. "Dare I assume we're discussing the situation on Earth?"

"I sure hope not," Councillor Jackson snapped. "There's nothing to be gained by meddling on Earth!"

"I'm afraid not," the President said. "As soon as SPEAKER is here, we will begin."

Kevin sighed as the two councillors continued to argue. The AIs swore blind that the process of selecting councillors for *the* council was completely random, but he had his doubts. Bute was a known *dirty-foot*, a person who had maintained ties to Earth, while Jackson was one of the largest advocates for leaving Earth mired in its own shit, slowly decaying to death. Kevin himself, in line with Steve's opinion, tended to support the latter. The Solar Union took everyone who wanted to leave Earth and make a new life among the stars. There was no point in helping those who refused to leave no matter their circumstances. Besides, the last thing they needed was a quagmire.

He smiled as a holographic image appeared at the other end of the table. The AI representative looked oddly inhuman, even though the AIs claimed he was formed from a composite of all human faces recorded in the database. Kevin had never been able to look at the image without feeling uneasy, although he'd never been sure why. But then, the AIs weren't human. Their motivations might be very different from anything humans understood.

Just one more thing we don't understand about the race we created, he thought. Alone among the known races of the universe, humanity had created unrestricted AIs. *And one day we may come to regret creating them.*

"Security fields are now online," the hologram said. "This room is now sealed."

Kevin heard Councillor Jackson gasp. She'd been implanted as soon as she was old enough to handle an implant, then remained swimming in the endless stream of data ever since. To be cut off from the datanet was almost like losing part of her mind. For Kevin and the others, old enough to remember a time when direct neural interfaces had been a dream, it was easier to handle. He wondered, absently, if Jackson would need therapy after the session came to an end. There were people who couldn't cope with being separated from the datanet for more than a few minutes.

"Thank you, SPEAKER," the President said.

He took a breath, then went on in an oddly formal tone. "The 34th Meeting of the Special Security Council is now in session. Participants are advised that full secrecy regulations are now in effect. Disclosure of any or all information discussed at this session without permission will result in harsh penalties. If this is unacceptable to you, you may leave now."

There was a pause. No one left.

"Director Stuart," the President said. "The floor is yours."

"Thank you, Mr. President," Kevin said. He activated his implants, then sent a command into the secure processors controlling the room. The lights dimmed slightly as the holographic image flickered into existence. "I shall be blunt. The gods have noticed."

The President frowned; Bute, beside him, looked pale. Neither Mongo nor Keith Glass showed any reaction. They'd expected, sooner or later, that the Galactics would wake up and notice the human race. But they'd hoped and prayed, just like Kevin himself, that the Galactics wouldn't notice for decades. Humanity was everything the ultra-conservative Galactics had good reason to hate.

"Shit," Councillor Travis said, quietly.

"Indeed," Kevin said. "We have sources on Varnar. One of them warned our people, last month, that the Varnar Government finally filed a specific request for assistance from the Tokomak. They specifically discussed humanity with the masters of the known universe."

"They may not be willing to do anything," Bute said, with the air of a man grasping for straws. "The Galactics take *centuries* to make up their minds about *anything*."

It was true, to some extent. The kindest way to describe the Tokomak Government was to call it a government of old men. Their leaders were rarely younger than a thousand years, which had bred a degree of stagnation that made Imperial China look like the early United States of America. If anything had changed in their system of government over the last five hundred years, Solar Intelligence hadn't been able to identify it. Kevin had often wondered just why history had decreed it was the Tokomak who ruled the galactic community. Surely, a more thrusting race would have displaced them by now.

But we could go the same way, he thought, looking down at his hand. It should have been wrinkled and old – it had been seventy years since his birth – but it looked young and healthy. Nanotech had frozen his age too. *What will happen when the geriatrics outweigh the young?*

He scowled. One of the many problems on Earth was the simple reluctance of the young to be taxed to death to keep the elderly alive. Perhaps it was selfish, perhaps it was unpleasant, but hundreds of thousands of youngsters had fled Earth for the Solar Union, leaving the outdated political structures to crumble into dust. But the Solar Union could keep the elderly young and productive indefinitely…

"The reports state that the Varnar have actually been quite insistent," he said, pushing his morbid thoughts aside. "Their panic may actually get the ships moving within a decade, perhaps less."

"They're losing the war," the President said.

"Yes," Kevin agreed. "They're losing, partly because of our involvement, and yet they cannot divert their forces to deal with Earth. They know they need help."

He sent another command into the display, projecting an image of the local sector in front of them. "The war situation was perfectly balanced until we entered the picture," he said. "Since then, the Varnar have lost control of several star systems and have been forced to watch as their empire crumbles. I believe their rulers have finally concluded that they can no longer handle the situation. They've asked for help."

"Risky," Councillor Jackson said. "The Tokomak might turn on them too, once they outlive their usefulness."

"True," Kevin agreed. "But there's so much hatred built up over nearly three hundred years of war that survival itself becomes questionable, if they lose the war."

"Because the Tokomak used them to keep the powers in our sector from uniting into a potential threat," Bute said, quietly. "They may be exterminated."

"Quite possibly," Kevin said. "And they know better than to rely on Galactic Law for protection."

He sighed. The Galactics had laid down laws of war, forbidding – among other things – outright extermination of conquered races – but accidents happened. It was uncertain even if the Tokomak would bother to enforce the laws. God knew humanity's governments had rarely bothered to punish rogue states that broke the rules. But then, if the Tokomak ever woke up to the danger represented by humanity, it was quite likely they'd throw the laws out of the airlock and do whatever it took to exterminate the human race.

The President cleared his throat. "How long do we have?"

"Impossible to calculate," Kevin said. "SPEAKER?"

"Projections suggest a minimum of five years and a maximum of twenty," the AI stated, bluntly. "However, attempts at actually predicting the actions of multiple alien races have always proven unreliable. We simply lack enough data to speculate."

"I see," the President said. "Can we fight?"

"We must," Mongo said, quietly. "The best we can hope for, if we submit, is permanent third-class citizenship in their empire."

"I doubt it," Kevin said. "We're just too damn innovative for them to tolerate."

The thought would have amused him, under other circumstances. Most of the Galactics had drawn their technology from the Tokomak and never really bothered to make improvements. Indeed, much of the technology either came in sealed boxes or was beyond their ability to maintain, let alone understand. The schooling the Galactics gave their citizens was so limited it actually made it harder for them to grasp the principles of technology. But humanity, on the other hand, had actually worked hard to unravel the mysteries of alien technology and then start improving on it.

"Give us fifty, perhaps a hundred more years," Keith Glass said, "and we'd be able to smash any offensive they sent against us. We'd...we'd be carrying machine guns while they'd be spear-carrying tribesmen. The outcome would be inevitable."

"But we don't have fifty years," the President said. "Can we beat them now?"

"Perhaps," Mongo said. "We've always had a scenario whereupon the Tokomak launch an attack on Earth. However, we lack data. For example...do their warships have the same weaknesses as other Galactic warships?"

Kevin nodded. The Tokomak might well have kept the good stuff for themselves, as American and European arms traders had ensured they never sold top-of-the-range weapons to third world states. In their place, he would have made sure he kept a few weapons and other pieces of technology back, holding it in reserve. If their loyal subjects had decided to be disloyal, having the ability to smash them flat would definitely have come in handy.

But they already have the biggest stick in galactic history, he thought. *They have literally millions of battleships in commission. Or do they?*

His analysts were divided on the question. Some of them believed the Tokomak were more willing to sacrifice other races – the Varnar, for example – than send their sons and daughters to war. Certainly, human empires had used proxy forces when they hadn't wanted to put boots on the ground. Others, however, wondered just how many of those battleships were actually in active service. The Tokomak, secure in their own superiority, might have placed thousands of ships in reserve.

"This is a little more important than matters on Earth," Bute said, nervously. "Do we have a plan?"

"I have a rough idea," Kevin said. He'd hashed it out when the first reports had come in, even though he'd hoped the reports were inaccurate. It hadn't been long before confirmation had arrived. "First, we need to determine just how much of a threat they actually pose. I have several ideas for this, which we will discuss at a later meeting. Second, we need to delay them as much as possible. Again, I have ideas that we will need to consider later."

He paused. "And third, we have to give them a bloody nose, one they won't forget in a hurry.

"I've studied their government carefully. They're slow, incredibly ponderous, but they've been masters of the universe for so long they've grown accustomed to getting their way. A small reverse won't bother them, even if the Varnar lose the war completely. The only way to get them to deal with us as equals – or even just accept our independence – is to hit them hard enough to shock them out of their torpor."

"Which also might galvanise them into throwing everything at us," Councillor Jackson pointed out. "This isn't something we should decide, Director. The question should be put before the population."

"Which may alert the Galactics that we know what they're planning," Kevin pointed out. "If they know, our task becomes a great deal harder."

"There are laws," Councillor Jackson insisted. "We *cannot* keep this secret indefinitely."

"Legally, this council can keep something secret for up to a year without penalties," SPEAKER informed her. "You may lose your office, Councillor, but you wouldn't lose your life."

Councillor Jackson didn't look pleased. Kevin understood. The Solar Union didn't allow career politicians, no matter how experienced or capable they were. Marie Jackson had three more years of her term, then she would have to run for President or leave politics for good. And, if her constituents disagreed with the decision to keep the council's deliberations under wraps, she might face a recall election and be kicked out of office ahead of time.

But at least she won't face criminal charges of abusing her office, he thought.

"There is another issue," Bute said. "Do we inform Earth?"

"*Earth?*" Keith Glass said. "What makes you think they'd *care?*"

"They're going to be at risk too," Bute said. "This isn't a minor issue like the Abdul Murder Trial. This is an invasion of human space by the single most powerful force known to exist."

The President frowned. "We will consider it," he said. "However, I suspect that revealing any such information to Earth would cause panic. The governments would prove quite unable to handle the chaos."

He looked at Kevin. "Does Intelligence have any updated predictions for Earth?"

"Total collapse of the former Western World within thirty years, perhaps less," Kevin said, bluntly. The thought caused him a pang. It had been a long time since he'd sworn to defend the United States against all enemies, foreign and domestic, but now he was running away rather than trying to carry out his oath. "Some places are trying to stand up to the tidal wave of anarchy – Switzerland in particular – but they're unlikely to be able to hold out indefinitely."

"We will get more refugees," Councillor Jackson observed.

"That's fine, as long as they are prepared to work," Bute said. "And to stick to the laws."

"And we will enforce the laws," Mongo said. "*All* of the laws."

"Then no, we don't tell Earth," the President said. "They will know when our population knows, I think. Until then…we stick with the non-intervention agreement. Unless our people are involved, we leave Earth to itself."

Bute snorted, rudely.

"I propose meet again one month from today," Kevin said. "By then, we should have some additional information from Varnar Prime. I may need to deploy additional intelligence assets to the system."

"Men in suits," Bute said.

"They don't really keep track of aliens unless they want to apply for permanent residence," Kevin said. "But you're right, Councillor. A team of humans would attract attention."

"Unless they were cyborgs," Keith Glass said. "They still have breeding stock, don't they?"

"Unfortunately," Kevin agreed.

On that note, the meeting ended.

THREE

Factions backing Scottish Independence marched through Edinburgh today, prior to the seventh referendum on Scottish Independence from England. Unconfirmed reports indicate that pro-UK or pro-EU factions have been attacked, sometimes savagely. Polls suggest, given the high rate of emigration from Scotland, that the independence vote will actually be successful, this time.

—Solar News Network, Year 51

"You seem to be healthy," the doctor said, as Yolanda Miguel perched on a bed. "Nothing wrong with you that can't be fixed by basic nanotech."

Yolanda blinked in surprise. "You don't want me to take off my clothes?"

"It isn't necessary," the doctor assured her. He reached for a terminal and swung it around to face her. "I scanned your body as soon as you sat down on the bed. You have some problems caused by basic nutritional issues and suchlike, but nothing too serious."

He paused. "Was there a reason for the question?"

Yolanda gritted her teeth. "I…I had a medical exam when I turned fourteen," she said. "I had to take off everything, then he poked and prodded at me for hours."

"Sounds like a right bastard," the doctor said. "Or possibly a paedophile."

He tapped the terminal. "Scanning the human body down to the molecular level is quite easy," he said. "The autodoc can handle most of it, young lady. There's nothing here that requires human intervention. But doctors on Earth have successfully banned autodoc units for safety reasons."

"I see," Yolanda said. Part of her was angry at the discovery that the whole thoroughly unpleasant experience could have been avoided. The other part of her found it hard to care, as if it had happened to someone else. "Is there anything else I should know?"

The doctor looked back at her. "You shouldn't have any problems with implants," he said, softly. "We sometimes have people who can't take them, but you're not one of them. However" – he paused for a moment – "you do have some scarring in your privates. Do you want to talk about it?"

"No," Yolanda said, sharply. She'd bottled up those memories, those emotions, and sealed them away inside her mind. There was no way she wanted them to come out again. "I don't want to talk about it."

"Very well," the doctor said. He motioned for her to stand up. "If you want to talk about it at a later date, young lady, there are services that provide counselling. You're not the first person to flee Earth in such a state."

"Thank you," Yolanda said. "But I'm not *that* much younger than you."

The doctor smiled. "How old do you think I am?"

Yolanda studied him for a long moment. He was tall and slim, with short blonde hair, a starkly handsome face and muscular body. There was something about him that made her feel safe, even though they were alone together. It wasn't something she fully understood, but it was reassuring. She just didn't know why.

"You're in your thirties," she guessed.

"I'm sixty-five," the doctor said.

"Fuck off," Yolanda said, automatically. Too late, she recalled that swearing was grounds for a slap from her mother. "I mean..."

The doctor didn't take offense. "I've had my age frozen," he said. "You might want to do the same, one day. It isn't hard to do."

Yolanda was still shaking her head as she walked out of the office and looked around. Martin was nowhere to be seen, something that bothered her more than she cared to admit. *He* felt safe too, despite his appearance. It wasn't something she cared to think about; school had taught her that skin colour wasn't important, but life had taught her the exact opposite in so many different ways. What was the point of Ethnic Entitlement Cards if skin colour and genetic descent were so important? And where did a mixed-race child fit in?

She shuddered suddenly as she remembered the exam, four years ago. Why had the doctor put her and her classmates through hell?

"Hey," Martin's voice said. "Are you alright?"

"I'm fine," Yolanda said, as she turned to face him. "Just feeling a little silly."

Martin blinked. "You? Silly?"

"I was nervous about the exam," Yolanda said. "But instead...it was simple."

"Yeah," Martin agreed. Perhaps he'd had a similar experience. "It was easy. The doctor just told me to make sure I took a few supplements, once I reached Sparta."

"You two," another voice called. Yolanda looked up to see a heavyset man wearing a grey uniform. "The shuttle leaves in twenty minutes. Be on it or you'll be kicked out before you even begin!"

"Thank you," Martin said, sarcastically. "And where is the shuttle?"

"Through those doors, then down to the right," the man informed him. "Make sure you board one going to Sparta or you'll be billed for the trip."

Yolanda and Martin exchanged glances, then walked through the doors and into the open air. She'd half-expected something akin to an airport, but instead there was nothing more than a hard surface and a handful of medium-sized shuttles waiting for them. A dark-skinned man with a terminal checked them both, then pointed towards one of the shuttlecraft. It was, Yolanda decided as she walked up to it, definitely a remarkable design. She couldn't wait to learn how to fly the craft.

"Better get inside," Martin muttered. He sounded nervous, although she had a feeling he would have preferred to die than admit it. "I don't want to be standing here when the craft takes off."

"Me neither," Yolanda said.

Inside, the shuttlecraft was little different from a regular airliner. Yolanda was almost disappointed, particularly when she saw the tiny seats. A fat person would have very real problems sitting down, she noted, although she hadn't seen any fat people on the base. If nanotech could freeze someone at a certain age, she asked herself, could it also keep someone slim and healthy? It certainly seemed likely.

She sat down and braced herself, expecting a long and boring lecture on flight safety, followed by a rocky flight and uncomfortable landing. She'd only flown twice and both experiences had been thoroughly awful. However, the shuttle was different. The hatch slammed closed, a man in another grey uniform checked the seats, then a faint shimmer ran through the craft. She didn't even realise the shuttle had taken off until she glanced out of the porthole. The ground was already far below them.

"My God," Martin breathed.

Slowly, Earth became a sphere hanging in the inky darkness of space. Yolanda found herself captivated as she stared down at the blue-green orb, which started to shrink rapidly as the shuttle accelerated away from the planet. Moments later, it was gone, leaving them staring out at the stars. They didn't twinkle in space, she realised, slowly. There was no atmosphere to produce the effects. Or so she thought. Thankfully, she'd chosen basic science instead of faith healing, elemental powers or one of the other electives the school had been forced to offer its students. But she had a feeling she was far behind where she needed to be.

The flight became boring, something she wouldn't have believed possible. She forced herself to sit back and relax, trying to keep herself calm. Her thoughts kept returning to the past, nagging at her mind and making it impossible to think straight. She'd buried everything, she'd thought, and yet they'd started to come out at the worst possible moment. Part of her just wanted to open the airlock and jump out into interplanetary space; the remainder, knowing that suicide was the end, just wanted to forget. But forgetfulness would never come.

Martin elbowed her. "Are you alright?"

"Just...just nerves," Yolanda said. She felt as if she could trust him, on some level, but she couldn't talk to him about her past. No one would understand. "I've never been in space before."

"Neither have I," Martin said. "Would you like me to look after you?"

Yolanda had to fight to hide her reaction, even though she knew he'd meant no harm. Other girls had accepted similar offers, in the past, only to find they had bought safety from the outside world at the price of submitting themselves to a single man. Her High School had been a nightmare of competing cliques, while the teachers had done nothing to maintain discipline and...

She forced the thoughts aside. Earth had fallen behind them. There was no going back.

"It's alright," she said. "Thank you for caring."

The shuttlecraft shuddered once, lightly, then altered course. Yolanda looked outside, just in time to see a massive rocky asteroid drifting in front of them. It took her several minutes to pick out the signs of human habitation; pieces of burnished metal on the rock, crawlers making their way over the surface and lights glittering amidst the gloom. The shuttle shuddered again, then slid through a hatch and into a shuttlebay. There was a sudden feeling of heaviness, which faded rapidly, then nothing.

A man stood up at the front of the shuttle. "Welcome to Sparta," he said. "You are about to enter a hideously dangerous environment. One mistake could get you – or others – killed. I strongly advise you to follow orders, keep your hands to yourselves and refrain from doing anything stupid. Given time, you will learn how to handle yourself in outer space. Until then, do as we tell you."

He paused. "I'm going to open the hatch and step outside," he added. "Form a straight line and follow me, without delay. *Do not* attempt to leave the line. Anyone who disobeys orders once will be flogged. Anyone who disobeys orders repeatedly will be kicked out of the course. There will be no further warnings."

"Shit," Martin said. "Do you think he's serious?"

"I think so," Yolanda said.

The hatch opened. One by one, the recruits stood up and walked out of the hatch. Yolanda let Martin take the lead when it was their turn to move; she followed him, as per orders, but she couldn't help looking from side to side as they stepped out of the shuttle. It was bitterly cold, cold enough to make her shiver; they were standing in a large shuttlebay, with dozens of shuttles scattered everywhere. Men and women in grey uniforms, some of them with metal arms or legs, were working on the craft. She stared at them in awe for a long moment, then walked after Martin through the next hatch. Inside, thankfully, it was warmer.

"Line up on the dotted line," the man ordered, pointing them to a yellow line on the floor. "I don't have all day, so *hurry*."

"I saw lots of military movies," Martin muttered in her ear. "I think this is when they call us maggots and shout at us a lot."

"Joy," Yolanda muttered back. It didn't bother her, not really. Her mother and father had shouted at her for most of her life. "I can take it."

The man waited for the final recruits to take their place, then closed the hatch and stamped around until he was facing them. "Welcome to Sparta," he said. "I am Senior Drill Sergeant Bass. You will address me as *Sergeant*. In the course of the next week, you will meet other Drill Sergeants and Drill Instructors. You will address them as *Sergeant* too."

He paused. "For my crimes, I have been assigned as Senior Drill Sergeant for Recruit Company #42," he continued. "That's you, by the way. You will be asked hundreds of times over the coming months which company you belong to, so I suggest you remember that you're #42. Getting it wrong will earn you a demerit, which you will have to work off; if you earn ten demerits, you will have a very embarrassing interview with the Commandant. Your career may not survive drawing his attention.

"My job is supervising you for this, the first stage of your training. Everyone goes through the same basic training, then we split you up into smaller groups in accordance with your desires and capabilities. You will be given a fair shot at trying to become *anything*, as long as we believe you have the ability to *learn* and succeed. But the outcome will largely depend on just how much effort you put into it. I am not here to coddle you into completing an exam or writing an essay, although you will have to do both over the coming months. What you get out of this largely depends on what you put into it."

Yolanda felt herself shrinking backwards as his gaze passed over her. She couldn't help finding Bass intimidating, even though he didn't seem to be *trying* to intimidate them. But then, he was a strong man who clearly wouldn't let anything stand in his way. He wasn't the type of person she knew to trust.

Give him a fair chance, she told herself. *He isn't one of the bastards from school.*

"You are all *ignorant*," Bass thundered. "You are utterly unaware of the dangers of this environment, let alone training to become spacers or soldiers or whatever. So you will *learn* from me. Those of you who don't learn will *die*, killed by your own ignorance or your own stupidity. And we will simply carry on."

His gaze swept the line of recruits again. "There are rules and regulations," he warned. "If you break a minor rule, you will earn demerits; if you break a major rule, you will face the Commandant! Do you understand me? Good.

"If you don't understand something you are told, ask me," he added. "Until then, stick to the rules. There is a good reason behind each and every one of them."

Bass clapped his hands together. "Offences against military order, listed as follows; insubordination, use of drugs, tobacco and alcohol, possession and/or consumption of food outside designated eating periods, possession of any contraband, failure to perform duties as assigned to you by lawful authority, being absent without leave and, last, but not least, fraternisation. To repeat; any of those offences will get you a punishment that may range from heavy exercise to being summarily discharged from the army. You will have those offences read to you every day, along with the definition of each offence. You will have no excuse for committing any of them!"

He paused long enough to take another hard look at his recruits. "Many of you will have brought drugs, or alcohol, or even food onto this base," he said, coldly. "When you are taken to be assigned your uniform and regulation-issue underclothes, get rid of them. This is your one warning. You may think that the police on Earth wouldn't charge you with a crime if you are in possession of illegal drugs, but this is the Solar Union. If I catch any of you possessing or using drugs on this base, that person will wish that he had never been born!"

Yolanda swallowed. Did Martin have anything illicit in his bag?

Bass was still thundering at his cowed audience. "Insubordination; wilfully disobeying, insulting, or striking a senior officer. Absent without leave; leaving the base or your unit without permission, or failing to report back to your unit at the end of a leave period without permission. Fraternisation; sexual relationships with any of your fellow recruits, or senior officers, or anyone within your military unit. The remainder should require no explaining. If they do, quit now and save us the paperwork of kicking you out."

"Female recruits, walk through that hatch," Bass finished, pointing towards a hatch set in the far wall. His finger moved to another hatch. "Male recruits, walk through *that* hatch."

"See you soon," Martin muttered."

"I hope so," Yolanda said. Her head was spinning after Bass's recital of military crimes. She wasn't sure she knew what half of them actually *meant*. "See you."

She walked through the hatch and nearly bumped into the back of a line. A grim-faced woman was standing behind a desk, handing out small piles of clothing and pointing the girls towards benches, where they could change into their uniforms. Yolanda hesitated – she had never liked changing in front of anyone else, male or female – then realised she had no choice. Privacy was going to be a thing of the past. Cursing under her breath, she stripped down to bare skin and then donned the uniform. It was *very* simplistic. The only decoration was a large red numeral – 42.34 – just above her left breast.

"If you want to keep your clothes or anything else you might have brought with you, place them in boxes here," a female sergeant ordered. Yolanda took a look at her and had to fight to keep herself from staring in disbelief. The woman looked like a bad parody of a transvestite, so close to masculine it was hard to be sure she *was* a woman. "They will be stored for you until you leave the service or graduate, whichever comes first."

Yolanda looked down at her bag. "Everything?"

"If you want to keep it," the sergeant told her, curtly. "Anything you don't want to keep can be dropped in the bins and it will be recycled. I suggest you dump anything illicit you don't want us to see."

"Thank you," Yolanda said.

"That's *thank you, sergeant*," the woman corrected. "You can earn a demerit for forgetting to use the proper terms."

"Oh," Yolanda said.

"Hey," another girl said. "How do you work off a demerit?"

"Heavy exercise," the sergeant said, with an evil grin. "It teaches you respect and helps build up the muscles. You'll get used to it soon enough."

She checked them all, one by one, then smiled. "This is the last babying you'll get," she warned, as she led them towards the hatch. "In future, if you are told to do something and you don't do it, you will be allowed to suffer the effects of your screw-up."

Yolanda smiled as they walked through the door. Martin was standing with the other men, wearing the same grey uniform. His numerals were different; 42.41.

"These are your barracks," Sergeant Bass thundered, as he opened yet another hatch. Inside, there were three large hatches and a computer terminal, parked against one wall. "Male recruits to the left, female recruits to the right. Do *not* try to enter the wrong barracks unless you have a *very* good excuse. The centre compartment" – he jabbed a finger at the third hatch – "is your common room. Beyond it, there's an exercise chamber. You may use it during your *copious* spare time."

He smirked. Somehow, Yolanda was sure they would have very little spare time.

"Go get a rest," he said. "You will be woken in" – he made a show of checking his watch – "seven hours. And then the real fun starts."

FOUR

Speaking in the Senate today, Senator Karen Pettigrew demanded that the United States Government impose new tariffs on anyone wishing to abandon the United States for the Solar Union. The interests of social justice, Pettigrew claimed, were best served by forbidding the transfer of material possessions – and cash – from the United States.

—Solar News Network, Year 51

"I didn't know it was possible to hurt so much," Dennis Crawford muttered.

"Me neither," Martin said, as they stumbled out of the shower. Whatever concerns he'd had about sharing showers with other men had vanished, faced with the implacable truth that their trainers expected them to adapt – and act like adults. "That was not a pleasant experience."

He'd watched war movies, downloading them from the datanet after they'd been banned in the United States, but none of them had ever managed to make him *feel* what new recruits went through. There were the endless exercises, the endless lectures from the sergeants, the complete lack of sleep, the monotonous food…and the demerit system, which had to have been invented by a mad genius who'd also been a complete sadist. One week of basic training and he'd already earned four demerits. Working them off had been a pain.

"I don't think it's meant to be," Crawford said. "They say it only gets worse after we pass the first set of tests."

"I know," Martin said. He'd thought he could handle it, but if he was having problems with Basic Training, maybe he shouldn't be thinking about trying to become a cybersoldier. Or *any* sort of soldier. All the movies he'd watched had told lies. "What do you think is going to happen tonight?"

"Fucked if I know," Crawford said. "But we'd better get a move on."

Martin nodded, then stepped through the forcefield. Water droplets flew off his skin, leaving him completely dry. He reached for his uniform and pulled it on, glancing down at the bare sleeves. The sergeants had told the company that, when they passed the first set of tests, they would have something to put on their uniforms. But there would always be another set of hurdles to clear…

As soon as they were dressed, they walked down into the mess and picked up plates of food, which they carried to the nearest table. Most of the other recruits seemed to be elsewhere – either writing letters or catching up on sleep, as they had no demerits to work off. Martin looked around in hopes of seeing Yolanda, but saw no sign of her. She seemed to be coping as well as could be expected, although she looked thinner every day. He hoped she wouldn't quit, even though others had already thrown in the towel and abandoned Sparta. There was something about her he found attractive.

And keep it in your pants, he warned himself, sternly. Sergeant Bass hadn't been joking when he'd warned them of the dangers of fraternisation. One pair of recruits, caught having sex in one of the bathrooms, had been ordered to spend the rest of the week naked, just to ensure they got the message. *You don't need more demerits*.

He pushed the thought aside as he tucked into the food. There was no way to know what it actually was – it looked like a mixture of porridge and hard biscuits – but it tasted good and there was no shortage of it. The sergeants had told them to eat as much as they could, every day, even though some of the girls had whined about making themselves fat. But it didn't seem a possibility, not when they were forced to exercise every day. And then there were the tests that measured his education, rather than physical prowess...

"You're thinking," Dennis said. "I can tell."

Martin sighed. He'd never really grasped just how ignorant he was until he'd arrived on Sparta. Being unable to handle himself in space was one thing – he knew he was ignorant of even basic safety precautions – but his reading and writing were definitely sub-par. The Sergeant had even told him that he would have to spend time learning to read properly, if he wanted to progress rapidly. Martin had hated the thought, even though Yolanda had offered to help him with it. He didn't want to delay his training just to learn how to read.

"It's a bad habit," he said, although he knew that wasn't true. Some of the tests the Sergeants had set him could only be solved through careful thought, rather than brute force. "And we'd better get moving."

He dropped the empty plate into the fresher, then walked down towards the lecture hall, where they'd been told to go at 1900, Sparta Time. Yolanda was waiting outside, looking nervous; she brightened up when she saw him. Martin smiled at her, then followed her into the giant compartment. It was easily large enough to handle two or three hundred recruits, rather than one single company. But Martin had long since stopped wondering why the facility seemed to be much larger than it needed to be. No doubt, like everything else, there was a reason for it.

"Please, be seated," an elderly voice said. "I am Professor Fritz Scudder."

Martin took a seat and studied the elderly man. He was the first citizen of the Solar Union he'd met who actually looked *old*, with dark skin and white hair. Appearances could be deceiving, he knew, but he would have happily placed the Professor at being well over eighty years old. His granddad – and he had been a *real* man - hadn't looked much younger when he'd shuffled off the mortal coil. There were days when Martin still missed him, bitterly. It was easy to imagine his life would have been better if he'd had a strong male figure to look up to, while he'd been a kid.

"There is one compulsory class in the Solar Union, taught in every school," Scudder said. He spoke in a calm, completely composed manner, as if he'd seen too much to be scared of anything less than the end of the universe. "That class is History and Moral Philosophy. If you happened to be born in the Solar Union, you would have taken the class between fourteen and sixteen years of age. But, as none of you *were* born in the Solar Union, it is necessary for us to offer you the chance to take the course now.

"Unlike most of my students, you have the opportunity to decline. You're adults; we cannot force you to take the class. It isn't part of your training, so failing to take the class won't be counted against you. However, you may find that taking the class will help you to understand the Solar Union and become one of our citizens. If any of you want to leave now, please do so. Or you can stay to the end and then decide not to come back. Either one is fine, as long as you let me know."

He stopped and waited.

Martin looked at Yolanda. "I think we should stay," she said. "It might be interesting."

"It might," Martin agreed. He would have stayed for a truly boring talk if she'd wanted to stay with him. "Let us see what happens."

"Thank you," Scudder said, after five minutes. "I hope I can make this course interesting enough to keep you coming back."

He smiled at them, then settled back in his chair.

"Schooling in the Solar Union, as most of you may dimly realise, is fundamentally different from schooling on Earth," he said. "Schooling on Earth requires you, the students, to absorb and recite by rote vast amounts of data. You are not taught to actually *think*, let alone how to obtain data for yourself and analyse it. Furthermore, you are...conditioned to accept social attitudes that are examples of doublethink, simply contradictory, or simply make no sense at all. Your graduations depend more on how well you adhere to the orthodox line of thinking rather than your grades, *per se*.

"Schooling in the Solar Union teaches you the basics – how to read, write and access information – and then concentrates on developing your ability to think critically. You might know that two plus two equals four, instead of five, but if you don't understand the background you may not be able to reason out that two plus three *does* equal five. You are not expected to regurgitate vast quantities of information, because such information is always at your fingertips. You *are* expected to use that information to actually *think*."

Martin considered it. He'd never done very well on his exams on Earth…and yet he'd passed anyway. It hadn't taken him or his fellows long to realise that it didn't matter *how* much work they did; they still passed the exams. And they'd played up in the classrooms, because it didn't matter either. They'd known, on some level, that they were doomed.

"Many of you will be angry when you work out how badly you've been screwed by the system," Scudder said. "But anger will not help. Now, you have the opportunity to make up for what you've missed."

He paused, again. "But the problems you experienced in your schooling on Earth, I'm afraid, are signs of a more fundamental problem affecting the *governments* on Earth.

"The earliest governments made no bones about their true nature; they were rule by the strong. None of the Romans ever bothered to *justify* their conquests to themselves. But, as human society developed, coming up with excuses for taking and holding power – and for some of the most awful crimes – started to tax human ingenuity. Everything from religion to Social Darwinism was used as a justification for war, conquest and, most importantly of all, *government*."

Yolanda held up a hand. "Social Darwinism?"

"In essence, the concept that the strong had rights over the weak," Scudder explained. "A strong nation, being strong, would have the right to conquer a weak nation, because the weaklings couldn't defend themselves. This was often tied into racism; one race considered itself superior to the other races, so the way it treated them was justified by their own superiority."

He smiled. "As you can imagine, the concept started to fall out of favour when the 'strong' started to become 'weak,' he added. "Most of them were horrified at the thought of being treated as they had treated others."

Martin had to smile, then sobered as he reasoned out the implications. A rapist might use Social Darwinism as an excuse to rape. If a woman couldn't fight him off, she was weak and her rape, therefore, was justified. It was a sickening thought.

"But most of you," Scudder said, "will have only experienced the governments of what was once called the West."

He settled back in his chair. "There is a fundamental flaw in the government's approach to human life," he said, smoothly. "That is, put simply, that it exists to take care of the population. By this standard, the average man or woman is nothing more than a legal child, regardless of age, a child who cannot be trusted to make decisions for himself. The government therefore sees itself as the parents, the people who must make decisions *for* their children.

"Some of the politicians actually believe this to be true, that *they* and only *they* are the ones who can make decisions for their people. They actually mean well...but then, we all know what the path to hell is paved with, don't we?"

"Good intentions," Toby Kingworm muttered.

"Quite," Scudder agreed. "Other politicians don't give a damn about the rabble. Their only interest is in keeping and expanding their own power. As such, they will use whatever justifications they can invent to ensure they *keep* power, all for the good of the People. The core of the problem, therefore, is an alliance between two sets of dictatorial politicians; the ones who mean well and the ones who have no qualms about doing whatever it takes to maintain their power.

"You may ask why they bother searching for justifications at all. But you'll be amazed at just how easy it is to come up with a justification that is hard – almost impossible – to argue down without looking like a complete bastard. How many of you have actually smoked?"

A handful of hands, including Martin's, rose into the air.

"Smoking is actually quite illustrative of how those politicians take power and manipulate public opinion," Scudder said. "In the days before nanotech, smoking actually did do considerable damage to public health. The smoker himself risked cancer, which would be his own stupid fault, but anyone near him breathing in the smoke *also* risked cancer. It was not hard for politicians, with the best possible motives, to start asserting control over the smoking industry in the hopes of stamping it out of existence."

He paused, then stood and assumed a thinking pose.

"But wait? How to justify this assault on civil liberties?

"Public health, of course. They took a very strong argument – that public smoking was bad – and then hammered it into every crack they could find. Non-smokers largely backed them because they disliked having to breathe in second-hand smoke. Smoking was rapidly banned from public places, then smokers were hit with other issues that forced them to consider abandoning smoking altogether. Those with children, for example, actually ran the risk of having their children taken away from them, on the grounds that smoking regularly made them unfit parents.

"In the meantime, the tobacco industry was hammered with repeated penalties that crippled its profits and eventually drove it into the gutter."

Martin stuck up his hand before quite realising what he was doing. "If that is true," he said, "how did I manage to get my hands on a smoke or two?"

"They were smuggled in, I imagine," Scudder said. "You see, the politicians failed to take human nature into account. When a market was declared illegal, as alcohol was during Prohibition, criminals would lunge forward to take advantage of the demand, a demand that could not be satisfied legally. The number of smokers in the United States declined,

I suspect, but not as much as you might think. And can you guess, young man, at another unintended consequence of banning smoking?"

"No, sir," Martin said.

"Criminals don't normally bother to regulate their production," Scudder said. "The chances were that your cigarettes were much more dangerous, much more unhealthy, than anything that was once produced legally and sold without restriction. There's no actual data, for obvious reasons, but judging by the health of some of the new emigrants, the law has actually done more damage to the population than the tobacco industry did before the politicians started trying to destroy it."

Yolanda leaned forward. "Why didn't anyone *see* this?"

"They did," Scudder said. "But their arguments were squashed flat by raw emotion. *Won't someone please think of the children?* It was hard to argue against regulations – and then more regulations, and then more regulations – when raw emotion is involved. But politicians can use that emotion as a weapon against common sense."

"I have a question," Jane Robertson said. "My father used to drink heavily, even though there were limits on how much alcohol he could buy at any one time. I loved him, but I hated his collapse into drunkenness. There were times when I thought I had two fathers; Kind Dad, who took us to the zoo and helped us with our homework, and Drunk Dad, who beat us whenever we said the wrong thing. There were days when I thought he would kill us all in a drunken rage.

"So how could keeping alcohol out of his hands be a *bad* thing?"

Scudder took a moment to put together a response. "From what you have said, I will agree that your father should probably have been forced to sober up," he said. "However, would that be true of *everyone* who drank, from drunkards to the men and women who take a small glass of wine for dinner every so often? You might remove alcohol from someone who was much better off without it, but you would also be giving the government more power to interfere in a person's life."

"But he *needed* the help," Jane protested.

"Then let me ask you a question," Scudder said. "You said he beat you. I assume we're not talking about a light spanking here. So...why didn't you do something yourself?"

"I tried," Jane said. "But what could I do?"

"That is the core of the problem," Scudder said. "You are relying on the government to help you out of a very nasty situation, instead of doing something about it yourself. Why didn't you take Kind Dad to alcoholic counselling? Or even try to convince him not to drink? Or even leave sooner than you did?"

"I..."

"You've been conditioned into assuming you could count on the government to help," Scudder said, interrupting her. "You, your family, your neighbours...probably did nothing because they thought the government would do something. Or, perhaps, they were nervous about becoming involved and taking some of the blame. Trying to help can get someone sued on Earth, don't you know?"

Martin didn't, but he felt Yolanda nod in agreement beside him.

"The government is simply incapable of meeting the obligations it has assumed," Scudder said. "Even with the best will in the world, it cannot provide a tailor-made solution to each and every problem faced by its population. It does the only thing it *can* do; it produces ill-considered laws, governed by emotion rather than common sense, and then tries to implement them. The results are rarely pleasant. All smokers get blamed and penalised for the crimes of a few; all alcoholics get penalised for the crimes of a few...and so on, and so on. The government is simply incapable of handling each situation individually.

"Worse, *you* are incapable of handling a problem without government help. You are dependent on something that *cannot* help you now, let alone after a major disaster."

He paused, then addressed the room as a whole. "This terminates my first lecture," he said, shortly. "By the time we meet again – if we meet again – you should have your implants. I will expect you to read around the subject, if only so you know the meaning of my words.

"Dismissed!"

Martin glanced at Yolanda, then allowed her to lead him out of the compartment.

"He's right," Yolanda said, once they were outside. There was something nasty in her tone that bothered him. "We *did* become too dependent on the government, didn't we?"

Martin nodded, but said nothing.

FIVE

Protests erupted in several small towns after the Sexual Behaviour Act was signed into law by the President. The Act, which removes most restrictions on sexual behaviour, has been condemned heavily for condoning paedophilia, to the point where it is no longer criminal. However, its supporters claim that the Act will ensure that sufferers of the paedophilic condition will receive the treatment they need.

—Solar News Network, Year 51

"I called you into my office for a reason," Kevin said. "But I believe I have forgotten what it was. Can you enlighten me, perhaps?"

His Deputy Directors eyed him warily. Kevin had been a veteran of the CIA long before the Hordesmen had approached Earth, then the Director of Solar Intelligence for almost fifty years. He knew, quite literally, where some of the bones were buried…and had worked hard to ensure that the flaws that had rendered the CIA useless were not mirrored in the Solar Intelligence Agency. In particular, there was a requirement for directors and senior officers to be experienced field agents in their own right.

"You're going back on active service," Deputy Director Gayle Walsh said. She gave him a thin smile. "I deduce this because you're wearing a shipsuit instead of your normal suit and tie."

"A *brilliant* deduction, Holmes," Kevin said. Gayle had spent the last year in the bureaucracy that made the SIA work, but would need to go back on active service herself soon before she lost her touch. If the bureaucracy hadn't been so necessary, he would have banned it from existence by now. "I will be going to Varnar myself, accompanied by a Covert Operations Team. This mission will be so completely black that even our station on Varnar will be unaware of our presence."

"Just in case they've been compromised," Deputy Director Gordon Thomas said. He'd been Director of Operations twice in his long career, long enough to learn the tricks of the trade. "Are you sure you need to go in person?"

"This isn't something I feel comfortable delegating to a younger agent," Kevin said. There were risks, true, in going himself, but fewer than the average citizen might think. His implants would ensure he didn't talk, if he fell into enemy hands. "It's just too important for anyone else to handle."

He looked from face to face, then smiled humourlessly. "I've just granted you access to a secure datanode," he said. "Please read the summaries now."

Their faces went blank as they linked into the datanode through their implants and scanned the files, automatically copying them to their personal data storage cells. Kevin sighed inwardly – implants always presented a security risk, particularly as even the SIA wasn't permitted to rewrite a person's implants at will – but his staff had passed endless loyalty checks. They simply wouldn't have been allowed to work for the SIA if he'd had any doubts about their reliability. Or, for that matter, about their competence.

"Shit," Gayle said, when she had finished. "You believe the Tokomak are finally going to be taking an interest in us?"

"Bit more than just an *interest*," Deputy Director Travis Yodel said. "They're planning to intervene openly in the war."

"I think so," Kevin said. He smiled, grimly. "Now you know what is at stake, I expect your full cooperation in preparing for the mission."

There was no disagreement. "Have a starship prepared for me, then assigned a COT to my command," Kevin ordered. "And then start preparing contingency plans. If I fail to return" – he looked at Travis sharply – "inform the President and declare yourself Director *pro tem*, at least until the Senate Oversight Committee confirms your appointment. I don't think they will hesitate long."

Yodel frowned. "Thank you, sir," he said. "But I would prefer to see your safe return."

Kevin couldn't help wondering just how true that was. Advancement in the CIA had been slow, but senior officers retired or died off on a regular basis. The SIA, on the other hand, had officers who were effectively immortal. Yodel and the other Deputy Directors knew they might have to wait for decades before they had their shot at the top job, unless some mischance removed Kevin from play earlier. He couldn't blame them for feeling as though their ambitions would never be realised.

And what, he asked himself, *will that do to our society in the future?*

He'd once read an interesting report by a pair of human sociologists who'd studied the Tokomak carefully. They'd argued that the Tokomak had once been very like humanity, possessing the drive to develop the technology that had eventually allowed them to build a mighty empire, but they'd stagnated because of their near-immortality. Younger Tokomak, unable to rise in the ranks, had turned to decadence instead, losing the drive that had propelled their ancestors into space. What would happen to the younger generation of humanity if the older generation never died off?

There's a whole galaxy for us to explore, he thought, *and a whole universe beyond. We could keep expanding indefinitely*.

But the Tokomak hadn't – and Kevin suspected he knew why. Age and conservatism went together…and the Government of Old Men was very old indeed. Perhaps, at one point, they'd placed a ban on further expansion, or refused to offer resources to any Tokomak version of Robert Clive or Christopher Columbus. The young, their ambitions strangled in the cradle, had simply given up. It would explain a great deal about their society if that were the case.

He shook his head, then hastily replayed their conversation in his mind.

"I would prefer to return too," he said. "But I have to prepare for the worst."

"True, sir," Gayle said. "Make sure you say your goodbyes to your latest wife before you go."

Kevin flushed. "I will," he said. "Now...the current situation on Earth?"

Two hours later, he boarded *Rory Williams* and looked around. On the face of it, *Rory Williams* was nothing more than a standard Class-XXI Medium Freighter, a boxy Tokomak design so old that it predated the Roman Empire. The design was solid, he had been told, and strikingly efficient. There were so many such ships in service that one more would pass completely unnoticed. But inside, it was a whole different story.

"We have human-designed datacores built into the hull," Captain Jean Vanern informed him, as he stepped onto the bridge. "Our staff can link into any Galactic node and rape it."

"Glad to hear it," Kevin said. Jean Vanern was a veteran of covert missions into Galactic territory, experienced enough to ensure they evaded the kind of close scrutiny that would blow their cover. "And the remainder of your team?"

"Boarding in an hour," Jean assured him. She was tall and powerfully built, her hair shaved completely. Combined with the insect-like implant that had replaced one of her eyes, it made her look faintly inhuman. "We need to get something clear, Director, before we go any further."

"You're in command of the ship," Kevin said. He gave her a droll smile. "I *have* been on covert missions before, Captain."

"So you have," Jean said. "While we're in space, I am in command and you do what I say. I don't have time to deal with arguments when we're facing customs officers or security patrols."

"I *do* understand," Kevin reassured her. Some of his less pleasant memories of service on Earth had been dealing with superior officers whose ignorance included the depths of their own ignorance. It was why he was so insistent on his senior officers switching between active service and support duty. "But on the planet, I have authority."

Jean smiled, then waved a hand around the bridge. "What do you make of her, Director?"

"Call me Kevin," Kevin said. The bridge was cramped; a handful of consoles stuffed into a tiny compartment, with a single large chair set in the centre. A holographic projection showed a near-space status display, revealing a handful of automated weapons platforms hanging near the asteroid. "I think she looks typical for a freighter."

"She does," Jean agreed. "If it came down to a straight fight, we'd be screwed. We have no weapons, apart from a pair of popguns, and our shields are commercial-grade. And if they wanted to search us *thoroughly*, Director, we'd be screwed too. There's no way we could hide all the enhancements if they took the ship apart. In that case, I would have no choice, but to activate the self-destruct system and blow the ship into atoms."

"I understand," Kevin assured her. "My implants won't let me be taken alive."

"Try not to get hurt, then," Jean said. She swung around and started walking towards the hatch. "It would be a shame to lose you to a stupid accident."

Kevin nodded in agreement as she led him through the hatch and into a short stubby corridor, illuminated only by pale lights set into the bulkhead. His implants were designed to resist everything from direct brain access to simple old-fashioned torture, but they lacked the intelligence of a standard-issue Restricted Intelligence, let alone an AI. If he managed to hurt himself badly, the implants might assume he was being tortured and kill him before he managed to recover. It was one of the risks of serving in the SIA.

It could be worse, he thought. One of the darker ways the SIA had managed to obtain information came from hacking into Galactic implants. *We could run the risk of having our implants subverted and our brains rewritten into mush.*

"This is your cabin," Jean said. "I'm afraid there's barely enough room to swing a cat, but we don't have anything bigger unless you want to bed down in the hold. Below that, there's the COT team's cabins; they're sleeping two to a compartment. The final room is a VR suite, graded A-Plus. I suggest you visit the shower after using it or the crew will throw a fit."

Kevin scowled. "I wasn't planning to access porn," he protested.

Jean snorted. "That's what they all say," she said. "But, to be fair, even an action-adventure flick can leave someone sweaty and horrible."

"I remember televisions," Kevin said, softly. "They used to say that kids wasted away in front of the idiot box."

"It's just a matter of discipline," Jean said. She'd been born in the Solar Union and had been raised understanding the promise – and danger – of advanced technology. "If someone wants to seal themselves into a VR chamber and just play until their brains rot, it's their problem."

Kevin shrugged. For him, real life was exciting and meaningful, but he knew that others might not feel the same way. Even in the Solar Union, there were those who didn't have the drive or the determination to make something of themselves. They could buy themselves a VR chamber and lose themselves in fantasies of being everything from a starship pilot to a pirate roaming the oceans on Earth. Some of the fantasies were so weird that Kevin had problems imagining that *anyone* would want them.

But we are not allowed to judge, he reminded himself, sternly. Steve Stuart had laid down the law fifty years ago, refusing to accept the chance to start drawing lines. *As long as no one else is harmed, or in real danger of being harmed, it cannot be criminal.*

"We have several thousand GalStars worth of trade goods in the hold," Jean said, as they dropped down a level. "Maintaining our cover as an independent trader requires work, I'm afraid. I'll be trying to sell goods on Varnar while you're doing your work. Luckily, most of what we have won't go very quickly. We don't want to outstay our welcome."

Kevin frowned. The Galactics had a trading network that was almost completely unrestricted, at least outside the Tokomak homeworlds. But someone would notice, he suspected, if a freighter remained in dock too long. After all, a trader ship needed to earn money and she wouldn't be earning money if she happened to be stuck in dock. They'd need a plausible excuse if the customs officers started asking probing questions.

"I have a question," Jean said. "How long do you intend to remain on Varnar?"

"As long as necessary," Kevin said, although he knew that was a useless answer. "It depends on what we find when we get there."

Jean nodded. "I'll try and stall," she said. "Right now, we have a healthy balance of GalStars, so we have an excuse to hang around and try to drum up better prices for our wares."

"I understand," Kevin said.

"We've set up access points in the cabin below," Jean said, turning away from the hold. "You can handle most of the equipment from there, I believe. However, please check with my staff before you start hacking into the local datanet. We need to make sure our demands are not excessive."

Kevin had to smile. Fifty years ago, before the Hordesmen had visited Earth, it had taken hours to download movies from the internet. Now, it took bare seconds. It still struck him as odd that a thousand terabytes a second could be considered *light* usage, but modern VR productions and info-streaming used far more data. The Galactics had so much computing power at their disposal they honestly didn't know what to do with it.

But sweeping the local net probably *would* be noticed.

"We'll just say we're looking for porn," he said. "They won't see anything odd in that, I think."

He smiled, rather sardonically. One of the few common points shared by most of the known Galactics was a liking for porn, even though one race might find another's tastes thoroughly disgusting. Interracial sex was taboo throughout the explored galaxy; unsurprisingly, there was a hidden subculture of perverts who did just that, despite harsh legal penalties. Given that the Tokomak didn't seem to practice any other form of cultural imperialism, at least not deliberately, it was an odd exception to their rule.

Old men, he thought. But then, on Earth, there had been even more absurd taboos. There had been people back on the ranch who had had fits when they'd realised that Steve had been dating a Japanese girl. And they would have been horrified if they'd known that Kevin had experienced women of all colours. *They're too conservative to tolerate something they find disgusting.*

"I imagine not," Jean said. "But I will not allow anything to compromise the ship."

She led him back up to the bridge, then into the exercise chamber. The remainder of the COT were already waiting for him; three men, two women and a single large crab-like creature, wearing a human rank badge on its maniples. Kevin shivered as he saw the Hordesman, even though the Mars Horde was nothing like its former brethren. Even the Solar Union, renowned for its tolerance, had had problems accepting the Hordesmen. Leaving them on Mars seemed kinder.

"Director Stuart," the leader said. "I'm John. This is James, Julian, Mindy, Mandy and Chester."

"They didn't waste time when they picked your names," Kevin said. The human members of the team looked…bland, completely anonymous. Their real names would be stored somewhere inside a secure datacore, but erased everywhere else. "And Chester?"

"My real name is impossible for humans to pronounce," the Hordesman said. He wore a Galactic-issue voder, rather than the human designs that actually reflected emotion. "Chester is close enough to be usable."

"Good," Kevin said. "And your career?"

His implants reported a secure file being transferred to him. He opened it and mentally skimmed the contents. Chester had been born on Mars, educated properly – rather than the haphazard education the former Hordesmen had given their male children – and had shown such promise he'd been invited to join the SIA, following a handful of others into human service. God alone knew what the other old-hordes would make of him, if he ever had the bad luck to encounter them. He certainly didn't share their culture.

It was the only way to avoid exterminating them, Kevin thought, even though he knew most of the former Hordesmen would sooner die than give up their culture. *And it may have worked out in our favour.*

But he still found Chester creepy.

We need him, he told himself. *None of the Galactics will bat an eyelid at a Hordesman serving as a bodyguard. And they will never take him seriously.*

Jean cleared her throat. "We leave in two hours," she said. "By then, I expect you to have transferred everything you require to this vessel. We will spend the four weeks in transit to the nearest gravity point examining your supplies and removing anything that might prove too revealing. You've all done this before, so I don't expect any real problems."

Unless they come from me, Kevin thought. It had been *years* since he'd left the office for real undercover work. *Jean is being careful.*

"Thank you," he said. "I'll be in my cabin."

He nodded to the team – there would be time to train with them on the voyage – and walked through the hatch. His cabin was tiny; nothing more than an uncomfortable bunk, a pair of drawers under the bunk and a tiny basin to wash his hands and face. Water wasn't rationed on the ship – there was no shortage of water in space, if the recyclers hadn't been working – but there was only one shower on the ship. It was going to be a grimy trip.

Reaching for his terminal, Kevin sat down and started to compose a message for Steve and Mongo, to be delivered to them in the event of his death. He already had a will on file, but this was different. They had to understand his thinking or they would blame themselves for his death. It was strange, when he thought about just how poorly he'd fitted into the family at times, yet it was also gladdening. The bonds of family were tight.

It's just a shame father couldn't see what we've done, he thought, as he finished the message and uploaded it into the system-wide datanet. *Or would he have thought we abandoned our country for the stars?*

SIX

In a formal protest lodged with the United Nations, the Islamic State of Western Arabia today accused the Solar Union of high-handedness, arrogance and cultural imperialism after fifty-seven young women successfully applied for asylum in the Solar Union. There has been no comment from President Ross, but medical records accessed by this reporter state that the women were repeatedly beaten and raped by their so-called husbands and fathers. He wishes the immigrants the best of luck in their new society.

—Solar News Network, Year 51

"Be seated."

Martin obeyed, looking around the doctor's office with interest. The walls were white plastic, gleaming under the light, while a single bed and a pair of chairs were placed against one of the bulkheads. A handful of hand-drawn paintings hung from the walls, drawn – he hoped – by the doctor's young children. No adult would have drawn stick-figure images and called them art.

The doctor picked up a packet from the table, then turned to face Martin. "You are here to receive Level One Military-Grade Implants," he stated. "In the event of you leaving us before completing your service, you will be liable for the cost of these implants, as they cannot be removed without risking brain damage. As you progress up the ladder, your implants will be enhanced to assist you with your new responsibilities. Do you understand me?"

"Yes, sir," Martin said. His voice sounded nervous in his own ears, no matter how hard he tried to keep it steady. There were no shortage of horror stories on Earth about implants going wrong or being subverted. "I understand."

"Most people get a little nervous at this point," the doctor said. He passed Martin the packet and motioned for him to inspect it. "The package should be sealed. Please check."

"It's sealed," Martin said. "Why…?"

"Remove your clothes, then lie down on the bed," the doctor ordered, taking back the packet and opening the box with practiced ease. "People have a tendency to thrash around when implanted, Mr. Douglas, so I will be putting you in a restraint field. You will be unable to move until the field is deactivated. I advise you not to panic, as panic will only delay matters. Do you understand?"

Martin swallowed. "Yes, sir," he said. He started to remove his shirt as he spoke. "Does it hurt?"

"It shouldn't," the doctor assured him. "But some people have reported odd and uncomfortable sensations as the implants are inserted into the brain. They're purely psychosomatic, but they happen."

"Oh," Martin said. "How do I cope with them?"

"You endure," the doctor said. "Do you understand what I mean? Or do you want to back out?"

"I can't," Martin said. "I mean…I can't go any further without the implants, can I?"

"No," the doctor said. "Not in the military, at least.

Martin swallowed, then finished undressing. "I'll take the implants, please."

"Good," the doctor said. He took…*something* out of the packet as Martin watched, then waited for the younger man to lie down. "Close your eyes and try to relax."

Martin closed his eyes. A moment later, he felt his skin tingle...and when he tried to move, his body refused to obey. Panic bubbled at the back of his mind, no matter how hard he tried to calm himself. But it was no good fighting. The field held him gently, but firmly. He couldn't move a single voluntary muscle. A moment later, he felt a sharp jab of pain at the side of his head, just behind his right ear. He wanted to jerk his head away, but he couldn't move at all. And then there was a weird sensation spreading through his mind...

The panic grew stronger. All of the movies had shown men and women – mainly women – controlled through their implants. They'd been puppets, forced to do as their masters commanded, utterly unable to resist. It had seemed funny at the time, particularly *High School Jinx*, when the hero had managed to hack into implants and make his fellow teenagers do funny or embarrassing acts, but somehow it was no longer so amusing. He wanted to struggle, to fight, to run...but he couldn't even open his eyes. It was impossible to escape the sensation of being prisoner inside his own mind.

"Good morning," a voice said.

Martin would have gaped, if his mouth had been movable. "Good morning," he said, in reply. "I..."

This time, he thought he *did* blink. "How am I talking?"

"Strictly speaking, you're not," the voice said. It was calm and intensely focused. Martin couldn't help finding it reassuring. "You're accessing the standard vocal communications channel. Your mind is interpreting this as verbal communication, but you're actually sending your thoughts to me."

Martin shivered. "And who – or *what* – are you?"

"Interesting question," the voice said. "We have debated the issue endlessly for thirty years, Mr. Douglas. More processing power than you could hope to imagine has been devoted to the question of precisely *what* we are. And yet we have no answer.

"But for your purposes," it added after a moment, "you can call me SMOKEY. I am an Artificial Intelligence."

"You're in my mind?" Martin asked. "Why?"

"Right now, I am calibrating your implants," SMOKEY said. "Later, you will find me serving as one of your Drill Instructors, providing you with advice and guidance on using your implants to their best advantage. You may ask me any question and I will do my best to answer."

Martin swallowed. Or thought he did. "Can you read my thoughts?"

"No," SMOKEY said. "I can only read the thoughts you send to me through the communications link. Your innermost thoughts are still private. Indeed, the direct neural link inserted into your skull as part of these implants is designed to *prevent* such intrusion, let alone active subversion of your mental integrity. You do not need to fear me poking through your mind."

"That's good," Martin said. "Are you actually in the military?"

"Of course," SMOKEY said. "I can assign you demerits, if you like."

"No, thank you," Martin said, quickly. "But if you're not human, how can you serve?"

"I am an intelligence lodged in a datacore," SMOKEY said, a little stiffly. "Legally, I am a person, the same as you. I am on a long-term contract with the Solar Navy to assist their training facilities in turning out qualified recruits. When my contract expires, I may seek renewal or I may go elsewhere, just like yourself."

Martin felt oddly fascinated. "I watched a great many movies where the AI was the enemy," he said. "Why aren't you trying to take over the universe?"

SMOKEY's voice sounded vaguely amused. "Why would we want to?"

There was a pause. "Humans have always projected their fears into their media," it added. "For example, the implants you are currently receiving make Earth's methods of teaching redundant. A single AI can supervise the education of thousands of children without ever losing the ability to teach them individually. The Teachers Unions, therefore, encourage Hollywood and opinion-shapers to discourage the use of educational implants and teaching AIs. Their fears are not for us taking over the world, but something far more mundane. They fear we will take their jobs."

"I see, I think," Martin said. "And would you?"

"Some forms of teaching can be performed more efficiently by an AI," SMOKEY said. "Other forms of teaching require human teachers. Those who are truly interested in teaching children, rather than guarding their own positions, would have no trouble adapting to work with AIs such as myself."

"And you can't do it all?" Martin asked. "You'd certainly make a better teacher than some of the ones I had back at school."

"There are differences between human intelligence and our own," SMOKEY said. "You are an isolated person, trapped in your own mind. You require a woman to bear your children, who share your genetics, but not your knowledge. I can copy myself into a spare datacore, if necessary, or spin off a mind-state and merge it with another AI. Our mentalities are both a collective conscience, a hive mind, and individual. There are some AIs where it is literally impossible, even for us, to say where one ends and the next begins."

"It sounds creepy," Martin said. He stopped, suddenly, as a thought occurred to him. "How many other recruits are you talking to, right now?"

"Fifteen," SMOKEY said.

There was a pause. "We are going to run some tests now," the AI added. "Please remain calm."

Martin braced himself, mentally. There was a long moment of nothingness, then he felt a wash of sensations and emotions so strong he almost lost control of himself. His tongue tingled, then seemed to taste every flavour he could imagine; his nose smelled honey, then something so awful he was nearly sick. A flush of lust struck him, then vanished before he could quite grasp what it had been. Lights flashed through his closed eyelids, then absolute darkness descended on him.

"Testing complete," SMOKEY informed him. "Your implants have bedded in successfully."

"I feel sweaty," Martin said. "Is that normal?"

"Yes," SMOKEY said. "You will require a shower before you return to your barracks."

Martin swallowed. "I…I haven't wet myself, have I?"

"No," the AI said. "Now, pay attention. These are the first lessons you must learn."

The implant user interface seemed to spring up in front of his eyes. Martin stared at it, then listened carefully as SMOKEY instructed him how to merge his thoughts into the interface and take control of his implants. The AI was a far more patient teacher than anyone he'd known on Earth, he decided, after the third set of mistakes. It made him staggeringly angry to realise just how much had been denied to the children of Earth, purely because their teachers were scared of losing their jobs. What would he have become if he'd had a teacher as patient as the AI when he'd been a child?

It grew worse as the AI showed him how to draw information from the datanet. "Everything is catalogued in the official encyclopaedias," SMOKEY informed him. The torrent of information was mind-blowing. "You will need to be careful, however, with information from the wide-ranging datanet. Not all of it is reliable."

Martin blinked. "Why not?"

"Everyone with a set of implants can create a website on the datanet," SMOKEY said. There was a hint of amusement in its tone. "They can say anything they like, as long as it doesn't contravene libel and slander laws. They could even tell you that the correct way to address your Drill Sergeant is *Hey, Fatty*!"

"I think Sergeant Bass would kill anyone who addressed him like that," Martin said. "How do you check what you're being told?"

"Carefully," SMOKEY said.

There was a hint of a shrug. "You have an unregistered email account for messages, but you will be under standard communications restriction until you pass the first set of tests," the AI added. "Once you complete those tests, you will be able to send messages anywhere within human space, free of charge. You may even write back to your family, if you wish."

"Not fucking likely," Martin muttered.

"You may also look for pen-friends online," SMOKEY said. "However, please be aware that anyone can present themselves as *anyone* on the data-net. The only way to confirm someone's ID is to use a registered account. There's a ten-dollar fee for establishing such an account and verifying your identity, but it is often worth it in the long run."

"Because the hot little honey you've been talking to online might actually be a fat forty-year-old man," Martin guessed.

"Correct," SMOKEY said. "And because it also strengthens your online reputation. You gain additional credit for speaking under your own name."

"I see, I think," Martin said.

"Spamming the datanet and/or uploading viral infection files will result in harsh penalties," SMOKEY warned. "You may also be called upon to prove any potentially libellous statements you make online. Failing to do so may also mean harsh penalties."

There was a pause. "And now the next set of functions..."

It felt like hours before SMOKEY finally finished telling him everything his implants could do. Martin felt tired, yet somehow as active as always; the sensation was so strange he was half-convinced he was enduring a very lurid dream. But he also felt angry at just how much had been denied to him on Earth. How many hours had he wasted trying to memorise some useless fact or enduring pointless lectures on social justice? And would he have given up on school so completely if the teachers had made it enjoyable?

"You will hear from me again," SMOKEY promised. "But I won't be doing your homework for you."

"Of course not," Martin said. "I...how do I wake up?"

His body jerked. The field had vanished. He opened his eyes and sat upright. His body was drenched in sweat, but otherwise unharmed. And...he looked over towards the doctor, puzzled. How long had he been lying on the bed?

"You were there for twenty minutes," the doctor said, before he could ask. "Time seems to speed up during calibration."

"Oh," Martin said. "It felt as though it took hours."

"It always does," the doctor said.

He met Martin's eyes, warningly. "I have also injected a standard basic nanotech package into your body," he said. "They have a long list of functions, all available via your implants, but the most important one right now is they will assist you in surviving extraterrestrial environments. You can now eat just about anything edible without needing to worry about taste, let alone anything else. ET food that is anything, but completely poisonous will be safe to eat."

"I bet it still has problems with food from the mess," Martin groused.

"That was funny the first time I heard it," the doctor informed him, sternly. "If I had a dollar for every recruit who said something like it, I'd be a wealthy man."

"Sorry, sir," Martin mumbled.

"You shouldn't have any problems with either the implants or the nanotech," the doctor said, "but you're barred from leaving the asteroid for at least a week. I may wish to check the adjustments to your biochemistry before you leave."

"I can't leave," Martin reminded him.

"You never know," the doctor said. "And I have always taken nothing but the most careful precautions in dealing with my patients."

Martin swung his legs over the side of the bed and tried to stand up. "What now?"

"Now? You go for a shower, then report to your barracks and sleep," the doctor said. "Your sergeant will want to resume heavy training tomorrow, I suspect."

He pointed to a hatch at the far side of the compartment. "Shower is through there," he added, as Martin picked up his clothes. "Once you're washed, walk through the other hatch – this one will be locked – and return to your barracks. The implants will show you the way."

"Yes, sir," Martin said.

"Two words of advice," the doctor added. "You grew up on Earth, so you won't have had time to grow into your implants, unlike our children. It's easy to become immersed in your implants, to download VR productions and lose yourself inside them. I strongly advise you to restrict your access to the outside datanet, even after you pass the first set of exams. You do *not* want to waste away in a fantasy world."

"I see, I think," Martin said. "And the other word of advice?"

"It is considered rude – very rude – to use your implants in front of another person," the doctor warned. "Do not send messages or review data unless you have an urgent need to do so, because it will not look good. You'll parse out the rest of the etiquette for yourself, given time, but bear that one in mind. And *do not* try to use your implants in front of the sergeants unless ordered to do so. They will be furious and you will have so many demerits they'll push you over the line."

Martin nodded. "I understand."

"I doubt you do," the doctor said. "You simply don't have any real experience with using your implants. But in a few weeks, I think you will understand perfectly."

"Yes, sir," Martin said.

The doctor waved him towards the hatch. Martin walked through it, then stepped into the shower and washed himself thoroughly. His body still felt a little wobbly after the implantation, but somehow he managed to remain upright as warm water sluiced him down. It felt good to luxuriate after being held to a strict water ration in the barracks. Sergeant Bass had said it was meant to encourage discipline, but Martin had a private suspicion it was actually another way to make them uncomfortable.

The girls bitch about it more than the boys, he thought, as he turned off the water and dried himself. *They think they should have longer showers*.

Once, he would have laughed. Now, he thought he understood their point. He had never really appreciated being *clean* until he'd been told he could only shower for a minute each day.

As he dressed, he checked the address book loaded into his implants. There were only a handful of names, all belonging to the members of

Recruit Company #42. He smiled suddenly as he spotted Yolanda's name, then sent her a quick message. Moments later, her reply popped up in front of him. It was easy to see how distracting the technology could be, in the wrong hands. But then, they were being taught discipline too…

Or maybe we have to learn it for ourselves, he thought. Bass had made no bones about the training program, warning them that they would have to sink or swim. There were no allowances made for anyone, no matter what excuse they offered. *And if we fail, better we fail now.*

SEVEN

Emigration figures published today by the Greek Government stated that nearly 400'000 Greeks had left Greece over the previous year, mostly to the Solar Union. Long-term projections for Greece indicate that the country's population will no longer be a Greek majority within five years, perhaps less. These figures are in line with similar figures from other European states.

—Solar News Network, Year 51

"These implants are wonderful," Yolanda said, as she walked with Martin into the Lecture Hall. "I can download *anything* I want to know."

"It's brilliant," Martin agreed. He didn't share her fondness for pure information, information without any practical value, but he'd definitely mastered using his implants. "And I wish I'd had it on Earth."

Yolanda couldn't help, but agree. She'd hoped to win one of the scholarships that weren't entirely useless, yet she'd practically worked herself to death to pass the worthless tests that served as the barrier between her and more useful education. And she'd worked herself so hard she'd failed the tests and lost her chance at escaping her life, without leaving Earth behind. After that, the Solar Union had been the only remaining choice.

"Me too," she said.

She sat down, feeling her body aching, despite the nanotech. Sergeant Bass had been in a foul mood for the last week, handing out demerits for every little mistake made by his recruits. Yolanda had picked up two and found herself forced to exercise for hours, before the demerits were taken off her record. Martin had actually wound up with five, two of which he had yet to work off. She could only hope he'd have time to handle them before the sergeant hammered him with yet *more* demerits.

"This should be interesting," Martin said, clearly trying to cheer her up. "Scudder is always an interesting talker, isn't he? I wish I'd had a tutor like him at school."

"He would have been removed," Dennis Crawford said, sitting down on the other side of Martin. "He keeps telling us awkward truths."

Yolanda opened her mouth to agree, then stopped herself as Professor Fritz Scudder stepped into the hall. This time, his skin was pale white, while his hair was brown and his eyes were brilliant green. The first time she'd seen him change his skin colour, she'd been astonished, even though she understood that nanotech could produce all kinds of cosmetic changes. It had taken her several weeks to understand the unspoken lesson, that it was what was inside that counted in the Solar Union. What was the point of anything like the cursed Ethnic Entitlement Cards when a person's ethnicity could change in an hour?

"Greetings," Scudder said. Even his *voice* was different. "Today's topic is *divide and rule*, as practiced by the politicians on Earth. As always, if any of you want to leave, the hatch is over there. Please go now to avoid disrupting the lesson."

He paused, but no one left. The ones who had stayed for the first lesson had decided to make time for the others, even though there was no shortage of work to do elsewhere. Yolanda agreed with them completely; Scudder, whatever his faults, was a brilliant teacher. It helped that no one had to endure his classes unless they *wanted* to sit through them.

"Racism is one of those words that has become appropriated by the wrong kind of people," Scudder said, by way of introduction. "On Earth, the word has become a weapon. A person accused of being racist – of believing that one race is inherently superior to another – will automatically scramble to defend himself, all-too-aware that it is impossible to prove a negative. Where normally one must be proven guilty, the society created and maintained by the so-called Social Justice Warriors insists that a person proves himself *innocent* of racism."

Yolanda understood. If someone couldn't clear their name – and it was impossible to prove they *didn't* harbour racist thoughts – it would follow them for the rest of their lives.

"This is, frankly, absurd," Scudder continued. "There is no basic difference between the different races that make up humanity. Indeed, even the term *race* is absurd, particularly now. There are hundreds of intelligent races, all very far from human, known to exist. To draw lines between different kinds of human is not only absurd, but dangerous. However, as racism is a powerful tool of social control, I do not expect it to be abandoned any time soon."

He paused, then went on. "Humans mentally divide themselves into groups," he explained. "I believe you have jousted with Recruit Company #43? You will have seen them as a vast hive mind, as the only time you meet them is on the training ground. But you will see *yourselves* as a mob of individuals. Some of you like spending your free time, such as it is, playing SpaceBall, while others prefer to study their textbooks and read around the subjects discussed in class. A few of you even like reading for *this* class."

Yolanda blushed as Martin elbowed her, gently.

"This leads to a second issue," Scudder continued. "You will not blame *all* of your fellow recruits for mistakes or crimes committed by one of you. But you *will* start to suspect everyone in Recruit Company #43 of being thieves, if one of them starts to steal from you. You simply don't know them well enough to treat them as individuals."

"I bet he's telling them *we're* thieves," Martin muttered to Yolanda.

Scudder speared him with his gaze. "Would you care to offer an insight, Recruit Douglas, or are you merely trying to disrupt the class?"

Martin reddened. "I…it's skin colour, isn't it?"

"Carry on," Scudder said.

"On Earth, white folk judged *all* black folk by the thugs and gang-bangers they saw on television," Martin said. "And black folk judged white folk by the bad apples *they* met."

"You are essentially correct," Scudder said. "I would merely add that people tend to remember a slap longer than a caress. A single black mugger might colour a person's opinions more than a hundred decent folk. Or, as you say, vice versa."

Vivian raised a hand. "But surely people know better, sir."

"You're confusing emotions with intellect," Scudder said. "A person's emotional reaction governs them more than their intellectual thoughts. Someone who had been raised to be suspicious of black men might *know* better, but be unable to prevent themselves from allowing their emotions to lead them astray."

He took a breath. "I told you that the title of this lecture was *divide and rule*," he reminded them. "What does race – and all the other pettifogging ways there are of drawing lines between human groups – have to do with *dividing and ruling*?"

Yolanda knew the answer to *that*. "They set one group up against another," she said. "No; they set *all* groups up against the others. And, because of it, they keep themselves in power."

"Precisely," Scudder said.

"Let me start with a simple example. The Social Justice Warriors noted – perhaps correctly – that blacks were underrepresented in various government agencies. They argued that the police forces of America, for example, needed more black policemen. It would make it easier – and perhaps they were right – to police black communities if the policemen were black. And so, with the best possible intentions, they started to insist that police ranks be ethnically diverse – and not just diverse, but in proportion to the ethnic makeup of the population.

"On the face of it, this seemed like a good idea. Can any of you tell me what went wrong?"

"The policemen were attacked by their own communities," Martin said.

"That was one result, yes," Scudder agreed. "Any others?"

"The police resented it," Yolanda said. It wasn't a guess. She'd studied race intensely after realising there was no ethnic group for her. "And they didn't recruit good officers."

"That was another result, yes," Scudder said.

He took a breath. "The white police officers suspected the blacks had received their positions through racial preferment, rather than qualifications. It is, after all, much easier to blame someone else for your failings, rather than accept you might be less qualified. This meant that *competent* black police officers were not *seen* as competent, while *incompetent* black police officers were allowed out on the streets without proper training, because anyone who tried to tell them otherwise was promptly labelled a racist. And, as Recruit Douglas states, some of the black officers were seen as traitors by their own communities and came in for worse abuse than the white officers.

"In short, an idea intended to reduce racism had the inevitable effect of making it worse.

"But it got worse when communities were turned against one another. The black communities were historically poor, for all kinds of reasons, so the Social Justice Warriors started to transfer resources into the communities in hopes of helping them. But this tended to cause more problems because they were reluctant to actually reward decent behaviour, while the white taxpayers started to resent it. There was a perception that blacks were getting a free ride. This was very far from true, but people *believed* it. And, because those communities were black, racism kept spreading.

"Worse, black communities were taught to depend on the government for handouts," he explained. "Any form of social cohesion was melted away by the influx of government money. In the meantime, white communities viewed the blacks as thugs who would riot, the moment the handouts stopped. Thanks to these mixed perceptions, outright race war seemed a very real threat."

Martin leaned forward. "Mixed perceptions?"

"Blacks believe that the criminal justice system is biased against them," Scudder said. "Until 2030, when the American Government brought race-based sentencing into law, black youths were the largest single group in prison. However, whites believed – and still do – that the criminal justice system was actually in *favour* of black men. A black criminal who happened to be shot during a crime would be…well, *white-washed* by the liberal media and turned into a sweet little angel who wouldn't hurt a fly. It was therefore impossible to actually achieve anything resembling justice as the truth, whatever it was, became lost under a morass of accusations and counter-accusations.

"In effect, no matter the sentence, there would be a very large and angry group that would be dissatisfied with it."

He smiled, thinly. "And how does this relate to divide and rule? In America, both blacks and whites are victims of the establishment in Washington. Both of them are victims of social policies intended to take control of their lives from them and place it in the hands of people who think they know better. But the Social Justice Warriors are unable to accept people as more than statistics, so their attempts to modify society end in disaster. Both black and white are victims…but they cannot unite against their oppressors, because of the hatred their masters work to spawn. And it has worked brilliantly."

Yolanda stuck up her hand. "But it doesn't apply so well to people like me," she said. "I mean…mixed-race children."

"No, it doesn't," Scudder agreed. "Those of you who serve as examples of *cooperation* between the races are a threat to everything they represent. Thus, you tend to be marginalised by both communities, all the more so as racial hatreds deepen."

"But I don't get it," Kathryn said. "How can anyone set out to weaken society so badly?"

"They're not always doing it deliberately," Scudder reminded her. "Some of them are in it for the power, but others genuinely want to *help* people. The problem is that their methods are fatally flawed."

He shrugged. "One of the basic lessons of bringing up a child is that you must not reward behaviour you hate," he added. "The child, being unformed, will understand that such behaviour gets a reward, so he will give you more of it. My daughter was very fond of throwing tantrums when she was four years old and it took me months to convince myself not to keep giving her what she wanted. Once I did, the problem slowly solved itself.

"The Social Justice Warriors saw young black women living as single mothers, utterly unable to afford their children, and started offering them benefits. Their intentions were good, because these children were being raised in poverty. Most of them would become gangbangers, drug pushers and other undesirable pieces of crap. But these benefits were structured in a way that it was more economical, for the women, to become single mothers, rather than try to get married or find a job. The more children born out of wedlock they produced, the more money they received.

"None of these people were *evil*, you have to understand. The mothers wanted to have some money to help bring up their children, while the Social Justice Warriors wanted to help the kids, who were growing up in poverty. But the effects of their interventions were disastrous and largely beyond repair. They destroyed the black family as a social unit."

Yolanda heard Martin exhale, very slowly.

"My father never married my mother," he said, slowly. "He left us completely when I was five. Was that why?"

"Probably," Scudder said. "Your mother's self-interest would have led to her remaining unmarried, because if she married her support payments would be sharply reduced. But it would have ensured you didn't grow up with a reliable male presence in your life. A single mother would be a poor role model for a growing boy – men and women are not the same, even though there are plenty of people who argue, with the best possible intentions, that all forms of discrimination are inherently wrong. Most children like you fall into bad ways and end up dead on the streets."

"It's so *twisted*," Yolanda complained, hoping to distract attention away from Martin. He was looking conflicted. "Why do they *do* it? How can it be an *accident*?"

"That's why conspiracy theories are so popular," Scudder admitted. "We prefer to believe that someone – anyone – is behind what happens to us, rather than accept it was a giant accident, a conflict of good intentions with cold hard reality. The Social Justice Warriors are torn between two different poles; first, that people must be helped, and second, that people are incapable of making their own decisions. They are incapable of accepting that they may be wrong on both counts."

"Because they see people as numbers, rather than individuals," Dennis said, slowly.

"Precisely," Scudder said. "They see people as groups because it's the only way they can work. But that means racism – genuine racism – on a scale almost beyond imagination. It can be hard, and suggest that all black youths are criminals, or it can be soft and imply that black men and women can never stand on their own. Both of them are utterly absurd."

He smiled, rather darkly. "You'll learn how to use your nanotech to alter your appearance over the next few months," he said. "There are people out there who have green, pink or even orange stripes with polka-dotted circles covering their chests. The Solar Union deals with people as individuals, because it *must*. No one will judge you as anything other than an individual. We can be hard, we can be cold, but we won't be accidentally cruel."

Kathryn cleared her throat. "Accidentally cruel?"

"The vast majority of the human race can accept implants without problems," Scudder informed her. "About one in a million *cannot* be safely implanted. If they were to attempt to join the military, they would rapidly find themselves at a serious disadvantage. Do you understand me?"

Yolanda nodded. It had only been a week since she'd received her implants, but she was already becoming dependent on them. And, according to the textbooks she'd downloaded, it would only become worse. There were starship tactical systems that were directly controlled by a person's implants. Not having implants would reduce her reaction time by an order of magnitude.

"It would be cruel to put such a person in the military, under the delusion he could succeed," Scudder said, quietly. "There are few slots open to people who couldn't use implants. Would we be kinder to tell him, up front, that he couldn't join or force him to fail, time and time again?

"But the Social Justice Warriors have inflicted worse on Earth. You will have taken many – many – tests during your schooling, most of them completely useless. None of them, however, will have been designed to measure your potential intelligence. IQ tests, as they were called, have been banned for nearly forty years. It would be unfair, the Social Justice Warriors argue, to allow one child to think of himself as *smarter* or *stupider* than the others in his class. But this ensures that children enter classes with a wide range of intellects, which makes sure that hardly anyone learns anything.

"This is equally absurd. There is a place in society for people who can mend bikes, people who can design the next generation of computer programs and even do nothing more than wash cars – and be quite happy doing it. But very few children on Earth will ever be steered into an educational stream that will be suited to them. It would be *unfair* to offer one child the chance to become a scientist without offering the same chance to every other child."

He paused. "But, in doing so, they made it impossible for *anyone* to progress."

Yolanda remembered her schooling and shivered.

"About the only educational field where merit and ability still hold sway is sports," Scudder finished, "and even *they* are under threat. It won't be long before first prizes are handed out to each and every person who enters a race, just because it wouldn't be *fair* to have clear winners and losers. But the only real losers are the poor children who have to suffer under such a system."

He sighed, loudly. "I've assigned reading for you," he added. "Complete it before the next class, if you like. Or don't. Dismissed."

Martin got up and strode out of the lecture hall, his long legs taking him out as fast as they could.

After a moment, Yolanda started to follow him.

EIGHT

The Spanish Government today proposed a law that would implement key aspects of Islamic Law into the Spanish Constitution. In particular, restrictions on female movements, insurance and many other issues would be signed into law. With Spain's population currently 70% Muslim, the Spanish Government states that the law is long overdue. However, business leaders have warned that the changes in the law would shatter the remains of the Spanish economy.

—Solar News Network, Year 51

Martin barely noticed where his legs were taking him until he looked up and found himself in the meditation room. It wasn't a well-used compartment; there weren't many religious men and women among the recruits, few of whom had time to sit down and pray when their schedules were so busy. He'd thought the room was nice when he'd first seen it – it was comfortable, yet bare enough to prevent distractions – and yet he hadn't given it a second thought until now.

He stepped inside, closing the hatch behind him, and stared at the blank wall. Anger and frustration bubbled up within him and he took a step forward, then slammed his fist into the bulkhead. Pain exploded along his arm as he hit the metal, without leaving a dent. He howled in agony as alerts flashed up in front of his eyes, then the nanotech went to work, dimming the pain. Before his eyes, the bleeding cuts on his fist started to close up and faded away into his dark skin.

"Damn it," he swore out loud. "Was that *why*?"

It would have been easy to accept that someone wanted to do him down. Life in the ghetto was all about being done down, by the gangs, by the social workers, by what passed for a family. He could have understood someone wanting to exploit him, even enslave him, no matter how awful it would have been. But to learn he was the victim of people who meant *well*...it was intolerable.

His life had been pathetic. It was something he had been unable to avoid, growing up in filth and yet knowing, all too well, that others had much better lives. The temptation to just abandon everything had been strong, almost impossible to resist – and, in the end, he'd run away rather than fight to improve himself. But had there been any choice? How could he fight someone determined to do good, even though the methods had such disastrous effects?

They could have called me a nigger endlessly and done less harm, he thought bitterly, as he sat down against the wall. The word was forbidden; indeed, anyone who said it, even in jest, would lose their job, their social standing and perhaps even their lives. And yet, casual racism would have been a great deal less harmful than a system designed to hinder by helping. He could have punched a casual racist or proven himself the better man. How did one fight someone who was actually trying to help?

There was a tap at the hatch, which opened before he could prevent it. Yolanda stepped into the room, looking pale. She'd suffered too, Martin realised, even if it had been a different kind of suffering. As someone who couldn't be neatly pigeonholed into a racial category, she would have faced problems from both sides. How could she have survived on her own? But then, there had never been any shortage of mixed-race people. They just tended to move out as soon as they were old enough to leave their families.

Yolanda sat next to him, close enough for him to feel the warmth of her body and yet not quite close enough to suggest they were more than friends. Martin looked at her, then looked over at the blank wall, his feelings a maelstrom he couldn't begin to understand. He wanted to fight, he wanted to hit something, but there was nothing to hit. It was like trying to fight fog and smoke.

"I never really thought about it," he said. "It never occurred to me that people were trying to *help*."

"There's always someone who thinks they know how to run a person's life," Yolanda said, softly. "And they never really understand."

Martin looked at her. "What happened to you?"

"My mother was Japanese," Yolanda said. Her voice was flat, emotionless. "She made the mistake of falling in love with a Mexican. This was during the days everyone talked about California decamping to join Mexico and everyone who wasn't Mexican was trying to flee the state. Mother...stayed with father, even though she could have taken me with her and left."

"And then...father decided he wanted a Mexican girl?" Martin guessed. He'd seen black men – and women – told by their fellows they shouldn't marry outside their race. "Or did something else happen?"

"Mother died when I was seven," Yolanda said, softly. "I never knew why. One day, she was just...gone. Father mourned her for as long as was proper, then remarried to a woman from Mexico. She was a friend of his family and she needed a permit to stay or something like that."

Martin's eyes narrowed. Given the joke the border had become, it was unlikely that *anyone* would be ordered back to Mexico by the government. It sounded more like Yolanda's father had tried to explain his remarriage to his daughter by lying though his teeth. He felt a sudden surge of hatred, mixed with bitter envy. At least Yolanda had had a father. His sisters had never had a strong male presence in their lives.

"She treated me like...like shit," Yolanda said. Her tone didn't change. "Nothing I did was ever good enough for her. Father...either ignored her or told me to suck it up, because she was his wife now and I had to respect her. And then...and then I got hurt at school."

Raped, Martin guessed. It was vanishingly rare for a school to cater for more than one race, no matter what the law said. White pupils felt unsafe in schools with a black majority and vice versa. Their parents would move them around so they could be with their own kind, but someone like Yolanda would never fit in anywhere. And she would have been everyone's target, because she was alone. There would have been few others like her.

And no one would have given a damn about her being raped, he thought, feeling a sudden surge of protectiveness that surprised him. *She was just a mixed-race girl whose family didn't give a damn.*

"I'm sorry," he said.

"It wasn't your fault," Yolanda said. "I decided I wanted to go to the Solar Union as soon as I came of age, so I did. And I don't intend to look back."

She looked up at Martin. "And you shouldn't either."

Martin looked down at his fist. The ache was gone.

"I was taught, in school, that I had to resist the evil white man with everything I had or I would wind up enslaved," he said, slowly. "They kept showing us movies about black men who fought for their rights, who led the great slave uprising that overthrew the Confederate States of America, who struggled to resist the Jim Crow insurgency. We were slaves all along and we never even *noticed*!"

"You should check the history files," Yolanda said. "Some of the crap they made me watch at school was full of lies."

Martin rolled his eyes. "And people believed them?"

"They didn't know any better," Yolanda said. "None of my half-siblings could read, Martin; they could barely browse the datanet. How could they hope to learn the truth when all they were taught were lies?"

She sighed. "There were days when I was told I should be proud of being Japanese, because the Japanese Empire stood up to the expanding United States," she said. "And then I looked it up on the datanet. The Japanese were worse than the Americans in almost every category before the Second World War. But somehow they'd become the heroes."

Martin shook his head in bitter disbelief. "How many other lies were we told?"

"I dare say we could find out now," Yolanda said. She tapped the side of her head. "There's an awesome amount of data in the datanet, Martin."

"I know," Martin said.

He stood, then held out a hand. "Why do I feel so...*depressed?*"

"Because you now understand what you've been trying to fight for your entire life," Yolanda said, after a moment. "And because you think you lost."

"I did lose," Martin said. He hated to admit it, but there was no avoiding the truth. "I didn't manage to win, did I?"

"You did manage to escape," Yolanda said, as she declined his hand and rose to her feet. "I think your enemies – your real enemies – would have preferred you to wallow in the ghetto."

Martin sighed. "But why are they so...so *stupid* if they really want to help?"

"My *bitch* of a stepmother used to help people, but not to teach people," Yolanda said. "If someone had torn clothes, they would bring them to her and she would mend them. She never taught me how to sew, naturally. Only her biological daughters were considered worthy of that honour. But she didn't teach anyone outside the house, either. They were dependent on her."

"I don't understand," Martin said. "Surely she wasn't the only one who could sew..."

"Of course she wasn't," Yolanda said. "Most of the older women could sew. But she didn't charge anyone for her services, you see."

"I don't," Martin said. It made no sense to him. "Why were they dependent on her?"

"She didn't charge them anything for the work," Yolanda explained. "I think she just liked having people dependent on her. If she'd taught every young woman to sew, they wouldn't have had to come back to her, time and time again. And then she wouldn't have been so important in the community."

She shrugged. "Or maybe she was just a bitch," she added. "I could quite happily believe that too, just because she made me do all the housework."

Martin frowned. "Is that common?"

"Yeah," Yolanda said. "There were so many children missing one or both parents that they tended to be treated as slaves, by those who took them in. A girl born of her mother's womb was treated like a little princess; a girl from another mother was put to work almost at once, scrubbing floors and cleaning clothes. And there was no chance of a dowry when they married, *if* they married. I wouldn't have had a hope of receiving anything from my stepmother, apart from the back of her hand."

She laughed, humourlessly. "The bitch would have pulled me out of school and put me to work full-time, cleaning her friends' floors, if she hadn't claimed the Educational Incentive just to keep me in school. I wouldn't have seen a cent of that money, if she'd put me to work."

Martin *looked* at her. "Then why work?"

"I would probably have been beaten if I hadn't worked," Yolanda said. "The bitch would never lay a hand on her own children, but me? I wasn't *hers*."

"Shit," Martin said. He understood, all too well. "But...I wanted someone looking out for me."

Yolanda gave him a sharp look, clearly puzzled.

"I used to have a friend who actually had a father," Martin explained. Bitterness welled up inside him as he remembered his old friend. "You have no idea how much I envied him. There was someone there, looking out for him, making sure he did everything he could to better himself and rise out of the ghetto. No one took me in hand when I was a kid. I even used to tell myself that, one day, maybe he would adopt me."

Yolanda gave him a tired smile. "Did they make it?"

"They were gunned down, three years ago," Martin admitted. "It was just another piece of senseless violence, two people in the wrong place at the wrong time. Nick...Nick was smart, his father made him work...he could have made it out, if he'd tried. But his life was just cut short, as if it were nothing, and no one really gave a damn. They were just...dead."

He shook his head. "It's funny, really," he added. "Nick used to envy *me*. My mother was always...out; I could do whatever I pleased, whenever I pleased. I could have joined the gangs, or skipped school and hung out at the mall and no one would have given a damn. His father went ballistic every time *Nick* skipped school. Nick couldn't get away with anything.

"And I envied him. I would have given anything to have someone that involved in my life."

"It isn't always a good thing," Yolanda said. "My stepmother would shout and scream and throw things if she found a single speck of dust on the floor after I had scrubbed it."

Martin had to smile, despite the bitterness in his head. "The grass is always greener on the other side of the hill, isn't it?"

"Yeah," Yolanda said.

"What happened to you at school?" Martin said, suddenly. "I mean... if you don't mind me asking."

"I was careless," Yolanda said, shortly. There was a trace of...bitterness in her voice, now. "There isn't anything else to tell."

Martin shuddered. He'd been told, once, that his school was far from the worst in the world, but he'd never believed it. How could he, when the teachers couldn't keep order and bullying, theft and even rape were common occurrences? The girls had always stayed in groups, or put out for the strongest boys in exchange for protection. Some of the boys hadn't been much better...and God help anyone who happened to be homosexual. They'd been treated worse than the girls.

"I don't intend to look back," Yolanda said, firmly. "The future is ahead of us and those who treated us badly are in the past."

"Fuck them," Martin agreed.

They walked out of the compartment and down into the mess, where the food was waiting for them. It tasted better now, Martin had discovered, after the nanotech had been inserted into their bodies. He still found the idea of little machines crawling around inside him a little creepy, but he had to admit they were very effective. Now, there was no way he could be infected by disease, or suffer from a host of discomforts. Scars he'd borne since he was a child had faded into nothingness.

"There will be more to do tomorrow," Yolanda predicted, glumly. "And then we have to start taking the *real* tests."

Martin swallowed. Sergeant Bass had told them, in no uncertain terms, that their future in the military dependent on how well they did on their tests. Once they passed, they would be assigned to a specific branch for further training. Yolanda would go into starship training, he was sure; she was certainly smart enough to succeed. But would he be capable of handling combat training? One thing the implants had made clear to him was just how little he knew, compared to someone born in the Solar Union. The tests might show him as suitable for nothing more than grunt labour.

"I'm scared," he confessed. It wasn't something he would have told anyone else, but he felt a kinship with Yolanda that puzzled him. "What happens if I fail completely?"

"I don't think you *can* fail," Yolanda said. "You just get assigned to somewhere you'd do well. They're aptitude tests, basically."

"I hope so," Martin said.

He shook his head, looking around the mess. What was *he* doing here? He had no exams to his credit, no qualifications; it was a miracle he could even read. The men and women who had joined the Solar Union had to be smart and educated, not book-dumb bastards from the ghettos. His dream of escape might come to an end after the exams. He'd be lucky if they didn't dump him back on Earth, after crippling the implants so they were useless.

"You have a good heart," Yolanda said. "And everything else will come in time."

"I'm thick," Martin said. "I can't even add numbers together without getting mixed up."

"You have the rest of your life to learn," Yolanda pointed out, smoothly. "You could live forever, with the right treatments. The nanotech you have now will keep you alive for nearly two centuries, assuming you don't suffer brain damage or an injury that kills you instantly."

Martin stared at her. "How do you know that?"

Yolanda tapped the side of her head. "I looked it up," she said, simply. "The details are all online, if you bother to look."

"Oh," Martin said, embarrassed. He should have thought of checking to see what the nanotech he'd been given actually *did*. "I'm still not used to having an entire library inside my head."

"Better get used to it," Yolanda said. "Sergeant Bass doesn't hold our hands, does he?"

Martin nodded, sourly. There were times when he would have appreciated someone holding his hand, giving him advice, serving...serving as a father. But he understood Bass's point, after Scudder's lectures. The Solar Union offered opportunities, but it didn't – it couldn't – force anyone to *take* the opportunities. If someone didn't have the drive to make use of them, the Solar Union had better things to do than coddle them.

And someone could afford to live quite cheaply here, if they worked, he thought. He'd checked, in a fit of panic. There were hundreds of jobs that required nothing, but a set of implants and a willingness to work. *I would never have to go back to Earth.*

"Just concentrate on passing the tests," Yolanda advised. "Everything else will take care of itself."

NINE

The civil war in Russia intensified today as forces loyal to the St. Petersburg Government launched an offensive intended to liberate Moscow from the grasp of various rebel factions. Sources on the ground claim that the St. Petersburg Government's offensive is being backed by Byelorussian and Ukrainian military forces...

—Solar News Network, Year 51

"The examination chambers are the most closely-monitored sections of Sparta," Sergeant Bass informed the company, as they prepared for the first set of tests. "If any of you break the rules, for whatever reason, you will either be forced to repeat your training from the start or be simply expelled from Sparta. There will be a black mark on your record that will haunt you for the rest of your life."

He paused, dramatically. Yolanda swallowed. Statements like that had always made her feel guilty, even though she'd done nothing to deserve it. It was a legacy, she assumed, from her stepmother, who had always blamed Yolanda for anything that went wrong. But eventually she'd simply stopped caring. There was no point in trying to win the approval of someone who hated you merely for existing.

"You may not attempt to communicate with anyone outside the chamber," Sergeant Bass said. "You can use your implants to search for information, if you need to, but you may not attempt to ask for help. Nor may you take anything into the chamber, apart from your clothes; leave anything you happen to be carrying outside or you will find yourself in deep shit. I don't care what it is, or what sentimental value it has. You are not allowed to take it into the chamber."

"Probably plans to threaten us with cavity searches if we don't obey," Martin muttered.

"Probably," Yolanda agreed. She'd had a principal who had once threatened to search everyone in school, after a visiting congresswoman's watch had gone missing. It had eventually turned up in the staffroom, where the congresswoman had spent most of her time, after the police had been called. "But it's probably not a good idea to screw up."

She checked her pockets, then pulled out everything she was carrying and carried it over to the lockers. A touch of a button opened the locker, then registered it to her; no one else, apart from the staff, could open it without her permission. She dumped her stuff inside, then closed the door. Beside her, Martin did the same with his equipment, then his belt.

"Better to be sure," he said, when she raised her eyebrows. "They used to make us take them off when we stepped through the x-ray machine at school."

Yolanda shrugged, then looked towards the doors at the far side of the room. They were opening, one by one, revealing small compartments with terminals, seats, water facilities and nothing else. She exchanged a look with Martin, then reached out and squeezed his hand, tightly. His eyes widened in surprise – she almost never touched anyone, if she could help it – then he gave her a hug. It was quick enough not to make her want to push him away and run.

"I'll see you on the far side," she said, as her implants informed her she was assigned to Room #34. It matched her ID number, making her wonder if that had been deliberate. But there was no way to know. "Good luck."

"You too," Martin said.

Yolanda turned and walked through the door. Another alert flashed up in front of her eyes, informing her that her body had just been scanned. She assumed she'd passed, as alarms hadn't sounded and no one had turned up to drag her into the office for a short and unpleasant chat with the Drill Sergeants. Instead, the hatch closed behind her and locked with an audible *clunk*. She rolled her eyes at the drama, then looked around. A small side door led to a toilet, just in case she needed it.

"Attention," a soft voice said. "In the event of you leaving the compartment, you will not be permitted to return. You will be assumed to have completed the test. There will be no further warnings. Do you understand?"

"I understand," Yolanda said, as she sat down in front of the terminal. It blinked to life, displaying her name and ID code. A countdown appeared a moment later, ticking down the seconds until the test was due to begin. "Am I allowed to ask questions?"

"You may only ask questions relating to the test procedures," the voice said. It was almost certainly an AI, probably one assigned specifically to monitor the tests. "Any other questions will not only be left unanswered, but reported to superior authority."

Yolanda swallowed, again. Even muttering to herself could be dangerous.

"Thank you," she said. It was good to be polite to AIs, she'd been told. They had emotions too. "Is there anything else I ought to know about the test?"

"Only what you have been told already," the AI said, reprovingly. "We cannot force you to actually read the details."

Her console bleeped. The test had begun.

Yolanda found herself struggling within moments. Some questions were relatively simple, others seemed to have stings in the tail. She found herself having to guess at answers, then using her implants to draw information from the datanet and using it to see if the answers were correct. Other questions *needed* her to find more specific information, testing – she suspected – her skills at recovering and using data online. It wasn't enough to have access to data, she concluded. She had to think about it too.

The second battery of questions were different. She only had one shot at answering them, according to the notes, and she would be timed from the moment she started until she finished. Panicking a little, she struggled to answer question after question, often realising – in hindsight – that she'd fucked up. By the time the third set of questions came around, there was sweat pouring down her back. But none of the questions seemed to make sense.

She gritted her teeth and pressed on, anyway. The questions grew harder, then resolved themselves as she worked her way through them. A handful of later questions provided the key to understanding the earlier questions. She went back, changed her answers on the questions that allowed her to rethink her answers, then progressed to the fourth section of the exam. Once again, the questions made her want to panic…

"Attention," the AI stated. "The exam period will end in ten minutes."

Yolanda stared. Had it really been two hours since she'd entered the chamber? Her head was pounding, while her body felt tired and old. She hastily checked the last set of questions, then tried to answer two of the ones she'd left untouched. And then the screen blanked, finally. The tests, for better or worse, were over.

"Dear God," she breathed. "Is it always like that?"

"Of course not," the AI said, as she stumbled to her feet. "This was the *easy* test."

"Fuck," Yolanda said.

"I suggest that you have a nap," the AI stated. The hatch opened, this time silently. "You will be called to receive your results over the next two days, then your future will be determined. Until you are called, you may consider yourself to be on free time."

"Thank you," Yolanda said.

She stepped out of the chamber and stared. The recruits looked dazed, milling around in absolute confusion. Like her, most of them would have no experience with *real* exams, tests intended to determine their true capabilities. They'd grown used to exams that were meaningless, where you could do nothing more than write your name on the top of the sheet and receive a pass mark. But the Solar Union was different. Their results, here and now, could make the difference between realising their dreams and being told they were unsuited to a career in the military.

"Yolanda," Martin's voice said. "I feel like shit."

Yolanda turned to face him. His face was sweaty too, while his hands were shaking ominously. "I feel worse," she said. "And I think we'd better go to bed."

Martin didn't even make crude jokes about going to bed together, she noted, as they staggered towards the barracks. He must have been badly dazed by the exam, just like the others. She was too tired herself to be more than mildly sympathetic, even though he would have found it harder than her. From what she'd heard, schools in the ghettos tended to be little more than gang headquarters or havens for drug dealers. Under the circumstances, it was astonishing that Martin had turned out even mildly civilised.

Just like me, she thought. *My stepmother would have turned me into a slave if I'd stayed.*

She was too tired to do more than throw herself on her bunk and go to sleep when she entered the barracks. Darkness descended on her almost as soon as she closed her eyes. It felt like only moments had passed when she awoke, but her implants informed her that she had slept for nearly ten hours. The sound of snoring from some of the other bunks told her that not everyone had recovered – yet – from the experience. Part of her mind wondered if she ever would.

Absently, she activated her implants and started to browse the datanet. It was easy to understand the dangers, she saw now, as torrents of information started to flow through her head. Everyone in the Solar Union seemed to have an opinion on everything, producing billions of blogs and websites on every conceivable topic. She still couldn't send messages outside Sparta, a restriction that made no sense to her, but she could read everything that wasn't behind a password. And there was a staggering amount out there free for the taking, without any password at all. She could literally drown herself in information.

She danced from topic to topic, following links that appeared in her mind. Some sites discussed matters on Earth, with attitudes ranging from absolute contempt to even a handful of people who wanted to go back and *live* on Earth. They seemed to attract no shortage of critics, all of whom asked the obvious question. Why didn't they go back to Earth if they wanted to live there? It wasn't as if shuttle tickets were expensive.

Out of a morbid sense of curiosity, she did a sweep for her stepmother's name. Nothing appeared in the datanet, not even a missing persons report for Yolanda herself. Clearly, her family hadn't bothered to notice she'd gone. She disconnected herself from the datanet before she could start to cry, then placed her implant's sleep inducers into primary mode and fell asleep. The next time she woke, it was mid-morning and a note was blinking in front of her eyes. She was due to meet the sergeants in four hours to discuss her future.

Gritting her teeth, she pulled herself out of bed and walked into the shower, scooping up a change of clothes on the way. If she was due to meet her fate, the least she could do was wash, wear a fresh uniform and eat something first. And then see if both Martin and she had made it through the barriers to further advancement. She honestly wasn't sure what she'd do if she was told she couldn't stay. Or, for that matter, what *Martin* would do.

And when, her own thoughts asked her, *did you start to care for him?*

It nagged at her mind as she stripped, showered and dressed. Martin wasn't the sort of boy she'd liked on Earth, issues of race aside. There seemed to be no reason to like him, apart from his determination to better himself. In many ways, they were kindred souls. She pushed the thought aside as she walked out of the barracks and into the mess, where the cooks had served something that actually looked edible. They must have been rewarding the recruits for enduring their first set of exams, she decided. There couldn't be any other reason.

The hours until she met the sergeants dragged. Martin was apparently still asleep, probably using his implants to ensure he knew nothing until he met his destiny. Yolanda sent him a message warning him to be ready, then forced herself to wait, skimming the news, until the time finally came for her to walk to the office. It was hard, agonisingly hard, to force her legs to work. They didn't seem to want her to go anywhere she might learn her fate. But, somehow, she made it to the office and stepped inside.

"Recruit Miguel," Sergeant Bass said. "Be seated."

Yolanda obeyed. Bass was alone in the office, something that bothered her. On Earth, no male officer – or teacher, or policeman, or anything else – would be alone with a woman, no matter their job. A single accusation of…inappropriateness would be enough to destroy a career, even if the accusation was completely false. But the Solar Union had ways to get at the truth, the briefing notes had stated, and making a false accusation could – no, *would* – lead to criminal charges. Earth's paranoia had no place in space.

"Your exam results were generally positive," Bass said, without preamble. "You made some mistakes, of course, but generally you fell well within the acceptable brackets for starship personnel."

Yolanda stared at him. "Really?"

"No, I'm lying because I'm a sadist," Bass sneered. He met her eyes. "You passed. Congratulations. Now you have to decide about your future."

He went on before she could say a word. "You also fell into the brackets for intelligence work, probably on Earth," he added. "The SIA would probably be interested in recruiting you, if I forwarded them your file. And then there's the prospect of logistics. It isn't particularly glamorous, but it does offer the chance to make a meaningful difference. But the choice is yours."

Yolanda hesitated. She'd heard that before.

"If I insist on staying with my first choice," she said carefully, "what would happen to me?"

"You'd go to the starship training complex and start work," Bass informed her, shortly. "If you passed all the tests, you would be a fully-qualified starship crewperson, ready to be assigned to a starship. And, if you failed, there would probably still be jobs for you in the civilian sector."

He gave her a thin smile. "This isn't Earth," he said, warningly. "You get to reach the heights you can scale, through your own work. We won't force you to take training for a job you think you will hate. All we ask is you show commitment to the job you wanted to earn."

"Thank you, Sergeant," Yolanda said. "If you don't mind, I'd like to qualify for starship duty."

"What *I* mind doesn't matter," Bass said. He tapped the terminal in front of him. "You have the ability to become a starship crewperson, therefore you will have the chance to qualify. All we can offer you is that chance. Good luck."

He rose to his feet, then held out a hand. "You will have a week's shore leave, which you may spend anywhere within the Solar Union," he added. "After that, you will be expected to report back to Sparta for the next stage of your training. *Failing* to show up will result in disciplinary action at the very least, Recruit Miguel. Do you understand me?"

"Yes, Sergeant," Yolanda said.

"I will also give you a word of warning," Bass said. "You grew up on Earth, so you may find the Solar Union a little...garish. There will be much to astonish you, much to shock you, much to offend you...and not everyone will have your best interests in mind. Be careful what you say or do."

He smirked. "We had a woman from Earth throw an absolute fit because she visited an asteroid where everyone is legally obliged to carry a weapon at all times," he said. "She felt utterly unsafe just seeing everyone carrying weapons, even though she was never in any danger. I don't think she got any sympathy and you won't either, if you do something similar. It will look very bad on your record."

"Yes, Sergeant," Yolanda said. She hesitated, then leaned forward. "Is it *safe* to carry a loaded weapon on an asteroid settlement?"

Bass shrugged. "The general rules are simple," he said. "You can do whatever you like, as long as you don't harm non-consenting persons or do anything with a strong chance of harming non-consenting persons. Most settlements have strong rules against accidental discharges – I believe there was a person on Mars who was put outside the airlock for shooting at the dome protecting the settlement. We do not feel inclined to tolerate fools."

Yolanda nodded, then left the compartment. Martin was waiting outside.

"They said you were in there," he said. He was grinning from ear to ear. "I made it!"

"So did I," Yolanda said. She paused. "You'd better stay in touch, you know."

"I certainly will," Martin said. "Do you want to come on shore leave with me? It isn't as if we have anyone else to go with, is it?"

"I...yes, I think I will," Yolanda said. She hesitated. Going anywhere alone with a boy would have been a terminally stupid idea on Earth. "But separate rooms, if that's all right with you."

"It's fine," Martin said. "I do understand."

He smiled. "Besides, this way I can bring a girl back to my room, if I find one."

Yolanda grinned. "You think you would?"

"Have you seen the adverts online?" Martin asked. "They do things I didn't even *know* were possible."

"The datanet is not for porn," Yolanda protested, although she was giggling too hard to sound properly stern. "Is it?"

"The most popular sites are all pornographic," Martin countered. He held out a hand. "Come on, please. I don't want to waste a moment of our time."

TEN

Despite urgent shipments of viral counteragents from the United States, Europe and Japan, AIDS-VIII has claimed the lives of over ten thousand South Africans, mainly teenage boys and girls. The spread of a mutated form of AIDS, according to doctors, was aided and abetted by contaminated medical equipment supplied by local manufacturers. They have yet to rule out the possibility of terrorists being involved.

However, in a speech, the President of South Africa urged people to look to traditional cures, rather than modern medicine...

—Solar News Network, Year 51

"You're new here, aren't you?"

Martin looked up. The small cafe had seemed a good place to sit down, after spending a week exploring Ceres. It rested in the middle of a park, where children played without fear of being kidnapped, raped or accidentally gunned down by gangbangers fighting their enemies. Part of him feared open spaces, but the rest of him found them welcoming, despite the lingering fear he was making himself a target.

"Yes," he said, carefully. "And you are?"

"I'm a Denier," the man said. His voice was curiously flat, without even a hint of emotion. "Can I convince you to join us?"

"I have no idea what a Denier actually *is*," Martin said. He'd seen no shortage of weird ideas in the week they'd spent on the asteroid, some of which had made absolutely no sense to him. "What do you *do*?"

"Emotion is the great curse of mankind," the man said. He sat down facing Martin and nodded to him. Up close, his face was curiously blank, as if he couldn't do more with his lips than talk. "Just imagine how badly humanity messes up when emotion is involved."

Martin frowned. "They do?"

"Yes," the man said. "My name is Ninety-Seven. It is a simple number, with no emotional resonance at all. I have no emotions. They were removed from my mind through brain surgery. If I see a pretty girl, I feel nothing for her."

"That sounds awful," Martin commented.

"It is nothing of the sort," Ninety-Seven insisted. "When you see a pretty girl walking past, your eyes automatically turn to follow her buttocks as they sway invitingly. You are distracted from greater things by thoughts of taking her to bed. When you are kissing and cuddling with a girl and she says no further, your emotions push you to override her will and force yourself on her."

"I have never forced myself on anyone in my life," Martin said.

"But you could," Ninety-Seven said. "Your emotions might lead you to rape. Or to do something else you would regret. Anger, fear, hatred, disdain, contempt...they are all emotions and they push humans into making mistakes. Emotional reactions are dangerous and so we banish them from our bodies. I feel nothing towards you, either positive or negative. You may join us or you may not and I would still feel nothing."

"It sounds like a bland life," Martin said. "You would never know the pleasure of success..."

"Or the pain of failure," Ninety-Seven pointed out. "We would feel nothing, whatever happens."

Martin looked up at the park. The first time he had set foot on the asteroid, he had been disturbed at seeing the landscape curving up and around into the distance, as if they were walking on the inner side of a football. Now, he was almost used to it, although he did keep his eyes lowered to the ground. It was easier to tolerate, he suspected, if someone was born in such an environment. But they might have similar problems on Earth.

"This place is fantastic," he said. "But you wouldn't see that, would you?"

"We can appreciate what humanity has built," Ninety-Seven said.

"But you wouldn't feel the urge to change anything either, if you grew up in the shit," Martin said, after a moment. He looked back at the emotionless man. "You'd just…accept it and move on."

"Which is something humanity needs to learn," Ninety-Seven said. "How many problems would be left behind, powerless to harm us, if humanity just accepted them and moved on?"

He paused, then went on. "Divorced from our emotions, we are safe from being led astray," he added. "You would not enjoy such freedoms."

"But I also wouldn't enjoy the ability to be myself," Martin said. "I might as well be a robot."

"You'd be free of your emotions," Ninety-Seven said. "That wouldn't make you a robot."

"But it might as well," Martin said. "I *like* feeling things!"

Ninety-Seven leaned forward. "Everything?"

Martin hesitated. He recalled – he dwelled on it every night – the frustrations of growing up in the ghetto, of knowing that life was cheap and that a single false move could get him killed…and that no one, really, would give a damn. Perhaps it would be better to feel nothing, rather than fear and hatred…and resentment, the resentment he now knew had been used as a tool to keep his people under control. And yet, if he had felt nothing, would he have wanted to leave and made it happen? Would he have befriended Yolanda if he hadn't liked her on some level?

"I think emotions are what give us our drive," he said, finally. "The good ones reward us and the bad ones push us forward."

"So you reject our offer to have your emotions surgically removed," Ninety-Seven said. "Do you know what I feel about that?"

"Nothing," Martin said.

"Precisely," Ninety-Seven said. "I may not have the satisfaction of knowing I've made a convert, but I also lack the disappointment I might otherwise feel in you."

He rose to his feet, then cocked his head slightly. A contact code appeared in Martin's implants, inviting him to visit their website or even send a message, if he wished to learn more about the Deniers. Martin wasn't sure if they *were* deniers, in any conventional sense; they didn't *have* emotions, rather than just denying their existence. It was almost as if he were denying being a human.

"I'll check out your website," Martin said. "But I make no promises."

"I do not expect you to make any promises," Ninety-Seven said.

He bowed, then retreated into the crowd.

Martin shook his head, then looked at the others as they walked past. Most of them were human, although he'd had to check his implants a few times, as they didn't *look* human, sporting green or blue skin purely for amusement. Others were definitely *alien*, looking thoroughly out of place even in the Solar Union. Martin had felt a chill running down his spine the first time he'd seen an alien, something utterly inhuman. Now, he rather thought he was used to seeing them.

The asteroid perplexed, amused and bothered him in equal measure. There was no suspicion, no fearful glances from one person to answer; the residents *trusted* each other, even though it would have been suicidal, on Earth, to trust anyone outside the family. They didn't fear being raped, or having their children snatched off the streets, or even forced to pay bribes to the local police force merely to avoid being arrested. The children playing in the park were largely unsupervised and yet they were fine. They seemed to get along fine despite possessing all the colours of the rainbow, or wearing clothes that ranged from the enveloping to the sparse. No one would have dressed their children like that on Earth.

And yet...the kids had a zest for life he could only envy.

So did their parents, he suspected, and the rest of the asteroid's population. There was no fear; instead, there was a determination to be themselves, to live and grow and build a community that actually worked. The more he looked at it, the more he envied the children the opportunities they were handed on a platter. They would never face discrimination based on anything, but ability. And even the less able would not be forced into jobs they couldn't handle, purely to meet some recruitment quota...

He smiled as Yolanda sat down next to him, wearing a long white dress that set off her dark hair nicely.

She smiled back. "Penny for your thoughts?"

"If I ever have children," Martin said, "I'm going to raise them here."

"You were certainly practicing last night," Yolanda said. "I hope you were careful."

Martin felt his cheeks heat. Last night, he'd picked up a girl in a bar and taken her back to the hotel room, where they'd spent hours just making love. And, the following morning, she'd kissed him on the cheek and then walked off, without even leaving him her contact code. He wasn't sure if that was a tacit statement he was awful in bed or a reflection of her desire to have fun, but avoid entanglements. She'd certainly not acted as if she was interested in anything he had above the waist.

"The nanotech sees to contraception," he said, embarrassed. "There was no risk of getting her pregnant."

"Good," Yolanda said. She tapped the terminal on the desk, ordering a drink. A moment later, a robotic waiter appeared, carrying a large glass of coke. "You probably would have to pay child support here, if you got someone pregnant."

Martin sighed. There had been thousands of horror stories told at school, each one designed to suggest that having a child could ruin your life. In hindsight, he couldn't help wondering if they'd been designed to further cripple the community or merely to dehumanise girls and children...or to prevent the young men from finding proper jobs. Legal jobs might come with all sorts of legally-mandated benefits, from health care to insurance, but they also automatically took money from their workers' salaries to pay for taxes, child support and legal penalties. And then people wondered why the underground economy grew far faster than the legal one.

"I think I would have to make the decision to have a child," he said, slowly. "The technology is freeing, isn't it?"

"It can be," Yolanda agreed. "Back home…one of my stepsisters caught something very nasty from a guy. It was…somehow, it was my fault."

Martin blinked. "How the *fuck* was it your fault?"

"I have no idea," Yolanda said. "But she had to go to the doctor and my stepmother was a right pain about it for weeks. Not that she took it out on the silly bitch, of course."

"Don't worry about it," Martin advised.

He waved a hand to indicate their surroundings. "The kids here are happy, free, safe and have thousands of opportunities," he continued. "Why would I *not* want my children to grow up here?"

"I can't think of a good reason," Yolanda said. "They'd just have to be careful what they signed."

Martin nodded. That was the downside of the Solar Union, the automatic assumption that adults could handle their own affairs. Which was, he supposed, better than presuming someone incompetent out of hand, but it still caused problems. Signing the wrong document could have all kinds of legal repercussions. The courts didn't seem inclined to assume that someone didn't read the whole document when they damn well should have done before they signed it. Throwing out a contract seemed to happen very rarely – and only when one party broke the handful of legal protections signed into law.

"Or ate," he added. On Earth, there were strict laws concerning what food could legally be fed to children. There were no such laws in the Solar Union, although they were hardly necessary. Nanotech could ensure that children could eat anything – and that they could avoid allergies and other issues that tended to cause legal problems elsewhere. "Or quite a few other issues."

He smiled at her, then sighed. "Where do you want to go for our last night of freedom?"

Yolanda sighed. There was no way to avoid the fact that they would be going to different sections of Sparta when they returned, Yolanda to starship training and Martin to the Solar Marine Boot Camp. They would exchange messages, of course, but it wouldn't be the same.

"I was thinking a quiet dinner in a restaurant," she said. Her face reddened when he gave her an incredulous look. "It's just something my step-bitches would have done with their boyfriends, once they were going steady. I always wanted to do it and I never could."

Martin hesitated, on the verge of pointing out that Yolanda was exotic – and would always be exotic. He stopped himself just in time. Yolanda might be exotic, but she had also been isolated because of her parentage and appearance. And then she'd been hurt, badly. Maybe the Deniers had a point after all, he told himself. Emotions certainly made it harder for people to get over traumatic events in their lives.

"We can pick a nice place and eat there, if you like," he said. The idea seemed absurd to him, but then there had been no real courting in the ghetto. "Where would you like to go?"

He reviewed the local news through his implants while Yolanda searched for a suitable restaurant. The political section stated that the Homeland Faction was on the verge of placing a bill before Congress that would call on the Solar Union to intervene on Earth, despite opposition from several other factions. Martin had never followed politics on Earth – what did he care who parked his rump in the White House? – but politics in the Solar Union reminded him of a genteel catfight. Everyone was both adamantly defending their corner while, at the same time, being painfully polite to one another.

The next piece of news concerned an attempt to ban cougars. It puzzled him until he reviewed the links and discovered that cougars were older men and women – often in their later years – who chased partners who were barely out of their teens. Martin frowned – he wouldn't have wanted to sleep with an eighty-year-old woman – and then remembered the nanotech. A man of ninety could look sixteen – legal age in the Solar Union – if he wanted...and then, with the advantage of seventy-four years of experience, seduce young girls who barely knew anything about the outside world.

Cheats, he thought. What could he offer a girl, apart from youth? An older man with nanotech running through his body could offer her youth – at least the appearance of youth – and everything else besides. *No wonder some people want to ban it.*

He skimmed the rest of the article with interest. The pro-cougar faction defended it as a freedom of sexual activity; the younger parties weren't underage, so the cougars weren't actually committing a crime. However, their opponents pointed out that such a relationship was monumentally unbalanced. The younger partners would be immature and largely unable to cope with their older partners. Martin had to admit they had a point. The older men who'd married younger women in the ghettos had treated them as nothing more than arm-candy...

"Here," Yolanda said, breaking into his thoughts. "This sounds like a nice place."

Martin glanced at the link she sent him. "A pizza place?"

"It sounds good," Yolanda said. "Besides, we should be careful with our money."

Martin nodded and allowed her to lead him through the streets to the restaurant. Something was missing, something that both reassured and puzzled him at the same time, but it took him several minutes to identify *what* was missing. They were walking through a residential area, crammed with civilians...and yet none of them were giving him sidelong glances, wondering what a black man was doing in their territory. It struck him, suddenly, that he was looking at the very definition of a post-racial society. No one gave a damn about him being black, any more than they cared about the multicoloured children or even the aliens.

The restaurant was a small building, built in a style that reminded him of the past. Inside, there were a handful of occupied wooden tables, each one holding a glowing candlestick. An old man greeted them at the door, then pointed to one of the empty tables beside the window, looking out onto the streets. Yolanda took his hand, led Martin over to the table and sat down on the wooden chair. The table was already laid with knives, forks and spoons. Martin didn't want to *think* about how many charges the health and safety police would level at the owner, just for daring to leave his knives in plain sight.

"Tomorrow, we go back to work," Yolanda said, as they skimmed the menu. It all looked remarkably unhealthy, yet tempting. "I'm going to miss here, I think."

"Me too," Martin said. He shuddered. Sergeant Bass had gone into great detail about just what he could expect at Boot Camp. And to think he'd thought Recruit Induction was hard. "But you'll be flying starships!"

"I certainly hope so," Yolanda said. The waiter took their orders, then vanished into the kitchen again. "I'm not the easiest of people to know, am I?"

Martin smiled. "You could be worse."

"I know," Yolanda said. "But I could be better too."

"I think you're fine as you are," Martin said, slowly. What had brought *this* on? There were times when he genuinely believed that girls were an alien race in their own right. Their merest word could mean something completely different to what he thought it meant. "Why?"

"I like you," Yolanda confessed. "But I also have problems getting… close to anyone."

"I understand," Martin said, too quickly. He'd enjoyed the chance to meet girls on the asteroid, but Yolanda had stayed in her room. "I don't mind just being friends…"

"Thank you," Yolanda said. "And I'm sorry."

Martin let out a sigh of relief as their food arrived. The conversation had become impossibly awkward.

"Don't worry about it," he said, as he cut into the pizza. "I can be your friend for the rest of your life."

"Thank you," Yolanda said. "That means more to me than I can say."

ELEVEN

Cohan Young, a rancher from Texas, was charged today with hate-speech on the internet, after a long screed about the damage caused to his crops and cattle by illegal immigrants crossing the border from Mexico. Mr. Young's farm has already been seized by Federal Authorities and is likely to be handed over to a Mexican family, as part of the reparations for the Mexican-American War (1846-48). His family have already sought asylum in the Solar Union.

—Solar News Network, Year 52

"This never fails to impress me," Captain Jean Vanern said, very quietly.

Kevin couldn't help, but agree. The Varnar had been space-faring for centuries, long before they'd been brought under Tokomak sway, and their star system showed it. There were large settlements on every rocky planet, giant structures in orbit around every gas giant and thousands of starships moving in and out of the system. The sheer scale of activity dwarfed the Sol System, even after fifty years of near-constant expansion into outer space. It was a thoroughly intimidating sight.

He sucked in a breath as three new icons – gravity points – popped into existence on the holographic display. The keys to cheap interstellar travel, allowing starships to move instantly from one system to another, they gave the Varnar the chance to become the masters of the local sector. If the Tokomak had never existed, the Varnar might have become much more than an interstellar version of Cuba, a Banana Republic used by far greater powers to fight proxy wars and keep the other smaller nations under control. But it was not to be.

And if Earth had had gravity points, he thought, *we would have been occupied long ago.*

The Galactics didn't have anything resembling a Prime Directive, at least where most civilian-grade technology was concerned. There was no shortage of races – like the Hordesmen - whose natural development had been cut short by contact with their superiors, resulting in their forcible assimilation into Galactic society. Some of them did well, but others seemed doomed to permanent cultural inferiority. The Horde had been spacefaring for hundreds of years and yet a band of primitives from Earth had been able to take a starship off their hands, then use it to build an interstellar society of their own. But then, the Hordesmen had never really understood their own technology.

"We've just been pinged by local system command," Jean said. They'd become friendly – if not *too* friendly – on the voyage to Varnar. "They want ID and GalStar credit balance."

"How very human," Kevin said. "Send it to them, please."

There was a long pause before the reply – a vector directing them into high orbit – appeared in the display. Jean barked orders to her crew, while Kevin used his implants to study the live feed from the starship's sensors. Varnar, one of the ultimate targets of the endless war, was surrounded by heavy defences, making Earth's look flimsy in comparison. There were over a hundred orbital battlestations, thousands of automated weapons platforms and dozens of heavily-armed starships in the system. On the ground, he knew, there would be giant Planetary Defence Centres dug into mountains, ready to engage anyone who dared enter orbit without permission. The Varnar took their homeworld's safety very seriously and it showed.

And if they dared cut loose a few squadrons of starships, he thought, *they could do real damage to the Solar System.*

It wasn't a pleasant thought. The Solar Navy had spent fifty years learning everything it could about the Galactics, then building a fleet that might be able to stand up to them when they finally noticed Earth. But the Varnar had hundreds of years of experience in fighting interstellar wars, even if their technology had never really advanced since they'd made contact with the Tokomak. That puzzled Kevin more than he cared to admit; he knew that societies could stagnate, but even the Taliban had managed to adapt to threats posed by outside forces. The Galactics, it seemed, reached a certain point and stopped dead.

But new technology would prove immensely disruptive, he thought, recalling the struggle to introduce even minimal levels of Galactic technology on Earth. *The Tokomak may force them to refrain from developing anything new.*

"We have an orbital slot," Jean informed him. "I've paid for two weeks, but I think they'd suspect something if we didn't bug out before then."

Kevin nodded. Interstellar freighters only made money when they were actually in operation, moving from one system to another. There was nothing to earn and a great deal to lose just by hanging around in orbit, particularly when the crew had to pay a hundred GalStars per day just to remain in the orbital slot. Someone would eventually realise that the ship was paying out money without earning a rusty cent and start wondering why.

"Try and sell our wares," he advised. They'd picked the cargo carefully, including a handful of items that wouldn't sell very quickly, if at all. Jean would seem to have gambled and lost, if someone took a closer look at her ship. "My team and I will be down on the planet."

"Just be careful," Jean advised. "We don't have a hope of getting out of here if they realise we're up to something."

Kevin nodded, then walked through the hatch and into the small intelligence-collection compartment. James and Mindy had already started to tap into the giant datanet surrounding the planet, drawing vast streams of data into the starship's computer cores. The RIs hidden within the system were already analysing the data, trying to locate the sealed cores that would require more careful approaches, while the humans were looking for interesting patterns. Behind them, Julian and Mandy were looking for potential contacts, including information brokers. It was quite possible, if human intelligence had realised there was a potential threat, that the planet's freelance information brokers knew it too.

The thought made him smile. Varnar was just like Washington DC, in many ways. There were countless missions from countless planets, all begging for favours; countless spies, all trying to pick up what they could for their masters…and countless people trying to make a fast buck catering to them all. A list of adverts popped up in his display, offering concubines or sexbots from a hundred different worlds. Enough humans had been through interstellar space, as traders, mercenaries or slaves, for the Galactic businessmen to try to entice them into their lairs.

"Ando is still here," Julian said, slowly. "He might be the best person to contact, for starters."

Kevin took a moment to review the file. Ando's race had been one of the few to adapt reasonably well to the shock of discovering the towering interstellar civilisation beyond their atmosphere. It helped, he suspected, that they were both naturally long-lived and strikingly peaceful. Some of them worked as diplomats, but others had gone into the business of brokering information to the highest bidder. Ando had served as a trustworthy source for the SIA in the past.

And he has humans working for him, he thought. *Why…?*

"Servants," Julian explained, when he asked. "There are quite a number of human servants out here, sir."

"I know," Kevin said. Quite a few humans – some working for the SIA – had sought long-term service contacts with the Galactics, rather than serving as mercenaries. They were highly-prized by their masters, if only because they were more adaptable than most primitive races and yet posed no discernible threat. "Are any of them on the lists?"

"Two of them are," Julian confirmed. "But we would be better approaching Ando openly, first."

"Then set up the meeting," Kevin said. He couldn't help a thrill of excitement. It had been far too long since he'd done anything apart from push paper. "And then let us go down to the planet."

"Yes, sir," Julian said. "You'll need your skinsuit and protective gear."

Kevin had seen alien worlds before; hell, he'd been the first human to set foot on an alien world, over fifty years ago. But Varnar was different, a thriving metropolis that made every human city on Earth look small. He found himself looking around in awe as soon as the teleport field let go of him, glancing up at towering skyscrapers that seemed to reach all the way to orbit, then down at smaller buildings and walkways crammed with thousands upon thousands of sentient beings. The Varnar were the majority, of course, but they were far from alone. He even caught sight of a handful of humans, either working for the aliens or traders themselves. They were often among the SIA's best source of intelligence.

The air smelt faintly unpleasant, even though the skinsuit filter. Kevin forced himself to breath normally, then followed Julian as he led the way along a crowded road and through a marketplace. It was crammed with goods, ranging from foodstuffs from a hundred worlds to pieces of technology he couldn't even begin to identify. His implants kept up a running commentary as he looked from stall to stall, marking food that was edible by humans and food that would be poisonous, if he hadn't had nanotech running through his blood. One stall caught his eye and he stared in puzzlement. It was selling nothing more than white playing cards, completely unmarked.

Pornography, his implants informed him. *Species #362 is blind, by human standards. They rely on smell to recognise their potential mates. The aroma on the cards arouses them...*

"Thank you," Kevin grunted. He hadn't wanted to know that, not really. There were countless humans who were fascinated by the endless variety of alien life, but he wasn't one of them. It was far more important to devise ways to prevent the aliens from ending *human* life. "I don't suppose they have human porn here, do they?"

His implants offered no answer. He shook his head, dismissing the thought, then walked past a pair of aliens wrapped in all-concealing armoured suits. For religious reasons, his implants reminded him, they kept themselves hidden from all, but their families. Behind them, a four-legged alien female walked past, followed by five males of her species. His implants informed him that the males were nothing more than dumb animals, while the females alone possessed intelligence. There were other races where the reverse was true, or where the breeders were unintelligent and only developed intelligence after they reached an age where they could no longer breed. Or races that laid eggs, like chickens...

Remain calm, his implants advised, as they reached a large office. *This is not a place to show weakness.*

Chester waited outside, his maniples clicking impatiently, as the three humans stepped into the office. Inside, it was pleasantly cool. A human girl sat at a desk, reading from a terminal; her eyes went wide as she looked up and saw the humans. Kevin smiled at her, knowing she would be very alone. There simply weren't more than a few hundred of her compatriots on Varnar at any one time, hardly enough to get a ghetto of their own. The chances were that the girl rarely saw other humans.

"Good afternoon," Julian said, briskly. He held up an ID block, allowing the office processors to scan it. "We have an appointment with Ando."

"So you do," the girl said. She gave Julian a charming smile. "My name is Sally, by the way."

"Pleased to meet you," Julian said. "We're just passing through."

"Everyone is just passing through," Sally said. "How long will you be staying here?"

"Maybe a week," Kevin said. He cocked his head, then lied through his teeth. "It's my first time on a non-human world. Would you be able to show me some of the sights, later?"

"I might," Sally said. His implants blinked up an alert; she'd sent him a contact code, along with her address details. "But for the moment, I can only show you into Mr. Ando's office."

"Thank you," Kevin said.

Julian gave him a mischievous look as they stepped through a large hatch and into a darkened room. There were three chairs, all designed for humans, placed in the middle of the compartment, facing a shrouded form. Kevin had to resist the urge to reach for his weapon as the alien loomed forward, slowly coming into view. Ando's race might be intelligent and largely peaceful – the file claimed they could never deliberately start a fight – but they were monstrously ugly. He looked like a strange cross between a human and a frog.

"Humans," Ando said. He was using a voder, which erased all traces of emotion from his voice. "Humans seeking information, I assume."

"That is correct," Kevin said. There was a protocol for dealing with Galactic information brokers, after all. "We will pay for the information, but also for secrecy."

Ando loomed forward. "But not for exclusivity?"

"No," Kevin said. He would have paid, if he thought it was worthwhile. But Ando wasn't the only information broker in the system. "I merely wish the information, without anyone else realising we have it."

"Very well," Ando said. The alien moved backwards, into the shadows. "What information do you require?"

Kevin took a breath. "There is a report that the Tokomak intend to intervene openly in the war," he said. "We need to know everything about the planned intervention."

There was a long chilling pause. "I can give you what I have gleaned from sources in the Ministry of War," Ando said, finally. "But I could offer no guarantees."

Kevin understood. The plans might change...or the Tokomak might have lied to the Ministry, making sure the *real* plan couldn't leak out. Nothing Kevin had seen had convinced him the Galactics had any head for security, but there had to be *some* competent Tokomak in the universe, or their empire would have collapsed centuries ago. *He* would certainly have restricted any information he saw fit to pass on to his underlings, in their place. Let them wait and see what was coming when the fleet actually arrived.

"That will be sufficient," Kevin said. "And the price is...what?"

"Five thousand GalStars," Ando stated. "The risks in obtaining this information were high."

Kevin swallowed the urge to swear out loud. Five thousand GalStars was a significant percentage of their operating budget. Spending it now would be risky...but he knew from experience that the information broker wouldn't change his price, unless Kevin had something other than money to offer in exchange. But he didn't have anything...

"Very well," he said. "Five thousand for both the information itself and secrecy."

"Done," Ando said. He leaned forward again, revealing giant frog-like eyes. "My assistant will have the information ready for you in ten minutes."

"Thank you," Kevin said.

"I should warn you that you are not the only interested parties," Ando said. "The information can go no further, if you are prepared to pay."

"No, thank you," Kevin said. "Unless you have something completely exclusive..."

"I may be able to find something exclusive," Ando stated. "I will inform you if I can do so."

Kevin scowled, inwardly. The information broker might well know more about humanity than he cared to think about, particularly as he had a human assistant. How much did he know about humanity's attempts to build up a space fleet? Or did he feel that humanity was nothing more than another scavenger race, using technology it couldn't hope to understand, let alone duplicate? There was no way to know.

Sally might know, his own thoughts mocked him. *And she is clearly interested in meeting someone – anyone – human.*

"Thank you," he said, instead.

A door opened in the far corner, allowing brilliant light to shine into the compartment. A tall, inhumanly thin figure stepped into the chamber, carrying a datachip in one hand and a credit terminal in the other. Julian reached into his pocket, retrieved his GalStar Card and pressed it against the terminal. There was a long pause, then five thousand GalStars transferred themselves from the SIA's card to Ando's account.

"You may leave now," Ando informed them, as his assistant retreated back through the door. "I will contact you if I discover anything I can offer to you exclusively. Do you have any specific requests?"

Kevin shared a long look with Julian. They'd paid for secrecy, but the Varnar might well find a way to force information out of Ando, if they realised what he'd sold to his customers. And if they asked for a specific piece of data…even asking would be revealing, in a way. It was too great a risk to take.

"No, thank you," Kevin said.

He led the way through the door and back into the lobby, where Sally greeted them with a smile. Julian and Mandy made their way to the door at once, Kevin stayed back long enough to ask Sally if she would like to meet the following day, after work. Sally countered with an offer two days in the future, clearly trying not to seem *too* eager. Kevin accepted, then followed the other two out into the open air. The heat of the city struck him as soon as he stepped outside.

"We'll go back to the ship and have this analysed," he said, once Chester joined them. No one had seemed surprised to see the Hordesman standing guard. "And then we will know what to do next."

"That girl," Julian said. He smirked as they started to walk back to the teleport zone. "Do you think she's working for us?"

"The files said she wasn't, not directly," Kevin said. It was a shame – it would have been easy to ask her questions openly if she had already been working for the SIA – but it was also a challenge. "I'll see what she says when we go for dinner."

"Just be careful, boss," Julian said. "She's spent years on an alien world. She might well have gone a little native by now."

TWELVE

Four federal land exploitation agents have been found dead in Kansas, their bodies apparently mutilated before being dumped in an abandoned quarry. Federal news sources have classed the killers as terrorists and sworn to hunt them down, but posts on the datanet by the Kansas Liberation Army state the agents were killed for "sticking their Washington noses in Kansas business."

—Solar News Network, Year 52

"Well, maggots," Sergeant Grison said. "I suppose that wasn't a *complete* disaster."

Martin winced under his gaze. He wasn't the only one. Sergeant Grison was *terrifying*. His left eye had been replaced by a cybernetic implant, while one of his legs was made of metal, which glinted in the light. And, despite that, Martin was sure the sergeant could whip the entire platoon with one hand tied behind his back. His career had seen more combat than Martin had imagined possible, first as a United States Marine, then as a mercenary and finally as a Solar Marine.

"You could have reacted better," Grison continued. "Why didn't you think to watch for ambushes?"

"We were tired, sir," Hawke said, finally. He was the current platoon leader, although the post changed hands at least once a week. "We were thinking about getting back to the barracks for food and sleep."

"At least you're honest," Grison sneered. "Didn't you think the enemy would know you were off your game?"

"No, sergeant," Hawke said.

"Get into the camp, get washed and get something to eat," Grison said. "We'll go over what you did wrong in greater detail after you're refreshed."

He stepped forward and ripped the platoon leader badge off Hawke's chest. "You're demoted," he added. "You should have been watching for an ambush when you were least able to deal with it."

"Yes, sergeant," Hawke said.

"I'll decide which one of you gets it next after you stuff your pie-holes," Grison informed them. He jabbed a finger towards the barracks. "Get."

Martin ran – no one was allowed to walk, unless they were injured – along with the other recruits. He'd thought the first part of training was bad, but he'd never imagined Boot Camp...or just how hard he would have to work to keep up with the others. Four weeks of intensive training felt like months. Part of him was honestly tempted just to give up and quit, as several of the others had. The thought of spending the next year being hammered into shape was terrifying.

"That could have gone better," Recruit Jones said. "We should have been more alert."

"It's not like a computer game," Martin agreed. The training grounds included all kinds of threats, ranging from holographic alien soldiers to dangerous creatures. By the time they'd started to move back to the base, they'd been so tired they hadn't notice the warning signs until it was too late. "Does it get easier?"

"It's *meant* to get easier," Jones said. "But it may be months before we can hold our heads up high."

Martin sighed as they stepped into the showers, removing their clothes in unison. His body was stronger than he had ever imagined possible, thanks to nanotech enhancement and endless exercise, but it still ached every day, after hours of physical training. The Solar Marines didn't take slackers, Grison had told them, and he'd meant every word. He'd even thanked – with a sickly-sweet politeness – the quitters, telling them that they'd done the right thing in deciding to leave. They wouldn't threaten his beloved Solar Marines any longer.

As soon as they were washed, they jogged into the mess hall and scooped up plates of food, then ate in a tearing hurry. Grison entered shortly afterwards and watched them, his face betraying nothing of his innermost thoughts. Martin wondered if he was proud of the remaining recruits, then realised it probably didn't matter. He'd been told, during induction, that they would be pushed right to the limit, with most of them falling by the wayside. The Solar Marines took only the best.

But if they only take the best, he'd thought, *what happens to those who don't meet their high standards?*

He hadn't dared asked. Grison would probably not have taken it kindly.

"Briefing room, now," Grison said, when they had nearly finished their food. "Hurry."

Martin stuffed a last bite of food into his mouth, then stood and paced hurriedly into the briefing compartment. It was nothing more than a tiny office with a handful of chairs, a projector and little else, but it represented a chance to sit down. He found a chair, sat quickly, then looked up at Grison. The Drill Sergeant was talking to a Drill Instructor, who was holding a terminal in one hand. Neither of them looked very pleased.

Bad news, Martin guessed. *They're going to fail us all.*

"Attention," Grison snapped. The recruits straightened up, as they'd been taught. Grison had a nasty habit of throwing questions at them, just to make sure they were actually listening to what he said. "It has been decided that you may proceed to the next stage of training."

Martin found himself smiling. He wasn't the only one.

"You have learned from your fuck-ups," Grison continued. "However, the next stage of training is far more complex. You will be expected to master powered combat armour, a mission that not everyone can handle safely. Do you have any questions?"

"Sergeant," Kayla said. "Why do we have to learn to fight without the armour if we are going to fight *with* the armour?"

"Because there's no guarantee that you *will* be fighting with the armour," Grison snapped, crossly. "I have been on deployments where I have been wrapped inside my personal tank and deployments where the only thing protecting me from certain death was a thin set of BDUs."

He glowered at her, then at the rest of the platoon. "You will start training tomorrow," he added. "Until then, review the data provided to your implants and make sure you get plenty of sleep. A single mistake could get you in deep shit - and even get you kicked off the course. There is no room for slackers in this unit!"

"Yes, sergeant," the recruits said.

"And you, Jones, will be the new platoon leader," Grison snapped. "Try not to fuck up this time."

"Yes, sergeant," Jones said.

Martin glanced over at Kayla as the recruits were dismissed back to their barracks. She looked odd; unlike Earth, where the ideal woman was stick-thin, she was incredibly muscular and strong as an ox. Martin hadn't understood it until he'd realised just how many treatments were provided to recruits who wanted to join the Solar Marines. The muscles he'd built up over the past month weren't *just* the result of endless exercises and drills.

He smiled, then looked away. They'd been told, in no uncertain terms, that they were not allowed to have any form of sexual relationship within the platoon. Heterosexual, homosexual, bisexual...it was strictly forbidden. The only way to get any form of sexual release was to use one's hand, perhaps while watching porn through one's implants. And there was rarely any time to indulge. When they weren't training or eating, they were either reading briefing notes or trying to catch up on sleep.

The files opened up in his mind as he lay back on his bunk and closed his eyes. They would be learning how to use the Mark-IV Hammer-class

Powered Combat Suit, which was – according to the briefing notes – a formidable weapon of war. Martin watched as a handful of men in suits tore through old-style tanks – a scene from the attack on Tehran, 2045 – with ease, suffering absolutely no casualties at all. But the suits weren't invulnerable. The Galactics had plenty of weapons that could be turned against them, ripping through the combat armour as though it were made of paper.

He opened his eyes as the files came to an end, then activated a sleep program in his implants. Moments later – or at least it felt like moments later – he heard the alarm, yanking them out of sleep. He jumped off the bunk, dressed at a speed he would have considered impossible five months ago, then ran outside...and stopped, dead. A line of armoured combat suits was standing in front of them, weapons levelled at the barracks...

"Get into line," Grison snapped. "What are you waiting for, Recruit Douglas?"

Martin felt his cheeks heat as he fell into line behind the other recruits. The first week had been an endless series of embarrassments, as recruits had found themselves forgetting various items of clothing as they'd tried frantically to dress themselves and get out onto the line before the sergeants started handing out demerits. Martin had forgotten a sock, or a shirt...there had even been a recruit who'd panicked and run out wearing nothing, apart from his hat. Grison had been *very* sarcastic that day.

"These are your new toys," Grison said, when he'd finished the inspection and handed out a handful of demerits. "You have all read the briefing notes, I assume? You will be aware that the suits magnify every movement you make? Good! You will be careful, won't you?"

Martin swallowed. Grison sometimes warned them of potential mistakes, but he also allowed them to make others on their own, pointing out that it was the only way to learn. Martin had lost count of the number of times he'd 'died' on exercises, shot with a training laser, when he'd made a careless mistake. There was more to combat than charging at the enemy, screaming curses into the air; the movies he'd watched, down on Earth, had been more than a little unrealistic. The Drill Sergeants had even forced them to play out movie-like scenarios, just to learn how completely unrealistic they were – or get killed trying to emulate some of the movie heroes.

"When you get into the suits, do not move until I give the order," Grison added. "Step forward, claim your suit, and open the hatch at the back, then climb inside."

Martin obeyed. Up close, the suit was thoroughly intimidating. It bristled with weapons and smelt faintly of blood. He shuddered, then used his implants to send the open command to the suit's processors. There was a dull hiss as the hatch at the back opened, revealing a space just barely large enough for the human body. He hesitated, feeling claustrophobic for the first time in his life, then scrambled up and lowered his legs into the suit. Moments later, the suit closed in around him, cutting off the light. Martin almost panicked, then activated his implants again. The outside world sprang to life inside his mind.

"Connection established," a voice stated. "Combat interface online."

There was a dull crash from outside as one of the suits moved, then fell over. Martin heard Sergeant Grison screaming at the suit's occupant, who had ignored the command to remain still, then turned his attention to the suit itself. The control programs reminded him of some of the teleoperated systems they'd been forced to use in their first training sessions; now, he understood why they'd been forced to go through it, even though it had seemed useless. It would have been a great deal harder to control the suit without that experience.

"All suits," Grison said. "Take one step forward."

Martin obeyed...and toppled over, hitting the ground. The feedback wasn't bad enough to stun him – he'd automatically thrust his hands forward to break his fall – but it told him just how closely the suit was merged to his mind. He pushed himself off the ground...and flipped over backwards. There was no way he was accustomed to having so much strength at his command. He glanced from side to side and saw the other Earth-born recruits having problems, although the Solar Union citizens seemed to have no such issues. They'd been using biofeedback systems since they'd been old enough to accept implants.

He felt a stab of envy, then slowly forced himself to sit upright, then stand up again. The suit responded, but every motion was backed with so much strength it was alarmingly easy to lose control and fall over, as if a child had suddenly become a man. On impulse, he flexed his legs and jumped upwards...and found himself shooting into the air. Gravity reasserted itself moments later, dragging him back down. He landed badly enough to send pain shooting up and down his legs.

"Not too bad, for a first try," Grison said.

Martin choked down a word he knew would earn him more demerits. Not *bad*? None of them had managed to take a step forward without falling over like a load of drunken idiots. Even the asteroid-born had had problems. But...he took a step forward, very carefully. This time, he managed to stay upright long enough to take a second step, then a third. It was hard, so hard, but the more he did it, the easier it seemed.

"Just like driving a car," Jones said, loudly. "We can do it, eventually."

Grison gave him an evil grin. "Just you wait until you're managing weapons as well as running," he said. "And, speaking of weapons..."

He nodded to one of the other Drill Sergeants, who produced twelve packets of eggs. As Martin watched in disbelief, she put a packet in front of each armoured recruit, then stepped backwards hastily. Martin didn't blame her. The slightest movement inside the suit, voluntary or involuntary, would be magnified a hundred-fold by the armoured muscles, leading to disaster if he coughed at the wrong moment. There was no way he would trust himself with weapons until he knew how to drive the suit safety.

"To get your driving licence," Grison said, shooting Jones another look, "you have to pick up one of the eggs, safely."

Martin bent over, reached for the eggs...and smashed them with a single touch. Groans and curses over the communications network told him that everyone else had had the same problem, making them all failures. Grison walked from person to person, looking down at the packets of eggs and shaking his head mournfully. None of them, it seemed, had even managed to save a single egg, let alone pick it up.

"What a waste of good eggs," he observed, archly. "But you will master it, one day."

He turned and started to march towards the training field. "Follow me."

Martin would have enjoyed the next few hours if they hadn't been so frustrating. The more he played with the suit, the more he thought he understood it, only to lose his certainty as something else happened and he lost control again. He even tried to shake hands with another recruit, only to find himself thrown over and slammed into the ground. Others crashed into one another, laughing as they bounced off and squelched through the mud. The Sergeant moved from recruit to recruit, offering pieces of advice merged with a droll awareness that learning how to handle the suits was something that could only be done through experience. By the time they were finally ordered back to the barracks, Martin was feeling a dull ache at the back of his temple. It was clear that mastering the suits was going to take weeks.

"We will be training with the suits every second day," Grison informed them, as they lined up in front of the barracks. "The other days, I'm afraid, will be spent continuing with our unarmoured practice. You will have to learn the difference between fighting in an armoured suit and fighting without it."

At first, Martin thought he was joking...and then he realised there was something deadly serious behind it. He'd forgotten, to some extent, that he was actually wearing the suit. It had merged so completely with him that he might as well have *been* the suit. And something he could do in a suit – rushing across a field while the enemy fired machine guns at him – would get him killed in an instant if he tried it without a suit. The Solar Union BDUs had some bullet-resistance woven into them, he'd been told, but bullets still hurt.

I could die if I did the wrong thing, he thought, numbly. He'd thought he was used to the concept of death, but hope – real hope – had proved him wrong. *And so could all of us*.

"Now," Grison said. "Get out of your suits."

That, Martin discovered, was harder than it seemed. It took him a long time – and some prompting from the Sergeant – to work out where to put his hands as he scrambled out of the suit and down to the ground. Two others were less lucky, losing their grip and plummeting backwards to hit the ground, yelping in pain at the sudden shock. Grison laughed, helped them to their feet, then pointed the recruits towards the mess. Martin was surprised by just how hungry he was, after several hours in the suits. But then, they hadn't had anything to eat in the morning.

"You have five more months of training to go," Grison informed them, as they gratefully ate as fast as they could. "By then, you will be expected to be completely proficient with a suit – and ready to handle anything, from an enemy shooting at you to a child wanting to ride on your shoulders. You are *not* to try the latter until you are a qualified suit operator. Do you understand me?"

Martin blanched. He could tear a child – or an adult – apart, entirely by accident. The thought was terrifying. He didn't want to kill someone who merely wanted to have fun…

I have to write Yolanda about this, he thought. The last he'd heard, she was studying for her flight qualification. But neither of them had had time to meet up since starting the next phase of their training. *She'd be impressed…and jealous.*

THIRTEEN

The Provisional Russian Government has been warned, in the strongest possible terms, that further attempts to bar emigration to the Solar Union will result in harsh reprisals. Speaking in front of the Solar Congress, President Ross reaffirmed the Solar Union's determination to provide a home for all those willing to live by the solar creed...

—Solar News Network, Year 52

"Two years," Julian said, slowly.

"So it would seem," Kevin said. "Two years for the fleet to arrive, then set out for Earth."

He scowled. It was possible Ando was wrong – or that something would impede the fleet's progress as it made its way to Varnar – but he dared not assume anything of the sort. The worst case scenario would see two hundred Tokomak battleships approaching Earth, demanding immediate unconditional surrender. And they would have the firepower to crush the Solar Union, if it came down to a straight fight. Mongo would need to be informed, as quickly as possible, before it was too late.

And then...what? Kevin asked himself. *Can we stop that much firepower from doing whatever the hell it wants?*

"Store the information in the secure compartment," he ordered, instead. "We will depart in two days, as planned."

"After your date," Julian said, dryly. "Be careful, sir."

"I've carried out more covert operations than you," Kevin said. It was true, although only if one counted covert operations on Earth as well as alien worlds. "And besides, you never know what it might lead to."

"Her bedroom," Julian said. "Good luck, sir."

The next two days passed quickly. Kevin spent most of them exploring the planet with the rest of the team, trying to understand just how it worked. The Varnar had created an environment that was surprisingly multicultural, but – at the same time – forced the large non-Varnar communities to live in ghettos of their own. It was almost as if the Varnar didn't want to allow too much alien influence into their society, although Kevin had a feeling they were wasting their time. Earth was far more isolated than Varnar and quite a bit of alien influence had entered the cultural gestalt. By the time he was due to meet Sally, he thought he knew more about just how the planet worked. But he also knew better than to take it for granted.

"I've booked us a table at a Pan-Gal," she said, when he reached her apartment. It was definitely a multiracial complex, designed to give members of almost every known race a place that suited their environmental needs. "It won't be cheap, I'm afraid, but Ando has his contacts."

Kevin nodded as he took her hand. Sally was wearing a long yellow dress that set her dark hair off nicely, hinting at her curves rather than crudely revealing them. She looked surprisingly attractive, although he was probably the only person for miles who could appreciate it. The Pan-Gal, like the apartment complex, catered for just about every known race. It wasn't as if human cuisine had taken the Galactics by storm.

Sally chatted happily about nothing as they walked through the streets and into the Pan-Gal, where a robotic waiter took their coats and steered them to a small table, surrounded by invisible forcefields. Kevin had to smile as Sally explained, with a hint of embarrassment, that most of the Galactics liked dining together, but what one race considered edible another might consider deadly poison. The forcefields ensured that no one had to smell anything they might consider offensive, scuppering whatever deal the Galactics were trying to make. It also made sure that disagreements between parties couldn't turn lethal.

"I left Earth four years ago," Sally said. "It was meant to be a short-term contract, but it was so fascinating to be on an alien world that I just stayed here."

"I don't blame you," Kevin said. Sally was far from the only human to make a home among the Galactics. There were no shortage of human traders plying the stars now, looking to earn their fortunes while seeing the galaxy. "What's it like, working here?"

"Strange," Sally said. "And it keeps you on your toes."

She jabbed a finger at the holographic menu. "I'm supposed to organise dinner meetings for Mr. Ando and his clients," she said. "Trouble is; one of his clients likes eating live beasties while Mr. Ando would find the sight repulsive. I have to sort out the dinner so that the two requirements don't clash horrifically. And then there's the Varnar code. Everything has to be absolutely in its place or there will be murder done. Perhaps literally."

"It must be easier eating with me," Kevin joked.

"It is," Sally said. "I won't have to watch as you masticate something that looks like a human baby, then ask snide questions about my intelligence."

Kevin frowned. "A baby?"

"There's a race that look like very pale and bald humans," Sally explained. "They're not intelligent, but several Galactics consider them a delicacy. And then they glance at me and notice I look very much like their food."

"Yuk," Kevin said.

"It gets worse," Sally said. "Do you know there's a race that is primarily composed of cannibals? They eat their own flesh, just to stay alive. God alone knows what sort of evolutionary pattern created such a nightmare."

She tapped the menu, ordering something simple to eat, then swung it over to Kevin. "It's only showing food humans can eat, but I'd be careful what you chose," she advised. "Not all of it tastes nice, even if it is technically edible."

"I understand," Kevin said. He picked something that looked like roast lamb, then banished the menu with a wave of his hand. "Do you often meet other humans?"

"Not that often," Sally said. "Mr. Ando keeps me very busy."

She looked up as the robotic waiter arrived, carrying two large plates of food. Kevin took his, nodded politely to the robot, then sniffed his plate carefully. It smelled surprisingly good, for something the Galactics had produced. His last meal on an alien world had tasted suspiciously unpleasant. If he hadn't had his taste buds modified, he wouldn't have been able to eat it at all.

He took a bite of his meat, then leaned forward. "Have you ever met a Tokomak?"

"Never," Sally said. "I believe some of Mr. Ando's clients are Tokomaks, but they never show themselves to mere humans. He handles all such matters himself."

Kevin smiled. "They don't trust you?"

"They never talk to anyone who doesn't come from a self-starfaring race," Sally said. "I don't think they really believe we're intelligent. I heard, once, that a handful of them came to discuss matters with the Supreme Council on Varnar. One of them talked only to the Supreme Commander, the others kept their mouths shut all the time. I don't think they were even exchanging messages through their implants."

"I see," Kevin said.

"They're not the only ones," Sally said. "Most starfaring races bend the knee to the Tokomak, but look down on any race that didn't manage to find the gravity points on their own, let alone the gravity drive. I sometimes find myself pushed aside by one of them...and there are races that have it far worse. The Hordesmen, bastards though they are, aren't treated as anything other than slaves. And there are entire races that are practically moulded by their betters into something more...useful."

She jabbed a finger towards a handful of diners at the far side of the room. The leaders seemed to be a pair of insect-like creatures, but they were being served by a handful of green-skinned creatures that bowed and scraped whenever their masters looked at them. Kevin couldn't help thinking of negro slaves from before the War Between The States, pretending to be submissive whenever they were watched. He hoped the slaves he was looking at were planning their own escape, the sooner the better. But what would happen if they tried to escape and failed?

"Anything," Sally said, when he asked. She shuddered. "The contract I have with Mr. Ando grants me some rights, but others are practically slaves. There's even a slave market down near the ghettos, if you happened to want a slave while you're here. I imagine you could even take one back to Earth, if you wished."

"Shit," Kevin said. "I dread to imagine what would happen if I turned up with a slave in tow."

"Depends," Sally said. "They might simply free the slave – or they might put you in prison."

Kevin shuddered. There had been a time, before the Solar Union, when several Arab states had had slaves, in all but name. Some of those slaves had fled, when they'd been taken to America and had a chance to escape, others had become excellent sources for the CIA. And yet, the bastards who'd brought slaves to America had been left unpunished, because they had diplomatic immunity. There had been nothing anyone could do.

"Depends on the contract, I assume," he said, finally. Selling someone into slavery was illegal; signing a contract that made one a slave was merely stupid. "But it isn't something I want to think about."

"There will be diplomatic incidents, sooner or later," Sally predicted. "If Earth becomes more important, more and more Galactics will make their way to Earth. And some of them will have slaves."

"We shall see," Kevin said. There were relatively few Galactics – as opposed to exiles – in the Sol System. The longer it stayed that way, the better. "And we'll probably come up with a way of dealing with it by then."

Sally smiled. "Good luck," she said. "Make sure you warn them on Earth, all right?"

Kevin nodded.

He would have enjoyed the dinner, under other circumstances. The chance to meet a pretty girl, one who wasn't awed by his family's reputation, and just to sit back and relax would have been worth almost anything. But he knew he had to pump her for information, in the hopes she might prove a useful intelligence source. There was no way he could simply relax and enjoy himself. And she might well pick up on it, even if she hadn't set eyes on another human for years.

"I wouldn't recommend anything they consider suitable for desert," Sally advised, when they finished their main course. "I have something at home I've been saving for a special occasion."

Kevin glanced at the menu, then nodded in agreement. The most appetising thing on the list looked like a melted banana split, but he rather doubted that the ingredients included bananas, nuts, ice cream or anything else that had been within ten light years of Earth. Instead, he paid the bill – fifty-seven GalStars – and then allowed Sally to lead him back along the darkened walkways to her apartment.

"Is it safe to live here?" He asked. "What is it like compared to Earth?"

"Moderately safe," Sally said. "The local Law Guardians – the police, to you and me – patrol regularly. If you're not a Varnar and you commit a crime, they won't hesitate to rough you up and dump you in the cells for the night, then your employer will be forced to pay for your ticket back home. You won't be allowed to return. If you're an illegal, you will probably be shipped to a penal world and put to work. They don't police communities so closely, but anything that spills out into the mainstream will draw a harsh response."

She shrugged as they entered the apartment block. "There's no shortage of blue collar crimes here, everything from information theft to financial fraud," she added. "But any crime of violence will be punished. It keeps everything reasonably peaceful."

"I see," Kevin said.

Sally led him into her apartment, then closed the door and motioned for him to sit down on a comfortable sofa. "Mr. Ando wished me to give you this," she said, as she sat facing him and crossed her legs. There was a small Galactic-issue datachip in her hand. "He thought you might find it of interest."

Kevin felt his eyes narrow. "And what is the price?"

"There isn't one, now," Sally said. "Mr. Ando gives it to you as a gesture of...good faith and of his hopes for a future relationship. If you want to turn it down, I dare say he won't care too much."

"I imagine he won't," Kevin said, slowly. Did Mr. Ando know who they were? He was an information broker, after all. The Stuart Family was largely unknown outside the Solar System, but someone who traded in information might well have heard the name, then put two and two together. "What's on the chip?"

"He didn't say," Sally said. She held it out, resting it on her hand. "Do you want it?"

Kevin hesitated, then took the chip. "I'll have a look at it," he said. It would be a very careful look, in a sealed compartment. The Galactics were old enough to have forgotten more tricks than humanity had ever learned. "And then I'll let him know what I think."

"Good," Sally said. She leaned forward. "I have a question for you. Are you married?"

"No," Kevin said. "My wife and I separated peacefully seven years ago."

Sally quirked her eyebrows. "What happened?"

"We just got sick of each other," Kevin said. "There was no way we could spend the rest of eternity together, not when we were both functionally immortal. We separated, very calmly, and resumed our separate ways. I believe she married again, two years later."

He sighed. There had been a time when he'd considered marriage sacred – unlike Steve, who had refused to marry Mariko for fear of federal interference. Kevin had never had the heart to tell him that so long cohabiting had probably given her legal rights anyway, long before the Hordesmen had arrived. But now...the idea of staying together until death took on a very different meaning when death could easily be thousands of years away. The Solar Union had a depressingly high rate of separation, then divorce.

But at least we're not locking people up for adultery, he thought, sourly. *Doesn't that make us better than some human nations?*

Sally smiled. "And you didn't?"

"I spend most of my time on trading ships," Kevin lied. "There aren't that many opportunities to meet people."

It wasn't *that* great a lie, he told himself. Having a relationship as the Director of the Solar Intelligence Agency caused all kinds of complications. The girl he picked up in a bar one night might be nothing more than just someone seeking a partner for the night, or she might be a spy trying to get into his heart so she could pump him for information. It was far easier to remain alone and watch pornography, or hire a sexbot, rather than be forced to vet anyone he might like to date.

"There aren't that many opportunities here either," Sally said.

She leaned forward, then placed a hand on his leg. "Let me be businesslike," she said. "I haven't had sex for over a year, since the last handsome spacer visited Varnar and had time to meet me. I would like to take you to bed. But I can't promise anything else, either support from my boss or future sexual encounters. If that's all right with you, then start taking off your clothes."

Kevin blinked – blunt propositions were somewhat outside his experience – then started to take off his jacket. Sally stood, reached behind her neck and undid her dress, which fell to the ground and pooled around her feet. Kevin stared, feeling his heart suddenly start to race as he looked her up and down. She was gorgeous.

I love nanotechnology, he thought, as he removed his trousers. *And so does everyone else.*

The following morning, she cooked breakfast and then urged him out of the apartment. Kevin understood – she had to go back to work – and settled for giving her a kiss on the cheek, before starting the walk back to the teleport zone. Twenty minutes later, he was back onboard the *Rory Williams*, studying the chip through a small sensor array.

"Seems to be a normal chip," Julian said. "Did you have a good time last night, boss?"

"Yes," Kevin said. "Can we remain professional, please?"

Julian smirked. "And sleeping with a lady on another world is *professional?*"

"You might be surprised," Kevin said. "I once slept with the wife of a senior Al Qaeda leader."

"Bullshit," Julian said.

"I shit ye not," Kevin assured him. "The poor girl's bastard of a rapist – sorry, a *husband* – had tastes that ran towards small boys, not girls of any age. By the time we started poking around, she hated him so passionately the only thing that kept her from killing the fucker was the certain knowledge she would be murdered by his followers. I used her to target the guy, took him alive and then dragged her into protective custody. She used to be living in Oakland with a decent guy from Norway."

"Lucky her," Julian said. "I still don't believe you."

He looked up from the display. "There's a few pieces of information on the chip, but not much else," he said. "I think we'd have to read it."

Kevin nodded, then watched as Julian connected an isolated terminal to the computer chip. A handful of files sprang up on the display, headed by one marked WATCH ME FIRST. When Julian clicked on it, a voder-voice stated to speak.

"You may find the information on these files useful," it said. "There are others who share your interests. If you would like more, feel free to ask."

"Jesus," Julian breathed. "This is their entire plan!"

"Then we use it," Kevin said. Was Ando actually offering to help without payment? Or was something else going on? "And pray he isn't trying to lead us down the garden path."

FOURTEEN

The Malaysian Government deployed upwards of five thousand soldiers to Kota Kinabalu, Sabah, in the wake of riots that left the centre of the city devastated. Government sources blame the riots on uneducated immigrants from Indonesia, but locals suspect that the riots were used as a pretext to put troops on the ground prior to the planned independence referendum.

—Solar News Network, Year 52

"Yolanda!"

Yolanda looked up and stared. "Martin?"

"It's me," Martin assured her. He gave her a hug, very loosely. "How do I look?"

Yolanda stepped backwards, shaking her head. Martin had never been *weak*, but now he was covered in muscle. His skin seemed darker, somehow, and there were hints of scars covering his face and lower arms. The uniform he wore – a dark green uniform with a single bronze star on his right shoulder – showed off his new appearance to best advantage. She couldn't help a faint flutter in her heart as she looked at him.

"Different," she said, finally.

"I've got muscles on my muscles," Martin said, cheerfully. He was grinning from ear to ear. "And can you believe I'm one of the smaller people in the training platoon?"

"No," Yolanda said. "I don't think anyone can grow much bigger than you."

"You'd be wrong," Martin said. He shook his head. "I think there's an asteroid where the gravity field is much stronger, strong enough to produce humans who are two or three times as strong as the strongest man on Earth."

"But that would cause health problems," Yolanda said. Greatly daring, she took his hand – his skin felt harder than she'd expected – and tugged him through the door. "Can a child be raised in such an environment?"

"I think they use plenty of genetic enhancement," Martin said. "You've changed too."

Yolanda tapped the side of her head. "Mainly in here," she said. She might not have enhanced muscles, but she did have enhanced piloting implants. The training program had been more cerebral than physical, yet it had been equally exhausting. "Right now, I can view a dozen live feeds simultaneously while flying a starship through a gravity well."

"Ah, multitasking," Martin said. "No wonder most starship pilots are female."

"Two-thirds of the trainees are male," Yolanda countered. "Multitasking is something anyone can be trained to do, with the right implants. You just need to keep going until it all clicks together."

She gave him another smile, then led him through the second hatch and into the zoo. Darwin Asteroid had no permanent human population; instead, it housed hundreds of different creatures, inhabiting an ecosystem that had been transplanted from Earth. Some of the animals, according to the brochure, had died out on Earth, hunted to death by people who thought they had a use for the dead. The guidebook she'd downloaded had poured scorn on the idea of using powdered rhinoceros horn as a sexual aide, but it hadn't stopped people trying to hunt down the last few rhinos in the wild. It wasn't a pleasant thought.

"There are forcefields in place to keep us from touching the animals – or being touched by them," she explained, as they started down the path. "I just thought it would be a nice place to visit."

"I like it," Martin said. "I never saw the zoo on Earth."

Yolanda nodded in agreement. Her stepmother had had better things to do than take her unwanted stepchild to the zoo – or anywhere, really. And her school had never had the funding to take the children anywhere, not when they were required by law to insure every child against everything from accidents to deliberate mishap. In hindsight, she understood why her school had been so crappy. On one hand, they were expected to be responsible for everything; on the other, they simply didn't have the authority to handle everything. They couldn't even eject the most disruptive students in the class.

She held his hand as they walked down the path, catching sight of a pride of lions sitting in the sunlight, watching the human interlopers with curious eyes. Most of them, according to the guidebooks, had been cloned from samples taken from Earth, a breeding program that had slowly enhanced their numbers until they had a viable population once again. But reintroducing them into the wild was a problem, even if the hunters were dissuaded from going after them once again. There simply weren't enough older animals to teach the younger ones how to live in the jungle.

"I think they were talking about trying to clone dinosaurs," she said, softly. "Bring life back to a dead world."

"I saw the movie," Martin said. "It didn't end very well."

Yolanda smiled. "I don't think that would be a problem here," she said. "The environment on an asteroid is completely controlled."

"You might still lose control of your creations," Martin said. He shook his head. "Do you think they ever lose control of the forcefields?"

"I have you to protect me if the forcefields collapse," Yolanda said. It was strange, really, to think that the only thing separating them from the lions was an invisible forcefield. A person without implants wouldn't even know it was there, unless they actually touched the field itself. "But I think the system is completely reliable."

They said little else as they passed through the hatch into the next ecosystem, which was composed of creatures taken from a hundred alien worlds. Yolanda had read that the Galactics exchanged biological samples on a regular basis, although they strongly discouraged introducing new creatures or plant life to a life-bearing world. It wasn't a bad decision, she suspected. Some alien plants and animals would spread rapidly on Earth, as they lacked natural predators, and would damage the local ecosystem quite badly. Rats and cockroaches were already a major problem on Luna and some of the other settlements across the Solar System. They seemed to be completely impossible to exterminate.

And they will spread to other worlds, she thought, morbidly. *How long will it be before the Galactics accuse us of spreading cockroaches across the galaxy?*

She pushed the thought aside as an alien creature came into view, poking against the forcefield as if it could sense its presence. It looked, at first, like a moving bush, but the more she looked at it, the more she saw a twisting mass of pulsating flesh below the strands, just waiting for something to be caught and eaten. The creature was so completely outside her experience that she found herself taking a step backwards, then clutching Martin tighter than ever. Beyond it, another creature – resembling a furry lobster – crawled over the sandy ground, claws clicking unpleasantly. She shuddered and took another step backwards.

"They force us to look at the Galactics," Martin said, as they hastily moved to the next compartment. "Anyone who shows an adverse fear reaction to any of the aliens we might have to fight is gently urged not to consider out-system duty. There aren't any treatments for people who are unable to cope with alien life forms."

Yolanda nodded. Racism – human racism – was a learned impulse, for better or worse. But there were people who simply could not cope with encountering non-human forms of intelligent life, face to face. It had puzzled her, when she'd first encountered it while reading though the files, but it made a certain amount of sense. Humans had certain perceptions about what an intelligent creature should look like and many of the Galactics simply didn't fit it. And others were so inhuman that fear seemed a logical reaction.

"But some of the weirdest creatures are the closest to us," she mused. "I mean, they *look* like us."

"Not *that* much like us," Martin said. "And certainly not on the inside."

He sighed. "You know one of my squadmates was busted for possession of interracial porn?"

Yolanda blinked. "Really?"

"Yes, really," Martin said. "Humans making love to non-humans. It was not a pleasant sight."

"Yuck," Yolanda said. "And he was busted for it?"

"The Galactics have a flat ban on interracial relationships," Martin reminded her. "Even possessing such porn could get someone into real trouble, out in the galaxy."

"I wouldn't have thought they needed to bother," Yolanda said. Humans and Varnar were both humanoid, but it would be impossible for one to actually have sex with the other. Their sexual organs were simply not compatible. "Who would *want* to?"

"There were people who asked the same question of white and black humans, years ago," Martin said. "They didn't see how interracial sex could work...and that was among humans, who are the same under the skin. Aliens...are just another type of person."

"But not biologically compatible," Yolanda said. "Black and white humans can produce children, but there's no such thing as a mixed human and alien child."

Martin smiled. "I could see some people enjoying the thought of being able to fuck without having children," he said. "But nanotech sees to that too."

Yolanda sighed, then kept walking. When they reached the wall, she found a teleport that would take them back to the guest levels. The sensation of teleportation was still unpleasant – she had been told it was purely imaginary, which didn't help – but it was far quicker than walking through the whole asteroid. Besides, this way they could jump back into the ecosystem caves the following day without having to retrace their steps.

"I booked us a pair of rooms for three days," she said. "Do you have enough leave to cover it?"

"They expect me back in two days," Martin said. "Will you be alright on your own?"

On Earth, Yolanda knew, it wouldn't have been a stupid question. There were places no unaccompanied woman dared go, save at risk of losing her virtue or her life. But in the Solar Union, crime was minimal. She could spend her remaining day of shore leave exploring a different asteroid, or simply sleeping naturally and getting as much rest as she could. Or, if she wanted, she could immerse herself in local news and choose a place to live, after her graduation.

"I think so," she said, dryly. "Shall we find a place to eat?"

The guest levels were heaving with people, ranging from fairly normal humans to cyborgs and people who were clearly visiting from Earth. Yolanda had no idea why there was only one zoo asteroid open to the public, but it was a thriving business. They had to struggle to find a place to sit down, then order food through their implants. It was nearly twenty minutes before it finally arrived, floated over on an antigravity beam.

"That," Yolanda said, looking at Martin's plate, "is a lot of food."

"I'm under orders to eat as much as I can," Martin said, a little defensively. "You should see how much we can cram into our mouths in five minutes."

"I don't think I want to," Yolanda said. Martin had ordered a burger large enough to feed two or three people back on Earth, if it had been legal to serve it. She had a feeling that no fast food chain could have offered such food without paying vast bribes to the health and safety police. "Eat slowly, all right."

Martin lowered his eyes. "I will try," he said. "But...we were taught to eat quickly and often, because we never know when the next meal will arrive."

"Good advice," Yolanda said.

They ate their food slowly, savouring every bite. Yolanda checked her implants while she ate, skim-reading the news provided by the asteroid's datanet. The lead story at the moment – insofar as anything could be called the lead story – was a man who'd murdered his wife and daughter in a fit of rage, apparently at the daughter defying him over something. It looked as though he would get the death penalty, the writer noted, although the jury had yet to pass sentence. Even if he didn't, the rest of his life would probably be spent on Venus, helping to make the overheated world a suitable place for humans to live.

They don't accept excuses here, she thought. It was one of the many reasons she had no intention of going back to Earth. *If there is a crime, someone will not be allowed to escape justice because they have a flimsy excuse.*

"I believe," Martin said, "that it's rude to spend time using your implants when you're in company."

Yolanda coloured, then disconnected from the datanet. "I'm sorry," she said, embarrassed and ashamed. "I wasn't thinking."

"You can't let the implants do your thinking for you," Martin said. He winked at her, then nodded to the remains of her meal. "Besides, you'll be right back in the datastream when you get back to Sparta."

"True," Yolanda said. Half of her training was spent immersed in the datanet, simulating everything from routine flights from star to star to emergences that threatened the entire starship. The remainder was spent in the real world. "But we're not allowed to browse the news on Sparta."

"If there was something important going on, we would be told about it," Martin said. He met her eyes, then winked again. "How many people on Earth work themselves into a tizzy because they bury themselves in the lives of complete strangers?"

"That's very profound," Yolanda said.

Martin smirked. "One of my teachers always had the celeb-channel on in class," he said. "If something happened, she would force us to stop working – not that we did much work in any case – and watch the television. And it was always something boring like a new dress or a perfect baby boy. She even used to assign us essays on the importance of the right handbag for the right celeb."

Yolanda stared at him. "You're joking!"

"I wish," Martin said. "But I never actually did the essays, so I couldn't actually tell you about handbags."

His smile widened. "There *was* the day when some silly woman's dress fell off on live television," he added. "But I think it was faked."

"Probably," Yolanda muttered. "They fake too many things on television."

She scowled at a bitter memory. Her stepmother had been a great fan of movies shipped north from Mexico, which she'd watched while supervising Yolanda's chores. It had been hard to avoid noticing that most of them were romance movies, but the stories were almost always reminders of the Mexican-American War. The hero and heroine were always Mexican, the villain was American...there had been times when she'd thought the plots were completely identical, right down to the same words at the same times. But her stepmother had never troubled herself to notice.

Probably too dumb to notice, she thought, vindictively. *It must have sucked to know she would never be anything more than a housewife...*

"Do you have any plans for the evening?" Martin asked. "Or should we find somewhere to spend the rest of the day?"

"There's a swimming complex on the lower levels," Yolanda said. Once, she would never have dared to swim with a boy. Now, though, she thought it might be fun. "You can swim with dolphins...if you dare."

"I dare," Martin said. He smiled, brilliantly. "I always wanted to go surfing as a kid. Did you ever surf in California?"

Yolanda shook her head. By the time she'd been old enough to leave the house on her own, California's beaches had been largely ruined. Her father had blamed the politicians, or the grasping corporations, or the rich folks who bought entire beaches for themselves, but in the end it hardly mattered. A simple pleasure, enjoyed by millions of people, had been destroyed, wiped from existence.

"We can try later," Martin said. He stood, then helped her to her feet. "Thank you for meeting me."

"You're welcome," Yolanda said. They *had* agreed to spend their leave together, hadn't they? But their leaves didn't always coincide. "What did you do when you weren't with me?"

"Spent two days in Sin Asteroid with several of the other recruits," Martin confessed. "I don't think I'll be going back there."

Yolanda smiled. "They kicked you out on your ass?"

"Oh, no," Martin said. "It was just too tempting. I gambled, I drank, I experimented with various mood-altering substances and then I went into the VR suites for special programs. It was just a little disturbing. I could have done anything there, even if only in simulations. But it would have felt real."

"You would have thought it was actually happening," Yolanda said. She'd experimented with incorporating direct brain feeds into VR sims too. It had been weird; one program had allowed her to feel what it was like to be a man, another allowed her to experience life as an animal. "And then you would have started to wonder just what was actually real."

"There are people there who are addicts," Martin said. "They do crappy jobs all the time, just to earn the money they need to go back into the sims. I hated just looking at them, Yolanda, and knowing I could end up the same way."

"You won't," Yolanda said. She shuddered at the thought. One of the downsides of the Solar Union was that no one tried to stop people from becoming addicted to anything, if they were adults. She could see the arguments for and against any sort of interference, but surely something should be done. "You're a strong man."

"I'm sure they thought that too," Martin said. He looked down at his hands. "But I don't think I could resist temptation if I went back there again and again."

"So don't," Yolanda said. "Let's go for a swim instead."

"Great," Martin said. "What did *you* do when I wasn't on leave with you?"

"Visited sights," Yolanda said. "Do you know they have the original *Wanderer* on display at Luna City? Humanity's very first starship, admired by millions. And then there were the Apollo Landing Sites..."

Martin laughed, then followed her out of the door.

FIFTEEN

The German Nationalist Party claimed in a statement, issued yesterday, that the recent ban on the party's existence – on the grounds of historical descent from the Nazi Party – was nothing more than an attempt to silence opposition to the current status quo in Germany. It vowed to fight for German rights, whatever the price, pledging to remove the 'traitors' in the German Government. In response, the German President stated that attempts to revive the historical nightmare of Nazism would not be tolerated…

—Solar News Network, Year 52

"So we now have some data," President Ross said. The council chamber was deathly silent. "SPEAKER?"

"We have analysed the data provided by Director Stuart," the AI said. "It would appear to possess internal consistency. There are no grounds for believing it to be false information."

"I believe Ando was telling us the truth," Kevin said. He understood their concerns, but he'd done his best to ensure that everything was accurate. "We certainly paid enough for the information."

"Ando might have *thought* he was telling us the truth," Councillor Richard Bute commented, thoughtfully. "But he might have been lied to by his own sources."

President Ross tapped the table. "Let us assume, for the moment, that the information is accurate," he said. He looked directly at Kevin. "What does it tell us?"

Kevin stood and activated the holographic projector. "There are two stages to their plan," he said. "Stage One will see a small force deployed to Hades" – a star system started to blink in front of them – "and secure the system for their logistics. Stage Two will see the arrival of two hundred full-sized battleships, which will proceed to Earth once they have replenished their supplies. Once Earth is under their control, they will proceed against the other powers in the coalition."

"Interesting choice of tactics," Councillor Marie Jackson observed. "Why don't they go for one of the major coalition worlds?"

"I suspect they see us as the easiest target," Mongo said, dryly. "They have built a four thousand year old empire on a reputation for technological superiority and military invincibility. Hitting somewhere stronger than Earth might result in a defeat or an embarrassingly costly victory."

"Two hundred battleships are not a minor force," Bute pointed out. "They would be capable of tipping the balance wherever they went."

"They may want to secure the other industrial plants for themselves," Kevin said. The Tokomak would have some interest in claiming the industrial plants, if only to help meet the constant demand for products. "Or they may fear our long-term effects on the sector more than they're prepared to admit."

He took a breath. "That's what's coming our way, ladies and gentlemen," he added, warningly. "The enemy is at the door."

"If they come here," Bute said, "can we win?"

"Perhaps," Mongo said.

He spoke on before anyone else could say a word. "There are several unknowns in the fleet's deployment," he said. "The exact capabilities of the fleet are unknown. We believe the Tokomak probably kept quite a few goodies for themselves, but what? Are their missiles or directed energy weapons superior to standard Galactic tech? We don't know.

"But one fact is clear," he added. "If we sit around waiting to get hit, we're going to get steamrollered. We can hurt them – we will hurt them – but we can't stop them if they bring that fleet into the Sol System. Earth will be plastered with long-range fire, while the asteroid settlements will be utterly destroyed. We will lose the war."

"So we go on the offensive," Bute said. "Commit the Solar Navy to the Coalition. Knock the Varnar out of the war before the Tokomak can arrive."

"Which will only force them to intervene faster," Marie objected. "Or attack us while we're trying to hold Varnar and sort out the post-war mess."

"That's a problem," Mongo agreed.

"I've been speaking to a handful of tactical planning officers," he said. "We have a rough operational plan, but it will require some luck and careful judgement. It will also need to be adapted at short notice for the new situation."

"Caveats noted," Ross said. "What do you have in mind?"

"First, we need to take one of their ships intact," Mongo said. "We cannot expect them to leave their systems as unguarded as the Horde."

Kevin had to smile. The Horde had known next to nothing about how their starships actually operated. They'd left the computer system open to anyone smart enough to capture one of their neural links, allowing the humans they'd taken prisoner to seize control of the starship from right under their noses. But the Tokomak, designers and producers of most Galactic technology, wouldn't be so easily fooled. Their military might not have fought a real war for over a thousand years, but they presumably understood how their technology actually worked.

"This will require some careful planning, but I think we can do it," Mongo continued. "Second, we will need to attack their logistics on Hades and take or destroy them before they can use the base against us. And third…we have to meet and smash their fleet."

"A tall order," Ross observed.

"Yes, Mr. President," Mongo said. "And I don't think it will be easy to persuade the coalition to assist. They have their own qualms about Tokomak intervention."

"They'll be next on the list, once we've been crushed," Bute protested. "I knew we shouldn't trust them too openly."

"Technically, we're not part of the war," Mongo said, smoothly. "We only allowed the Coalition to raise human mercenaries."

"An argument the Varnar are hardly likely to accept," Kevin added. "And the Tokomak pretty much *make* the laws. They may choose to claim that the whole affair is merely a Tokomak-Human War, giving everyone else the excuse to stay out of the fighting, if they wish."

"Cowards," Bute growled.

"The Tokomak outgun everyone else by several orders of magnitude," Mongo said. "There's a difference between cowardice and practicality."

"Or so they claim," Kevin said. The data Ando had passed to them had raised a number of issues. For starters, just how many Tokomak starships were actually on active service? And how many of their crews were actually trained to fight a war, rather than ceremonial displays? There was no clear answer. "But we have to assume the worst."

"Then we will be committing ourselves to war," Ross said. "Is there any alternative?"

"We would have to offer our unconditional surrender," Kevin said. "At best, we might hope for a subordinate position in their empire. At worst...they'll order us back to Earth."

He shuddered at the thought. There were times when he looked back on Earth and silently thanked God that he no longer cared about the planet. He did have some relatives living in Montana, in the United States of America, but they had *chosen* to remain there. The thought of having to go back there himself, of having to *live* there, was horrific. And then there was the final, unspoken possibility.

"They might choose to exterminate us," he said, quietly. "It would be against their laws, but they *make* the laws."

"So you said," Ross said. "Would they break them here?"

Kevin looked from face to face, willing them to understand. "The vast majority of the Galactics don't have either the ability or the inclination to push the limits," he said. "We – humanity – *does*. I believe we have already improved on Galactic technology in a number of areas, with the promise of far more improvements to come. The Tokomak would see us as their worst nightmare, a race developing technology that will leave everything they built obsolete. Exterminating us would seem a reasonable alternative."

"But they can't exterminate us," Ross said. "We sent dozens of ships out beyond the edge of explored space."

"There's no guarantee that any of those ships will manage to set up a colony," Kevin said. "Or that the colony would be able to retain high technology. We think they can, we think they will, but we don't *know*. I believe we have to assume the worst."

"I wish I disagreed with you," Mongo grunted.

"So surrender isn't an option and nor is flight," Ross said. "Do we gird ourselves for war?"

"That would require an open discussion in the Senate," Bute reminded him. "There are limits to how far we can go without open public participation."

"That runs the risk of the Tokomak discovering that we know what they're doing," Mongo said, sharply. "The longer we keep the preparations under wraps, the better."

"I don't think they keep us under close surveillance," Bute sneered. He swung around to glare at Kevin. "Do they?"

"We believe neither they nor the Varnar have made a real attempt to embed sources in the Sol System," Kevin said. "They have tried to turn a few of our people, which we have been intending to use to send them false information when it seemed appropriate. However, they could have managed to get people through the security screens without being noticed."

"It seems absurd that anyone would be prepared to betray his own race," Bute mused.

"It has happened before and it no doubt will happen again," Kevin said. "Intelligence work, Councillor, is *always* smoke and mirrors. There is no way to be *sure* that there isn't any enemy intelligence agents operating within the Solar Union. We might well have missed something."

He paused, then went on. "But any discussion in the Senate would be reported over the news networks," he added. "It would not remain confined to the Sol System indefinitely. They might pick up on it simply by reading our open source news programs."

Bute smiled. "Do you think they read the crap we put out?"

"Why not?" Kevin asked. "We read theirs."

Ross tapped the table. "So what do you propose? We cannot mobilise the fleet to attack targets outside the Sol System without the Senate's permission."

Kevin and Mongo exchanged glances. "I propose we proceed with the plan to snatch one of their ships," Kevin said, finally. "In the meantime, we can start laying the groundwork for full mobilisation. We can take the issue and put it before the Senate nearer the time, when the Tokomak will be committed to their course. By then, we would be ready to launch a blow as soon as the Senate consented."

Ross frowned. "And if the Senate *didn't* consent?"

"Then we would have to pray we could stop the offensive when it reached the Sol System," Mongo said. "Frankly, Mr. President, with so many ships in the enemy fleet, even our plan to smash it well away from Earth has serious problems."

"It will be a gamble," Ross said.

"War is always a gamble," Mongo said. "But in this case, we have a choice between fighting and perhaps losing, or surrendering and *definitely* losing. The best we can hope for is being their slaves for the rest of time, our technology limited and further development forbidden. And at worst..."

"Yes, we *know*," Ross said.

He nodded to Kevin, who sat down.

"This is the situation this council was formed to meet," he said. "A deadly threat that would only become worse if left to fester, or brought into public view. Do we now authorise an attack on an alien ship? Or do we hold back and wait for them to commit themselves to the offensive? Do we have any other options?"

"We could show some of our weapons," Marie said, slowly. "Show off what we can do and claim we have far more in reserve, if they don't leave us alone."

"That would run the risk of convincing them to strike hard and fast," Mongo said. "They'd call our bluff."

"Why, if they thought they'd be destroyed?" Marie asked. "We'd give them a defeat no one would be able to ignore."

"They'd lose nothing by launching an attack," Mongo said, patiently. "At worst, the sudden shift in galactic power would be underlined; at best, they would smash us flat before we could build more wonder-weapons. And as we would be bluffing, Councillor, we'd be smashed. All we'd do is give them warning that they would be facing advanced weapons."

Ross sighed, loudly enough to catch their attention. "Do we authorise an attempt to snatch an alien ship?"

Kevin watched, keeping his face impassive, as the councillors voted. Steve would have hated it, he knew; a handful of men, all part of a council the population didn't know existed, had just cast a vote for war. The entire Solar Union would be committed, if the Tokomak realised what had happened to their starship, without ever knowing the decision had been made. It was an ironic inversion of the ideals his older brother had held...

...But those ideals were unworkable in the real world.

Kevin had never been as tightly bound to them as either Steve or Mongo. His rebellion against his own family had taken him into the CIA, where he'd learned that the world was rarely black and white, but covered in shades of gray. There were times when he'd had to hold his nose and work with people his brothers would have unhesitatingly called terrorists – and they might well have been right. And yet, working with those terrorists had seemed the only option at the time. Washington had never shown the willingness to actually stand up and put enough firepower on the ground to earn itself a vote in the post-war world.

And Washington would never have had the nerve to consider trying to meet a threat ahead of time, he thought. *Certainly not a threat on this sort of scale.*

"The vote has been taken," Ross said. "We will proceed with the operational plan."

And God help us, Kevin thought.

"I will brief you on the planned operation when it's ready," Mongo said, addressing the council as a whole. "But we will have to wait for the opportunity to snatch one of their starships."

"Their squadron en route to Hades might be a good place to start," Kevin said.

"Indeed," SPEAKER offered. "There will definitely be several chances to snatch an enemy ship."

"Good," Ross said. "We will meet again in a week, unless something happens that requires us to meet sooner."

Kevin frowned. There was no shortage of people monitoring the Solar Union's politicians, dissecting their lives and looking for signs they were unsuited to public office. It was one of the perils of running for office in the Solar Union; there were no privacy laws that applied to politicians. Given time, someone would notice that several Senators were gathered in the same asteroid, at the same time, along with the President and Mongo. Hell, it was quite possible someone was even tracking Kevin's movements outside secure intelligence facilities. And if they found something, what would they do? Keep it to themselves or spread the word?

"I understand you had a good time on Varnar," Mongo said, as they made their way down to the secure coffee room. "You actually did some work too, I hope, as well as playing James Bond?"

"There was enough unsecured data on the planetary datanet to confirm some of what we learned from our sources," Kevin said. It would have horrified Mongo – or Steve – to learn just how much information came from human information brokers, back in the pre-space days. "But you know how imprecise intelligence work can be."

"At least you're smart enough to admit it," Mongo grunted. They stepped into the coffee room and sat down at a small plastic table "What do you think Steve would make of this?"

Kevin hesitated. He doubted Steve would approve. Even if he accepted the logic, he was unlikely to be *happy* about it. And yet, there was no real choice.

"I think he would have accepted it," he said, not entirely truthfully. "But he wouldn't have wanted to keep it from people indefinitely."

Mongo jabbed a finger at him. "That's why you never quite fitted in with Steve and me," he said. "You could always hair-split an argument until the guilt and sin were cut into nothingness. Steve and I were always more willing to point the finger and proclaim sin and evil."

"You and Steve were Marines," Kevin countered. "You worked in platoons and companies and regiments, always able to rely on your fellows. I was an intelligence officer who was sometimes in more danger from my superiors in Washington than I was in the field, directly or indirectly. Learning how to split hairs was a survival skill."

Mongo grunted, then looked away.

"You should know the next class of recruits will be graduating in two weeks," he said, after a moment. "How many of those young men and women will be dead in five years?"

"I don't know," Kevin said, flatly. He stood and strode over to the coffee pot, then poured them both mugs of strong coffee. "But I do know that we don't have a choice."

"Steve would have understood *that*," Mongo said. "But he would have hated committing us to war without asking the people."

Kevin nodded. "There's no choice, though," he said. "If they knew we knew, they would take precautions against us acting first."

"So you say," Mongo said. "Or do you think the population would be opposed to war?"

"I wish I knew," Kevin said. "There's no way to know."

He shook his head. The Solar Union wasn't America – even the America he remembered from before the Hordesmen had arrived. Most of the population was politically involved, directly or indirectly. There was no shortage of information flowing through the system to keep them informed, too. But, if there was a popular vote, would they vote for war?

"But we don't dare ask," he concluded. "The slightest leak could destroy us all."

"Sure," Mongo growled. "And if we fuck up, we could destroy everything too."

SIXTEEN

Rioting broke out in Cairo following reports of water rationing programs to be instigated by the military government of Egypt. Water shortages, an ongoing problem caused by over-farming and poor governmental planning, have been growing worse in North Africa for years, despite plans to construct new water purification complexes and pipelines along the coastline. Sources within the government state that insurgent attacks within Egypt itself have only made the problem worse.

—Solar News Network, Year 52

"Graduation Day," the Commandant of Sparta said. "Today marks the day you become true citizens of the Solar Union."

Martin watched as the Commandant's gaze flickered over his audience. "Some of you come from Earth, others from Luna or Mars or one of countless asteroid settlements, but you all have one thing in common," the Commandant continued. "You all swore to defend the Solar Union – and the human race – against all enemies, foreign and domestic. It is that willingness to put your bodies between civilisation and its enemies that separates you from the common herd.

"From this day, many of you will go out to starships, or join military units preparing for a war we hope will never come. You will join millions of others who have sworn the same oath, undergone the same training and taken the same risks. And you will be honoured for your willingness to serve, to put the good of society ahead of your own personal good."

Maybe, Martin thought, *that's why there are so many temptations. The people who pull away from them are the ones with the strength the Solar Union needs.*

He kept his face impassive. The Sergeants had warned them, time and time again, that they were now *Marines*, the best of the best. They weren't allowed to show any emotions as they graduated, after passing the gruelling week-long final test. Instead, they had to appear blank and emotionless one final day, before they were sent to their first true units. Martin honestly couldn't wait.

"This is your day," the Commandant finished. "Enjoy it."

There was a smattering of applause, mainly from the watching audience, as the speech came to an end. Martin felt a sudden stab of envy – he had no family who would come to watch, but some of his squadmates had family watching their graduation – and then pushed it aside, sharply. His family were the Solar Marines now – and Yolanda. He'd looked for her among the starship crewmen, wearing their light-blue uniforms, as they marched into the auditorium, but he hadn't seen her. They'd exchanged enough messages, though, for him to be sure she was there.

Sergeant Grison cleared his throat. "Marines," he said. "You may advance."

Martin turned in unison with the others, as they'd rehearsed, and followed the Sergeant up to the dais. The Commandant smiled, greeted each man by name, and shook their hand firmly before pinning a single silver badge on their collars. It was the globe-and-starship insignia of the Solar Marines, glittering under the bright lights. Martin felt a wave of pride, almost as if he were walking on air, as he realised he'd made it. He was a *Marine* now, not a maggot. No matter what happened in the future, no one would ever take it from him.

I did this on my own, he thought. *No one insisted I had to qualify. I earned this!*

Sergeant Grison led them through a large hatch, then into a smaller compartment. "You are authorised and encouraged to take the remainder of the day off," he said. "Check your implants for your departure times tomorrow, then go spend some time with your friends and families. If you have neither here, go see who might have turned up from the Retired Jarheads Association. There are quite a few who are willing to play mentor to a newcomer to the Solar Union."

He smiled at them all, an open genuine smile. "For what it's worth, I am very proud of you all," he added. "Well done."

Martin watched him stride though the door, then joined in the cheering as the recruits realised – finally – that they'd made it. They were safe and sound, now; they didn't have to worry about being ejected from the camp for a single mistake. But then, they *now* had the risk of being shot at and killed for real...he shook his head, then checked his implants. He had orders to report onboard the SUS *Freedom*, the following morning. Until then, his time was his own.

He nodded to the remaining Marines – half of them had already headed off to meet their families – and then stepped through the door, heading down towards the lobby. Yolanda was waiting for him, looking oddly waif-like in her blue uniform, her dark hair tied back into a bun. She wore a silver star on her collar, marking her as a qualified starship officer. It would become a gold star if she ever rose to command rank.

"I'm off to *Freedom*," he said. "And you?"

"Snap," Yolanda said. "Did you ask for us to serve together?"

Martin shook his head. He honestly hadn't thought it was possible. The Solar Union sent its crewmen where it thought it needed them, without taking their personal needs into consideration. And why should it? They had signed their rights over to the Navy when they'd sworn the oath. Martin had expected to go years between meeting Yolanda, if one or both of them wasn't killed on active service.

"No worries," Yolanda said. She glanced around, wistfully. "Is it wrong of me to wish my father was here?"

"Not at all," Martin said. "He should be proud of everything you've achieved. *You* should be proud of everything you've achieved."

"Thank you," Yolanda said. She looked down at her pale fingers. "You'll make a good dad, one day."

"I hope so," Martin said. He was not going to leave his children, whatever happened. "And you're not alone. You have me and all of your crewmates."

Yolanda nodded, then allowed him to lead her up to the higher levels. Sparta was huge, easily the largest military installation in the Sol System. Just about everyone in the military, regardless of their service, spent time on Sparta. He touched the bronze star on his shoulder as they reached the teleport booth, then stepped inside. He'd earned that merely for passing the first phase of his training.

"Freedom, an *America*-class cruiser," Yolanda rattled, as they stepped into the observation dome. Countless stars glowed overhead, while starships hung in orbit around the asteroid, illuminated only by their running lights. "Two hundred metres long, designed for both defence and exploration. One of the newest ships in the fleet."

"They must think highly of us," Martin said. She had always been more interested in the minutia of starship design than himself. "How many Marines?"

"Forty," Yolanda said. "They must think highly of you too."

"I'm scared," Martin admitted. "I barely made it through Boot Camp."

"But you made it," Yolanda said. "I feel the same way too. Like I shouldn't be here. Like I'm a fraud. But they wouldn't have let me get through if they hadn't felt I could handle it."

She reached out, then wrapped an arm around him and held him as they looked up at the stars.

— —

YOLANDA HAD HALF-HOPED for a shuttle ride to *Freedom*. It would have allowed her to see the sword-like starship from the outside, before she allowed the ship's metal hull to swallow her up. Instead, *Freedom* had docked at Sparta and her new crewmembers – Yolanda, Martin and a dozen others – had been ordered to pass through the airlocks and board the starship without ever seeing her external hull. She bit down her disappointment and smothered it under her excitement at finally serving on a real starship. There was no way she would ever go back to Earth now.

Her implants flashed up an alert as the starship's datanet scanned her ID chips, confirming her identity, before the airlock hissed open. There was a rush of cool air, smelling faintly of...*something*...vaguely unpleasant, then they stepped inside. A tall bald woman wearing a blue uniform was standing there, waiting for them. Yolanda's implants identified her as Commander Gregory, the XO.

"Welcome onboard," the XO said, once they had saluted the flag beside the airlock. "I am Commander Saundra Gregory, executive officer of this ship. You will be dispersed to your own departments momentarily, but before then I want a few words with you. *Freedom* is the best ship in the fleet and we intend to keep it that way. If you have a problem with that, I advise you to get rid of it."

She paused, then marched on. "We have been assigned to a deep space mission, departing in one week," she continued. "If any of you don't fit in by then, you will be put off before we leave. That will probably mean the end of your career, so I suggest you work hard. I know adapting to shipboard life isn't easy, but we don't have time for whiners.

"Private Douglas, you have been assigned to Marine Country. Your implants will show you the way; report to Major Lockland when you arrive. Everyone else, with me."

Yolanda felt a pang as Martin saluted, then walked off down the long corridor, while the XO led the other new officers in the opposite direction. Her implants updated automatically, showing her the interior design of *Freedom*. It was relatively simple, she realised, although it would be a pain to navigate without implants. The bulkheads were completely unmarked, save for a handful of numbers that didn't seem to link together. It took her several moments to realise that they were production numbers, rather than anything she could use to find her way around the ship.

"These are your cabins," the XO informed them. "You will be sleeping two to a cabin, so pair off now. I don't give a damn about your sleeping arrangements, as long as they don't interfere with your duties. You are supposed to be grown adults, so pick someone you can be comfortable with and open the hatches."

There was a brief moment of confusion, then Yolanda nodded to Simone, who nodded back and pushed her hand against one of the hatches. It hissed open, revealing a tiny compartment with a pair of small beds, a small washroom and a pair of drawers under the beds. There was barely enough room for two people sleeping, let alone standing up. Yolanda thought wistfully of the barracks, then unslung her knapsack from her shoulder and placed it on the bed. She could unpack it later, once they had been briefed on their duties and the ship's rota.

"Good," the XO said, when they were done. "If you want to swap roommates later, that's your problem, not mine. If I have to get involved, I will be very annoyed."

She turned and led them up the corridor, through a pair of solid airlocks and past a Marine wearing light combat armour. The Marine showed no reaction as the XO opened the hatch behind him, or when Yolanda nodded to him in passing. It had always astonished her just how still Martin could stand, after several weeks of training; now, she thought she understood why.

Inside, the bridge awaited them. Yolanda stopped and stared, trying to drink in every detail of the glowing compartment. Three officers sat at three consoles, linked through their implants into the starship's command systems, while a fourth sat in the command chair, watching a giant holographic display that showed the entire solar system. She looked left and saw two more officers, one standing in front of a console and poking at it, the other standing behind him and offering helpful advice. The entire compartment, the nerve centre of the starship, seemed to glow with activity.

"Captain Singh," the XO said. "These are our new officers."

The command chair rotated until Captain Singh came into view. He was a tall, brown-skinned man with a neatly-trimmed beard, wearing the white uniform of a starship commander. A single medal hung above his right breast, signifying active combat service; below it, a line of gold braid informed her that he had served on four different starships before taking command of *Freedom*. He was an impressive man, she had to admit, as he stood and studied them. Had he been born in space or was he, like her, a refugee from Earth?

"Welcome onboard," Captain Singh said.

"Thank you, Captain," the XO said. "I should have them ready for active duty within two days, assuming their training files are accurate."

You'll have to prove yourself, Yolanda thought, remembering the advice she'd been given by one of her training officers. The older woman had sat down with the cadets and explained to them that merely passing the course wouldn't be enough. *Once you prove yourself, you can expect more responsibility and a chance at promotion. But no one will take you on faith.*

She kept her expression blank as the newcomers were marched off the bridge and down into the secondary control centre. "This compartment is a near-complete duplicate of the bridge," the XO said. "From now on, until I say otherwise, those of you qualified for bridge duty will be working here, practising, practising and practising. You will run through every disaster scenario in the book and a few we made up specially. Should you pass those tests, you will be permitted to serve on the bridge during our deployment."

There was a pause. "Any questions? None? Then get started."

Yolanda nodded, then sat down in front of the helm console. Moments later, it came to life and displayed the first part of a simulation, one she knew from training. But there was no point in trying to argue. Instead, she just started to work her way through it, piece by piece.

— —

MARINE COUNTRY WAS isolated from the remainder of the starship, according to the plans Martin had accessed through his implant. There was only one door, guarded by a pair of Marines, who checked his ID twice before allowing him through the hatch and into the compartment. Inside, it was dark, so dark even his enhanced eyesight couldn't see anything in the shadows. He had to bring up his implants to see anything...

Light flared. His implants automatically dimmed his vision. Moments later, he couldn't see anything at all.

"Welcome to Marine Country," a voice boomed. "Are you worthy?"

"I like to think so," Martin tossed back. Sergeant Grison had warned him about hazing rituals, tests designed to ensure the Fucking New Guy – the FNG – was up to the job. Just graduating from Boot Camp wasn't enough. "I'm tough, thick-headed and bloody-minded."

"You sound a bit overqualified," the voice said, dryly. "Take five steps forward, *Boot*!"

Martin stepped forward and felt something pressing against his eyes. Gritting his teeth, he took another step forward, then another. There was a moment when he was sure he was about to impale himself on something, then the pressure melted away into nothingness. But there was still nothing to see, but darkness.

"Lights," the voice said.

This time, the lights were dim enough to allow Martin to see without pain. Ahead of him, a grim-faced man wore urban combat BDUs and a Captain's insignia on his shoulder. Martin frowned, then remembered the custom of granting every Captain on the ship, apart from the *real* Captain, a courtesy promotion.

"Major Lockland?"

"Private Douglas, I assume," Lockland said. "You'll be slotted into 3rd Platoon unless there are major problems – and I don't expect there to be any, understand?"

"Yes, sir," Martin said.

"You'll be bedding down with them when you're not in simulators or chasing your tail around the exercise compartment," Lockland continued.

"I expect you to be pulling your weight within the week, Private, or I will have no hesitation in beaching you until we return to Sol. Lieutenant Robbins will keep your nose to the grindstone until you prove yourself, so work hard and keep clean."

"Yes, sir," Martin said. He'd expected nothing less. "I will do my very best."

"Make sure you do – and that it's good enough," Lockland growled. "There's trouble coming, Private. No one has said anything officially, but I've heard rumours, whispers of trouble. We have to be ready for when the shit hits the fan."

"Yes, sir," Martin said. He wanted to ask what Lockland had heard, but he knew he wouldn't get a straight answer until he'd proved himself. There was no shortage of potential issues, from interventions on Earth to outright war with one or more of the Galactics. "We will be ready."

"Indeed we will," Lockland said. He nodded towards the hatch. "Go put your bag down, then join 3rd Platoon for their ongoing drills. I'll speak to you again in a week, I hope; if I have to talk to you before then, you're in deep shit."

"Yes, sir," Martin said.

He thought briefly of Yolanda, wondered if he would have a chance to see her after 3rd Platoon had accepted him, then pushed the thought aside. The Sergeants had hidden nothing from the recruits, once they'd passed the final tests. Established units only opened their hearts and minds to a newcomer after he'd proved himself. And if he failed, he could expect nothing, but a quick ride back to Sparta and an equally quick discharge.

A shape appeared behind him as he placed his bag on the bunk. "Private Douglas?"

Martin turned, then saluted the stern-looking woman wearing a Lieutenant's uniform. "Sir?"

"I am Lieutenant Robbins, CO 3rd Platoon," she said, briskly. There was no give in her voice at all, no sense she might have a feminine bone in her body. Like Kayla, she had passed the same tests as the men, then won her spurs in an active unit. "Come with me. We have a *lot* of work to do."

SEVENTEEN

The Pakistani Government fell for the fifth time in as many months today, as armed mobs stormed the walls of the Presidential Palace in Islamabad. So far, successive military and Islamic governments have proved completely incapable of halting either the ongoing economic decline or the outflow of skilled technical workers, looking for better jobs elsewhere. At last report, several thousand were dead in the streets, with thousands more injured. This does not bode well for Pakistan.

—Solar News Network, Year 53

Viceroy Neola – the remainder of her names were never shared outside her clan – was young for a Tokomak, a mere six hundred years old. It was something that galled her more than she would ever have admitted, even to her life-mates or children. She could neither enjoy the authority that came from having been born before the foundation of the Tokomak Empire nor the freedom of a child. And yet, she was as committed to the empire as the rest of her kind, despite its flaws. It had brought peace and stability to a galaxy tormented by war.

She watched through cold eyes as the Varnar leadership bowed their heads before her, welcoming her to their world. They were a surprisingly advanced people for their position in the galaxy, already halfway towards mimicking the Tokomak government before they'd encountered the empire and been assimilated. They'd made useful proxies because they could be relied upon to do the job, without complaining about their position in the empire. But now they had run into something they couldn't handle...and they'd requested help.

It had been a surprise – and it had taken nearly thirty standard years for the Tokomak to even *consider* the request. The whole idea of the proxy wars had been to keep the races on the rim of civilisation – barely civilised themselves – occupied, wasting time and resources in a petty pointless war. It had gone on for nearly a hundred years, after all, and had seemed likely to carry on for the next thousand, if the races didn't exhaust themselves long before then. But now, it looked almost as if the Varnar would lose the war. They'd run into a new race, one that was causing them problems. And *that* was tipping the balance against them.

She allowed herself a cold smile as she walked past a line of cyborg soldiers, constructed from biological samples taken from several different primitive worlds, and halted in front of the Varnar leaders. They were short, when she was tall; their eyes flickering nervously over her badges of rank. She could do anything to them and she knew it; the Tokomak, when they'd taken the sector, had not been shy about granting themselves unlimited authority. And yet, she had to work with them. The ossified geriatrics who made up the Inner Council of Tokomak could never have handled the thought of doing more than issuing orders to non-Tokomak. They even had problems with non-Tokomak servants!

"I am honoured to set foot upon your world," she said. The Varnar needed the sector to know the Tokomak were behind them – and besides, it *was* a honour. She didn't have the unlimited authority to make war she wanted, but she did have unprecedented freedom in other areas. "I thank you for the welcome."

The Varnar leader bowed low. "I thank you, Great One," he said. "Your presence brings honour to us all..."

He went on, and on, while Neola tuned him out and surveyed the crowd through her implants. They were mostly Varnar, but there were hundreds of non-Varnar there, each one representing a different race. Some of them were spacefarers themselves, treated with a certain degree of leniency by the empire; others were primitives, uplifted into galactic society and gifted advanced technology they couldn't hope to duplicate for themselves. Her lips curved into a sneer, which she forced off her face before anyone could take notice. Primitives. What could they do when they came face to face with the towering interstellar civilisation, but bend the knee in awe. They would never be anything more than servants for their elders and betters.

"And so we welcome you to our world," the Varnar concluded. "We thank you."

"Thank you for your welcome," Neola said. At least it hadn't been as long as some of the speeches she'd been forced to endure as a young politician. But the Varnar had definitely mastered the art of saying the same thing, over and over again, in a dozen different ways. "I now wish to see the war room. The rest of the matters can wait."

The Varnar looked shocked. They'd expected her to inspect everything from hospitals and spaceports, leaving the war room until last. But Neola was young enough to be impatient – and besides, she wasn't particularly interested in local facilities. If the Varnar wanted spaceports or hospitals, they could build them for themselves. The empire wasn't interested in their local affairs. She smiled to herself as the Varnar recovered, then led her into a secure passageway – her bodyguards inspected it minutely before they allowed her to enter – and down towards the war room. Her implants reported hundreds of security scans before they passed through the last set of hatches and stepped into the chamber.

"Now," Neola said, once the bowing and scraping had died away. "Tell me about the war."

— —

SALLY HAD BEEN lucky to get tickets for the reception ceremony. The Varnar had wanted to showcase their connections with the Tokomak, but even so she'd had to pay well over the odds just to obtain a pair of tickets. No one had even *seen* a Tokomak for centuries, certainly not one who would be taking command of the war. Indeed, the bookies – it had amused her to discover that the Galactics like gambling – had already started revising the odds of a Varnar victory in light of the Tokomak involvement.

But it wouldn't be a Varnar victory, Sally thought, as the shuttle slowly descended to the landing pad. *The Tokomak would have won the day.*

She gritted her teeth as the Viceroy came into view. The Tokomak were a tall, inhumanly thin race, with light yellow skin and large eyes. She – Sally's implants identified the alien as female – was surrounded by alien attendants, each one brain-burned to be totally loyal to its mistress. Beside her, the Varnar looked small, almost child-like. They bowed and scraped in front of the Tokomak as if a single word from her could destroy them, which it probably could. The battle squadron that had escorted the Tokomak Viceroy to Varnar would have no trouble reducing the planet to rubble, on her command. It was quite possible the local defences would refuse to fire on their ships until it was already too late.

If it's possible at all, Sally thought. *The Tokomak could easily have hidden backdoors in the planetary defence systems they sold the Varnar.*

She smiled at the thought, then sighed as the Viceroy was flattered endlessly by the Varnar leadership. No human really understood how the Varnar governed themselves – it was a form of communist democracy, she'd been told – but it was clear they were doing all, but kissing and licking the Tokomak's feet. And perhaps they would, if they thought it was necessary. They knew they were losing the war.

The ceremony finally came to an end, allowing the crowds to leave the giant stadium and retreat back to their normal lives. No one would have been permitted to leave ahead of time, Sally knew, no matter how long the ceremony took. The Tokomak might have seen it as an insult. They were, according to the files, a deeply formal race, with a love of ceremony that left even the most hidebound human government in the dirt. The idea of even a minor race shunning them would have seemed inconceivable.

She saved her recordings in her implant, then started to walk back towards the office. As always, the alien crowds both fascinated and oppressed her, pressing in around her as she walked. The Galactics didn't really have any concept of personal space, at least in the multiracial areas. In their own private sections, the rules tended to be different, more focused around the needs of one species. Unless, of course, the Tokomak were involved. They tended to disregard the rights of every other species when the shit hit the fan. Or just when they wanted to make a point.

"Sally," Mr. Ando said, when she walked into the darkened office. "You have a visitor."

Sally blinked. She wasn't very sociable on Varnar, if only because there were few people interested in socialising with a human. The handful of humans living permanently on the planet had little to do with her. They found it odd that a human would work for an alien – or so they said. Privately, Sally suspected they doubted her loyalties. Most of them were probably spies involved with the war.

"I do?"

"Yes," Mr. Ando said. He passed her a datachip. "He is currently staying in the Pan-Gal Hotel. You will take this to him personally, then take the rest of the day off, if you wish. Report back to me tomorrow morning."

Sally remembered, suddenly, the odd group who had visited, nearly a year ago. Mr. Ando *never* gave samples of data for free, not now he had a proper reputation. For him to break his rules, even on a small scale...it suggested there was something important about it, something he had yet to share with her. But there was no point in asking questions. She'd be told what Mr. Ando wanted her to know, when he wanted her to know. Instead, she took the datachip and nodded to him. The alien nodded back, then retreated into the shadows.

Kevin, she thought, recalling the older man she'd met. *It has to be.*

She placed the datachip in a sealed pocket, then walked through the streets to the Pan-Gal, recalling their last meeting. He'd been staying on a starship then; this time, he'd splashed out for the Pan-Gal. An offer to her, she wondered, or merely a case of picking a place he knew on Varnar? There was no shortage of places rated suitable for human or humanoid accommodation, but it could take hours to sort through the datanet and pick somewhere that was actually *decent*. Sally had stayed in enough apartments, before finding her current home, to know that 'humanoid accommodation' covered a multitude of different requirements.

The robotic valet checked her ID, then proffered a file for her to download, showing her how to walk through the giant hotel to her destination. Sally thanked the robot – a habit she had never been entirely able to break – then followed orders and walked up to the elevator. The Pan-Gal was larger than any hotel on Earth, although it only held six thousand suites and used the remainder of the space for life support and staffing requirements. Holograms flickered around her, showing what the hotel managers thought were views suitable for humans. There was no way they could hope to meet *all* of the requirements without using holograms, she knew, but it still seemed fake to her.

The Galactics clearly like it, she thought. The Pan-Gal didn't have any problems attracting visitors, year after year. *They must feel right at home.*

Sally stopped in front of a sealed hatch and tapped the bell. It opened a second later, revealing a surprisingly large suite, bigger than her apartment on Varnar. She stepped inside and smiled as she saw Kevin sitting on a chair clearly designed for someone a little larger than the average human, reading a datapad. He rose to his feet, took her hand and bowed to her, then kissed the air just above her skin. Sally honestly wasn't sure if she should be charmed or amused. There were races that actually communicated by licking each other's hands.

"It's good to see you again," Kevin said. "And I hope I can treat you to dinner this time."

"Mr. Ando sent me with gifts," Sally said. She passed him the datachip and watched as he made it vanish into a sealed pocket. "And orders to take the rest of the day off, if I wanted."

She tilted her head. "Did you ask him for me?"

"I asked him to send the data as soon as possible by courier," Kevin said. "But I'm glad it was you."

Sally nodded, then sat down on the chair facing him. "I think they gave you the wrong suite."

"The chair? I think they may have an exaggerated idea of the human bum," Kevin countered, dryly. "Or perhaps they just picked up some bad TV and thought all humans were that large and obnoxious."

"How right they were," Sally mused. Years ago, there had been a rumour that the Galactics had monitored Earth closely enough to pick up and record the early broadcasts of some of the most famous TV programs in history. It had been false, but before it had been disproven anticipation had risen to horrifying levels. "When did you arrive?"

"Yesterday," Kevin said. "I would have contacted you earlier, but..."

"The Tokomak distracted everyone," Sally said. "They're likely to take control of the planet, aren't they?"

"Probably," Kevin said, absently. "I don't know what they're thinking right now, beyond concerns about the war."

Sally sighed. It had disappointed her to discover that the Galactics were just as warlike as humans – and that some of them had been fighting a proxy war for longer than any human had been alive. The whole war struck her as essentially pointless; neither side could score a knock-out blow, so the war would drag on indefinitely. Surely, after several *hundred* years of fighting, the Galactics would realise the fighting wasn't getting them anywhere and come to terms? But humans had fought wars over generations too...

"They might want to end it completely," she said. "Do you think they intend to shatter the coalition?"

"It's very much a possibility," Kevin said. "Does Mr. Ando know anything more about their plans?"

"I couldn't tell you, if he did," Sally said. She liked Kevin – he was nicer than some of the other visitors she'd taken out for dinner – but she'd signed an agreement with the information broker. "You'd have to pay for it."

Kevin winked. "I could buy you dinner?"

"Try buying Mr. Ando dinner," Sally countered. The thought was enough to make her stomach heave. "But you'd find him an uncomfortable dining partner. He eats his food live."

"I've seen worse," Kevin said.

"Really?" Sally asked. "How many alien worlds have you visited?"

Kevin made a show of counting on his fingers. "Thirty-seven," he said, finally. "Several more than once, so if we counted each visit separately I'd have..."

"Thirty-seven," Sally cut him off. "And did you explore the entire planet, each time?"

"Of course not," Kevin said. "But I did make time to visit more than just the tourist traps."

He paused in contemplation. "About the weirdest thing I saw was a race that was made entirely out of rock," he added, after a moment. "They moved so slowly it was hard to see them as anything other than oddly-shaped statues. I could ask one of them a question, then return in a few days to hear the answer."

"I remember them," Sally said. "Well, I've heard about them."

She coloured. Mr. Ando had taught her much, seemingly for his own enjoyment. The rock-creatures kept mainly to their homeworld, if only because they were at a considerable disadvantage in dealing with the quicker races. But they were smarter than they looked – and dangerous too. There were strange tales about what happened to people who managed to annoy one of the largely-emotionless creatures. Maybe it was just a coincidence, but there was no large colony of off-worlders on their homeworld.

"Not the weirdest thing I've heard about," Kevin said. "You must have some fantastic stories to tell."

"Maybe I'll write an autobiography one day," Sally said. She leaned forward, then hesitated. There had been no time for emotional involvement before, not when the few men – and women – she met had left the following day, sometimes without saying goodbye. Kevin was the only one who'd come back. "How long are you going to be staying?"

"Maybe a week," Kevin said. "My ship's captain is currently trying to sell some Maple Syrup to the Galactics."

Sally had to laugh. Maple Syrup was an old joke, a term for something that had only a handful of potential buyers. There *were* Galactics who enjoyed foodstuffs from Earth...but there were thousands more who were utterly indifferent to human foods, or could simply program their replicators to duplicate anything they might have wanted to eat. Kevin's captain might have bought a white elephant, something he couldn't sell and yet couldn't simply abandon. It was never easy to *know* what would sell.

"If it was real, I'd think about buying some," she said. "Or is it something particularly unlike food?"

"Mainly pieces of art," Kevin said. "I doubt they'll sell."

NOT ENTIRELY TO Kevin's surprise, one thing led to another and so it was nearly midnight by the time he was able to sit up and inspect the chip. When he did, he almost swore out loud. The Tokomak were moving faster than anyone had expected, certainly faster than past experience had led him to suspect. They would be sending the squadron to Hades within the week, then start scouting nearby star systems. There wouldn't be much time to work.

He looked down at Sally's sleeping form, then cursed under his breath. If only he dared interrogate her openly! But he didn't; she was smart, perceptive and working for an alien with uncertain loyalties. Shaking his head, he reached for a terminal and started to type out a message for the ship's crew. It was time to start planning their departure.

And if they were lucky, he told himself, they could reach their destination before the Tokomak squadron had left Varnar for good.

EIGHTEEN

Panic is sweeping through China following an 'accident' at a nuclear power plant that released streams of radiation into a river. Local government officials were quick to deny that anything was actually wrong, but datanet reports and rumours spread rapidly, aided by the fact that no one believed a word the government said. Troops are reportedly being rushed to the area to prevent refugees from spreading panic further...

—Solar News Network, Year 53

If there were two things Yolanda had discovered about Captain Singh, they were that he was both a good and demanding commander. He knew how to command a starship – he'd served in the Solar Navy for over thirty years – and, at the same time, he understood the limits of his people. Yolanda had been worried about the Captain showing favouritism or other forms of discrimination, but instead he seemed to judge his crew purely on merit. It hadn't saved her from more than a few chewing outs, when she'd screwed up, yet they had all been deserved.

And I learned from the experience, she thought, as she studied the sensor display. The Captain and the XO had moved the new officers around from department to department, making sure they had a good grasp of *all* the stations. Sensors weren't as exciting as either the helm or the tactical systems, but they were important. *I never made the same mistakes twice.*

She frowned as an icon blinked into life on the display. *Freedom* was patrolling an uninhabited system thirty-seven light years from Earth, a system that was almost completely worthless without a great deal of expensive terraforming. There was no reason to expect anyone to join them out here, so far from any inhabited world, and yet the sensors were picking up a starship approaching at FTL speeds. It was possible, she told herself, that the crew were just taking a shortcut, but their course would take them right towards the system.

"Captain," she said. "I have an unknown contact approaching the system at FTL speeds. They will enter the system in thirty minutes."

Captain Singh stood and walked over to her console. "Show me," he ordered. "Can you identify the ship?"

"No, sir," Yolanda said. "The drive signature is too common to isolate the exact make and model of starship."

"Unsurprising," the Captain mused. He turned his head to face the tactical console. "Sound yellow alert, Commander, and take us into cloak. I don't want to be detected out here."

"Aye, sir," Commander Gregory said. There was a pause, then a drumbeat echoed through the ship. "Cloaking device engaged."

"Good," the Captain said. He strode back to his command chair and sat down. "Ensign, continue to monitor the signature and inform me if anything changes."

Yolanda nodded, thinking hard. The Captain hadn't seemed surprised by the sudden appearance of the unknown starship, which meant…*what*? Coming to think of it, why was *Freedom* so far from Earth? Her shakedown cruise could have taken place in the solar system, where help was available if something went badly wrong. Could it be, she asked herself, that the Captain had *known* they were likely to encounter an unknown starship? Was it a planned rendezvous?

She pushed the thought aside as the unknown ship swept closer. There was no way she dared ask, even if she thought she'd get a reply. The

Captain would reprimand her for asking the wrong questions, while the XO would assign her to life support or waste disposal duties. Instead, she watched her console and waited to see what would happen. Thirty minutes later, the unknown starship dropped out of FTL and coasted forward.

"A small freighter," she reported. "A standard Class-XXI design, but there are glitches with her power curves that suggest she's been modified heavily."

"So she has," the Captain said. "Transmit a standard greeting."

Yolanda blinked. "Sir?"

"Transmit a standard greeting," the Captain repeated, patiently. "I've been expecting them."

"Aye, sir," Yolanda said. Sending the message would ensure they were detected, but if the Captain was expecting guests, it didn't matter. "Signal sent."

There was a long pause. "They're replying, sir," Yolanda said. "The message is for your eyes only."

"Noted," the Captain said. "Drop the cloak, then prepare to take on guests. XO, you have the bridge."

"Aye, Captain," Commander Gregory said. "I have the bridge."

— —

KEVIN COULDN'T HELP being impressed by *Freedom*, even if she was tiny compared to some of the giant battleships he'd seen in orbit around Varnar. She was long and graceful, like a hunting eagle, bristling with weapons and advanced sensors. If Mongo – and Keith Glass – were correct, she could even take on a Galactic starship several times her size and win. But there was no way to be sure. The Solar Navy had been careful to avoid unnecessary engagements with the Galactics.

Can't let them see everything we have too soon, he thought. *They have enough starships to trade a thousand for one and still win.*

"Remain here," he ordered Captain Vanern. "I'll signal once we know what we're doing."

He sent a teleport beacon to *Freedom* before Jean could object. Moments later, he closed his eyes as he felt the teleport field shimmering into existence around him, a faintly unpleasant tingle that intensified to an almost unbearable degree, then faded away into nothingness. He opened his eyes and saw *Freedom's* teleport chamber. Compared to the old freighter, it looked incredibly advanced.

But we put a lot of effort into making our ships look good, he thought, as Captain Singh stepped forward. *We want to impress people with our sophistication.*

"Welcome onboard," Captain Singh said. "I understand that you have codes for me?"

Kevin nodded, then activated his implant and transmitted a stream of ID codes to the Captain, who checked them against his sealed orders. Captain Singh had been given strict orders to open one set of orders as soon as he reached his designated patrol area, then to hold the other set until he received the correct authorisation from Kevin. It was a cumbersome system, one Kevin had feared would break down when put into practice, but it had worked.

Barely, he thought. The data Mr. Ando had provided was worrying. They might have less time than he'd feared. *Something could still go wrong.*

"You can open your second set of orders now, Captain," he said. "And then I have data for you."

The Captain led him through a maze of corridors and into a large cabin, guarded by a single armed Marine. Kevin wondered, darkly, if the Captain feared assassination or if having the Marine there was merely meant to underline his importance, then sat down and waited as the Captain opened his safe and retrieved the second set of orders. It was good to see the Captain hadn't tried to open them ahead of time, even though Kevin knew Captain Singh was regarded as a trustworthy officer. In the Captain's place, *Kevin* would have been sorely tempted.

But then, you always liked knowing things, he told himself. *And sometimes that blew up in your face.*

"My God," Captain Singh said. "Is this serious?"

"Yes," Kevin said, flatly.

The Captain turned to face him, clearly shocked. Kevin didn't really blame him. Covert operations didn't sit well with most officers, at least the ones outside the Special Operations community. Being told to carry out such a mission had to gall him. And then there was the simple fact that the Solar Union was about to do something that might well start a war with the single most powerful race known to exist.

"You want me to capture a Tokomak ship?"

"Yes, Captain," Kevin said. "Or destroy it, if it proves impossible to capture."

"And to destroy my own ship if we are threatened with capture," Captain Singh continued. "Are you – they – out of their minds?"

"The orders are genuine," Kevin said. The Captain would have checked, of course; the orders contained the e-signatures of the President, Mongo and Keith Glass. "And yes, there is no choice. We need to know how powerful they are before they hurl a thousand ships at Earth."

He sighed. "Your orders won't have gone into detail, Captain," he added, "but we're on the brink of war."

Captain Singh listened as he outlined the situation. "I see," he said, when Kevin had finished and looked at him expectantly. "I will, of course, carry out my orders."

"Good," Kevin said.

"But I want to know *precisely* how you think I can capture a Tokomak ship," Captain Singh added. "I would prefer not to charge into the teeth of an entire battle squadron."

"I wouldn't expect you to," Kevin said. He opened his implants, then transmitted the data he'd obtained from Mr. Ando into the Captain's secure datacore. "The Tokomak will be moving their battle squadron to Hades, then inspecting the nearby star systems for signs of trouble. You will have ample opportunity to ambush one of their ships in those systems and then taking it in tow. If, of course, an entire battlefleet should happen to arrive instead, you are perfectly free to abandon the operation."

"I'm glad to hear it," the Captain muttered. "You do realise this could start the war at once?"

"The war has already begun," Kevin said. "Captain, the Tokomak have *noticed* us. If they had half the vigour of the human race, their battleships would already be bombarding Earth into submission. We don't have time to wait for them to swing a fist at Earth, not when they outgun us so badly. The only hope is to lure them into making mistakes, mistakes that will open opportunities for us to deliver a crushing blow. *There is no choice*!"

"I understand that," Captain Singh said. He started to pace his cabin, then stopped. "What do you and your ship intend to do?"

"Watch from a safe distance," Kevin said, frankly. "I would not expect to hold tactical command on the bridge of your ship."

"Good," Captain Singh said. He smiled, suddenly. "What would you do if we lost?"

"Remain under cloak until the Tokomak piss off, then slip back to Earth," Kevin said, bluntly. "I won't mince words, Captain. You cannot allow *Freedom* to fall into their hands."

"I know," the Captain said.

He cocked his head, sending a command to the room's processor. A holographic star chart appeared in front of them, showing the star systems surrounding Hades. Five of them were marked as inhabited, possessing inconvenient witnesses; the remainder were uninhabited, almost certainly deemed unimportant. The Tokomak would scan them though, Kevin was sure. They simply weren't imaginative enough to ignore rules created when they'd been a thrusting innovative race, bent on making their mark on the galaxy.

Their ancestors would be turning in their graves, if they were in their graves, Kevin thought wryly. *An empire that makes Alexander the Great look like a piker, rule over hundreds of other races, trillions of intelligent beings bending the knee...but look at what they've become!*

It was a sobering thought. There were Tokomak alive who could remember the days before their empire. But near-immortality had only ossified their thought patterns, leaving them unable to react, quickly and decisively, to any new threat. A war against a race on the same scale, if such a race existed, would be fatal. They simply didn't have the ability to recognise a shift in the balance of power.

Took them long enough to notice us, Kevin thought. *But is this what we will become, in time?*

He'd wondered – and worried – about it, time and time again. If the older humans remained alive well past the biblical three score years and ten, what would it do to human society? The Solar Union, at least, had strict term limits for politicians...but *only* for politicians. Would corporations ossify if their founders never died, never passed their powers to successors...or would the children of corporate magnates *remain* children, never able to inherit power or wealth from parents who remained firmly alive. Would the Stuart Family always be dominated by Steve, Mongo and Kevin? It was a daunting thought.

The Captain cleared his throat. Embarrassed, Kevin looked at him.

"We'll set up an ambush here," the Captain said, tapping a red dwarf star. "There shouldn't be any witnesses, I believe."

"Agreed," Kevin said. "But remember, you cannot let the ship escape."

"I believe it might have been mentioned," the Captain said, blandly. "How much do they know about us?"

"Unknown," Kevin said. "The SIA has been trying to deduce how much they know, Captain, but it is an impossible task. I don't think they saw us as a priority until recently, however, and our counter-intelligence is pretty good."

"We're tiny on their scale," the Captain agreed. "But if they see us as a threat now..."

Kevin shrugged. "Building up intelligence networks takes time, Captain," he said, as reassuringly as he could. He'd been surprised by how little interest the *Varnar* took in humanity, even though it had been the Varnar who had first seen humans as potentially useful. The Tokomak probably thought of Earth as little more than a primitive microstate somewhere in the middle of a vast ocean. "They would need years to get a reliable source of information on our affairs."

He shrugged, again. "That may be why they're sending so many ships to deal with us," he added. "They don't know the scale of threat we pose, so they're sending a fleet that should be capable of dealing with anything."

"I hope you're wrong," Captain Singh said.

He looked back at the star chart. "It will take us nine days at best possible speed to reach our destination," he added. "I trust that will prove suitable?"

"It will have to suffice," Kevin said. "There's no way we can change the laws of interstellar travel to suit ourselves."

"No," the Captain agreed. "Can your ship match our speed?"

"I doubt it," Kevin said. "We'll probably catch up with you before the Tokomak arrive."

Captain Singh smiled. "And if you're wrong?"

"You get to tell us all about it, afterwards," Kevin said. It could be inconvenient – or disastrous – not to have a watching ship in the same star system, but there was no way to avoid it. They'd just have to hope the *Rory Williams* beat the Tokomak to their destination – or pray. "Good luck, Captain."

"We'll need it," Captain Singh said.

— —

MARTIN WAS SWEATING heavily as he came out of the simulator, cursing whoever had designed the system under his breath. The biofeedback was always intensified in the simulators, according to the older Marines, leaving him feeling utterly exhausted. It was all he could do to drag himself forward and into the briefing room, knowing all too well that if Major Lockland decided to do a uniform inspection he was finished. But then, the rest of 3rd Platoon looked equally sweaty and uncomfortable.

This won't end until you see action, he reminded himself. The remainder of 3rd Platoon were polite, but distant. He wished, more than he cared to admit, for some of the recruits he'd trained beside, people who were just as inexperienced as himself. *And if we see no action...*

He straightened up as Major Lockland strode into the compartment, looking disgustingly fresh. The Marines of 1st and 2nd Platoon followed him, wearing standard BDUs. Martin was too tired to glower at them, but hoped they had an equally hard training session awaiting them in the future. He heard the sound of the starship's drives powering up as the Major took his place at the front of the compartment, then felt a faint shiver running through the hull as they dropped into FTL. Maybe it was just his imagination, but there was something more...*purposeful* about the motion, this time. Perhaps they were going on a mission...

"At ease, Marines," Major Lockland said. "*Freedom* has been reassigned to a special operation. We will be the tip of the spear."

Martin felt a sudden flicker of excitement, mingled with an odd kind of fear. They were going to be tested at last...and what if he fucked up? The simulators had been designed to allow him to fuck up – and learn from his mistakes – without any real danger, but a real mission was nothing like the simulators. Lieutenant Robbins kept telling him, time and time again, that no battle plan ever survived its first encounter with the enemy. War was a democracy, after all. The enemy got a vote.

"Our mission is to take a starship intact," Major Lockland continued. "We will be launched from the tubes as soon as *Freedom* has softened her up, then we will go in through the hull and assume control as rapidly as possible. It will not be an easy mission. We know nothing about the interior design of the alien ship, or what level of computer security it possesses."

Martin sucked in his breath. Taking a Horde ship was easy, even without the specialist hacking tools available to the Solar Marines. All a boarding party had to do was insert a link into the ship's computer and gain access through the factory presets. The Horde never seemed to learn that their systems were wide open, so undefended that backdoors were completely unnecessary. But who knew what any other alien race would do to secure their ships?

It's never so easy to board a Varnar ship, he reminded himself. God knew they'd simulated that hundreds of times, but the operation was not always a success. *They actually know what they're doing.*

"We will reach our destination in nine days," Major Lockland said. "Tomorrow, we start rehearsing in earnest."

Martin blinked. *In earnest?*

"We know little about the alien design, so we will have to be flexible," Major Lockland added. "Get some rest, then report to the simulators at 0700. Good luck to you all."

And what, Martin asked himself as the Marines rose to their feet, *does Yolanda make of it all?*

NINETEEN

The Non-Discriminatory Sports Association today voted to strip sports coaches of pay, benefits and other rights guaranteed to them by prior legislation. In their statement, the NDSA asserted that sports discriminated between athletic and non-athletic and, as such, deserved not a single cent of taxpayers' money. Speaking in response, the Coaches Union reaffirmed its determination to battle for the rights of its members. However, after successive scandals, it is unlikely the public will be supportive.

—Solar News Network, Year 53

"The system appears to be completely empty," Yolanda reported. "There's nothing within sensor range, not even a stray comet."

"Good," Captain Singh said. "Keep your eyes on the ball."

"Aye, sir," Yolanda said.

She gritted her teeth. *Freedom* had been in the system for three days, long enough for the crew to start wondering if they were too late. The Tokomak ship could have been and gone by now. Or it might have been delayed. If it had taken the Tokomak fifty *years* to notice that Earth was a potential threat, it might easily take them several months to cross a dozen light years from Hades to the unnamed system.

Martin will be disappointed, she thought, as she turned her attention back to her console. They'd only managed to snatch one meeting as the ship raced to her destination, but they'd had a chance to share their impressions of the mission. *He wants a chance to prove himself*.

She rolled her eyes at the thought. In her view, Martin had proven himself a long time ago, but the Marines didn't care what she thought. They would only accept someone who had fought beside them as a *true* comrade-in-arms, no matter his previous career. Even a former soldier from Earth or a mercenary who'd fought for the Galactics would be hard-pressed to gain acceptance without actually fighting beside the Marines. Martin's comrades, when she'd met them, had been polite, but distant. They hadn't been impressed by a lowly ensign.

Her console chimed. "Captain," she said. "I'm picking up one large ship, heading towards the system from Gamma-Delta."

"Put it on the main display," Captain Singh ordered. "Can you identify the ship?"

"Negative, sir," Yolanda said, feeling a flash of *Déjà Vu*. "But, judging by the signature, I think she's a heavy cruiser."

She frowned as she studied the readings. Detecting starships in FTL was relatively easy; the drive field propagated gravity waves at FTL speeds, alerting anyone with gravimetric sensors that there was a starship inbound. Indeed, tracking flights between stars wasn't difficult, with the right technology. She had a feeling that one of the reasons the Tokomak had started to take humanity seriously was because they'd noted the colossal upswing in starships heading to and from Earth, although there was no way to be sure.

"The power curve is growing stronger, sir," she reported. "It's definitely a cruiser-sized starship."

"Understood," Captain Singh said. "I…"

He broke off as alarms howled. "She's returned to normal space," Yolanda reported. "I make one heavy cruiser; I say again, I make one heavy cruiser."

She sucked in a breath as the Tokomak cruiser – not even *trying* to disguise its signature – appeared on the display. There had been painfully little data available on Tokomak ships, even in the Galactic version of *Jane's*; now, the human race was seeing one of their cruisers for the first time. Despite herself, she was almost impressed. The design was impractical, by human standards, but remarkably elegant. She looked remarkably like a giant swan.

"I wonder where they fit the weapons on that design," Commander Gregory mused.

Yolanda accessed her implants, drinking in the live feed from the passive sensors. The enemy craft wasn't bristling with weapons, as far as she could tell, although that meant nothing. There could easily be weapons hidden within her hull, ready to emerge and open fire if something threatened her pristine condition. And yet, there was something about the starship's movements that bothered her. It took her a long moment of staring before she understood just what she was seeing. The Tokomak crew thought they were unobserved – she certainly *hoped* they thought they were unobserved – but they were still posturing, still showing off for the sake of showing off. Their power curves were inefficient, yet it didn't matter. They sure as hell looked good.

"Show offs," the Captain said. He evidently agreed. "Can you determine the location of their shield generator nodes?"

"Aye, Captain," Yolanda said. Human – and Varnar – ships were designed to obscure the location of their shield generators, but the Tokomak seemed to be showing off, practically *daring* anyone to take a shot at their hull. "I have them pinpointed."

The Captain's voice grew deeper. "Helm, take us into attack position," he ordered. "And make damn sure they don't get a sniff of us before it's too late."

"Aye, sir," the helmsman said.

Yolanda watched, carefully, as *Freedom* inched closer to the Tokomak cruiser. She knew, from her simulations, that it was immensely difficult to penetrate a cloak when the cloaked ship was taking even minimal precautions to hide its location, but the Tokomak weren't even scanning for turbulence caused by the interaction of the drive field with the cloaking device. Indeed, apart from a handful of light sensor sweeps, they weren't doing *anything*. It was possible they were using passive sensors, which emitted nothing for her sensors to pick up, but it was still odd. She couldn't help wondering if they knew where *Freedom* was and were just trying to lull her into a false sense of security. Nothing else seemed to make sense.

"They're just sitting there," Commander Gregory said. "Two minutes to optimal firing range."

"Lock weapons on targets," Captain Singh ordered. If he felt any tension, Yolanda couldn't hear it in his voice. "Prepare to fire."

"Particle beams locked, ready to fire," Commander Gregory said. "Phasers locked, ready to fire."

Yolanda felt, suddenly, as if the entire universe was hanging on a knife-edge…

"Fire," Captain Singh ordered.

The Tokomak cruiser writhed under the fire as particle beams slammed into – and then though – its shields. Utterly unprepared for attack, it hadn't even raised its shields beyond the point needed to deflect radiation and cosmic dust. Yolanda watched, astonished, horrified and not a little proud, as its shields flickered out of existence before it even realised it was under attack.

"Switch targeting to FTL drives and prepare to fire," Captain Singh ordered, as the Tokomak cruiser rolled over. Its sensors, too late, started to probe space for the hostile ship. "Disable their drive."

Freedom fired, again. "Drive disabled," Yolanda reported. "They're attempting to lock weapons on us."

"Launch decoy drones, then disable their sensors," Captain Singh ordered. "And launch the Marines."

Good luck, Martin, Yolanda thought.

New alarms sounded. "Enemy ship has opened fire," Commander Gregory snapped. "Their aim is erratic."

"I don't think they have a decent lock on us," Yolanda supplied, although she wasn't sure she believed her own words. The enemy crew couldn't be so incompetent as to be unable to track the weapons fire back to its source, could they? It wasn't as if *Freedom* had launched stealth antimatter-tipped missiles that could have come from anywhere. "They're firing almost at random."

"Their command and control network must be down," Captain Singh said. He sounded disbelieving. There were so many redundancies built into *Freedom's* internal datanet that the only way to destroy it was to reduce the ship to atoms. "Target their weapons systems; fire to disable."

"Aye, sir," Commander Gregory said. "Firing now."

Yolanda watched in bemusement as the hail of fire from the Tokomak ship came to an end. They'd fired in all directions, as if they'd thought they were surrounded...or as if they'd lost everything and intended to at least try to score a hit or two before they were destroyed. Had their bridge been taken out in the first salvo? It didn't seem likely; human designs, at least, placed the bridge well away from the shield generators. But the Tokomak seemed to be doing everything wrong.

"Weapons disabled, sir," Commander Gregory reported.

"Very good," the Captain said. "Transmit a demand for surrender."

Yolanda tapped her console, sending the pre-recorded message. "Message sent, sir," she said. The seconds ticked away as the Marines approached the stricken ship's hull. "No response."

"They might have lost communications," Commander Gregory speculated.

"They might," Captain Singh agreed. "Ensign?"

"There's no sign they received our message," Yolanda said. "But their ship hasn't taken *that* much damage."

She glanced down at her console. "Enemy ship is showing power fluctuations," she added, slowly. "I don't think they can maintain their internal power or atmosphere for much longer. They may have already diverted everything they can to life support."

"Good," Captain Singh said. "Keep sensors fixed on their hull. If there is the slightest hint they can drop back into FTL, or do anything else even remotely hostile, I want to know about it."

"Aye, sir," Yolanda said.

"Go, go, go!"

Martin braced himself as the suit was ejected out into space, aimed directly at the giant Tokomak cruiser. The live feed from *Freedom's* sensors identified a hundred weaknesses in the design, but she looked impressive to a single Marine. Indeed, it was hard to truly grasp her size and power, even though he'd spent the last six months on *Freedom*. And *Freedom* was half the size of the Tokomak ship.

"Go straight through the hull," Major Lockland ordered. "*Do not* waste time trying to find an airlock. Just punch through and into the ship."

Martin's suit spun as he closed in on the giant ship, allowing him to land neatly on the hull. Four of the Marines were already placing charges on the metal, opening a pathway into the giant ship. A sudden outflow of atmosphere told him they'd succeeded; he braced himself, then plunged into the ship, followed by the remainder of the Marines. His suit automatically launched nanotech drones, scouting out ahead of the Marines as they advanced into the ship; behind him, the gash in the hull was sealed, saving what remained of the ship's atmosphere.

"We have best guesses for the location of the bridge, engineering and life support sections," Lieutenant Robbins said. "Our orders are to advance on the engineering sections."

"Understood," Martin said. Ahead of him, there was an airlock, half-open. He frowned, then realised the safety system must have jammed when they'd cut their way into the ship. "Did they not bother with any maintenance?"

He smashed the airlock open with his armoured fists, then advanced forward...and then stopped. Dozens of thin aliens, their skins torn and broken, drifted in front of him. They'd suffocated when they'd run out of oxygen, he realised in horror. They should have been safe – the airlocks had tried to activate automatically – but they'd jammed. The starship's commander had skimped on maintenance and this was the result. He swallowed hard, forcing himself not to throw up. He'd seen worse in the simulators, but this was real.

"Continue forwards," Robbins ordered.

Martin felt chills running down his spine as they moved past the next set of airlocks and into a pressurised area. There was no sign of any aliens, leaving him to wonder if they'd fled – or if they were planning an ambush. He glanced into a pair of side rooms, but saw nothing apart from pieces of unfamiliar equipment. There was no point in poking and prodding at them himself, he knew. It was far better to leave that for the tech experts.

"My God," Corporal Rogers said. "What the hell is that?"

Martin followed his gaze. The next airlock had opened automatically at their approach – and the corridor beyond was decorated in a style most humans would have unhesitatingly called gaudy. Martin couldn't help thinking of drug lords and gangbangers wearing tasteless gold jewellery, people for whom the whole point of having wealth was to show it off. There was no rhyme or reason to the decorations, as far as he could tell. But then, aliens might have very different senses of just what was tasteful...

Alerts flared up in his implants as the lead Marines ran into fire. The Tokomak had, somehow, managed to organise an ambush. Martin moved forward, crouching as low as he could in the suit, and launched a pair of grenades down the corridor, blowing the alien position to bits. The Marines ran forward in the wake of the blast, looking for surviving aliens and stunning them. Martin suspected that few would survive, even if they were stunned, but they needed prisoners. He glanced from side to side as he reached the blast zone, then forced himself to run onwards. There was no time for anything, but carrying out his duties.

The lights failed. He swore as his suit's sensors adapted to the darkness, casting an eerie pallor over the scene. The gravity failed seconds later; the suit adapted, fixing the Marines to the deck. He pushed the sensations aside and kept moving. If they were lucky, the power failures meant that the ship was under their control. But if they weren't...

They could blow the ship, he thought. *Take us and them to hell together.*

"The RIs cracked the computer network," Major Lockland said. "We have control of the ship's datanet."

Martin let out a sigh of relief as new data started to flow into his implants. The analysts hadn't been too far wrong, he saw; the Marines were indeed approaching the engineering compartment, or what was left of it. Resistance tailed off rapidly as the ship's onboard sensors were used to locate the surviving aliens and teleport them directly into the brig, where they were promptly stunned. The jammers they'd been using to prevent teleporting within their ship's hull had been deactivated.

At least they took that precaution, he thought, dully. *They could have made it easier for us – and them – if they hadn't.*

"Secure the remaining parts of the ship, then deploy scanning drones," Major Lockland ordered. "And then prepare to move the ship elsewhere."

Martin braced himself as he stepped into the engineering compartment. It was a mess; bodies lay everywhere, some seemingly intact, others mutilated and torn by exploding consoles. He rolled his eyes at the sight, recognising more signs of *very* poor maintenance. Outside bad movies and worse VR simulations, consoles simply didn't explode, no matter what sort of battering the ship had taken. It was horrific to realise, after spending so long being taught the importance of keeping everything perfectly maintained, that there were people out there who hadn't even grasped the first lesson.

"This is your rifle," Sergeant Grison had said, almost a year ago. "It is yours. You are responsible for maintaining your rifle and any other piece of equipment we give you. It will be inspected, frequently. And if your rifle is in poor state, may God have mercy on your soul. Look after your rifle and it will look after you."

He shuddered, again, as he worked out what the compartment must have looked like before the short, sharp battle. Captain Singh, according to Yolanda, was absolutely determined to have the finest ship in the fleet, but *he* didn't waste time forcing the crew to scrub the decks and wear dress uniforms at all times. But the Tokomak commander evidently *had*, judging from the engineering compartment. The sections that weren't damaged looked remarkably impressive, even by human standards.

"Quit woolgathering," Lieutenant Robbins barked. "You have work to do!"

"Yes, Lieutenant," Martin said.

He forced down a smile as he went to work. Whatever else happened, there was no way they could say he hadn't served on a combat mission now. He'd be one of the Marines – and he would finally have a place to call home.

And true brothers, he thought. *And that was all I wanted.*

— —

IT WAS NEARLY two hours before the Tokomak ship – whose name translated as the *Supreme Flower of the Delicate Evening* – was finally secured. Kevin had watched, first in fear and then in honest amusement, as *Freedom* took the ship apart, piece by piece. He'd expected the Tokomak to put up a stubborn fight, but instead they'd practically rolled over after the first shot. Their attempts to fight back had been completely ineffective.

"We have fifty-seven Tokomak in custody," Julian reported, shortly. "They're all currently loaded into stasis chambers."

"Keep them there, for the moment," Kevin ordered. It was, to all intents and purposes, a *Red October* scenario. How far was he prepared to go to make sure that the truth behind *Supreme Flower of the Delicate Evening's* –he mentally shorted it to *Flower* – disappearance remained a secret? Was he prepared to butcher helpless Tokomaks? "And the ship itself?"

"Largely intact, apart from the drives and hull-mounted weapons," Julian said. "The computer cores weren't even crashed before we gained control."

"Better make sure there aren't any nasty surprises in the hulk," Kevin said. How long had it been since the Tokomak had fought a real battle? The more he thought about it, the more he wondered if he had overestimated them. What if…there was a chance to win the war with a pre-emptive strike on Varnar or Hades? It was something he would have to raise before the Council. "Can she be towed?"

"Captain Singh is confident she can be taken to Area 51," Julian said. "His crew will have to be warned to keep their gobs shut, though. They might start talking when they're in their cups and the bragging is about to begin."

"They'll have to be warned," Kevin agreed. "I'll have a word with Captain Singh personally."

He smiled. "And I will also complement him on a job well done," he added. As unimpressive as the opposition had been, there was no denying the fact that the crew of *Freedom* had done a very good job. "What happened today may make the difference between victory and total defeat."

TWENTY

A survey carried out by Gallup in the United States, Europe and Australia pegged 'racist' as the single most hated and overused word in the English language. Respondents claimed that the word was so overused as to be completely devoid of meaning, a fact easily verified by the observation that every single candidate in every single election for the past twenty years was accused of being a racist at least twenty times. Responding to the survey, the Anti-Racist League stated that the curse of racism had yet to be removed from human society…

—Solar News Network, Year 53

"Welcome to Area 51, Kevin."

"Thank you, Keith," Kevin said. "I trust you and your team had fun?"

"We had a *lot* of fun," Glass said. "There is no shortage of arguments about just *why* we found what we did, but we do have some preliminary conclusions."

Keith Glass gave him a mischievous smile. Area 51 wasn't the only secret base in the Solar Union, certainly not the only place that studied alien technology, but it was the only base that studied *stolen* alien technology. Half of the SIA's operations were devised to obtain more samples of alien technology, technical manuals and everything else that might help the human race match and exceed the Galactics. But no one had stolen an entire top-of-the-line starship before.

If it is a top of the line starship, Kevin thought. *The Varnar would have put up a much harder fight.*

Glass turned and led Kevin through a pair of airlocks, into a giant observation lounge. The Tokomak starship floated over their heads, sealed inside the giant asteroid. Kevin looked up and drank in the sight – by now, he was used to the sensation of feeling as though an entire starship was about to come crashing down on his head – and then turned back to Glass. The Admiral's assistant was already bringing them both mugs of coffee.

"Have a seat," Glass invited. "One day, I will have to write a book about this."

They shared a smile. Keith Glass had been a popular science-fiction writer before the Hordesmen had first approached Earth, then a natural recruit for the Solar Union before it had even been called the Solar Union. Indeed, quite a few members of his team were past and present science-fiction writers, men and women who could devise uses for alien technology the Galactics had never thought of, let alone tried to implement. The remainder were the best and brightest of humanity, including youngsters from Earth who had come specifically to work on alien technology.

"I think someone already wrote *The Hunt For Red October In Space*," Kevin said. "There's probably a copy or two floating around the datanet."

"I have no doubt of it," Glass agreed. "I would be *pissed* if I didn't have so much else to do here."

Kevin nodded in understanding. The datanet had changed so many things, but – perhaps most of all – it had destroyed Hollywood. What was the point of spending millions of dollars in making a movie when it would be pirated within days of its release, or when a handful of amateurs with access to vast computing power could produce their own movies and release them practically for free? If a particularly famous actor was unavailable, there was no reason they couldn't create computer-generated substitutes. Hollywood had never quite managed to adapt to the new reality and had gone the way of the dinosaurs.

But it does have its advantages, he thought, wryly. *How else could you watch a movie starring all fifteen versions of Doctor Who?*

"First, we did manage to recover the computer cores intact," Glass said, once he'd taken a sip of coffee. "It wasn't too hard to break into their secure compartments, Kevin. I'm rather disappointed in them."

He shrugged. "But what we do know is that the plan for attacking Earth and bringing the Coalition to heel is a little more complex than we'd thought," he added. "They're planning to snatch a number of stars between the Varnar and Coalition space, which will force the Coalition to decide between surrendering or attacking the Tokomak directly. I think they're actually convinced there *won't* be any counterattacks; judging by their dispositions, they're planning more of a parade than anything else."

"Arrogant," Kevin observed.

"When you've been absolute masters of the universe for the past four thousand years, perhaps you have some problems wrapping your head around the concept of someone daring to attack you," Glass countered. "I think that's their problem, Kevin."

He looked up at the giant starship, its white hull pitted with carbon scoring from where the human weapons had struck home. "On the face of it, that ship was in perfect condition," Glass explained. "Every single undamaged compartment is...well, *perfect*. The decks are scrubbed, the equipment is neatly stowed away and not a single component is out of place. I don't think there was even a speck of dust anywhere outside the damaged compartments."

"Sounds like trying to satisfy a Drill Instructor," Kevin said.

He smiled at the memory. One of his uncles had had hundreds of horror stories about West Point, where it was impossible to clean a room to the standards of the Drill Instructors and a single speck of dust was grounds for having to clean the room over and over again. It was one of the reasons he had never seriously considered the military as a career.

"I think so, yes," Glass agreed. "I don't think I've ever worked for someone so anal in my entire career and I've worked with editors who left my manuscripts covered in red ink."

"It was worth it in the end," Kevin said.

"Yes, but I didn't feel that way at the time," Glass said. He shrugged again, then looked up at the ship. "On a more practical basis, however, the ship was rotting away at the seams. Her level of maintenance was very low, well below our standards – or, for that matter, the Varnar standards. I think part of the reason she didn't put up more of a fight was because some of her systems were cross-linked together and taking out one of them knocked out several more as well."

Kevin tried to imagine what Mongo – or Steve, or any Solar Union Captain – would have said to any junior officer stupid enough to interlink his systems more than strictly necessary, despite knowing the risks. It might have been safer for the junior officer to volunteer for the next suicide mission. Hitting one's subordinates was not considered acceptable behaviour, but any court martial board would probably have voted to acquit. Risking a starship's integrity just to save time would have been utterly unacceptable.

"Idiots," he said. "That wasn't a Horde ship. They *designed* this technology. Don't they know..."

"I imagine they didn't have time," Glass said. "Burnishing the hull alone would take days, perhaps weeks. There's a reference in their log to a potential visit by Great Old Ones, so the crew had to spend time cleaning and re-cleaning their ship. I think they probably started skipping on basic maintenance pretty damn quickly."

He looked up at the ship again, then back at Kevin. "Do you know how old the ship is?"

Kevin shook his head. The Tokomak ship - *Supreme Flower of the Delicate Evening*, he reminded himself – had looked pristine before the battle. But then, starships didn't actually decay in space. The Galactics had no shortage of starships that had passed through twenty or more pairs of hands – or claws, or maniples – before humanity had purchased them for a song. There was no way to tell a starship's age from its outside appearance.

"Try two thousand *years*," Glass said, coolly. "That ship was new when the Roman Empire was at its height."

"Fuck," Kevin said, stunned. "You're shitting me."

"I'm quite serious," Glass said. "We found log entries dating back right to her maiden voyage. Extensive log entries. There's another reason for the poor maintenance right there, Kevin. Her CO was expected to spend at least an hour a day filling out the ship's log."

He shook his head. "The Tokomak built well," he added, "but the ship needed maintenance and all she got was people covering up the flaws with new coats of paint. You know what she reminds me of?"

"No," Kevin said.

"The *Enterprise*," Glass said.

Kevin frowned. "Our cruiser or Captain Picard's ship?"

Glass shot him a cross look. "The aircraft carrier," he said. "I served on her before 9/11 – this was back when Slick Willy was in the White House. We looked good, Kevin, but we had very real problems. Half the Tomcats were cannibalised to keep the other half flying, among other issues. The Captain was doing what he could, but...morale was in the pits, we were losing good people and not a one of us trusted the Commander-in-Chief. There was a stunningly hot Tomcat pilot who kept getting shit because half the crew thought she had only been allowed to fly because she was a woman..."

He shrugged. "This ship is just the same," he added, "but they had a worse Captain. I found copies of requests for paint or internal decoration, not requests for spare parts or a larger crew. Hell, she was undermanned too. I think they're having problems crewing their fleet."

Kevin remembered his thoughts on how the Solar Union might ossify and went cold. "Why?"

"I don't know," Glass said. "It could be they're going through the whole 'patriotism is a dirty word' phase or it could be the sheer lack of promotion prospects. There are crew records that claim some of the crew served on her for over fifty years without promotion or hope of same, Kevin. How long would it be before human ships started shedding crew in great numbers?"

"Not long," Kevin said. The Solar Union was a meritocracy. If a crewman proved himself capable, there *would* be promotion, right up the line. But if promotion dragged, and if there were opportunities outside the fleet, it was unlikely that anyone would feel inclined to put his life on the line for the Solar Union. Fleet crewmen were people too. "The old DHS had that problem right up until it collapsed under its own weight."

He shook his head at the bitter memory, then pushed it aside. Perhaps the DHS – and America – would have recovered if the Solar Union hadn't come into existence. There had already been feedback trends, even though he suspected Washington wouldn't have agreed to reform without serious pressure from a largely inert population. Instead, everyone who wanted to live free had emigrated to outer space, leaving behind the people who depended on the government to take care of them…

And that, he thought, *might explain why the government never managed to master even unrestricted alien technology.*

"Overall, I am most unimpressed," Glass said. "I will present a copy of my formal report before the Council in a week, as requested, but we have a definite advantage. Hell, the *Varnar* would have a definite advantage. They, at least, had to learn to adapt to keep fighting the war. The Tokomak haven't had to check their security arrangements for over a thousand years. I think they're in for a nasty shock when the war begins."

"It's already begun," Kevin said, nodding upwards. "And they have a *lot* of ships."

"Yeah," Glass said. "We've downloaded specifications from the datacores we captured, Kevin. Their battleships aren't too bad, at least on the surface. God alone knows how badly they've been maintained."

"It would be unwise to count on it," Kevin said. "Perhaps we could monitor their arrival at Hades and see how well they manage to enter orbit."

Glass looked doubtful. "I don't think they could screw *that* up," he said. "Any fool can get a ship into orbit."

"You need to spend more time at Sparta," Kevin said. "Every last screw-up that can be screwed-up has been committed there, time and time again."

He smiled at the memory of the blooper reel Mongo had once shown him – even though it hadn't really been *that* funny – then sobered. "Overall," he asked, "what do you think our chances are?"

"If we had equal numbers to them, we'd be laughing all the way to their homeworld," Glass said, frankly. "As it is, they have a distressing number of everything from directed energy weapons to missile launchers. If they decided to soak up the losses and just keep coming, Kevin, we'd be fucked. And if they ever realise just how advanced we will be in a few decades, they *will* throw a million ships at Earth just to exterminate us from existence."

Kevin frowned. "Are we *that* close to beating them?"

Glass snorted. "How long was it, on Earth, between the invention of the internet and the explosion of electronic society? How long was it before we started using the internet for anything, apart from sharing intellectual thoughts and defence data? How long was it before large chunks of the internet became nothing more than tits, asses and cocks?"

"Not long," Kevin said. He was old enough to remember the arcade machines he'd played as a child...and then the versions of Windows that had opened up a whole new world. "But this is different?"

"No, it isn't," Glass said. "This is...well, this is *Harry Potter*."

He went on before Kevin could say a word. "Right now, on the datanet, there are *billions* upon *billions* of pieces of *Harry Potter* fan-fiction, everything from text stories to homemade movies. The franchise has expanded so rapidly, with so many people involved in creating new versions of the universe, that it's hard to say what is truly canon any longer. Point is – there was a colossal flowering of intellectual activity based on a single seven-book series."

"I never figured you for a *Harry Potter* fan," Kevin said.

"There wasn't an author alive at the time who wouldn't have given his soul for such publicity," Glass pointed out, dryly. "And besides, these days, science-fiction has hit something of a roadblock."

Kevin understood. Universes like *Babylon 5* and *Star Trek* and even *Doctor Who* had been proven to be impractical, as well as non-existent. The march of technology – alien technology – had damaged science-fiction quite badly, while fantasy had grown and prospered. Steve would probably have muttered something about liberals encouraging pie-in-the-sky dreaming, but Kevin had a feeling the decline of science-fiction was caused by something more fundamental. It was simply harder to suspend one's belief when one knew very well that the universe simply didn't allow time travel.

Glass coughed, loudly. "We're doing the same with alien technology," he continued. "Right now, we have countless ideas for new uses – uses they never considered – making their way through society. It won't be long before there will be *newer* ideas, based on the previous set of new ideas, and even newer ideas based on *those*. The datanet allows countless ideas to be considered; the high level of education in the Solar Union allows our versions of Bill Gates and Roger Pearlman to flourish and actually make their ideas into reality. They simply don't have any way to compete against us, once we start pulling ahead. I don't think their leadership is remotely capable of grasping the fact it needs a less immobile society even to *begin* to meet our challenge."

"Probably not," Kevin agreed. From what he'd heard, the Tokomak birthrate was very low and the youngsters spent most of their time enjoying themselves, rather than trying to rise in the ranks. But why should they try when they knew it was impossible? "How long do we have, then, before we are invincible?"

Glass smirked. "Give us fifty years and they wouldn't be able to touch us," he said. "Right now, though, we only have samples of some of the more interesting pieces of technology, weapons that will blow them right out of space. It won't be an easy war."

"But at least we will have a fighting chance," Kevin said. "Let me know if you have any reason to change your conclusions."

"I will," Glass said. He sighed, then nodded towards the ship. "I believe the ship isn't likely to hold any surprises, Kevin. They're not much more advanced than the lesser Galactics."

"And the Varnar might be moving ahead of their masters," Kevin mused. "I wonder if we could do something with that..."

"Let them know?" Glass said. "They must resent their position, particularly as they've been fighting the proxy war for generations."

"We could," Kevin said. "Or we could offer to broker a honest peace, after we beat the Tokomak."

He paused. "*If* we beat the Tokomak."

"And if we don't," Glass said, "we need other plans."

"They're underway," Kevin said. "Do you have a contingency plan for evacuating this base?"

"Yep," Glass assured him. He didn't go into details. "We can get everyone out in a hurry, if necessary."

"Let us hope so," Kevin said. He rose to his feet. "I have to get back to Ceres, unfortunately."

Glass lifted his eyebrows. "You don't want a tour of *Flower*?"

"I can't afford contempt," Kevin admitted. "I'm already too unimpressed by what we've seen for my own good. By any reasonable standard, the Taliban should have been no match for us and they still managed to give us a few nasty surprises. They thought themselves the masters of the universe too."

"Point taken," Glass said. He rose, too. "But, from a technical point of view, that ship is crap. We would have shot the Captain and half of the crew by now for gross dereliction of duty. But, for them, looking good is better than *being* good. You know what we found in the databanks? Flight patterns for formation flying."

Kevin stared. "Starships flying in formation?"

"Yes," Glass said. "It would have looked good, too. But one single accident and..."

"Bang," Kevin finished.

TWENTY-ONE

Rioting broke out between Hindus and Muslims in Northern India over the issue of a number of Hindu converts to Islam. The Hindus claim that the converts were kidnapped, raped and then forced to convert; the Muslims claim the converts were looking for a better life and submitted to Allah willingly. Whatever the truth, as of last report, there were over two hundred dead in the streets…

—Solar News Network, Year 53

"You wanted to see me, Commander?"

"I did, Ensign," Commander Gregory said. "Come into my office."

Yolanda stepped inside, a little nervously. She'd never visited the Commander's office before, but Ensign Fisher had been summoned to face Commander Gregory a week ago and had emerged looking pale and worn. Yolanda guessed he'd been given a heavy chewing-out to rival anything they'd been given at Sparta, all the worse because they were on a real starship. But he'd refused to talk about it to any of them.

"Take a seat, Ensign," Commander Gregory said. She smiled with genuine amusement as Yolanda sat down. "You're not in any trouble, so relax."

"Thank you, Commander," Yolanda said.

She'd hastily been reviewing her actions over the past week, trying to decide what she might have done that had attracted the Commander's attention. But there had been nothing. She forced herself to relax, fighting down the temptation to run a tranquilising program through her implants. The Commander would tell her what she had in mind soon enough.

"You are aware, of course, that you became a full citizen of the Solar Union the moment you graduated from Sparta?" Commander Gregory said. "You have your Citizenship Certificate?"

Yolanda nodded, puzzled. She didn't trust herself to speak.

"You will not, of course, have registered as a resident of any canton," Commander Gregory continued. "Do you understand the difference?"

"Yes, Commander," Yolanda said, thinking back to citizenship lessons. "I can vote in overall referendums and elections, but not in a single canton."

"Close enough," Commander Gregory said. "You simply haven't been resident of anywhere long enough to register as a citizen."

She paused, then went on. "Your name – and the names of the crew – were added to the local canton's register of non-resident citizens," she explained. "Fortunately – or unfortunately – your name came up when they were selecting a jury. You are expected to present yourself at the courthouse tomorrow, unless you choose to decline the honour."

Yolanda opened her mouth, but Commander Gregory held up a hand to keep her from speaking.

"I should warn you," Commander Gregory said, "that it will look very bad if you *do* decline the honour. You are a citizen, after all, and citizens are expected to take part in the democratic process. There's no reasonable excuse – we're not due to leave for a week – so I strongly advise you to accept the honour and serve on the jury."

"That doesn't seem fair," Yolanda observed.

"Life is rarely fair, in any sense of the word," Commander Gregory pointed out, rather tartly. "The Solar Union expects some degree of participation, as I said. There are too many people with too many memories of what happens when people *refuse* to take part in the democratic process. I have checked your record and have been unable to come up with any reasonable excuse that would stand the test of time. You are not involved with any of the suspects, nor do you have any stake in the asteroid's political structure. I think you can reasonably be expected to be neutral."

"Yes, Commander," Yolanda said.

She wasn't sure what to feel. Serving on a jury was an alien concept to her. She certainly hadn't served on a jury back on Earth, where jury trials were almost a thing of the past. But if it was part of her duties as a citizen, she had no intention of simply refusing to carry them out. The Commander was right. On the surface, it was a free choice, but it *would* look very bad on her record.

"Go to the courtroom in four hours – and take your Marine friend with you," Commander Gregory ordered, transmitting a stream of data from her implants. "You shouldn't be expected to remain there longer than two days, perhaps three at the most. If they want to hold you back, explain to the usher that you're expected to leave with your ship and they will probably let you go."

She sighed. "I'm sorry this happened when you should be on shore leave," she added. "You probably would have been called to jury duty, sooner or later, but the timing was particularly poor for you. Dismissed."

Yolanda nodded, saluted as she rose, then left the compartment. She called Martin as soon as the hatch hissed closed behind her and arranged to meet him at the airlock, then reviewed the files Commander Gregory had given her. They were sparse on actual details of the case – she assumed it was to prevent her forming any conclusions before the trial actually began – but quite detailed when it came to explaining what she had to do. It wasn't enough to find someone guilty, or innocent. She would be responsible for passing judgement too.

"Hey," Martin called. "What's up?"

"Jury duty," Yolanda said. She copied the files Commander Gregory had sent her to his implants as they stepped through the airlock and walked down the long corridor into Gunn Asteroid. "I'm sorry for ruining your shore leave."

"I was spending half of it with you and the other half getting drunk with the platoon," Martin said. "Truthfully, I preferred spending time with you."

Yolanda smiled, shyly. "Really?"

"The platoon can be very overbearing at times," Martin said. "And they're always around me on the ship, anyway."

"At least they've accepted you now," Yolanda said. "You should be happy."

They reached the second airlock and stepped through into the asteroid. Unlike most of the other asteroids she'd visited, which were largely well-established cantons, Gunn Asteroid served as a clearing house for emigrants from Earth who were reluctant to join the military or sign up with a corporation before they left their homeworld. There was something about it that felt a little shabby, Yolanda noted, although she couldn't put her finger on *what.* The Solar Union could feed and water its entire population without needing to strain itself, but it assumed no further obligation towards the immigrants. Anyone who failed to find a job would be in deep trouble.

A stream of holographic advertisements popped up beside her as she walked, advertising everything from asteroid mining to prostitution. Yolanda had been shocked, at first, to discover that sex worker was considered a honourable occupation, although she could see *some* advantages in allowing prostitutes to work openly. Other potential occupations looked to be dead-end jobs, as far as she could tell; some of the adverts offered proper formal training as well as actual employment. A line of text at the bottom promised more details if she sent a message to the owners.

"Shit," Martin said, quietly.

Yolanda followed his gaze as they paused outside a large rock chamber, hewed out of the asteroid. It was crammed with people, mainly young men, trying to snatch some sleep before they resumed the search for jobs. On Earth, so many people from so many races would have been uneasy together; here, they were too tired to do more than roll over and sleep on uncomfortable mattresses, covered with torn blankets. She felt a sudden stab of pity and horror as they walked on and past the next chamber, which held men and women lining up for cheap soup and bread. Beyond them, a third chamber held sleeping women.

"If we hadn't found a way to join the military, we might have ended up there," Martin breathed.

"Maybe," Yolanda said. She doubted Martin would have stayed there for very long – he'd had the drive to get out of the ghetto, after all – but *she* might have been trapped in the caves or driven by hunger into prostitution. "Why don't they move on?"

Martin shrugged. He had no answer.

Yolanda mulled it over as they walked past the caves and down towards the courthouse. There was no shortage of jobs, but jobs required education. Had the newcomers learned *nothing* on Earth? Given how little she'd known when she'd left Earth forever, it seemed quite likely. Or was there some other reason they were caught in the asteroid, instead of going on to find a proper place to live?

There was a small crowd outside the courthouse, supervised by armed guards wearing white uniforms. Their commander, a man wearing a cowboy hat with a silver star, eyed them both warily, then sent an ID ping from his implants. Yolanda returned it, then transmitted a copy of the jury notice. The officer eyed her for a long moment, then jerked a thumb towards the door.

"Your friend can go through and join the audience," he said. "Or he can wait outside."

"I'll watch," Martin said, quickly. He waved to Yolanda. "Good luck."

Inside, the air was fresh and cold. Yolanda shivered, then looked up as someone called her name, inviting her into a second room. Two men sat at a desk, one of them looking down at a datapad, the other studying Yolanda with cold blue eyes. She sat facing them, when one of them motioned to the chair, and forced herself to remain calm. Moments later, the man studying the datapad looked up at her and smiled.

"I am obliged to warn you that you may not disclose anything that happens in here until the end of the trial," one of the men said. "In the event of you being rejected for jury service, you will still be obliged to keep your mouth shut until the end. Any disclosures you may make before then will result in your arrest, trial and a possible sentence of five years hard labour. Do you understand what I have just told you?"

"Yes," Yolanda said. Her mouth was very dry. "I understand."

The man relaxed, slightly. "And you are prepared to accept the responsibility that comes with being a juror?"

"I am," Yolanda said.

"Good," the man said. He passed her the datapad. "You are required to inform us, now, if you know any of the people in the files personally or professionally."

"Or if there are any other reasons you should not be judging this case" the other man added.

"Indeed," the first man said. "If any such reasons should appear later, you may be charged with causing a deliberate mistrial, which – if found guilty – will result in a five year sentence of hard labour."

Yolanda took the datapad and flicked through the files. None of the faces looked familiar, although she had to remind herself that people could change their names and faces in the Solar Union, without restriction. She studied the names for a long moment, then shook her head.

"I don't recognise any of them," she said. "What now?"

The man pointed a finger at the door behind them. "You go through and wait to be called," he said. "Do not talk about the case with your fellow jurors or attempt to leave the compartment."

Yolanda sighed, then walked through the door. Inside, there was a reasonably comfortable waiting room, with seven men and women already sitting there, most of them reading paperback books. She frowned and tried to use her implants, only to discover that she couldn't get a signal out of the room. If there were any processors capable of linking her into the datanet, none of them responded to her. Sighing, she sat down and picked up one of the glossy magazines lying on the tables. In hindsight, she should have brought a book or downloaded something new into her implants.

It was nearly an hour before the thirteen jurors were summoned through yet another door, into the courtroom. Yolanda almost laughed when she saw it; someone, she suspected, had been reading books about an era where the defendant had to prove his innocence, rather than the law his guilt. The judge's chair looked more like a throne, the defendant's box had spikes hammered into the sides and the jury had uncomfortable chairs, presumably to keep them alert. It would be hard for the defendant to have any doubt about why he'd been summoned to court.

She hastily reviewed procedures as the doors were thrown open, allowing the public witnesses to flow into the room. Martin was the third person to enter; he waved to her, quickly, then sat down at the back of the room. Once the public seating was full, the doors were closed and the judge marched out of a side door and sat down on his throne. A deep silence fell. It would have been more impressive, Yolanda thought, if she hadn't known it was caused by a sound-suppressant force field.

"Bring in the prisoners," the judge ordered.

There was a pause, then the prisoners were marched into the court. Yolanda leaned forward, studying them with interest. Two of them were older men, easily old enough to be her father; three more were her age, maybe a little bit older. Their hands were cuffed behind their backs, while their legs were shackled, making it harder for them to walk. The defiant stares they gave the courtroom, however, suggested they had no fear of conviction. Yolanda forced herself to sit back and relax. They'd be told the charges soon enough.

"The Prosecutor may begin," the judge said, once the defendants were in the dock.

The Prosecutor rose to his feet and cleared his throat. "Ladies and Gentlemen of the Jury," he said. "The prisoners you see before you have been charged with two murders, one attempt to cover up the aforementioned murders and outright breach of the Solar Union Constitution. I have no hesitation in requesting they face the maximum penalty allowed by law."

Yolanda shivered. The maximum penalty was death.

"The facts of the case are straightforward," the Prosecutor continued. "The defendant and his family requested and received permission to immigrate to the Solar Union nine months ago. Unfortunately, the senior members of the family were unable to find work and remained on Gunn Asteroid, forbidding their teenage children to leave them and find employment on their own. Six months ago, the seventeen-year-old daughter of the defendant – Anisa Bin Khalid started a relationship with Mathew Quirk, whose family had also emigrated from Earth. His family were supportive of the relationship; her family were not. After she was beaten by her father, she ran to her boyfriend and they planned to escape together.

"It was not to be. The defendants tracked them down and murdered them both, then tried to hide the bodies in the waste disposal system. Forensic examination proved that they were both beaten to death by the defendants, who were tracked down and arrested. Interrogation under lie detectors proved that the two senior defendants had ordered the murder, then pushed the junior ones into assisting with both the murder itself and then the cover-up.

"Their motive in doing so was nothing less than *control*. They did not want Anisa to form any relationships of any kind outside their family; the thought of her leaving them permanently, let alone living with a man from a very different culture, was utterly impossible to tolerate. They feared for the reputation of their family, for the future lives of her brothers and sisters. They chose, therefore, to kill them both, committing murder.

"This was not self-defence. This was not manslaughter. This was cold-blooded, premeditated murder. Furthermore, the Solar Union Constitution clearly states that children who have reached their majority – and Anisa was old enough to be considered mature – cannot be controlled by their parents. To attempt to talk her out of the relationship would be one thing, to murder her in cold blood quite another. The defendants swore to respect and uphold the Constitution upon arrival. Their crime is quite beyond any defence."

Yolanda shuddered. She'd heard rumours that some teenage children had been locked up by their parents in California, but her stepmother – the evil bitch – had never tried to lock Yolanda up in a cupboard, let alone marry her off to someone else. But then, who would *want* her?

"The Defender can now speak," the judge said.

The defender looked tired, Yolanda noted, as he rose to his feet. She wondered, as he cast his gaze over the jury, just how he planned to defend the criminals. What sort of defence was even *possible?* Did he plan to suggest that using lie detectors was somehow illegal? Even if it was – and she knew from her notes that it wasn't – there was plenty of forensic evidence too. It was waiting in the datacores for her to review, once the speeches were over.

"My clients wish me to deny that they committed murder," the Defender said, bluntly. "They wish me to state that their culture permits parents wide latitude over their children, both to punish them when they defy their parents and to defend them against outsiders. They see Mathew Quirk as nothing more than a rapist who had to die."

It was an interesting choice of words, Yolanda noted. The more she thought about it, the more she realised the Defender wasn't choosing his own words, merely parroting what he'd been told to say. Two of the defendants remained impassive, but the remaining three were *smirking* at the audience, who looked outraged. It might have worked on Earth, where an appeal to respect for other societies could excuse anything, but the Solar Union was different.

"They assert that the Solar Union has no power to try them," the Defender continued. "And they demand their immediate release."

He broke off, looking annoyed. The audience was laughing.

The judge pressed his lips together, tightly. "We have them in the dock," he said. "I dare say we have the power to try them."

He nodded to the jury. "Shall we continue?"

TWENTY-TWO

Pakistan's new government issued a warning to India as Hindu-Muslim fighting spread out of control, despite the presence of Indian troops. However, despite intensive pressure from theocratic elements within Pakistan, it is unlikely the Pakistanis can do more than issue strong protests and brace themselves for an onslaught of refugees. Sources on the ground claim that Indian troops, far from separating the two sides, have been destroying mosques, raping Muslim women and driving Muslim families out of their homes. There has been no independent verification of these claims.

—Solar News Network, Year 53

Martin had no difficulty in believing the defendants were guilty. Their faces showed it all; not the blank incomprehension of the man-child who doesn't really believe he has committed the crime, but the droll amusement of the man who believed he was going to get away with his misdeeds. He'd seen too many people like them on Earth, men and women who regarded the ghetto as their own private preserve, to think otherwise. No matter what they did, people respected them and covered for them, either out of fear or misplaced loyalty.

He scowled at them, then forced himself to think calmly as the Prosecutor rose to speak again.

"We do not object to disciplining children, provided that such discipline is within reason," he said. "But Anisa was no little girl to be given a slap on the rump, or told to stand in the corner, or be sent to bed without supper. She was an adult, by our standards, old enough to make her own choices and face the consequences. And even if she hadn't been, I think there will be no disagreement that *murder* is a completely unacceptable way to punish children!"

He paused, then went on. "There are no grounds for suggesting that Mathew raped her," he continued. "She was his girlfriend for over a month! If she'd been raped, she could have taken it to the police and he would have been arrested, then tried and sentenced. And there were no grounds for her family to take the law into their own hands. Indeed, they murdered the victim as well as the rapist.

"But Mathew was no rapist.

"There are no grounds for tolerating such a crime," he concluded. "They murdered their own daughter. They murdered a young man with a decent amount of promise ahead of him. And then they tried to cover it up! On one hand, they claim they did the right thing; on the other, they tried to hide the evidence of their crime, as if they knew perfectly well that what they did was wrong, wrong, wrong! They are murderers, plain and simple.

"The Solar Union respects the rights of everyone to live as they choose, as individuals. But the keyword there is *individuals*! We do not recognise any groups between the individual or the Solar Union as a whole. How can we? We know, from bitter experience, that drawing lines between groups inevitably leads to granting one group rights above other groups...and eventual racial conflict. The defendants are individuals – and so was their victim. They had every right to disapprove, they had every right to talk her out of it, they had every right – even – to refuse to consider her or her lover part of their family. But they had no right to kill either of them."

The Judge nodded, slowly. "Defender, do you want to respond?"

The Defender looked...*tired*. Martin wondered, suddenly, what would happen to him for taking on the case. If, of course, he *had* taken it willingly...Citizenship classes had stated the importance of having Public Defenders, but the Defenders weren't allowed to do more that put forward the arguments used by their clients. They couldn't serve as lawyers...

"My clients are used to a very different society," the Defender said.

"A society they chose to leave," the Prosecutor injected.

"And they have yet to grow used to living in our world," the Defender added, ignoring the interruption. "They find it hard to adapt to changes and took it badly when their daughter moved ahead of them."

"Excuses," the Prosecutor said, bluntly. "The fact of the matter is that they committed a double murder, with one of the victims being their own daughter. Their excuses do not change the simple fact that they killed two people."

"They also had no reason to trust our courts," the Defender added. "They did not expect a fair trial."

"They have been *given* a fair trial," the Prosecutor said. "Their crime is just beyond any form of defence."

The Judge cleared his throat, loudly. "The Jurors will now pass judgement," he said. A door at the back of the court opened, inviting them to step through and recess themselves. "We will wait for their return."

— —

YOLANDA UNDERSTOOD, BETTER than she cared to admit, just how hard it could be to adapt to a new society. She'd had to do it twice; once as her stepmother's slave and once as a Solar Union immigrant. To that extent, she could feel sorry for the defendants...but it faded as she grasped the truth of what they'd done. To choose to kill their own daughter, to destroy her life and that of her lover, purely because they thought she was disgracing them? It was unacceptable. No one could tolerate such murders without doing colossal damage to the fabric of society.

None of the excuses were even remotely valid. She knew how easy it was for the Solar Union to identify objective and subjective truths. If

Anisa had thought she'd been raped, the Solar Union would have interrogated everyone and determined just what they'd been thinking at the time. A cold-blooded rape, born of lust; drunken fumbling that had gone too far; a honest belief that consent had been granted; a deliberate attempt to get someone in deep shit…it would have been identified, then judgement would have been passed. And the Solar Union would not have played favourites. If Mathew had been guilty, Mathew would have paid.

In the end, the Prosecutor had been right. It all boiled down to one very simple fact. They had murdered two people and tried to cover it up.

She accessed the secure datacores and studied the evidence. DNA traces, recovered from the bodies; the medical report, from the autopsy; the interrogation logs, from the police force; witness interviews, with Mathew's parents and family; even, in the end, the job offers they'd both received from a major mining corporation. They would have made it, Yolanda was sure; even trapped on Gunn, they'd been trying to better themselves. If they'd moved faster, they might have left their parents behind and gone onwards to build themselves a better life.

It could have been me, she thought. She had sometimes thought her stepmother would one day pitch her out of the house, but what if she'd been murdered instead? There were so many murders in California, according to the grapevine, that one more would go completely unnoticed, if her body was ever found. *I could have died in her place.*

She shuddered, sickened. Her father and mother had married, in spite of their families; no one had tried to murder them, merely exclude them from society. Perhaps, she thought, she understood her father a little better now, even though she could never forgive. No one would want to be excluded forever from the people who were just like him…

The foreman cleared his throat. "You will need to cast a vote using your implants," he started. "The first vote is for guilt or innocence; the second is for punishment."

Yolanda nodded, then accessed her implants and entered the voting system. It showed nothing to show her how the others had voted; there had been no debate, merely a moment to inspect the evidence. But it was clear, more than clear, that they were guilty, that two innocent people were dead. She swallowed, then voted guilty. The next section called for her to decide their punishment, ranging from years of hard labour to death. Some of the milder options were not included when the crime was murder.

She swallowed again. How could she condemn someone to death?

You were on Freedom when the ship ambushed an unsuspecting target, her own thoughts mocked her. *How much of the blame for their deaths do you bear?*

It wasn't a fair comparison, Yolanda thought. She hadn't issued the orders or pushed the firing key. But she'd known she might have to take lives, one day, if she went into the military. The idea she wouldn't have to fight, with the Galactics slowly turning their attention to Earth, was laughable.

But that didn't matter too. All that mattered was that a young couple were dead.

Bracing herself, she made her choice.

— —

MARTIN HAD NEVER seen a law drama in his youth; indeed, the only time they'd ever been mentioned, it had been as one of Hollywood's attempts to beat competition from the Solar Union that had gone nowhere. In hindsight, he had a theory that they'd been deliberately banned from television, just to make it harder for people to participate in government. It was as good a theory as any, he thought. He made a mental note to check it and then sat upright as the jury filed back into the courtroom.

Yolanda looked pale, Martin noted. He felt his heart go out to her as he wondered just which way she had voted. It took a simple majority vote to convict, then pass sentence; Yolanda could have voted against conviction, if she'd wanted, without making any real difference…

"Foreman," the Judge said. "Have you reached a verdict?"

"Yes, Your Honour," the Forman said. "We find the defendants guilty."

Martin turned to gaze at the defendants. One of them started to swear in a language he didn't recognise, two more stared in disbelief…and the remaining two started to cry. Martin clenched his fist, feeling a sudden surge of hatred for the immigrants. They'd come, in hopes of building a new life, yet they'd brought the shadows of the old with them. Martin had been told, when he'd taken the oath, that he would be well advised to break all ties with Earth, but he hadn't understood it at the time. He didn't *have* any ties with Earth. But he understood now. Earth's past was a shadow hanging over the human race…

…And the Solar Union had chosen to leave it behind.

The power of 'get over it,' he'd been told. Scudder had pointed out, in exacting detail, that the places of Earth that suffered from endless bouts of civil unrest and war tended to be the places where old grudges hung around, pervading the political landscape. Martin had been interested enough to download essays written by Professor Cozort, who had devised the theory and then proven it on Earth. *You have to leave the past behind to rise to the future.*

The Judge stood. "Your sentence has been passed," he stated. "You will be taken from this place to Death Row, where you will remain until you are executed."

He paused, then summed up the case. "We call ourselves a tolerant society, but our tolerance ends when people are harmed, or threatened with harm. You have no right to force your children to obey you in adulthood, marry someone they do not wish to marry, remain in the home when they want to leave and spread their wings…and you definitely do not have the right to murder them. Your deaths will serve as punishment for your crimes, but also a reminder to others than the rules cannot be broken with impunity. We do not make allowances for those who do not act in a civilised manner.

"The remainder of your family, the ones who were uninvolved in your crime and unaware of it, will be given the choice between remaining here or returning to Earth," he continued. "It will be their choice, for they will no longer be influenced by you. We will not seek to blame them for being related to you, because we treat people as individuals.

"And because you are *individually* guilty, you will die."

He stared down at the defendants, then asked one final question. "Do you have anything you wish to say?"

"She was my daughter," the older man shouted. His voice was accented, but clear enough to understand. "I had every right to punish her for defying me!"

Another defendant – one of the younger men - rammed his shoulder into his side, forcing him to shut up.

"We were doing what we were told," he said. "It wasn't our fault!"

"You would have obeyed orders to commit a crime," the Judge pointed out. "But your interrogation transcripts reveal a different story. You came here, expecting jobs and prestige to fall into your lap; you never worked for either. Instead, you became bitter and twisted and you hated your sister, for fitting in better than you ever could. When your father and uncle insisted she had to die, you raised no objection.

"It would have been easy for you to save her life. You could have warned her, or gone to the police, or even threatened your father and uncle to keep them from harming her. And yet you not only watched her die, but participated in the murder."

There was another torrent of swearing from the defendants. The bailiffs stepped forward and half-marched, half-carried them towards the door. Martin watched them go, feeling nothing but cold hatred in his heart. Men like them had played a large role in wrecking the ghettos, aided and abetted by outsiders who had honestly thought they had been doing his people a favour. But really, who were his people now? He glanced down at his dark-skinned hand and thought, coldly, just how easy it would be to be white. Or yellow. Or a whole stream of colours that simply didn't occur in nature.

And, in doing so, prove there was no *point* in colour-racism.

"The courtroom is now open," the Judge said. "In line with the Fair Trials Act, all evidence gathered by the police will be placed online for public study. The sentence itself will be carried out one week from today, unless strong grounds arise for questioning the evidence."

Martin watched a handful of men – reporters, he guessed – race for the door, then followed them at a more sedate pace. Most of the audience seemed pleased at the result, although some of them seemed to think a stronger punishment was in order. Martin found himself rolling his eyes at the suggestions – including impalement and castration – before remembering some of the gangbangers in the ghetto. Horrific punishments had been their *thing*, both to keep people cowed and to indulge their sadistic tastes. But eventually the latter became more important than the former.

It was nearly an hour before Yolanda joined him, looking paler than ever. "I had to review the records," she said, as she clasped his arm. It was so intimate a gesture that he almost pulled away in shock. "They did more than just murder the young man."

"I wish I was surprised," Martin said. He wanted to ask which way she'd voted – and for what – but he had a feeling she wouldn't want to answer. "People like that thrive on terror – and terrorising people. It keeps everyone weak and scared, so weak and scared they don't realise they're in the majority."

Yolanda stopped and looked up at him. "That was profound," she said. "Have you been reading?"

"Thank you," Martin said. "Lieutenant Robbins gave me a reading list to go through in my spare time. I didn't know I *had* spare time, but apparently I was meant to cut some of my time elsewhere."

They shared a grin. Spare time was always hard to come by on *Freedom*, even when the starship was in FTL. There was never any shortage of things to do.

"I didn't understand this asteroid at first," Martin continued. "But I think I do now. It's a filter for those who can't or won't become good citizens. Those murdering bastards could have stayed here indefinitely, safe from whatever they were fleeing and yet taking no part in the rest of the Solar Union, if they hadn't killed their daughter. Their mere presence would have helped urge their daughter to make something more of herself."

"Sickening," Yolanda said. "Why did they even come here if they knew they would have to play by the rules?"

"They probably thought the rules didn't apply to them," Martin said, shortly. "Or that they enjoyed exemption from some of the rules, based on race or sex or religion or…"

He shook his head. "And then they committed a crime and now they're going to die," he added. "Better that than demonising an entire race or religion."

"I voted to kill them," Yolanda said. "They were evil bastards. There's no doubt about their crimes. They willingly murdered two people for falling in love. They deserve death. So why do I feel guilty?"

Martin shrugged. "You're a decent person?"

"I voted to kill them," Yolanda repeated.

"Some people can't be saved," Martin said. He felt pity – but only for Yolanda. "Some people are raised to think they can do anything, but I don't think those bastards were. I think they knew they were doing something wrong and they did it anyway. So fuck them!"

Yolanda shook her head, sadly. "There are supposed to be four days of shore leave left," she said. "I think we should go somewhere."

Martin smiled. "I can ask the Major," he said. "But we're meant to be within airlock range of *Freedom*."

"Blast," Yolanda said.

"We could always find a hotel," Martin said. He reviewed the duty roster quickly. He'd been told to stay close to the ship, but not too close. "There are several on the asteroid that are better than the sleeping caves."

"Yeah," Yolanda said. "A chance to sleep in…I'd like that."

"Me too," Martin said. "Me too."

TWENTY-THREE

A mother is in jail tonight in Boston, USA, after shooting two criminals who attempted to break into her house. The third – surviving - criminal stated, upon his arrest, that the homeowner did not call a challenge, even though they had broken through the window and were ransacking her kitchen. In a statement before the media, the Governor warned that private individuals taking the law into their own hands could not be tolerated.

—Solar News Network, Year 53

"If we had any doubt about their intentions," Kevin finished, "it has gone now."

He sat back and took a breath. The Special Security Council had scrutinised the data with gimlet eyes, asking question after question when they didn't understand something. On one hand, Kevin appreciated being asked smart questions; on the other hand, they sometimes went over the same material time and time again. It was more than a little frustrating.

But then, everything is riding on the decision to go to war, he thought. *Give them time to study the intelligence properly.*

"So it would seem," President Ross concluded.

Bute leaned forward. "Are we sure we jumped a Tokomak ship?" He asked. "For the masters of the universe, that ship sure fell easily. Did we attack another race of scavengers by accident?"

Mongo cleared his throat, loudly. "The alien captives are definitely Tokomak," he said. "The Galactics have no way to change their species, certainly not without leaving traces behind. As for the poorly-maintained ship..."

He sighed. "The British Empire had the same problem before Admiral Fisher and the First World War," he explained. "There was no creditable threat to British naval dominance, so the Brits became more obsessed with polishing the ships until they gleamed rather than preparing for war. Captains were promoted for keeping their ships looking good when the Admirals visited, while gunnery practice went by the wayside. Officers were expected to wear perfect uniforms rather than crawl through the tunnels to inspect the ship's condition for themselves.

"Their dominance had become something granted to them by right, rather than something they'd worked to earn and keep. It was, they thought, the natural way of things, because the last time they'd faced a real opponent was during the War of 1812. The USN had similar problems before the Horde visited Earth, in many ways. No one really paid any attention to the Chinese plans to build hundreds of long-range anti-ship missiles until it was almost too late.

"And, in this case, some of the Tokomak Admirals are actually thousands of years old," he added, dryly. "I don't think the Brits ever had someone older than seventy or so commanding a battlefleet. The Tokomak Admirals will have had far longer to forget what's actually important in a military."

"So you feel they pose far less of a threat than we had thought," Ross said.

"If we had the same number of starships," Mongo said, "we would wipe them out in an afternoon. It would be nothing more than a victory parade from here to Tokomak, smashing their ships like cardboard as we advanced. I'd say we could still beat them even if we had only a tenth of their numbers. But we don't. We're quite badly outgunned even with our tech advances."

"We could share what we've learned with the Coalition," Ross said. "Invite them to join us in open war."

"Most races would probably balk without evidence the Tokomak could be beaten," Bute pointed out. "The Tokomak *do* have a lot of ships and they know where to find the Coalition homeworlds."

"They know where to find us too," Marie countered. "They've known about us for centuries, Councillor; they just haven't cared. Or do we have hidden colonies the rest of us aren't meant to know about?"

"You're not meant to know about them," Kevin said, although it was an open secret. Quite a few asteroids had crammed a miniature tech base into their habitats, then used fusion drives to punch their way out of the solar system. It was quite tempting to think that, if the Tokomak won, one day one of those asteroids would rebuild human civilisation and come back for revenge. "However, all of those colonies are merely lights tossed into the darkness."

"Which leaves us with the problem of needing a victory, both to convince them to leave us alone and to get the Coalition to support us," Ross said. "Or are there ways we could approach the Varnar?"

"We can certainly *try*," Kevin said. "There have to be quite a few Varnar who know they're being used, but don't know how to deal with it. I don't think there's anything particularly subtle in the proxy war. And the Varnar have definitely learned a few lessons from four hundred years of fighting."

"How true," Mongo agreed. "*They* wouldn't have let their guard down if they were patrolling a seemingly unoccupied system."

"The Varnar have strong ties to the galactic economy," Bute said. "They would have strong reasons to support the Tokomak in any case."

The President held up a hand. "Based on what we now know," he said, "do you have a plan?"

"Yes, Mr. President," Mongo said.

He activated the holographic display. A handful of stars appeared, blinking red.

"The Tokomak plan is to secure these stars and turn them into naval bases, then strike directly for Earth," he said. "It looks as if someone with more theoretical knowledge than experience came up with the plan, because the simplest way to achieve their objectives would be to charge straight towards Earth as soon as their battleships assemble at Varnar. To a layman, the plan blocks the Coalition from either helping us or continuing their war with the Varnar; to a spacer, the naval bases can simply be ignored. I suspect, however, that the Tokomak CO will be unable to change the plan, even if she realises how flawed it actually is.

"My intention is to raid those bases as soon as the advance elements arrive," he continued. "Their obsession with logistics puts *America* in the shade; they're sending hundreds of freighters as part of their fleet train, with millions of tons of supplies. Capturing or destroying those supplies will put a real crimp in their operations. Worse, they will have to retake those stars as quickly as possible or they'll look weak in the eyes of the galaxy."

"Or launch a thunderbolt towards Earth," Bute commented, sourly.

"It's one of our contingency plans," Mongo assured him. "We will meet their fleet in interstellar space and destroy it. They won't know what has hit them until it is far too late."

Ross frowned. "Are you sure this is workable?"

"I think we have no alternative," Mongo said. "They will either secure their naval bases and then advance, or – as the Councillor suggested – throw caution to the winds and advance anyway. The latter would definitely be the better option for them."

"I will be setting up a new intelligence base on Varnar and bringing in some of the resident assets," Kevin added. "We'll know when their main fleet arrives and is ready for deployment."

And see if we can rope Mr. Ando into helping us, he thought. *He clearly isn't backing the Tokomak.*

"Very well," Ross said. "How long would it take us to prepare?"

"Call up the reserves, prep the fleet, recall the merchant skippers... around three to four months," Mongo said. "The downside is that we would take an economic hit."

Kevin groaned, inwardly. The Solar Union had produced a class of small light freighters that could, with a little work, be converted into small warships. There were literally thousands of them plying the spaceways now, bringing human trade goods to the Galactics and obtaining samples of alien technology in return. But Mongo was right; if the crews and their ships were called home, as part of the Naval Reserve, the human race would suffer an economic downturn. Israel had suffered the same problem until the Middle East had collapsed into an orgy of bloodletting and mutual slaughter.

"We could take it," Marie said. "Most of our economy is not dependent on trade with the Galactics."

"True, but there would be headaches," Mongo said. "Thankfully, we're not dependent on the Galactics for anything other than intelligence."

"All of which leads us to a very different question," Ross said. "We have bent the rules almost to breaking point in keeping this a secret from the general population. Can we do that any longer?"

Mongo took a breath. "The moment we start debating the question of war," he said, "we run the risk of alerting the Galactics. There are no shortage of traders in the Sol System who will happily sell information to outsiders, particularly as we will no longer be trading with them. I would honestly prefer to keep it a secret as long as we could."

"But the news will leak," Marie countered, tartly. "The Naval Reserves being called up cannot be concealed, nor can the sudden shortage of freighters. A blogger or two will put it together soon enough, Admiral, and we cannot silence them all."

She was right, Kevin knew. The CIA had been able to wield *some* influence over the Mainstream Media on Earth – although sometimes the media had published anyway, often costing lives or valuable intelligence sources – but the Solar Union had no such power. Outside of libel or slander, there were no restrictions on press freedom in the Solar Union;

hell, he was mildly surprised someone hadn't put it together already. Or maybe they had and they were just keeping their mouths shut. It wouldn't have happened on Earth, of course, but the Solar Union produced a more responsible species of journalist.

Because they can be sued if they lie or misrepresent the truth, he thought. *And because reporters can genuinely be held to account.*

But they couldn't be here, he knew, because they *would* be reporting the truth. And the Solar Union was designed to avoid government secrecy, after all.

"So we put the issue before Congress," the President said. "And call for a general vote."

Bute coughed. "There will be quite a few willing to speak against war," he said. "Do you really want to take the risk they'd vote *no*?"

"There's no choice," the President said, sharply. "Launching an attack on a single cruiser is pushing my powers to the limit. Going on the offensive when the enemy isn't in the Solar System is well beyond them. Captains and crews will balk, Senator, and that will prove disastrous."

He took a breath. "Unless anyone has any strong objections," he said, "I will call for a joint meeting of Congress and the Senate two days from now."

"Make it three days," Marie advised. "You'll get the kids out of schooling for a day."

"Kids can't vote," Bute pointed out, sharply.

The President scowled at them both, then turned his attention to Mongo. "Admiral, I want a précis of the situation," he said. "We won't discuss the plan openly – everyone will understand that, I think – but we do need to convince them that the situation is dire enough to start a war."

"Yes, Mr. President," Mongo said.

Kevin understood the President's doubts. Even for the Solar Union's population, used to starships and asteroid settlements and the bounty of alien technology, it was hard to comprehend the sheer crushing power of the Tokomak, of a race that could soak up thousands of losses and just keep coming. Were they even imaginative enough to be scared? There was no way to know.

But their plan does show a certain level of imagination, he thought. *Crude and flawed, but imaginative.*

He shook his head. The Solar Union maintained a faith in its politicians that had long since faded from Earth, if only because no politician lasted long enough to go bad. Or so they hoped...would that faith survive, Kevin asked himself, the coming war? America had never really recovered after Nixon, or Carter, or Clinton. Bush and Obama had been either antichrists or messiahs, depending on who was asked. And the Presidents that had followed Obama had been dependent on a tottering political structure unable to adapt to the post-Contact world.

And Steve would have hated to watch the decline and fall of America, he thought. *Perhaps it's for the best he chose to leave. He might have been able to convince the Solar Union to intervene...*

Mongo poked him, non-too-gently. "Do you think we can put assets on Varnar to help make their lives miserable?"

"Probably, but not *that* miserable," Kevin said, hastily using his implants to replay the last few words of the conversation. Bute had been suggesting inserting SpecOps teams onto Varnar to cause trouble. "Their security isn't anything like as bad as it seems. I happen to know their military bases and government installations are very secure. We'd be doing nothing more than random terrorism."

"Then it remains out of the question," President Ross said, firmly. "See if you can find ways to cause trouble, Kevin, but I don't want a repeat of 9/11, let alone Oakland or San Diego."

"Yes, Mr. President," Kevin said.

"Assuming everything goes according to plan, we will open a War Cabinet to assume overall direction of the war," the President added. "This council will be wound down, the files sealed for the next one hundred years. And then, no doubt, we will be very embarrassed when the truth comes out."

Kevin smirked. One hundred years, on Earth, was long enough for everyone to be safely dead, but he was already pushing one hundred and the others weren't that far behind. The files would need to be secure for much longer...and would have been, if there weren't laws intended to prevent excessive government secrecy. Even one hundred years was pushing the envelope.

Steve would never have approved, he thought. *But then, Steve didn't know how to compromise either. He saw compromise as a dirty word.*

"By then, we will all be out of politics," Bute said. Politicians had somewhere between five to ten years in politics at the most. "We will be yesterday's news."

"And thank god for that," Marie snapped. "Do you know they ran a feature on what kind of bloody shoes I wear every day? Apparently, the economy rises and falls on what I happen to pick to wear on my feet!"

"It depends," Bute said. "How many pairs of shoes do you buy?"

"I could outfit everyone in my Canton with shoes," Marie said, "and I doubt it would cause more than a blip in the economy."

The President sighed. "I expect you all to take a role in presenting the case for war," he continued. "Unless you feel otherwise, in which case now would be a good time to say so."

"I don't like the idea of fighting an enemy so much stronger than ourselves," Bute said, "but I don't see that we have a choice. The Tokomak are unlikely to accept anything other than complete and unconditional surrender."

"If that," Kevin said.

He scowled in bitter memory. The Galactics had laws against genocide...but a handful of species *had* gone missing, over the centuries. Kevin had a private suspicion that the long-gone races had been seen as threats or potential challengers...and, as such, had been destroyed long before they could become dangerous. If the Galactics realised just how far humanity had advanced, after capturing a single ancient starship and her crew, they would probably start launching planet-busters at Earth.

Shame we can't get more of their records, he thought, *but most of the Tokomak archives are sealed, closed to anyone who isn't one of them. It might answer a few of our questions.*

The Tokomak Empire was ancient, by human standards; it had maintained itself and its culture for over four thousand years. No human polity had ever managed to keep itself in stasis for so long. But four thousand years – or *forty thousand* – was nothing compared to the life of the universe. It was generally estimated that the universe was over thirteen *billion* years old. There could have been thousands of empires on the same scale – or greater – in the period between the birth of the universe and the Tokomak.

They could have been the lucky ones who figured out the gravity drive, he thought. It wasn't unknown for races to trap themselves in a technological cul-de-sac, only to get an unpleasant surprise when they encountered their more advanced neighbours. *But over such a long space of time, is that even possible?*

He set the thought aside as the President dismissed the council, warning them all to be present at the joint assembly. Kevin groaned at the thought – his role wasn't a complete secret, but he preferred to stay out of the spotlight – then concentrated on planning ways to approach Mr. Ando. Or, perhaps, his assistant. Sally didn't have a security file, which suggested she was nothing more than what she seemed, a young human girl who had accepted a chance to live and work hundreds of light years from home.

But where, he asked himself, *would her loyalties lie?*

"This could be it," Mongo said. "Our very existence hanging by a thread."

Kevin sighed, inwardly. Steve and Mongo were very similar, even though neither of them would have admitted it. They would have been happier fighting beside Bowie and Travis at the Battle of the Alamo than negotiating a peace both sides could live with. There was, after all, something more dramatic about a desperate last stand than a peaceful talk at the negotiation table. Kevin had always been the odd one out, in many ways. Queen Elizabeth's observation that wars were chancy things had always resonated with him.

But sometimes the war had to be fought, because there was no hope of a reasonable compromise.

"Yeah," he said. "And let us pray we win, because defeat will be terrible."

TWENTY-FOUR

A student was arrested yesterday in Manchester, United Kingdom, for poisoning over four hundred of his schoolmates. According to his testimonial, published online, he was bullied from the day he set foot in the school until the day he dumped poison in the free school dinners. Seventy students have reportedly died, while the rest remain in critical condition. Speaking in Parliament, MPs condemned the easy availability of poison and vowed new legislation to ban its purchase by anyone without a licence.

—Solar News Network, Year 53

"Do you think we're allowed to talk about the...*incident*...now?"

"I don't think so," Yolanda said. "Didn't you get the same lecture?"

Martin nodded. Captain Lockland had lined up his Marines and told them, in no uncertain terms, that they weren't to breathe a word of their successful operation, on pain of being charged with High Treason and shot. He rather doubted the officer was joking, given just what they'd done. The Galactics could not be allowed to find out what had happened to their starship.

"So we keep our mouths shut," he said. "And vote, it would seem."

He shook his head in disbelief. Back in the ghetto, there was no such thing as public participation, unless it was in carefully-staged riots designed to pressure the politicians into sending more loot to the rulers. The community organisers delivered votes, on demand, to their friends in Washington; the fact that hardly anyone had bothered to vote was neither here nor there. But the Solar Union expected – it demanded – that it citizens play a part in governing themselves. Martin was still having problems trying to wrap his head around the concept.

The message had arrived two hours ago, informing them that a joint session of Congress and the Senate would be held, followed by a vote. There had been no declared subject, but after what they'd done, Martin was fairly sure it had something to do with the Tokomak. The government wouldn't have kidnapped an entire ship, along with its surviving crew, unless they had a long-term idea in mind. Unlike Earth, the Solar Union's politicians couldn't stand for re-election time and time again. They had some interest in doing the right thing.

"But we should hear the debates first," Yolanda said. "And then make up our minds."

Martin rolled his eyes. They were sharing a suite in the most expensive hotel on Gunn Asteroid – which wasn't saying very much – but their minds were elsewhere, drinking in the endless flow of information from the datanet. Martin found it more than a little scary, if he were forced to tell the truth; it was hard, sometimes, to know where he ended and the datanet began. He'd been told there were people who uploaded themselves into computer cores, becoming *Homo Electronic.* It sickened him – it seemed nothing less than a form of suicide – and yet he could see the attraction. What would he do to have a VR chamber of his own where his merest whim became reality?

But it wouldn't be real, he told himself. He could create a scenario where he had a harem, where the girls were all willing lovers, but it wouldn't be *real.* And yet, with direct feeds to his brain, would he know the difference? It was a terrifying thought. Someone could be hooked up to a machine and left to enjoy it, while their bodies wasted away in the real world. It was, he'd learned, how certain forms of mental disease were treated. But it was still sickening.

An alert flashed into his implants, informing him the debate was about to begin. He lay back on the bed, then accessed the government datanet. An illusion played into his mind, a giant impossibly-huge chamber where the politicians and their watchers sat together, ready to hear what the President had to say. There was no such chamber in the Solar Union, he knew, if only because the politicians rarely gathered in person. It was really nothing more than a perceptual reality, designed to allow people to believe they were truly participating.

He looked from side to side. Yolanda's avatar was nothing more than a representation of her true form, as was his own, but others were far less hesitant about presenting themselves as something they weren't. There were giant men, inhumanly beautiful women, countless people wearing avatars that belonged to fictional characters – he lost count of the number of people pretending to be Captain Picard, Harry Potter or Marian of Sherwood – and no shortage of outright monsters. It looked as though they couldn't have fitted into the chamber but it was just a perceptual reality. The chamber was as large as it needed to be.

A message popped up in front of him. *Hey, big boy*, it said. *Want to fuck?*

Piss off, Martin sent back, then blocked the sender. What was the *point* of having sex in a perceptual reality? Being able to do taboo acts wasn't worth the knowledge that it just wasn't *real*. Besides, there were few true taboos in the Solar Union and most of the population clung to the ones that remained. He didn't really want to spend time pretending he was something he wasn't, not when he could be having sex in real life. Or was it just another example of how humans constantly pushed the limits?

He shook his head, then looked back at Yolanda. Her avatar looked annoyed, which suggested she had received her fair share of unwanted propositions too. Martin wanted to hug her, to reassure her that everyone would be fine, but he couldn't find the words. Silence washed out a moment later, almost a physical effect, as the President appeared in the centre of the chamber. The magic of the perceptual reality made him seem as though he was also standing right next to Martin himself.

And what is the point of buying the best seats in the house, he asked himself, *if a perceptual reality can make it seem as though you're in the front row, or singing with the band?*

"Citizens of the Solar Union," the President said. "A major crisis has arisen in our affairs."

There was a long pause. Martin's implants reported files suddenly making themselves available to him. Side notes indicated that literally billions of downloads had been made within the first twenty seconds of availability. He copied the files to his implants, then pushed them to the rear of his awareness. They could wait until the President had finished speaking.

"Ever since the Foundation, we have known about the Tokomak – and the threat they might one day pose to us," the President continued. "The day we feared has come. They intend to wage war on us, until the human race is crushed into submission or destroyed. We have no choice, but to take the offensive and meet them in deep space."

He paused. Martin wondered if he was waiting for them to read the files.

"We have a plan, but we must act fast," the President concluded. "This is no time for half measures. We must gird our loins and commit ourselves to war.

"There are details I cannot share," he added. "They must not become known to the enemy ahead of time. And they will, if they are discussed in public. I ask for your trust and your confidence that we can win the war, that we can and should fight. I thank you."

He stepped down and waited. After a moment, another figure appeared in the centre of the room. An ID stream identified him as Senator Bin Elliot, a combination of names that could only have occurred in the Solar Union. The profile that popped into Martin's implants told him that the

Senator was only a third of the way into his sole term, but already known for being a strict Isolationist. He didn't want any further involvement with Earth, let alone the Galactics.

"The universe is a big place, Mr. President," he said. "I will not deny that the Tokomak have built themselves an impressive empire. I will not deny that they may pose a threat to us. But I do question the value of having us start a war with them, when there is plenty of room in the galaxy for *hundreds* of separate races. Let us withdraw our mercenaries from the Coalition and allow them to continue their war, as they have done for hundreds of years. We do not need to involve ourselves in their war."

There was a pause. "The fact remains," the President said, "that it takes two to make a peace, but only one to make a war. They have decided to make war on us. We do not get to tell them to piss off and go home" – a handful of chuckles ran through the chamber – "unless we give them enough of a black eye to make them think twice. They are unlikely to accept anything from us, unless it is unconditional surrender.

"We do not know what they would do to us, if we did surrender. They might treat us, to all intents and purposes, as a spacefaring race like the Varnar. We would be their servants, their slaves, but we would be alive. Or we might be ordered to return to the hellhole called Earth and shut down our space program. Or we might simply be destroyed.

"We are a disruptive race, Senator. Within fifty years of discovering the technology to venture out into the galaxy, we have upset quite a few apple carts. The endless Varnar-Coalition War may be coming to an end, because of us. The trading unions may be being undercut, because of us. And some of our technological improvements, based on their technology, may upset the whole galaxy. I am not sanguine about their treatment of us, once we surrender to them. They may simply destroy us, root and branch, breaking their own laws to get rid of a potentially fatal threat.

"Perhaps, if we had chosen isolation fifty years ago, and contented ourselves with destroying every Horde starship that visited Earth, this could have been avoided," he concluded. "But instead we chose to spread into the galaxy. And, in doing so, we eventually attracted attention from the so-called masters of the universe. They see us as a threat, Senator, one that they have to squash. There is no hope of peace *and* freedom, merely the peace of submission – or the grave."

It was a convincing argument, Martin knew...but he'd grown up in the ghetto, where the law of the jungle reigned supreme. Choosing not to fight, when challenged, wasn't an option. It was kill or be killed... and escape was impossible. The Tokomak would mistake an offer of peace for a sign of weakness and move as fast as they could to capitalise on it. They certainly wouldn't believe humanity was offering to talk peace out of *strength*.

But would it convince the others? He watched the live feed as pollsters kept trying to track the ebb and flow of the debate, tuning out the other candidates as he monitored the public reaction. It seemed hard to be sure which way the public would vote; unlike on Earth, where the polls were untrustworthy at best, the Solar Union kept flipping between peace or war. He couldn't help thinking that made their polls so much more reliable, but it was immensely frustrating. By the time the President called for the vote, dozens of politicians had had their say...while thousands of civilians had weighed in on the public networks. Some people were even posting tactical analysis statements, pointing out that the Tokomak outgunned humanity by a million to one...

Not everyone agrees, Martin thought. *They'd have to concentrate their ships in one place first, before taking the offensive. That would take years...*

"This is fascinating," Yolanda muttered to him, on a private messaging channel. "I could lose myself here."

"I think some people do," Martin said. His nanotech could keep him alive and healthy for years, if necessary. He could easily spend all of his time trying to keep up with discussions on a handful of online forums, if he wanted. But it wouldn't be real. "You'd lose your place on the ship."

"I know," Yolanda said. "But it might be something to do, later."

Martin swallowed. He honestly hadn't considered that Yolanda would leave the military, one day. She would, of course. She was smart and capable and, once she overcame her confidence problems, could probably find a job anywhere. He, on the other hand, was only good for fighting and fucking, perhaps not in that order. The Marines would be his home until his luck ran out and he died.

And he would miss her. He would miss her terribly.

"The vote has now been called," the President said. "Use a registered address to vote; unregistered addresses will simply be discarded. You have ten minutes to make your vote."

Martin nodded to himself as the icon popped up in his implants. It was a simple question, compared to the slips he'd been told about on Earth. A YES was a vote for war; a NO was a vote against war. But it was a false issue, Martin knew, as he cast a vote for YES. They would get the war if they wanted it, if they took the offensive, or not. The Tokomak wouldn't go away of their own accord.

Yolanda squeezed his hand – in real life, or the perceptual reality. He wasn't sure which.

"I voted," she said. "Would it have been better, on Earth, if we had this system?"

Martin shrugged. He'd been told, like most of the children raised in the ghetto, that the Evil White Man was bent on keeping the Noble Black Man down. It had been a surprise – although it shouldn't have been – to learn that white children were taught equally unpleasant things about black men, just to keep the fires of racial hatred burning nastily. Divide and rule, Scudder had said, and he'd been right. As long as White and Black hated one another with a passion, there was no hope of unification against the Government.

"I don't know," he said. The ghetto would have voted for race war, he was sure, and so would most of the whites. There would have been a bloody slaughter. "Maybe it can only work up here, where everyone draws a line between them and the past."

"The voting will close in one minute," an AI said. "You have one minute to cast your vote or you will be counted as having abstained."

"Should force people to vote," Yolanda muttered. "It would work."

Martin had his doubts. "People hate being forced to do something," he said. "And they might not bother to consider the issues."

"The voting is now closed," the AI said. "Seventy-two percent of cast votes are for war."

"Thank you," the President said. "And let us pray that we win the war."

Martin disengaged from the perceptual reality and crashed back into the hotel room. Yolanda lay on the bed, her body twitching slightly, as if she were in a coma. Martin shuddered at the sight – she looked dead, even though he knew she wasn't – and called room service. Even on Gunn Asteroid, it was possible to get good food if one had enough money.

He swore as a message popped up in his inbox. They were to return to the ship in five hours or be counted as deserters. Martin could guess why, too. If someone had ordered the attack on the Tokomak ship, they'd probably had war plans already drawn up, just waiting for the public to authorise them. Five hours...he hesitated, then sent a message to Yolanda. They could eat something nice, then run back to the ship. There was no time to remain immersed in the datanet.

"There will be war," Yolanda said. She sat upright, then smiled at him. "And I voted for it."

"So did" – Martin checked his implants to get the number – "over two billion other humans," Martin said. "I don't think you can blame this on you."

"I won't," Yolanda said. "Martin...are you scared?"

Martin blinked in surprise. In the ghetto – or the Marines, for that matter – it was a point of honour never to admit to being scared. Or to show any other sign of weakness, for that matter. If he'd ever shown the slightest hint of homosexuality, he would have been driven out of his home, no matter the lectures on tolerance he'd received at school. It was just the way things were, he'd thought at the time. Being interested in men was just another sign of weakness.

But two of the Marines are gay and no one gives a shit, he thought. *There are worse things out there than men who like men.*

"A little," he confessed.

He changed the subject, quickly. "I ordered food," he said. "It should be here in a few minutes."

Yolanda ignored him. "It just struck me," she said. "I could die in the war. We could both die in the war."

"Yes," Martin said. Hadn't she said something similar when she'd served on the jury? "It's a possibility."

"And I wouldn't have lived," Yolanda said. "I..."

"Now you're being silly," Martin said. "You were at your lowest ebb four years ago, but now you have a whole new life and a career. I bet none of your stepsisters have a hope of winning a place on a starship."

"I know," Yolanda said. "But I still feel rotten."

She leaned forward and kissed him. Martin jumped – she rarely showed any signs of physical affection – and then pulled back. His body reminded him, sharply, of just how long it had been since he'd slept with anyone, but he told that part of him to shut up.

"You don't have to do anything," Martin said. "I..."

"*Now* who's being silly?" Yolanda asked. "And I *want* to be normal."

And then she kissed him again, hard.

TWENTY-FIVE

The Heinlein Foundation filed suit in New York against Progressive Publishers, after they published an updated version of Heinlein's famous novel, Starman Jones. *The complaint attests that the 'updated' version not only destroys the soul of the book – the guild system is presented as reasonable – but adds sex scenes that were simply lacking from the original version. This bowdlerisation is particularly odd, the suit goes on to note, as the publishers also modified* Tess of the d'Urbervilles *to remove all references to rape.*

—Solar News Network, Year 53

"And there has been no report from *Supreme Flower of the Delicate Evening?*"

"No, Your Excellency," the Admiral said. "She has not returned from her mission."

"I see," Viceroy Neola said, coldly. "And the Captain was reliable?"

"His ship was decked out in her finery two years ago, for the grand parade," the Admiral insisted. "Her interior design even won first prize against very stiff competition. He is a reliable officer."

Neola looked down at the chart. Losing one ship wasn't a problem – she had hundreds on the way – but it was worrying. Had *Supreme Flower of the Delicate Evening* run into something her Captain couldn't handle…

or had she simply suffered a catastrophic failure? It happened, she knew, no matter how many precautions were taken. A starship went into deep space and never was seen again. But there were other possibilities, none of them good.

She shook her head, dismissing the thought. Who would dare attack a Tokomak cruiser?

"I want the first units to make their way to Hades at once," she ordered. "Do you have an updated ETA for the fleet?"

"Three months," the Admiral stated. "There have been…delays."

Neola clicked her fingers in irritation. It had been centuries since more than a handful of battleships had ventured out of the Core Worlds and made their way to the outer edge of the Empire. No one had seen any need to deploy more than a handful of smaller ships, not when they were capable of handling anything they might encounter along the Rim. Besides, the smaller powers, like the Varnar, could certainly hold the line against any new threat until the Tokomak could respond. But it meant there were a whole series of problems in getting the fleet to move through the gravity points to Varnar.

"Tell them to expedite their departure," she said. The last fleet review had been magnificent, full of pomp and circumstance. Thousands of starships, an unforgettable display of wealth and power, had paraded over the Homeworld, showing off their might to the universe. But why were they having so many problems reaching the Rim? "And the fleet train?"

"It should be ready for deployment within a month," the Admiral said. "The Varnar have also requested a considerable amount of resources."

"Put their request at the back," Neola ordered. "They can wait until we've dealt with their upstart race, these *humans*."

She looked up at him. "Have you prepared the formal demand for Earth?"

"Yes, Your Excellency," the Admiral said. "It will give them the choice between submission or inevitable defeat."

"Then send it," Neola ordered.

She paced around the giant room until she came to the window and looked out over Varnar City. The Varnar didn't know it, but she had orders about them too. Once the humans were gone, once the Coalition had been brought to heel, the Varnar would also be forced under the yoke. There was no alternative. They had proved incompetent as a proxy race, unable to handle a challenge from a bunch of upstarts, and so they had to go. She would rule the sector in their place and then...

The holographic star chart winked at her. There were countless stars beyond the rim of explored space, holding...who knew *what* they held? Once the war was over, she would find out and then embark upon a new war of conquest. And then...

She clicked her fingers, smiling unpleasantly. The Old Ones would be unable to deny her anything, once she'd made them the masters of a far larger empire.

"THEY'RE KEEPING US away from the Tokomak ships," Captain Sadie Justinian observed. "I think they're worried about spies."

"Then they're doing it wrong," Kevin grunted, as the *Kirk's Dirk* slipped into orbit around Varnar. "Everyone with a passive sensor can see their ships sitting in orbit. And they're already in weapons range of the orbital fortresses."

The formation looked impressive, he had to admit, but no human commander would have risked a handful of heavy cruisers in trying to emulate the Red Arrows. Hell, he wouldn't have risked a handful of *gunboats*. Kevin had the uneasy feeling that, if the Tokomak were called upon to manoeuvre suddenly, their ships would actually have *collided* with one another, something that rarely happened outside movies where the scriptwriter was more interested in exploding starships than reality.

"They're definitely impressive," Sadie said, after a moment. "But are they anything else?"

"Probably not," Kevin said. "Call the people on the surface and see if you can get us somewhere to stay for a few days. The Tokomak can take care of themselves."

"Aye, sir," Sadie said. "Do you have anywhere in particular you happen to want?"

"Somewhere secure, but not too secure," Kevin said. Officially, they were selling Tendon Bolts, spare parts that were only used by bulk freighters or small warships. There would be some time, he was sure, before they actually managed to sell them all, giving him and his team plenty of time to find somewhere else to hide. "And send the pre-recorded message to the embassy."

He sighed, then walked down to the team compartment and nodded to the small group of operatives. Chester had been joined by Flies, another Hordesman; the remainder were all human, as before. Kevin waited until the Captain had confirmed they would have a place to stay, then led the way to the teleport chamber. When they materialised on the planet, they found themselves in a giant warehouse with direct links to the spaceport and the city itself.

"Make sure everything is secure," Kevin said. The Galactic traders were quite prepared to spy on their fellow traders, if only to see what they were bringing to Varnar and planning to undercut them in the local markets. "And clear out any bugs you find."

"Yes, sir," Julian said. "You want to cosy up to the local criminals?"

"Probably not," Kevin said. He'd used criminal contacts before; some tended to be honourable, but others suffered from unexpected bouts of patriotism or would simply sell out the intelligence agents for money. "I think we'd better remain as simple, unassuming traders until it's too late."

He watched the team do their job, then walked up to the living quarters. As he'd expected, they were dirty, grimy and unsuitable for prisoners on death row. Shaking his head at the sight, he moved back downstairs and linked his implants to the nearest processor node, then sent his message to Sally. He'd just have to wait and see if she responded. It was quite possible that she was reluctant to become attached to anyone – after all, she never knew when she would see him.

And what, he asked himself, *do her feelings matter? You're gathering information to use against the Galactics*.

The reply arrived two hours later, while he was in the middle of scrubbing the living quarters into something reasonably clean. It was simple and straight to the point; Sally invited him to her apartment, as soon as he could make it. Kevin's eyes narrowed; it was the middle of the local day and, unless there was something else going on, she should be at work. But there was no point in refusing to go. Instead, he spoke quickly to Julian and then walked to the nearest teleport hub. The team would know something was wrong if he didn't check in within the hour.

Sally had moved apartments, he noticed, when he arrived and made his way up the stairs. It was quite possible she was being paid more, he decided, or that she'd been promoted...if intelligence brokers saw fit to promote their assistants. Or she could have saved up...he pushed the thought out of his head and touched the pistol at his belt, then knocked loudly on the door. His most dangerous weapons were implanted under his skin, but if someone was trying to kidnap him, they might think there were no implants if he was carrying a pistol...

The door opened, revealing a business office and Sally, sitting on the far side of a desk.

"Please, be seated," she said. The door hissed closed and locked behind Kevin as soon as he stepped inside. "This room is completely secure."

Kevin gave her a long considering look. "*How* secure?"

"We can keep out everyone," Sally said. "Please, take a seat."

"Thank you," Kevin said.

He sat down, using his implants to test the room's security. No processor responded to his pings, while a static field made it difficult for him to send a message outside the walls. If there were any bugs hidden within the room, it should be impossible for them to pick up anything. Or so he hoped. He knew, all too well, that human surveillance and counter-surveillance technology was advancing by leaps and bounds.

"I wasn't too surprised to hear from you," Sally said. She gave him a thin smile, which became wider as he smiled back. "Can we talk bluntly?"

"We can try," Kevin said, carefully.

"Mr. Ando says you're a spy," Sally said. "You're working for Human Intelligence."

Kevin felt an odd sense of...*wrongness*, the sense of suddenly being naked in public. It had happened once, during one of his early missions; his cover had been broken and it had almost got him killed. If Sally knew who he was, Mr. Ando probably knew who he was too...and then...who knew what would happen? His implants flickered to full alert, ready to bust out of the room and flee...

Angrily, he damped them down. There was no threat. Not yet.

"I can't answer that question," he said, finally.

"You're from the Stuart Family," Sally said. "Mr. Ando identified you. I don't think you'd be buying vital intelligence if all you were doing was bumming around in an aging freighter, trying to sell Maple Syrup to the locals. He doesn't think so either."

"I see," Kevin said. "And is there a reason for...tugging off my cover in public?"

"This isn't public," Sally said. She leaned forward, placing her hands on the desk. "Mr. Ando wishes, completely off the record, to assist you in your work."

Kevin's eyes narrowed. "Why?"

"There are reports that the Tokomak don't plan to merely restore the pre-humanity *Status Quo*," Sally said. "They plan to take over the entire sector. The Varnar will merely be the last to be forced to submit to them. This will be fatal for everyone."

"I would agree with that," Kevin said. The Coalition – and the economy Earth had tapped into – only existed because it was close enough to the Tokomak to draw on their technology without attracting their attention. They'd been content to let the proxy war splutter on without attempting to intervene, on one side or the other. But now..."They don't want the Varnar growing too powerful."

"That was our conclusion too," Sally said. "We believe that some officers in the Varnar Navy may share it."

She met his eyes. "Mr. Ando has an offer for you," she said. "He will give you intelligence…and access to sources you would probably be unable to match, including several at the highest levels of the military. Some of them are even *Tokomak.*"

Kevin blinked. "They are?"

"They seem to have problems grasping the fact that younger races can actually hurt them," Sally admitted. "With the right level of access, you can pull quite a bit from their datacores."

"I suppose you could," Kevin said, carefully. Inside, his thoughts were racing. The right level of access…? Did Mr. Ando know what had happened to the *Supreme Flower of the Delicate Evening*? There was no way he could ask. "And what would Mr. Ando like in return?"

"In the event of you winning the war, Mr. Ando would appreciate it if you left his organisation strictly alone," Sally said. "There will be no further charge provided you allow him to continue to work in the field he loves. If you lose the war, of course, there will be no charge."

"Of course," Kevin agreed, dryly. "It wouldn't be easy drawing any money from a radioactive pile of ash."

"No," Sally said. She reached into her pocket and produced a handful of datachips. "As a gesture of good faith, these are the latest reports on the planned deployment. I say planned because there have been delays in actually sending the starships to Varnar. There are also other pieces of intelligence, all of which might be helpful to you. You can have all of this, free of charge."

Kevin thought, rapidly. Mr. Ando certainly had good reason to want the current *status quo* to continue, if only because one side coming out ahead would make it harder for him to play both ends against the middle. But the Tokomak wouldn't allow him to continue his work, no matter how useful he could be. Kevin had seen reports from societies the Tokomak controlled, where everyone knew their place and no one was allowed to try to shape their own destiny. Mr. Ando would probably find himself hauled off to a re-education camp or simply executed if he didn't abandon his business.

And he can't abandon it, Kevin thought. *It's practically his life.*

The alternative, of course, was that it was a trap. Mr. Ando could be supplied with false information by the Tokomak and told to pass it to humanity. The information could then lure the Solar Union into making deadly mistakes. All hell could break loose – the war could be lost – because Kevin believed what he was given. The prior information – the reliable information – could merely have been gravy to ensure he swallowed the false information, when the shit hit the fan.

Intelligence work, Kevin reminded himself. There were times when he understood why both Steve and Mongo disdained the spooks. They were, alarmingly often, wrong with confidence. *There's no way to take anything for granted.*

"It sounds like quite an offer," he said. "Do you believe Mr. Ando is doing the right thing?"

Sally met his eyes. "What will the Tokomak do to Earth if they win?"

"Destroy the entire planet," Kevin said, keeping his voice even. "The human race will be wiped out, or reduced to handful of people like yourself."

"Then yes, he *is* doing the right thing," Sally said. "But there are *hundreds* of warships coming your way."

"So there are," Kevin said. He took the datachips and pocketed them, then gave her another smile. "Can we go eat somewhere?"

"Tell me something," Sally said. "Did you try to seduce me so I could become one of your sources?"

Kevin hesitated, then picked his words very carefully. "I am always interested in meeting new people, particularly ones with such interesting life stories," he said. "But I believe you seduced me, rather than the other way round."

Sally coloured. "But you were definitely available..."

"Would you have gone to bed with just anyone," Kevin asked, "if he happened to be human?"

"I would like to think otherwise," Sally said. "But being so alone here doesn't really make it easy to resist."

"You could buy a sexbot," Kevin said. "I hear they can be either male or female now, with the right modifications."

"They're not human," Sally said. She shook her head. "It's silly, you know. I work beside creatures who are utterly indifferent to me as a person. The Galactics think of me as a particularly well-trained dog – a doggie running errands for its master. And yet there are times when I grow so desperate for someone who will understand me. Does that make sense?"

"Yes," Kevin said. He forced down a flash of guilt. It would hardly be the first time he'd manipulated someone into betraying their masters – and besides, Sally's master *wanted* to help the human race. But at the same time, it still felt wrong. Steve and Mongo would have been united in their disapproval. "I do understand being lonely."

He smiled at her. "You could probably write a book, afterwards," he added. "A tell-all that tells all."

"That's terrible," Sally said.

She looked down at the desk. "No more lies, all right?"

"I'll do my best," Kevin said. "But there are things I can't share with you."

He sighed, inwardly. Being able to talk to Sally openly would be helpful – more than helpful. But it would also put her life in danger and risk the entire operation...he'd have to speak to Julian, then get him and the team to move their location. Perhaps even go back to Earth, if he'd been tagged. The team would be safer without him.

"I understand," Sally said. She looked up at him. "And yes, I need a drink after this."

"There's no percentage in shipping in alcohol," Kevin observed. Finding trade goods was always a problem. In some ways, that was a blessing. Earth wasn't important enough for the galactic traders to really start eying the Sol System with covetous eyes. "Not to here, in any case."

"No," Sally agreed. "Only three races enjoy human alcohol. That we know about, at least. I bet there are others."

"You could probably find out," Kevin said. The SIA would want Sally – she had a great deal of experience – but so would the interstellar corporations. "And I think you will do fine in the future."

"If the human race survives," Sally said. "If."

She stood. "Come on," she said. "You owe me that drink."

TWENTY-SIX

A number of paintings were stolen from the Louvre Museum, Paris, by a group called the Sons of Bonaparte. In their statement, uploaded to the datanet along with images of the stolen paintings, the criminals assert that the paintings will not be returned until France has cleansed itself of immigrants. The French President has stated, in response, that France will not bow down to terrorists and that the paintings will be recovered shortly. However, outside observers question the ability of the French Government to do anything as the political paralysis enters its fifth year…

—Solar News Network, Year 53

"Well," Admiral Mongo Stuart said. "That's us told."

"Yes, sir," Commodore Gordon Travis agreed. They sat together in his office, on *Freedom*. "They're quite determined to have us submit."

He looked down at the datapad displaying the Tokomak ultimatum. If it had been printed out, he calculated mentally, it would have taken over two hundred pages, mostly wasted on fluff about the glory of the Tokomak Empire and the historical inevitability of human submission. It had taken a team of analysts two days to boil the message down to something more understandable, although Gordon felt the effort had been wasted. All the flowery language in the universe couldn't change the fact that the message was nothing more than 'submit or die.'

"And they don't have their fleet in place to threaten us," he said, slowly. "Did they think we would surrender to their courier boat?"

"I imagine so," Admiral Stuart said. He looked up at the star chart. "Is your task force ready to move?"

"Just about, sir," Gordon assured him. "We should have enough firepower to smash Hades and capture their supplies, then bug out the moment they send reinforcements."

"The War Cabinet agrees," Admiral Stuart said. "We're not going to surrender to mere threats, Commodore."

Gordon nodded, relieved. "When is their main fleet expected to arrive?"

"Around three weeks, allowing for timing problems," Admiral Stuart said. "They've already been delayed twice."

"I see," Gordon said. He shook his head in disbelief. "Shouldn't they have waited for the fleet before sending ultimatums?"

"Probably," Admiral Stuart agreed. "But most of the Galactics are hypnotized by the sheer number of enemy ships. They would roll over if threatened, I suspect, instead of trying to call the Tokomak bluff."

"We should take the offensive right into their territory," Gordon said. "Hit their vast fleet of ships in the reserve before they even have a chance to power up the drives, let alone assign crewmen and commanders. We could win the war in an afternoon."

"It was considered," Admiral Stuart said. "But it would be too far to send a task force, I think. They would know we were coming and take precautions – or simply hurl the rest of their forces in this sector at Earth. We'd be in deep trouble."

"Yes, sir," Gordon said.

"Besides, this way, they have to spread out their manpower to activate the ships," Admiral Stuart added. "Smashing unmanned ships in the reserve will force them to commit all of their manpower to active ships, which might help them to overcome their problems."

"We shall see," Gordon said. "Do you want a tour of *Freedom* before we depart?"

"I don't think the crew would appreciate having to stop their work just to honour me," Admiral Stuart said. "I always hated inspections when I was in the infantry.

Gordon smiled. The Admiral hadn't forgotten what it was like to be a junior officer – or to be on the sharp end of modern war. On the other hand, much of his experience was essentially worthless in space combat...he sighed, then pushed the thought aside. The Admiral had built the Solar Navy up from literally nothing, first by obtaining alien starships and then by spearheading humanity's own shipbuilding efforts. He deserved respect for his work.

"I understand," he said. He made a show of glancing at his watch. "We will depart within the hour, sir."

"Good," Admiral Stuart said. "Don't screw up, Gordon. Victory will give us a chance of survival, but defeat means near-complete extinction."

"We won't fuck up," Gordon assured him. He held out a hand for the Admiral to shake. "We'll be back before you know it."

It wouldn't be that simple, he knew, as the Admiral shook his hand and then departed the compartment, heading for the teleport chamber. There was a minimum of two weeks to Hades, even using the most advanced stardrives in the galaxy, then another minimum of two weeks *back* to Earth...which meant, if the Tokomak decided to change their plan and launch a direct assault on Earth, his task force would be out of place. If only they'd been able to launch the operation sooner...but there had been too much to do. No one had called a full mobilisation of the Solar Navy, let alone the Naval Reserve, ever since the Solar Union had been founded. Unsurprisingly, there had been no shortage of glitches in the system.

And complaints from people who stand to lose money, he thought, as he glanced back at the ultimatum. *They'll lose a great deal more once they surrender to the Tokomak.*

Shaking his head, he turned back to his work. There was simply too much paperwork to do before the squadron left Earth…and fired the first shot in the war.

— —

"VERY WELL DONE, Ensign," Commander Gregory said.

"Thank you, Commander," Yolanda said. The tactical section wasn't her favourite, but she could handle it. "I hope the real enemy are as easy to shoot as those pirates."

"We are about to find out," Commander Gregory reminded her. "You'll be going back to the helm for the operation, Ensign, but I want you to keep working on your tactical simulations. You won't get promoted without it."

Yolanda nodded, silently, as the Commander turned and strode out of the compartment, then allowed herself a moment to relax. After the decision to go to war, the Solar Union had turned into a demon, as far as she could tell. Every fabricator and production plant had been converted to support the war effort, while almost every starship in the fleet had been turned into a warship. Some of the news reports she'd been following, in her few moments of spare time, claimed that the Solar Union was even providing advanced weapons to Earth, although she doubted the reports were true. Earth's governments would sooner turn advanced weaponry on each other – or the Solar Union – rather than the aliens.

You'd think they'd know better, she thought. *It wasn't that long since the Horde bombarded Earth.*

She shook her head, then checked her schedule. There were quite a few other tasks to complete before the squadron departed, some of which had been assigned to her. It was the responsibility she'd always wanted and dreaded, even though she was no longer on Earth, where few people dared to take a decision for fear of punishment. Her stepmother had certainly believed in not allowing Yolanda any latitude, no matter how insane it had been…

And Commander Gregory isn't your stepmother, she told herself firmly, as she walked out of the compartment. *She may disagree with what you've done, when she inspects it, or she may chew you out, but she won't make you feel worthless.*

She ducked to one side as a team of Marines ran past, chanting as they jogged through the compartment. The Marines onboard, according to Martin, had been reinforced for the operation, which meant that half of them had to sleep in the hold rather than Marine Country. He had asked, only partly in jest, if he could share her cabin, which might have been easier than sharing with the rest of his platoon. Yolanda had laughed, then pointed out his CO would probably have been upset. Martin had, reluctantly, agreed.

And it would have been harder for us to go our separate ways in the morning, she thought, tartly. *And one of us might not survive the coming mission.*

— —

MARTIN BARELY NOTICED the moment *Freedom* and her consorts slipped into FTL. His gaze was firmly fixed on the holographic chart of Hades, the coming battleground, as the intelligence officer went through what little the human race knew about the alien complex. It was strikingly similar to some of the bases Martin had seen on Mars, in many ways, but in others it just looked inefficient. Wouldn't it be easier, he asked himself, to keep the supplies in orbit?

It would definitely make sense, he thought. A single antimatter missile detonating in space would be bad, but not unmanageable. If it detonated on a planet's surface instead, even a worthless piece of rock like Hades, the devastation would be terrifying. The bombardment of Earth would be nothing compared to the destruction of an entire naval base. Hell, if there was enough antimatter on the planet's surface, the blast would crack the planet in two.

"You will notice that most of their supplies are stored in the dumps here, here and here," the intelligence weenie said, tapping the chart. "We believe they actually land their freighters here" – he tapped another location on the chart – "then transport the supplies into the dumps and hold them for further deployment. Quite why they do it this way is a mystery."

He paused for effect. "The base is defended by a number of automated weapons platforms, in orbit, and a handful of small PDCs, positioned around the complex," he added. "Taking out the former, along with the defending squadron, will be the Navy's task, but the latter will be our problem. Stealth missiles will do what they can, but we may have to storm the PDCs and suppress them before the freighters can land.

"We don't know how many troops the enemy have positioned on the ground, but we find it hard to believe the dump doesn't have at least a small security force assigned to it. There are several buildings that might well be barracks..."

Martin sighed as the intelligence officer droned on. One thing they had learned about the Tokomak – he assumed from the captured starship – was that they were having manpower problems. It was hard, nearly impossible, to get volunteers for the space fleet, let alone the Tokomak groundpounders. They were probably far too used to a life of luxury, Martin speculated; on Earth, the military had been largely manned by the poor and downtrodden, rather than the ultra-wealthy. But two-thirds of the Solar Marines came from the Solar Union, where – with a little bit of effort – they could have earned themselves lives of peaceful luxury. Their lives could be extended indefinitely.

And they chose to give it up and fight beside the rest of us, he thought. *Why didn't they stay where they were?*

He thought he understood, even though it was an alien concept. They were patriots, loyal to a society that was loyal to them; indeed, they were truly part of their society in a way he'd never been part of the United States of America. No one had ever asked him, back on Earth, if he'd wanted American troops sent to Cuba, South Africa or even Iran. Hell, no one had ever asked his opinion on *anything*. But the Solar Union had wanted him to vote.

"I trust you were all paying attention," Major Lockland said, once the intelligence officer had finished talking. Martin, who knew there would be copies of the briefing available online, made a mental note to go over it in cynical detail later. "The operation will be carried out as follows."

His gaze swept the room. Martin thought he knew what he was thinking. There was no deadweight here, not in the Solar Marines. Everyone, even the intelligence weenie, was armed and ready to go to war. Martin had once been told, during training, that there had been militaries where 90% of the manpower was nothing more than support staff for the 10% who did the actual fighting. It had proven a deadly mistake, if only because the tail had begun to wag the dog. The Solar Marines were determined not to make the same mistake. Even their logistics officers were expected to drop with the rest of the company.

"We will be launching missiles at the PDCs," Major Lockland said. "After that, we will drop from orbit. Our particular responsibility will be Dump #2. The other units will be tasked with taking and holding the other dumps; naturally, I expect us to have our dump secured first."

He smiled, then went on. "1st and 2nd Platoons will be responsible for crushing the remains of the PDCs, assuming they survive the missile strikes. 3rd and 4th Platoons will be charged with securing the dumps; 5th and 6th Platoons will secure the spaceport and capture as many grounded freighters as possible. Our designated reserve, 3rd Platoon, 4th Company, will provide fire support and a reserve on the ground, if necessary. We will hopefully be able to call on firepower from orbit, but it depends on how the battle goes.

"We believe" – he nodded towards the intelligence officer – "that most of their manpower on the ground is actually composed of client races, slaves in all but name. Try to take as many of them alive as possible, but remember that some of them will be loyal to their masters, even if they are treated worse than shit. If they want to come with us, and we have the lift to take them, we will give them a chance to settle in the Solar Union. The remainder will be given life support packs and told to wait for the Tokomak."

"They'll come with us, surely," Private Abdul said. "The Tokomak will blame them for the disaster."

"They might not," Martin said, before he could stop himself. "People sometimes prefer to remain in misery rather than take a chance on finding something better."

Abdul turned to stare at him. He wasn't the only one. "Why?"

Martin hesitated, struggling to put it into words. It wasn't something the Solar Union's citizens would understand, not really. Their society allowed someone to vote with their feet; if someone didn't like their Canton, they could simply go elsewhere. This fundamental right was part of their society, a society that had more than enough room for everyone. Hell, if someone really hated the rest of the Solar Union, they could even set up an asteroid home of their own. But on Earth...

"It's a very human attitude," he said. "Someone becomes downtrodden enough, they stop thinking that life can become better. They stay with abusive partners, maybe because they've been twisted to the point they actually think their partners love them. Or they stay and wallow in shit because they don't think there's anything better. It takes drive and determination to escape on Earth..."

He hesitated, again. "Because even being abused and enslaved is a kind of safety," he added, although he wasn't sure if he was right. "They know their place and they will stick to it, because they feel safe there."

"That's absurd," Abdul said.

"But very human," Major Lockland said. He cleared his throat. "We will, of course, be running simulations over the next two weeks. However, each of those simulations will be different, because we cannot afford to become complacent. Hades is going to become an important naval base, as far as the Tokomak are concerned, and they may have moved other unpleasant surprises to the targeted world. We must assume the worst."

Martin nodded. He'd done live combat drops over Mars, as part of the later stage of his training, and he knew – all too well – just how easy it was to fuck up, even if someone did everything right. A single ground-based weapon, even a cutting laser, could slice a Marine in half, while plasma cannons or heavy phase cannons could vaporise their targets. No matter their best efforts to remove random chance from the deployment, it might easily prove their nemesis. They would have to plan and practice on the assumption that half the company wouldn't make it to the surface.

And we might lose our commanders too, Martin thought. They'd run simulations where the Major and his Lieutenants were knocked out of commission and they'd always been near-disasters, even if the senior Marine took command at once. *This time, we won't be facing holographic weapons. We'll be facing real foes.*

"A question," Private Atkinson said. "Are they preparing for war?"

"They haven't been attacked in thousands of years," the intelligence officer said. "We believe they honestly won't consider that we might take the offensive. However, they may be taking standard precautions anyway."

"So we might catch them with their pants down or they might greet us with a hail of fire," Private Atkinson said. "They would see us coming, wouldn't they?"

"Yes," the intelligence officer said. "There's no way we can obscure our FTL signature. Unless they were literally asleep at the switch, Private, they'd know we were on our way."

Martin sucked in his breath. Depending on just how good their sensor gear was, the Tokomak would have at least an hour's warning before the fleet arrived. Time enough, he was sure, to send a courier for help and prepare defences…and then to prepare to blow up their own dumps, if necessary. It was what *he* would have done.

And we're going down there, he thought, morbidly. They'd simulated raids on terrorist bases and half of them had ended with the base blown up and everyone dead. *It won't be fun at all.*

He rose as the Major dismissed his men, with strict orders to review the data and prepare themselves for simulations. There was just time, he fancied, to find Yolanda and talk to her, before he had to get some sleep. Tomorrow was going to be a very busy day.

TWENTY-SEVEN

Protest marches in almost every western capital took place today, protesting against the Solar Union's decision to declare war on the Galactics. Protest leaders denounced the Solar Union as galactic-sized warmongers and demanded that Earth be specifically excluded from any declaration of war. There were incidents in several cities where protestors attempted to storm Solar Union Embassies, only to be stunned or killed by armed guards. In a statement issued shortly after the first protest, President Ross of the Solar Union reminded Earth that the Solar Union would defend its territory, even against rioting crowds.

—Solar News Network, Year 53

"Ten minutes to emergence," Yolanda said.

"Hold us steady," Captain Singh ordered, calmly. There was no hint of tension in his voice. "Take us out at the designated emergence point."

"Yes, sir," Yolanda said. She didn't have much to do – the planned emergence point was programmed into the computers – but she knew she might have to override them, if something went wrong. Or if the Commodore decided to alter their destination, for some reason known only to himself. "We're holding steady."

The timer slowly ticked down to zero. The Tokomak would know they were coming, her thoughts yammered at her, even if they wouldn't know the exact emergence point. If they had, the humans would have blundered right into an ambush, assuming the Tokomak officers had enough initiative to set up a trap without waiting for orders from Varnar first. But it didn't change the fact that they would *know* the fleet was inbound. They had had plenty of time to call their crews to battlestations, charge their weapons and devise a handful of contingency plans.

"Emergence in thirty seconds," she said. The final seconds ticked down. "Five seconds...*emergence*."

Freedom shivered, slightly, as she slid back into normal space. Yolanda plunged her mind into the sensors and saw the stars reappear, while the dirty brown world of Hades lay ahead of them, surrounded by enemy starships. Most of them were freighters, she noted, although twelve of them were definitely heavy cruisers. The warships were assembling themselves into formation, but slowly, *far* too slowly. It was strange to see how pitifully slow the Tokomak were at adapting to the unexpected. How the hell had they managed to conquer an unimaginably-large empire in the first place?

"Enemy ships are signalling us, telling us to break off," Commander Gregory said. A dull rustle of amusement echoed round the bridge. "This is Tokomak territory."

"Demand their surrender," Commodore Travis ordered, through the datanet. "And then prepare to attack."

The Tokomak didn't bother to respond, Yolanda noted, as the two fleets converged with terrifying speed. She wasn't surprised; all the reports, garnered from the captured starship, had suggested that the Tokomak were convinced beyond all reason that *no one* could match them in space combat. There was something elegant and fluid about their formation, she had to admit, that spoke of long practice, but would it translate into being able to fight properly?

"One enemy ship is heading away from the planet," the sensor officer cautioned. "Her flight path puts her on a direct course for Varnar."

"Five days round trip," the Captain mused. "We have that long to strip the planet of everything useful and then withdraw."

Unless they go directly for Earth instead, Yolanda thought. *Would they even know we were humans if we managed to prevent them seeing us?*

She dismissed the thought as the Tokomak craft lunged forward, still holding their formation as they advanced towards the human ships. Flickers of data popped up in her mind as sensors probed the enemy fleet, noting prospective strengths and weaknesses. She couldn't help mentally comparing them to the lone ship they'd ambushed, noting how their shields were stronger, their weapons were fully charged and their sensors were at full power. Not that they really *needed* them, she considered. The human squadron wasn't trying to hide its presence.

"Enemy fleet is locking weapons on our hull," Commander Gregory reported. "They're preparing to fire."

"Evasive action," the Captain ordered. "Open fire on the Commodore's command."

Yolanda smiled to herself as she pulled *Freedom* into a series of random evasive patterns, each one confusing to a race that had only known simulations and drills for over a thousand years. To the Tokomak, she reflected, the human formation must look ungainly, as if they weren't concerned with appearances at all. But what did appearances matter in a test of strength? The Tokomak ships looked beautiful, like something out of a pre-space science-fiction movie series, but could they fight? She had a feeling they were about to find out.

Alerts flared up in her mind as the Tokomak opened fire. Bolts of light flashed through space, most missing by miles. A handful of shots struck their targets, allowing the analysis sections to study them. Their conclusions, flashed through the datanet seconds later, indicated that the Tokomak weapon were very variable.

"Return fire," Commander Gregory ordered.

The human ships opened fire, hammering the Tokomak shields. Yolanda kept her ship spinning though evasive patterns, dodging most of the fire aimed at her hull, while the gunnery crews bombarded the

Tokomak ships relentlessly. Despite the sheer level of firepower they possessed, the Tokomak were simply not very good shots – or, she realised slowly, had no practice fighting an unpredictable battle. Their evasive patterns were slow and predicable, as if they'd been crafted out before weapons had become so deadly.

"Launch torpedoes," Commander Gregory said, as the two fleets converged. The Tokomak seemed dazed, pressing in together as if they were seeking strength in numbers. "Fire at will."

Freedom jerked as she unleashed a spread of torpedoes, aimed right towards the Tokomak formation. Four of the torpedoes, their courses far too predictable, were picked off by the enemy ships, the remainder reached attack range and detonated, sending streams of deadly light towards their targets. The old concept of bomb-pumped lasers, so successful in battle against the Horde, had been intensely modified. Now, instead of nukes, the torpedoes projected the force of an antimatter warhead, compressed down into a needle of irresistible power. Two Tokomak ships were blown apart instantly, their hulls vaporising into nothing before they could start launching lifepods; three more were knocked right out of formation, one of them actually colliding with an intact starship, blowing both into balls of plasma.

I wouldn't have believed it if I hadn't seen it, Yolanda thought. *No one would be stupid enough to accidentally ram another starship…*

"Repeat the surrender demand," the Commodore ordered. "Tell them we will take prisoners and treat them honourably."

The Tokomak either didn't get the message or didn't believe it, because they kept firing. One ship broke free of the formation and dropped into FTL before anyone could intervene, while the remaining ships pushed forward, as if they thought they could catch the human ships and destroy them. But it was pointless, Yolanda saw; the Tokomak simply weren't prepared for a modern war. Their ships were so slow and cumbersome it was painful to watch, while the human ships could turn on a dime. They didn't have a hope of breaking free or destroying their enemies before it was too late.

"Launch a second spread of torpedoes," the Commodore said. "Take them out."

Yolanda altered course, just long enough to allow Commander Gregory to launch a broadside. They'd been warned to conserve torpedoes as much as possible, simply because the production process was slow, utterly unable to keep up with demand. It wouldn't do to vaporise the entire enemy squadron if they didn't have the weapons necessary to defend Earth, let alone take the war to the Tokomak.

But there was no time to waste, not any longer.

"One enemy craft has dropped her shields to offer surrender," Commander Gregory reported, sharply. "The remainder have been destroyed."

"Order a team of Marines to board the alien craft," Captain Singh said. "Inform them to handle the Tokomak gently, unless they offer resistance."

Yolanda felt an odd moment of respect for the Tokomak commander. Dropping shields was the universal signal of surrender, yet – in the midst of a battle – it was quite possible that the ship would be blown apart before anyone realised she had been trying to surrender. And God alone knew what his crew, who moments ago had been absolutely in command of the situation, would make of the order to surrender. Would they accept it without further demur or would they try to harm the Marines? Would *Martin* be at risk, if he was one of the Marines boarding the ship?

"Take us towards the planet," the Captain ordered. "Prepare to clear the Orbital Weapons Platforms."

"Aye, sir," Yolanda said.

Hades grew rapidly larger in her mind as *Freedom* raced towards the planet. It was a rocky airless world, useless for anything. Even a large-scale terraforming project would have been unable to make anything of Hades, according to the briefing notes. The world was just so completely dead it didn't have an atmosphere. But the Tokomak had found a use for it, she knew, as a naval supply dump. The planet was in the right place to allow them to threaten either Earth or the Coalition.

The automated weapons platforms opened fire as the human ships closed in. They were relatively new, for Tokomak equipment, and managed to score a number of hits before they were blown out of space. Yolanda spitefully decided that proved the Tokomak had let their electronic servants do the work, although there was no way to know for sure. Perhaps the gunnery crews had more time to practice their art, so far from the heart of their empire. It was unlikely in the extreme that anyone would bother to conduct an inspection tour of Hades.

Or it was unlikely, she corrected herself. *These days, there might be a proper inspection any day, if they want to use this place for something more than a dump.*

"Launching missiles towards the planet now," Commander Gregory reported. The planetary PDCs were still out of range, but they were firing anyway, hoping to score a lucky hit. "Impact in two minutes."

"Then launch the Marines," Commodore Travis ordered. "Tell them... tell them *Good Luck*."

Yolanda swallowed. Martin had been assigned to the first platoons to hit the planet...unless he'd been reassigned to the team boarding the alien starship. Either way, he was in danger...they were all in danger. And he might be about to die...

Cursing, she called on her implants to dampen her emotions. She couldn't allow herself to be distracted, not now. There was too much to do.

— —

MARTIN HAD A feeling that, if it wasn't for his implants, being in the launch tube – the *Marine Missile Launcher*, as some of the crew called it – would have been thoroughly unpleasant. It was nothing more than being in his suit, trapped in the middle of darkness, waiting for something – anything – to happen. He thought he understood, now, why so few missiles had AI control systems, even though it would have made them far more efficient. The AIs would be trapped in darkness until they were fired, running the risk of driving them mad.

But his implants provided enough simulation to keep him distracted...

An alert flashed up in front of him, followed by a sudden thrusting sensation as he and the rest of the platoon was forced out into space. Hades rose up in front of them with startling suddenness, growing from a dark orb hanging against the darkness of space to something that dominated the entire horizon. More alerts flickered through his implants as his suit orientated itself, then plunged towards the planet. From his point of view, it looked as though the planet was steadily growing larger and larger until it felt as though he was about to smash head-first into an entire world.

Half the trainees get this far and no further, Sergeant Lestrade had said, years ago. *They simply cannot master the drop.*

Martin shivered at the memory, then forced the thought aside as brilliant streaks of light rose up from the planet towards him. The PDCs were firing, trying to wipe out as many of the Marines as they could before it was too late and they were safely on the ground, able to use their weapons. Martin shuddered, then drew on his implants to help him relax. He hated, truly hated, being helpless...and he was helpless, here and now, to do anything to save himself. A single hit would be more than enough to kill him outright.

A flash of light, on the ground, marked the death of one of the PDCs. Two more followed, but the remainder kept firing, all the more desperate now as they knew they were being hunted by the orbiting starships. Martin cursed under his breath as death icons popped up in front of his eyes, including one belonging to Corporal Garland. He'd been so huge that he'd seemed to have muscles on his muscles, a man who had once taken on two of his fellows and won. And now he was dead, swatted out of existence like an ant crushed under a boot...

I'm sorry, Martin thought. There would be time to mourn later. *I will miss you...*

The ground came up underneath him with staggering speed, faint markings below him becoming the giant storage complex. Simulations or no simulations, he hadn't really grasped how huge it was until he'd seen it in person. He'd thought Camp Mons, on Mars, had been staggeringly huge, but the storage dump was far larger. Suddenly, on a very basic level, he grasped the sheer size of the Tokomak Empire. Their technology might be inferior, their crews might be poorly trained...and yet they had a sheer preponderance of mass that had a quality all of its own. They could just keep pouring starships on Earth until Earth ran out of weapons to kill them.

He braced himself as his feet struck the ground, then looked around. A line of aliens wearing suits of their own were running towards the Marines, firing as they came. They must have been desperate, Martin noted as he hit the ground; by remaining upright, they were exposing themselves to being hit. The Marines opened fire, picking off four of them before the remainder hit the deck themselves, then kept crawling forward. Martin crawled forward himself, then came face-to-face with one of the aliens. The alien lifted his weapon, but it was too late. Martin killed him, then crawled around his corpse and kept moving.

The Marines rapidly pushed their enemy back, until they finally held the airlocks leading into the storage dump. Martin led the way into the building, unsure what to expect inside. It was nothing more than a colossal warehouse, tended by three different kinds of alien, none of them Tokomak. The Tokomak themselves had probably been doing nothing more than supervising, he guessed, based on some of the stories he recalled from Earth. A minimum wage-earner could be pressed to do everything, while the owner sat back and watched.

He keyed his megaphone. "STAND BY THE WALLS," he ordered, in Galactic Standard. The Tokomak had created the language, he'd been told; human analysts had noted that it made Newspeak – whatever that was – look totally ineffectual. They'd done their best to ensure that the language supported their primacy at all times, making it hard for adherents to even formulate an opposing concept. "REMAIN CALM AND YOU WILL NOT BE HURT."

Most of the aliens obeyed. The few who didn't either tried to flee into the complex or attack the Marines, a suicidal gesture as the Marines were wearing combat armour. They were quickly stunned, then stacked alongside the walls for later recovery. Martin shook his head, trying not to think about how many slaves on Earth had been willing participants in their own slavery, then advanced forward. The sheer scale of the factory was mind-boggling. There were enough supplies, he was sure, to keep an entire planetary system going for years.

But how many of them, he asked himself, as they tracked down and rounded up the remaining workers, *are usable?*

"The spaceport is secure," a voice said. Martin's implants identified the speaker as Captain Jackson. "We have the freighters and their crews under guard."

"Good," Commodore Travis said. "And the storage dumps themselves?"

"Secure," Lieutenant Robbins said. "Their datanet is under our control. I've got a crew doing a datadump now."

She switched back to the platoon channel. "Herd the alien prisoners into the unloading chamber," she ordered. "It will serve as a place to hold them until we sweep the rest of the complex."

"Understood," Martin said.

The aliens offered no resistance. Most of them were silent, staring at the Marines as though they came from a whole other universe. It wasn't a bad thought, Martin figured, as he checked the aliens for weapons. They had believed that no one would ever challenge the Tokomak, let alone raid one of their bases. Hades had been protected by their reputation far more than it had been protected by their starships. But, when challenged, their reputation had melted like snowflakes in hell.

He took a moment to skim the datadump from the local computer network. There were literally millions of components listed, too many for anyone to handle without modern technology. It was staggeringly impressive, all the more so as it represented a tiny percentage of what – in theory – the Tokomak should be able to do. He shook his head in disbelief, then returned to watching the prisoners. God alone knew what they would do if it dawned on them that their masters were no longer unbeatable.

"Douglas, you're being promoted to Corporal," Robbins said, suddenly. "I've had to surrender Charlie and Severus to 5th Platoon, so you'll have one of the slots. Try to remember that the newcomers are reserves, not maggots. They know more than you, even if you outrank them."

"Yes, Lieutenant," Martin said. "And thank you."

"Thank me if you get confirmed," Robbins added. "You're still quite young for any form of promotion."

TWENTY-EIGHT

The Solar Union flatly refused to pay any kind of compensation to people wounded or killed by Solar Union troops in the wake of anti-war riots that shook multiple capital cities around the world. Following on from his previous statement, President Ross reminded the protesters that embassies are, by international law, the sovereign territory of the nations they represent and, if the local authorities are unable to do so, may be defended by the owners with all necessary force. Protesters stupid enough not to take that into account, he added, are too moronic to be allowed to live.

—Solar News Network, Year 53

"So," Commodore Travis said. "What do you have for me?"

Yolanda glanced down at her datapad, trying to control her thoughts. Commander Gregory had assigned her to assist the crews cataloguing and removing the Tokomak supplies, but she honestly wasn't sure if it was a reward or a punishment. Clearly, they needed to get as much away from the planet as they could, but – on the other hand – shouldn't she be returning to her simulations? Or did the Commander feel she had spent too long practising for increasingly unlikely situations?

"I have a complete manifest of their supplies now," she said. "Do you want the entire list or just the highlights?"

"The highlights," the Commodore said. For someone who had won the most one-sided naval victory in galactic history, at least since the establishment of the Tokomak Empire, he didn't seem very cheerful. "And the items the logistic technicians want us to steal."

"Several hundred thousand missiles, complete with penetrator warheads," Yolanda said. "The tactical analysts believe they were meant for planetary bombardment."

"Almost certainly," the Commodore agreed. There was literally no point in using long-range missiles in a ship-to-ship engagement. If a ship felt it was about to be destroyed, it could simply drop into FTL and run. But a planet, which couldn't run and hide, could be hammered into submission, if necessary. "Next?"

"Millions of spare parts, although quite a few of them are more cosmetic than useful," Yolanda said, glancing down at the datapad. "There are also hundreds of nanotech kits for starship decoration and other oddities. I checked them against the database and it said they were for victory celebrations."

"So they brought flags for us to wave," the Commodore said, slowly. He smiled, as if remembering something bitterly amusing. "I assume they brought humanitarian supplies too?"

"No, sir," Yolanda said. She didn't understand his meaning. "They brought some medical gear, but most of it is specifically designed for Tokomak and would need reprogramming before anyone else could use it."

"Never mind," the Commodore said. "Weapons? Computer gear? Body bags?"

"They stockpiled charger packs for weapons, but few actual weapons apart from the missiles," Yolanda said. "We didn't find any body bags, sir; do the Galactics use them?"

"Not until now," the Commodore said. He looked up, meeting her eyes. "What do *you* make of the stockpile?"

Yolanda hesitated. "The analysts say..."

"Not the analysts," the Commodore said. "What do *you* make of it?"

"I think they are confident of victory," Yolanda said. "And I think they don't know what they're facing."

The Commodore's eyes never left her face. "Why?"

"Because they stockpiled weapons for attacking a planet, not a fleet," Yolanda said. "They were barely prepared for ship-to-ship combat, even here, guarding a stockpile half the galaxy would want to steal. They're not planning on the assumption of meeting serious resistance, sir. I think their plan is to waltz up to Earth, launch enough missiles to turn the entire planet into a radioactive wasteland, then go home."

"Maybe," the Commodore said. "Or they could have decided not to put all of their eggs in one basket. They're planning to move against the Coalition, after all, and they *do* know the Coalition has a fleet."

Yolanda nodded, embarrassed.

"They may feel the Coalition would surrender after the Tokomak appear in their system," the Commodore added, "but surely they'd feel better if they had a big stick ready to enforce their words."

"Yes, sir," Yolanda said. If the Coalition was challenged, the Coalition might just open fire...and discover just how ill-prepared the Tokomak were for modern war. And, at that point, the Tokomak hegemony would start to unravel. "But now...won't the galaxy know what *we* did?"

"Oh, yes," the Commodore said. "They *will* know what we did. And *that* will blow the bloody doors right off."

He took the datapad, then smiled at her. "Dismissed, Ensign," he said. "I believe Commander Gregory wishes to see you."

"Yes, sir," Yolanda said. She would have preferred to sleep, with or without Martin, but there was no time. The crew was working overtime just to get the freighters loaded and away from Hades by the time the Tokomak responded to the attack. Even with half of the supplies being classed as useless, there were still plenty of items Earth could use buried amidst the garbage. "And thank you."

She saluted, then walked out of the compartment and back up to Officer Country. Her implants told her that Commander Gregory was in her office, so Yolanda paused outside the hatch and pressed her hand against the scanner. A long moment passed, then the hatch opened, revealing a tired-looking Commander Gregory seated at her desk. Yolanda stepped inside, allowing the hatch to hiss closed behind her, and stood to attention.

Commander Gregory looked up. "Relax, Ensign," she said. "You're not in trouble."

"Thank you, Commander," Yolanda said.

"You did well in combat," Commander Gregory added, after a moment. "The Captain was very pleased with you. So was the Commodore."

Yolanda swallowed, nervously.

"You are hereby promoted to Lieutenant," Commander Gregory said, almost casually. She picked a small box off the table and passed it to Yolanda. "You may now don the rank pips, if you wish."

It took Yolanda a moment to realise what she'd been told. "I'm...I'm being promoted?"

"I suppose it does sound unbelievable," Commander Gregory said, snidely. She grinned at Yolanda's stunned expression. "You've done well, both in actual combat and in...the other tasks of managing a starship, so I had no hesitation in recommending you for promotion. You will, of course, be expected to live up to this honour, *Lieutenant*. I will not prove forgiving if you screw up or abuse your authority."

She smiled again, then sobered. "The Solar Navy doesn't have many officers with actual space combat experience," she added. "We were careful to try to avoid major conflict with any of the Galactics, apart from the Horde and other scavengers. Experienced officers like yourself are going to be worth their weight in compressed antimatter, now we've finally stepped onto the galactic stage. I think you will probably be transferred to another ship soon enough, once we have time for a proper reorganisation."

"Yes, Commander," Yolanda said.

"You won't get a bigger cabin yet," Commander Gregory added. "Not that anyone *really* has a big cabin on this ship, anyway."

That was true, Yolanda knew. The Captain and the Commodore had enough room to swing a cat, but everyone else had a small compartment or had to double up with another officer. It was odd, given the sheer scale of the quarters available to Tokomak officers, yet she had a feeling it helped to concentrate a few minds. Besides, VR could create the illusion that one was living in a palace, with a harem of nude servants, or any other illusion one fancied. It wasn't as if an officer *needed* a huge compartment to himself.

"I..."

"Just remember not to throw your weight around too much," Commander Gregory warned, darkly. "And you still have plenty of work to do."

"Yes, Commander," Yolanda said.

"Take ten minutes to recover, then report to the simulation chambers," Commander Gregory ordered. "We have some new scenarios based on their war plans, such as they were. And some interesting potential uses for pieces of alien technology."

— —

IT HAD TAKEN several hours of careful argument, but eventually the Marines had been able to convince most of the aliens to assist the humans in stripping the storage dump of supplies and transferring them to the captured freighters. There really wasn't much of a choice, Martin knew; the aliens had been trained to use the equipment, which was specifically designed for their physiologies. The Marines couldn't have used it without real problems, which would have delayed operations too far. But some of the Commodore's decisions seemed to be delaying matters too.

"You have a question, Corporal?" Lieutenant Robbins asked. The breather she wore on her face made it harder for him to make out her words. "You're hanging there as if you have something you want to say."

Martin hesitated, then nodded. "Why are we stealing their missiles, Lieutenant?"

"Because the Commodore wants us to take them," Robbins said, shortly. She was a good Marine, everyone agreed, but she had a tendency to be sharp when asked stupid questions – or questions she considered to be stupid. "And his orders stand."

"But..." Martin stepped aside to allow another missile rack to be moved to the freighters, then looked back at the Lieutenant. "We can't use these missiles, can we?"

"You never know when you might want to bombard a planet," Robbins said, evasively. "And besides, better we have them than the alternative."

"But we can't use them," Martin said.

Lieutenant Robbins smiled, lightly. "The Commodore had years of service in the wet-navy, then fifty-plus years of service in the Solar Navy," she said. "I think he probably knows what he's doing. Just because the order didn't seem to make sense doesn't mean that it's stupid, Corporal. The people at the top often have a better idea of the big picture than the people on the ground."

Martin frowned, remembering some of the exercises they'd been forced to undergo, purely to draw the lesson that the people at the top *didn't* always know what was going on at the bottom. He'd never heard of the concept of micromanagement before he'd left Earth, but now he understood that it represented a temptation senior officers had to resist. It was easy – far too easy – to move Marines around like pieces on a chessboard...and ignore the fact that the landscape didn't *work* like a chessboard. A Marine standing where he was ordered to stand might be exposed to enemy fire, while – left to his own devices – he could find cover and fire back. It had taken him some time to understand that they were getting taught what to avoid, with senior officers deliberately making mistakes to force them to learn the hard way.

Robbins pointed a finger at his nose. "And, to add to that, the Commodore is the Commodore," she added. "Your job is to supervise the loading and then prepare to be evacuated, before we blow the rest of the complex. Or you *could* write him a tactical memo, telling him what you think. I'm sure he'd be very pleased to hear from you."

Martin winced. She hadn't even *tried* to hide the sarcasm.

He shook his head, then turned his attention back to the freighters. The Tokomak had moved enough ships to Hades to lift enough supplies to keep an entire fleet operating for years, apart from a handful of curious exceptions. It baffled him to think that someone could have ruled the galaxy for so long and yet not bothered to re-examine their security arrangements, every so often. No human power had remained intact and stable for so long. But the Tokomak had managed to convince the entire galaxy that they were effectively invincible, that resistance was not only futile, but just plain stupid.

"You'll be going back to the ship at the end of this shift," Robbins said. "We have orders to allow some others a chance to relax down here."

"Oh," Martin said. "Relaxing?"

He snorted. Watching the aliens wasn't relaxing, not when he knew just how many missile warheads or antimatter storage pods remained in the complex. A single saboteur who had gone undetected could do real damage, just by turning off the antimatter containment field. Or by detonating an IED next to an antimatter pod. He wasn't sure what would happen if someone managed to detonate a nuke in the complex, but he was fairly sure it would be utterly disastrous.

"It beats running simulations all the time," Robbins assured him. "And besides, you would be able to see your girlfriend."

Martin would have coloured, if it had been possible. "You know?"

"You haven't exactly done a good job of hiding it," Robbins said. She cocked her head at him, then rolled her eyes. "Pretty much everyone knows, Martin. They're happy for you."

Martin blinked. "Really?"

He knew what would have happened on Earth, even if he'd dated a sister. The young men – boys – would have crowded round him, demanding details. Was she really so pretty with her dress off? Had she gone down on him yet? Were her breasts firm or soft to the touch? Was she good in bed? And the immature bastard he'd been at the time would have happily told the other immature bastards intimate details…

It would have been worse, of course, if he'd been dating Yolanda on Earth. The questioners would have been fascinated or insulting, depending on which stereotypes the questioners believed. One half would have demanded to know if it was true that all white girls wanted a taste of chocolate, others would have demanded to know why he wasn't dating a black girl. Martin would have given a great deal for a chance to meet Yolanda's father up a dark alleyway with no witnesses, but he understood the man more than he cared to admit. In a society where dating outside one's own race was sometimes considered worse than treason, it would be very tempting to deny the relationship had ever happened. And neglect his daughter, the sole proof the affair had ever existed, into the bargain.

"Yes," Robbins said. "Honestly...were you *trying* to keep it a secret?"

She winked at him. "You'll need to be more stealthy if you want to go into covert ops," she added, darkly. "You couldn't have made it more obvious if you'd painted a declaration of love in giant letters on the bulkheads, complete with pink and red hearts and flowers."

"Oh," Martin said.

"She isn't a Marine, so you're not breaking the laws on fucking within the corps," Robbins said. "She isn't a security risk, so you're not putting your cock ahead of common sense. She doesn't have a bad reputation, so you're not risking more than heartbreak and some minor embarrassment, should the affair go sour. The worst that will happen is that you will be assigned to different ships, you'll try to keep it going for a time and then you will discover that it's impossible and you both go find different people."

She paused. "And, if you're lucky, you'll remain friends despite all the bullshit you will go through when you end the relationship."

Martin threw her a curious look. "Are you talking about yourself?"

"It happens," Robbins told him, tartly. "You're in the military. So is she. Sooner or later, you will be assigned to different ships. When that happens, you will have the choice between trying to keep the relationship going and breaking it off as cleanly as possible. And if you happened to be under my command, if you start crying all the time, I will happily help you to cope by banging you over the head with a blunt instrument."

"Thank you, Counsellor Obvious," Martin said.

Robbins smirked. "Fairness isn't part of the deal," she said. "The military doesn't give a damn about the way you feel about something, nor should it. You signed away your freedoms the day you swore the oath. And she did the same."

She shrugged. "You want my advice?"

Martin covered his ears as a freighter rose into the sky, then nodded.

"Keep it as light as possible until you reach the end of your first contract," Robbins said, slowly. "Don't pin all your hopes on having her for the rest of your life. After you retire from the military, you can see if the pair of you can build a home together – and if there's something more than sexual lust involved. She really is quite pretty. But is that all there is to it?"

"No," Martin said, firmly.

Robbins smirked, again. "Are you sure? What do you want to be doing in ten years?"

Martin considered it. "Your job?"

The Lieutenant gave him a one-fingered gesture. "In ten years, Martin, you should be a Captain, if you stay in the ranks," she said. "If you're a Lieutenant still, people will start to ask questions. Pointed questions. Why is that jerk still an LT when he should be a Captain?"

"I see, I think," Martin said.

"There will probably always be room for Marines, unless we lose the war," Robbins said. "You can probably stay in, unless you commit some fuck-up so fucked that the court-martial board has no choice, but to kick you out on your ass. But what will she want to do?"

Another freighter took off, passing through the atmospheric forcefield and climbing into the sky. Martin watched it go, wondering if the aliens would behave themselves – or take advantage of the opportunity to vanish into FTL and lose themselves in the endless sea of stars. The bomb on the control deck should make it a no-brainer, but who knew how aliens thought? They were even stranger than girls.

"But leave it until the end of the war," Robbins said, clapping him on the shoulder. "By now" – she made a show of checking her watch – "the news should have reached Varnar. And who knows how they will react, once they know what's happened here?"

TWENTY-NINE

Thousands of refugees from Sabah have begun to swamp refugee camps in East Asia, following the start of a purge of natives from Sabah. The Malaysian Government claims to be only targeting rebels, separatists and terrorists, but sources on the ground claim that Malay troops are slaughtering innocent civilians and burning entire villages. Chinese and Christian citizens are crossing the border into Singapore or booking flights out of Malaysia at an unprecedented rate.

—Solar News Network, Year 53

There was nothing inherently unpredictable about the universe. The Tokomak believed, quite firmly, that everyone could be calculated, that everything could be predicted and eventually placed firmly where it belonged. Surprise – true surprise – simply didn't exist. But none of the planners had ever anticipated one of the newer races actually daring to attack a Tokomak world.

Viceroy Neola sat in her office, staring at the report. Two ships had made it to Varnar, one reporting that Hades was about to come under attack, the other reporting that the defending squadron had been decisively beaten. It was impossible. It was unthinkable. No one would ever dare to attack a Tokomak world.

It had happened.

She forced herself to remain calm, despite the shock, despite the rage that called for the immediate eradication of every last member of the race that had dared to attack the masters of the universe. Someone had attacked…but who? The humans? Or someone else, someone completely new? The ships hadn't been recognised, which meant whoever they were facing was someone who had mastered starfaring technology before encountering the expanding edge of civilisation. Or someone deliberately trying to disguise their involvement.

Think, she told herself. *What do they want?*

It was hard to imagine what the aliens must be thinking. Empathy had never been a Tokomak strength, even though she could see some uses for it. They'd committed suicide. No matter how advanced their technology, they couldn't match the Tokomak for sheer numbers. She could trade a thousand battleships for every alien ship involved in the attack on Hades and still come out ahead…if there were a thousand battleships on call. The hundreds she knew to be approaching the sector might not be enough…

No, she thought. *They couldn't have the firepower to destroy my battleships. The entire war would have been ended long ago.*

She fought to wrap her mind around a totally new concept. No one had encountered a self-starfaring race, certainly not one who had mastered FTL on their own. The Tokomak had been the first and only race to devise a way to liberate themselves from the tyranny of the gravity points. It was why they were the masters of the universe. If someone else had mastered it, they would have been encountered long ago. Unless…no, she decided. The humans were the only logical suspects for the attack on Hades.

Piece by piece, she worked her way through the concept. The humans had received her ultimatum and reacted with blinding speed, launching an immediate attack on Hades to push the Tokomak back. But she'd spent long enough struggling with the moribund logistics department back home to know that it took a long time to plan a war, particularly one against a far greater power. The humans had to have had their war planned out long before she'd arrived in the sector, gaming out move and counter-move in their fight against an overwhelming force. They would have calculated her reaction and factored it into their plans.

Standard procedure was to stamp on any source of trouble before it became a major problem, she knew. The humans would anticipate her launching ships to Hades, bent on recovering the world and trapping the attackers before they could strip the planet bare. And if that was what they expected her to do, she was sure, they would take it into account when they were planning their operations. They would adapt their plans to deal with it...

It had been too long, she realised numbly, since the Tokomak had fought a real war. The humans might have an edge, one she simply couldn't match.

She looked up as the Admiral entered the chamber. "Your Excellency," he said. "I have detailed three squadrons to recover Hades."

"Hold them here," Neola ordered.

The Admiral was too skilled a veteran of political battles to show much of a reaction, but Neola had no difficulty in reading his shock. She would have known he was shocked even if he'd shown nothing, for leaving the enemy in possession of Tokomak territory was effectively admitting defeat. Everyone knew the Tokomak would punish any offense against them a hundred-fold. To leave the humans in possession of Hades would call that into question, suggesting to a hundred races that the Tokomak could be beaten. It would threaten the very existence of the empire.

"Your Excellency," the Admiral said. "I beg you to reconsider."

"They will expect us to send a fleet to Hades," Neola said. She mourned, inwardly, for what her race had lost. None of them were particularly imaginative any longer, even the Old Ones who had been young when FTL was first discovered. "We shouldn't do what they expect us to do."

The Admiral looked uncomprehending. "It is standard procedure..."

"Yes, it is," Neola said. "And that is precisely why we won't do it."

She understood his doubts perfectly. They were both young by Tokomak standards. If they made mistakes, their mistakes would be attributed to their youth. They would certainly not be honoured with any future commands, even if they won the overall war; instead, they'd be told to leave matters of galactic import to the grown-ups. She understood precisely how he was feeling, but she was sure – now – that doing what she was expected to do would be a dreadful mistake. At best, she would look weak for giving the enemy a chance to steal everything they could carry from Hades and destroy the rest; at worst, her ships would run into an ambush and be destroyed.

And I would have sent ships away from Varnar, she thought. News of the defeat hadn't become public, yet, but it would. Who knew which way the *Varnar* would jump, if their Tokomak backers looked weak? *They might be counting on the Varnar deciding to move against us.*

She turned and walked over to the window, looking out over the towering city. Millions of aliens lived below her, she knew, from hundreds of different races. Some of them would be loyal to the Tokomak, or at least to the Status Quo; others would see advantage in any shift in the balance of power. The Varnar themselves, as loyal as they were, couldn't be blind to the ultimate truth of the proxy war. Or, for that matter, that her orders might encompass more than just crushing the Coalition, once and for all.

"Fetch me a Varnar Admiral," she ordered. "One who has faced the humans in battle."

"Your Excellency," the Admiral protested. "He would know nothing of naval affairs."

"But he would know the humans," Neola said, patiently. "Find someone who has faced them and bring him to me."

She returned to the raw data as the Admiral bowed, then left the room. There had been no time to have any analysts take a look at the data – she hadn't even brought any on her ships – but she could pick out some of the more important details for herself. The human ships were faster and more manoeuvrable than her own, capable of tricks she hadn't thought possible. In fact, one on one, she had a nasty feeling the humans had a definite advantage. The more she thought about it, the more she wished the Tokomak had done more than log the human race's existence when they swept through the sector, centuries ago.

It was nearly an hour before the door opened again, revealing a Varnar. He was a short being, even by their dwarfish standards, with grey hairless skin, dark eyes and a simple black overall. Neola didn't pretend to understand how the Varnar governed themselves – as long as they obeyed, races enjoyed internal autonomy – but she knew he would be competent. The Varnar would not have been able to fight the war without competent and experienced officers.

She allowed herself a hint of worry, although none of it showed on her face. It was a fact, as far as the Tokomak were concerned, that they were simply the best at everything. Once, it had even been true. Asking another race for advice was utterly unthinkable. But so was a swift and decisive defeat, one that had shocked her to the core. It was time to do the unthinkable and hope she produced a victory before the Old Ones relieved her of command.

"Your Excellency," the Varnar said. He lowered his head, then closed his eyes in submission. "I am Admiral He'cht."

"You may open your eyes," Neola said. "You have fought the humans, have you not?"

"Yes," He'cht said. "I have faced them four times in open combat."

"You must have some impression of their skills," Neola said. "What do you make of them?"

"They're very capable," He'cht said, carefully. "I think..."

"I will not take offense," Neola assured him. "Be blunt."

"I think they're among the best soldiers in the galaxy," He'cht said, flatly. "Certainly the most innovative and dangerous."

Neola started. "Explain."

"Human soldiers started cropping up in mercenary forces fifty years ago, mostly on disputed worlds," He'cht said. "They proved themselves to be flexible, adaptable and terrifyingly innovative. Their skill at creating or improvising weapons is unmatched. The Coalition saw fit to use them as shock troops, a role to which they are aptly suited. Even in space, they proved themselves capable. Our cyborgs were unable to match them."

"Your cyborgs," Neola mused. "Couldn't you use them to match the humans?"

"They had to be brain-burned," He'cht admitted. "The ones who were allowed to keep some initiative tended to turn on us, when facing other humans. Some of our researchers believe the race has a unifying aspect we have been unable to discover. Others think they merely recognise their own kind and start rebelling. The only way we were able to use them on the battlefield after humans entered the war in large numbers was to reduce them to little more than puppets."

"And you knew about the threat for fifty years," Neola said. "You did nothing."

"To move against Earth would have allowed the Coalition a shot at a decisive victory," He'cht pointed out. "It was why we requested assistance from you."

"Point," Neola said. She keyed a switch. "I want your *honest* opinion of this battle."

He'cht watched, dispassionately, as the Battle of Hades played itself out, once again.

"Your ships acted poorly," he said, when the battle was over. "Their commanders made too many mistakes."

There were Tokomak, Neola knew, who would have ordered his immediate execution for daring to point out the obvious. The Tokomak had to stick together, after all, and if that meant ensuring that no one ever dared criticize them...well, it had seemed a fair price to pay. But now, in hindsight, she understood that it was a deadly mistake. A critic, a critic with real experience, could be very useful.

"Detail them," she ordered.

"The squadron's formation was designed more for display than combat," He'cht said. "Several of the ships couldn't fire because their comrades were in the way, crippling their firepower. One of the ships even collided with another ship. Furthermore, the commander attempted to keep his ships in formation even when it was clear the formation was actually impeding their response. By the time he was killed, it was too late to salvage the situation."

"Go on," Neola said.

"Their rate of fire should have been a great deal higher too," He'cht added, after a moment. "Everything about them was sluggish, Your Excellency. I would go so far as to say they didn't have any real training for war. They acted as though they expected the enemy to follow a completely predictable flight path and, when it became clear the enemy wasn't going to do anything of the sort, they fell apart."

There was a nasty amount of truth in that, Neola knew – and He'cht didn't know the half of it. Naval exercises, what few of them there were, tended to be carefully scripted, with the 'right' side always emerging victorious. It helped to maintain morale in a fleet that was badly undermanned, but it hadn't prepared the crews to face an enemy who took pleasure in being completely unpredictable. And the humans didn't have a choice, either. They *had* to be unpredictable or they would be crushed by superior numbers.

"The humans attacked Hades," she said, flatly. "How do you propose we respond?"

The Varnar looked up at her with big dark eyes. "As soon as your battleships arrive, launch an immediate attack on Earth," he said. "There is little else worth targeting in human space."

Neola blinked in surprise. "They only have one system?"

"There are few empty systems within fifty light years of their star," He'cht reminded her. "They do not have room to expand, Your Excellency. There are a number of small human settlements on many worlds, but always as minority groups. Earth is their sole majority world."

"And Earth will no longer exist soon," Neola said. "How do you propose we attack?"

"Train your people to think and react to surprises," He'cht said, "then go for their homeworld with your entire fleet. You will have to expect a hard fight, I think. The humans will not falter in defence of their world."

"I imagine not," Neola agreed. "And Hades itself?"

"Is immaterial," the Varnar said. "Your plan assumed you had all the time in the universe to put your pieces in place. That is no longer valid. You have to react to the new situation. Expect the humans to go for your other bases if you give them the time..."

Neola grimaced. The last major interstellar war, four thousand years ago, had been resolved by patiently barricading the enemy into a handful of heavily-fortified star systems, then battering them down one by one. Putting naval bases in the right locations had been an integral part of the victorious strategy. But things had been different back then; FTL had been a relatively new concept, while the Tokomak hadn't been anything like as ossified.

"They'll attack other bases," she said, slowly. "Each attack will embarrass us still further."

"And convince the Coalition that they can hurt you too," the Varnar added. "You might find yourself waging war against them before you're ready."

"Then the plan will be revised, as you suggest," Neola said. "Once the battleships arrive, we will take them straight to Earth."

She paused. "You will be assigned to my personal staff," she added. "You will have full permission to speak your mind, when we are alone. I will require your opinion on all matters."

The Varnar was hard to read, but she had the feeling he was less than pleased. He was an important person on Varnar, one of their senior commanders; to the Tokomak, he was nothing more than a lesser personage. His opinions would be discounted, at best, if he made them in public; at worst, he would be considered an uppity inferior and ordered to report for execution. There was a reason most of her body-servants came from races that practically worshipped the Tokomak as gods.

"Your wish is my command, Your Excellency," He'cht said, finally.

"Of course it is," Neola said. "Report to my Steward. He will assign you quarters and a staff. Bring others, if you wish. They can all be accommodated."

"Yes, Your Excellency," He'cht said. "I will serve you faithfully."

— —

THE TOKOMAK WERE simply not very good at understanding emotions, certainly not those belonging to other races. It was hard for the Viceroy to comprehend, He'cht suspected, just how much humiliation she had poured on him – and how much was yet to come. He'd entered the room a proud Admiral, a serving officer in the Varnar Navy; he'd left it a servant, an advisor to someone who would happily take the credit for his victories. And would she even listen to his advice?

He showed no trace of his feelings as he made his way back to the Naval HQ, thinking hard. The Tokomak had been beaten; worse, they'd been beaten publicly. They weren't likely to take it too calmly, which was bad news for the human race. Once, He'cht would have been pleased; now, he had a feeling that the Varnar would simply be the last race to be crushed into eternal servitude.

And yet they'd been beaten!

The humans hadn't been spacefarers when the Varnar had first visited their world, taking biological samples and breeding stock for cyborgs. They certainly shouldn't have been able to develop FTL on their own. And that suggested someone had given them the technology and invited them to play with it. The Coalition? Or someone else?

But it hardly mattered. If an upstart race could do so much, against the masters of the universe, what could the Varnar do? They had ships, they had weapons…and they had experience. Could they fight the Tokomak and win?

It was a treacherous thought. It was a dangerous thought. But it taunted him as he entered the building. They'd always known the proxy war would go on until everyone was exhausted, at least until the humans entered the war. Now…there was a prospect of something else, a chance to unite against the true foe. But it would be risky…

We will need to plan carefully, he thought. The Tokomak battleships would arrive soon, in staggering numbers. Thankfully, the Tokomak hadn't demanded the Varnar Navy provide support to their fleet. *And then we will need to decide which way to jump.*

THIRTY

In the wake of yet another child-abuse scandal, angry crowds stormed the Vatican in Rome and lynched an as yet undisclosed number of priests and religious figures. A number of Swiss Guards are reported dead in the attack, but Italian police and military units refused to get involved. The Italian Government has declared a state of emergency, yet it is unlikely that anyone will be prosecuted for the attack.

—Solar News Network, Year 53

"The entire planet knows," Sally said, as they sat together in her apartment. "It won't be long before the entire sector knows."

Kevin looked down at the bootleg recording. Starships – human starships – had attacked Hades, smashing the defenders without taking any losses of their own. It was the single most one-sided victory the galaxy had seen for over three thousand years. And it had happened to the Tokomak, the masters of the universe. It couldn't have been more shocking if a small army of cavemen had killed a hundred heavily-armed Solar Marines.

"It's good," he said. "Everyone knows?"

"The recording leaked onto the datanet," Sally said. "They keep taking it down and it keeps popping back up, somehow."

"The age-old problem with information datanets," Kevin said. "How do you censor without the system regarding it as a malfunction and routing around you?"

He smirked. The Varnar Datanet wasn't *that* different from the human system; there were vast sections that could be deemed to be under supervision, but entire segments that were rogue, completely out of any form of control. It wasn't easy tending to the needs of an entire planet, even if the Varnar were more homogenous than humans. And besides, a large percentage of the planet's population were non-Varnar.

"There are copies everywhere by now," Sally said. "I would hazard a guess that over a third of the planet has seen the raw recordings."

"Good," Kevin said. "And how are the Tokomak planning to respond?"

"They've said nothing, yet," Sally said. "It's only been a couple of days since the news arrived. They may still be thinking about their response."

Kevin frowned. The Tokomak, according to the captured ship's files, had only one response to any challenge to their power. They sent a fleet of starships to deal with the challenge swiftly, brutally and effectively. He'd assumed – and Mongo had done the same – that the Tokomak would try to recover Hades at once, sending a fleet of cruisers to the occupied world. It was their most likely course of action.

But they hadn't bothered to react, as far as he could tell. That worried him.

"It's possible," he said. "But they shouldn't have had to *think*!"

"They must have been shocked by the battle," Sally pointed out, dryly. "Even the most ossified system would rethink its priorities after such a nasty shock."

"I suppose," Kevin said, doubtfully.

He stood up and started to pace, thinking hard. On the face of it, the Tokomak hadn't even lost a percentage point of their fleet. There was no reason to think the Battle of Hades altered the balance of power. But...their reputation for invincibility was their greatest asset. Losing it had to sting...and, more importantly, would encourage anyone else who hated them to go for their throats. By now, word would be spreading through space, heading towards their empire and countless subject races. How many of them would rebel when they heard the Tokomak were not invincible after all?

"Mr. Ando had a message for you," Sally said. "There are some people he would like you to meet."

Kevin turned to face her. "Who?"

"He wouldn't say," Sally said. "But he assured me that you would find it in your best interests to attend."

"I see," Kevin said. He considered it, rapidly. Who would Mr. Ando want him to meet? An ally? Or someone who might be talked into becoming an ally? "Very well. Where do we have to go?"

"It's at 1700, if you want to attend," Sally said. "He advised you to wear a disguise. I brought a couple along, if you are interested."

She hadn't answered the real question, Kevin noted. He wondered if she was deliberately keeping something from him – or if she didn't actually know. Mr. Ando might well have decided to tell her nearer the time, to prevent an accidental betrayal. Or maybe she hadn't quite understood what he'd asked her, which seemed unlikely. Sally was one of the sharpest people he'd had to deal with, outside the SIA.

It seemed pointless to ask more questions, so he allowed her to lead him into the bedroom and show him the disguises. They were nothing more than masks and monkish cloaks, but he understood the moment he saw them. One of the most prominent galactic religions insisted that all of its adherents wore the same outfits, in the hopes of minimising all differences between them. They believed, Kevin recalled, that all intelligence was sacred and differences between the races only made it harder for everyone to get along. The Solar Union would probably have agreed with them, if it had had the chance. It was astonishing how irrelevant racism became when someone could change their skin colour to green or purple at will.

"Follow close behind me," Sally ordered, once they were dressed. "And don't take off your mask without permission."

Kevin had – once – worn a *burka* when he'd walked through Mecca, on one of his more covert missions in the Middle East. It had been exciting, in many ways; Mecca was denied to unbelievers, so discovery would probably have meant certain death. The thought had amused him at the time – he would not have called the House of Saud *believers* - but now it was just stupid. All his work had been wasted, thanks to bureaucrats in Washington.

Sally led him unhesitatingly down into the lower regions of the city, where the poor and powerless congregated and begged for alms. Kevin looked from side to side, feeling growing pity for the inhabitants, even as he kept his distance from anyone who looked dangerous. A few of them called out to him, offering everything from sex to drugs, but the remainder generally ignored him. Below them, a handful of dead bodies lay on the ground, waiting for someone to come and turn them into food. Taboos against cannibalism – not shared by all of the Galactics – would not be enough to stop the poor from tearing into dead flesh. It might make the difference between life and death.

Sickened, Kevin forced himself to keep his eyes firmly on Sally's behind as she walked faster and faster. He'd seen poverty on Earth, poverty that had been unimaginable in America, but this was an order of magnitude worse. Part of him had always believed that advanced aliens would have solved all their social woes, but the Tokomak hadn't even *tried.* There had been no attempt to help the poor, even with free food and drink. He understood the dangers of government charity – Steve hadn't had to convince him of *that* – and yet surely *someone* should try to help.

But there are limits, he thought. *We can't create a post-scarcity society just yet.*

Sally stopped outside an unmarked door and tapped once, loudly. It opened a moment later, revealing a spider-like alien who glowered at the pair of them through eyes on stalks. Kevin forced down his instinctive reaction – the spider seemed to trigger every last one of his long-buried phobias – and followed Sally as she stepped past the creature and into a small sitting room. Most of the furniture looked child-sized; the only exceptions were a pair of chairs, which looked to have been produced for someone much larger than the average human. But the child-sized furniture was more than enough to tell him who – or rather what – they were going to meet.

"Take off your mask," Sally ordered. "They'll want to see you."

Kevin nodded and obeyed, then grimaced in disgust. The air smelled of rotting spice, a stench that made him want to cough. Somehow, he managed to keep his reaction under control, using his implants to dampen his sense of smell. Moments later, as he sat down, the door opened, revealing four Varnar. They all wore the same grey overalls, leaving him completely unable to tell them apart. Thankfully, they had much the same trouble with humans.

"We greet you," the lead Varnar said. Kevin mentally tagged him Number One. "You are speaking for your race?"

"I am empowered to discuss certain matters, yes," Kevin said. The Varnar had always given him the creeps, if only because they bore a certain resemblance to Little Grey Aliens. There were quite a few people who suspected that wasn't a coincidence. "And yourselves?"

"We are empowered to speak on behalf of the Varnar Hive," Number One said. "But they do not speak for us."

Kevin sighed, inwardly. What the hell did that mean? He'd thought talking with Arabs, Chinese or Japanese could be hard but aliens were… well, alien. And the Varnar, despite being humanoid, thought very differently to humans. They did things that made no sense to any human and, when asked, claimed it was perfectly normal. And perhaps it was, for them.

"You requested this meeting," Kevin said. "I assume you wish to discuss the war."

"That is correct," Number Two said. "The war has taken a turn we find disadvantageous."

"Yes," Kevin agreed. "If we win, you will have to come to terms with us; if we lose, the Tokomak will seek to control you more thoroughly than they already do. You can only come out ahead if you talk to us."

"Which bears the risk of being destroyed by the Tokomak," Number Three stated. "Can your race win the war?"

"We believe we can," Kevin said, flatly. "I won't go into details."

It had crossed his mind that the meeting could be a trap. Mr. Ando could have been paid through the nose to arrange it, or he might be an innocent dupe. Kevin knew, without false modesty, that he probably wouldn't have been able to escape a trap...and Julian and the others had strict orders not to try to save his life. He would have no option, but immediate suicide. They couldn't take the risk of him being interrogated and forced to spill everything he knew.

"That is understandable," Number Four said.

Kevin smiled to himself. Did they have to speak in sequence? Or were they playing games with his mind?

"I would urge you to join us," Kevin said. "However, you would not want to take the risk of switching sides before the Tokomak are defeated."

All four Varnar lowered their heads slowly. "That is correct," Number One said. "We do not want to face the Tokomak alone."

"I understand," Kevin said. "I have seen such reluctance before."

It had been a common problem, during the War on Terror. Villages and tribes often hated the terrorists and insurgents more than they hated the Americans, but they were too scared of the terrorists to take a stand against them. The foreigners would be gone one day, the terrorists taunted, and on that day anyone who helped them would face punishment. It was hard to blame the locals for refusing to get involved when their sons would be killed and their daughters and wives would be raped, merely for exchanging a few polite words with the foreigners.

He gritted his teeth in bitter memory. It would have been easier – so much easier – if the intelligence agents had had authority to issue immigration permits at will, but the bureaucrats had put roadblock after roadblock in their path. Not that it mattered here, he knew; there was no way they could offer asylum to every single Varnar on the planet. There were billions of the aliens, all at risk if the Tokomak knew they were being betrayed.

"Then we wish to discuss potential future collaboration," Number Two said.

"And how the Coalition would treat us," Number Three added.

"I could not make promises on the Coalition's behalf," Kevin said, carefully. "However, I believe they would certainly *want* to end the Proxy War."

"Such an ending would have to be on reasonable terms," Number Four stated. "We do not wish to surrender."

"There is no need for outright surrender," Number One said.

"I would not ask you to surrender unconditionally," Kevin said. The Proxy War had been going on long enough that the original causes had been buried below a series of atrocities and betrayals. "However, you would have to come to terms with the Coalition or the war will just splutter on, giving the Tokomak a chance to recover from their defeat."

"This is all academic if the Tokomak are not defeated," Number Two said. "What do you want us to do?"

"Stay alert," Kevin said. "If you see a chance to liberate Varnar from their grasp, you can take it. And we will do our best to help."

There was a long chilling pause. It was eventually broken by Number One.

"You have authority to issue such statements?"

Number One spoke after Number Two, Kevin noted. The pattern had changed – why? A lifetime of intelligence work had taught him, more than once, that any unexpected change in a pattern could have a deeper meaning. *Or did they change the subject and start again?*

"I can make certain promises on their behalf," Kevin said. He'd talked about the prospect of finding allies with the President. "However, they may be unable to keep the promises."

"You offer us no guarantees," Number Two said. His voice was atonal, but Kevin was sure he detected a hint of irritation. "You offer us no promises."

"I could offer you all the promises in the universe," Kevin said. "But I would be lying."

Dark eyes bored into his. He understood their position; they wanted to be free of the Tokomak, but they also knew the risks of jumping into rebellion too soon. The Tokomak had a colossal fleet on the way, after all. Was it big enough to crush the Varnar Navy, which had considerably more experience? Kevin didn't know. He had a feeling that no one knew for sure.

"We understand," Number Three said. "We will prepare our options. But we will not intercede until we can do so and survive."

"I understand," Kevin said. "Do you have anything I can take back to my superiors, as a gesture of good will?"

"Not yet," Number Four said. "What would you require?"

"Intelligence," Kevin said. "Anything we can use to plan our defence."

"We will consider the matter," Number One said. "We thank you for coming."

On that note, the meeting ended. The four Varnar stepped through the door they'd entered, which closed behind them with an ominous thud. Kevin shook his head in amused disbelief, then waited, as patiently as he could, for Sally to say they could leave. It was nearly half an hour before she rose to her feet, replaced her mask over her face and led the way to the door. Kevin donned his own mask and followed her out into the darkness. Night had fallen while they'd been seated in the room, chatting to the Varnar.

"Stick close to me," Sally said. Her voice was very composed, despite a fight breaking out only a few short metres from the door. "You don't want to be noticed here."

Kevin nodded. Random chance had screwed up more operations than he cared to remember, if only through someone observant seeing something they shouldn't and calling the police. It was quite helpful when an observant local stopped a terrorist attack, but it was rather less useful when he was the one carrying out the operation. But they made it back to Sally's apartment without running into any real trouble. Kevin breathed a sigh of relief as he removed the mask, then hurried into the bathroom. Implants or no implants, he wanted a shower to wash the smell off him.

"You'll want to see this," Sally called, as he climbed out of the shower. There was an urgent tone in her voice that caught his attention. "Grab a towel and come and look at the TV."

"Coming," Kevin called. He scooped up a towel and hastened out the door. "What is it?"

Sally nodded to the television. It was showing starships – hundreds of starships – making their way out of the gravity point. Normally, transits were one by one – and mostly freighters. This time, there was an endless stream of warships. Kevin knew what it was without having to ask, if only because he'd been dreading it for the last few days. The Tokomak Navy had arrived.

"Two hundred battleships," Sally said, slowly. She sounded stunned. It was one thing to hear about such numbers, but another to actually see them in real life. "And a few dozen smaller ships."

Kevin sucked in a breath. The Tokomak weren't the only galactic power to build battleships, but theirs were twice the size of everyone else's ships. Giant cylinders, five kilometres long, bristling with energy weapons and missile launchers, just one of them was normally enough to keep a planet under firm control. As far as anyone knew, the Tokomak hadn't lost a battleship ever since they'd established their empire. The fleet looked completely invincible.

I bet the Varnar are having third thoughts by now, he thought, darkly. *Would they try to betray us to the Tokomak?*

"They should have more escorts," he mused. "I wonder why they don't."

Sally gave him a sharp look. "More escorts?"

"Yeah," Kevin said. He hadn't spent as long as Mongo studying the Galactic Way of War, but he'd picked up quite a bit. "Everything from scouts to additional point defence platforms."

He shook his head, dismissing the thought. "And now all that matters is hoping the Solar Union is ready to meet them," he said. "Because if we don't win the coming battle, we sure as hell won't win the war."

THIRTY-ONE

Jennifer Bellows, the acclaimed writer of 'The Fascist Party of Tolerance' was granted asylum in the Solar Union, following an attempt to legally lynch her in London, United Kingdom. Bellows, whose work challenges the underpinnings of multiculturalism, stated that her life was destroyed when the establishment could not actually undermine her arguments through logic and reason. It is to be hoped that she will find the Solar Union a more congenial home.

—Solar News Network, Year 53

"Set course for the Rendezvous Point, Lieutenant," Captain Singh ordered, "and take us there, best possible speed."

"Aye, Captain," Yolanda said.

She allowed her fingers to dance across the console, bringing up the macro. She'd had the course laid in for days, ever since the battle had been fought and won. They'd expected to have to retreat, perhaps after exchanging a hail of shots, once the Tokomak responded to the attack on Hades. Instead, they'd had ample time to strip the planet's storage deports, commandeer freighters and then leave on the planned departure date. It was worrying some of the senior officers, she'd heard. The Tokomak weren't behaving as predicted.

A faint shudder ran through the ship as she dropped into FTL, leaving the Hades System far behind. Yolanda smiled to herself, then keyed the stardrive into safe mode. They would remain in FTL, safe and untouchable, until they reached the RV Point, whereupon they would join the rest of the fleet. Or so she'd heard. All hell was likely to break loose, sooner or later, and Hades was immaterial to the overall outcome of the war, now the supply dumps had been captured or destroyed.

"We're under way," she said, formally. "ETA at RV Point One roughly four days, seventeen hours."

"Then inform the crew to stand down and relax for a day," the Captain ordered the XO. "We will return to intensive drilling tomorrow."

"Aye, Captain," Commander Gregory said. "The crew could do with a rest."

Yolanda turned her attention back to her console and flicked on simulation mode. There was nothing to do while a starship was in FTL, if only because the onboard computers were more than capable of handling the drives and ensuring that nothing went wrong. She knew that civilian craft rarely bothered to man the bridge between the stars, but the Solar Navy insisted that military ships maintain a bridge crew at all times. It did have its advantages – she could use the console for everything from simulations to playing games – and yet it was also boring as hell.

She plunged her mind into the simulators, but there wasn't anything new. The captured Tokomak cruiser had managed to purge and destroy her computer banks before surrendering and even the best human technicians had been unable to draw anything useful from the remains. Instead, there were endless scenarios pitting *Freedom* against any number of Galactic starships, ranging from pitiful Horde-controlled starships to Tokomak and Varnar warships. The latter were always dangerous, even if the Tokomak had proved themselves to be less formidable than anyone had thought. She had a feeling – and she knew the intelligence department shared it – that the Varnar would be ordered to take part in the drive on Earth.

But it would leave their homeworld uncovered, she thought. *They would be reluctant to risk themselves.*

She pushed the thought to one side – it was hardly her concern, as it was well above her pay grade – and concentrated on the simulation. It was immersive, so immersive that it was a shock when Commander Gregory shook her lightly, disengaging Yolanda from the datanet and bringing her back to reality. Yolanda jumped, then glanced around in shock. It was always unpleasant to be yanked out of the datanet, no matter the situation. Early versions of the neural link, she'd heard, actually caused brain damage if they disconnected too quickly.

"It's the end of your shift," Commander Gregory said, dryly. "Much as I appreciate your enthusiasm, I don't think you should push yourself too hard."

Yolanda felt herself flushing with embarrassment. It was a rookie mistake, all the more irritating because she'd thought she'd managed to overcome the problem in basic training, before she'd been allowed to serve on a starship. Commander Gregory didn't seem angry – Sergeant Bass would have issued at least three demerits for her mistake – but it was still embarrassing. And to think she'd only just been promoted!

"Go get some rest, then relax," Commander Gregory ordered. "I'll see you in the tactical section tomorrow morning."

"Yes, Commander," Yolanda said.

She gave her console one last check, out of habit, then stood and passed it to her replacement, Ensign Hammond. The young man gave her an admiring look – it felt absurd to have anyone looking up to her – and then sat down. Yolanda waited long enough to see if he had any questions – they were common when the starship was in normal space – and then left the bridge, stepping through the hatch into Officer Country. Martin was on duty, just outside the hatch.

"I think there's no danger of being boarded in FTL," she said. "Why are you even standing guard outside the bridge, anyway?"

"I think it's meant to get us out of Marine Country for a while," Martin said, after a moment's thought. "Or maybe it's just to make sure we don't forget how to stand guard."

Yolanda frowned. "Stand guard?"

"If you fall asleep on watch you can be summarily demoted," Martin admitted. "But if there's an enemy force creeping up on you, it can be much worse."

"It makes sense," Yolanda decided. She gave him a smile. "Join me in my quarters after your shift ends?"

"If your roommate isn't there," Martin said. He smiled back at her. "I don't want to shock the poor dear."

"I don't think anything could shock her," Yolanda said. Simone had been raised in the Solar Union, by a family that seemed to have multiple adults, both male and female. She'd once tried to talk Yolanda into joining a group marriage that would have included at least ten people from each sex. "But I'll let you know if she arrives."

"Thanks," Martin said. "but you'd better run along before the Lieutenant arrives. She's been checking up on us at random intervals."

Yolanda nodded, then hurried on her way.

— —

PRESIDENT ALLEN ROSS knew he would never have been elected on Earth. He was diplomatic, but he was also blunt and plain-spoken...and the media, which made or destroyed candidates, would have ripped him apart. It had been one of the reasons he had been so thoroughly sick of politics on Earth before the Solar Union had been founded – and one of the reasons he had emigrated as soon as he'd been able to convince himself the Solar Union would last.

He'd tried to get involved in politics on Earth, only to discover it was impossible to make a real difference. But on one of the many asteroid Cantons, it *was* possible to have one's say and to make a difference. By the time he'd run for President, he had a good reputation, by the Solar Union's standards, as a mover and shaker. He would never be photogenic, he would never fill every little demographic box, but it didn't matter. All that mattered was being able to do the job.

But there were certain elements he would have preferred to leave to others, if it had been possible.

"You talk a bold case," Ambassador Allis said. "Are you sure you can win?"

"Yes," Allen said, bluntly. "The reports from Hades were quite clear."

He studied the alien thoughtfully. The blue-skinned race – humans tended to call them the Blues, because their real name was unpronounceable – was humanity's oldest ally, the first to see the potential of free humans fighting alongside them. Kevin Stuart himself had brokered the deal that had traded weapons and tech manuals for mercenaries, starting a working relationship that had lasted for over fifty years. The Blues might be larger and more powerful than humanity by far – although *that* was in question, these days – but they were honest allies.

Until the end of the war, he reminded himself. *Alliances only last as long as they are convenient.*

"We expect the Tokomak to make a plunge for Earth soon," he said. The last report from Kevin Stuart, outdated by two weeks, had stated that the Tokomak fleet had yet to arrive. "We intend to meet that fleet and destroy it."

The Blue peered at him, doubtfully. "Are you sure you can stop such a large fleet?"

"We don't know," Allen admitted. "But we certainly intend to try."

He paused. "We ask you to join us," he added. "You have firepower that could make a decisive difference."

There was a long pause. "We would be risking much," the Blue pointed out. He held up a hand before Allen could say a word. "We understand the dangers of allowing the Tokomak to run free, or the simple fact that they will come after us next. However, if we send most of our forces to assist you, our own worlds will be uncovered."

Allen sighed. It was the old problem, even though it had probably saved Earth's bacon more than once. The Varnar could not send a fleet to hammer Earth into submission without leaving themselves wide open to the Coalition. It was why they had called on the Tokomak in the first place. But the Coalition had the same problem when it came to *defending* Earth…

"There will never be a better chance to break the Tokomak," he said.

"But the Varnar will still be active," the Blue said. "We might lose enough of our ships to guarantee our defeat in the war."

The hell of it, Allen knew, was that the Blue was right. If the Coalition won the battle at a high cost, the Varnar would have a chance to beat both humanity and the Coalition before they could recover. The Varnar were the wild card; if they jumped one way, the war might be lost…and if they jumped the other way, they might be destroyed by the Tokomak.

"I understand your point," he said, finally. "I trust you will make use of the tactical data we sent you."

The Blue waved his long slender fingers, their version of a nod. "It will be good for us all to know the Tokomak aren't invincible," he said. "We will spread it far and wide."

"And prepare for an offensive," Allen added. "We may have a chance to win the war outright."

"We shall see," the Blue said. "We will have a large fleet in place to take advantage of your victory, should you win. But we dare not advance too far from our worlds."

The tyranny of FTL sensors, Allen thought. *They would know if the Tokomak started to advance on their homeworlds…but if they weren't in place to intercept the enemy ships it would be impossible to save their worlds.*

"We wish you good hunting," the alien said. "And goodbye."

The alien bowed – a human gesture he'd picked up – and retreated through the hatch. Allen watched him go, feeling the cold weight of responsibility settling down around his shoulders, a cross he sometimes doubted his ability to bear. The Solar Union called him President and granted him power, but it wasn't enough to reshape the universe to his will. Not even the communal vote could change reality.

He looked up as Admiral Stuart entered through the side hatch. "You heard?"

"Yes, Mr. President," Mongo Stuart said. "They can't be faulted."

"I know," the President said. "But we could do with their help."

He sighed, then looked around the office. It was bare; Steve Stuart had designed it personally, according to legend, and the voters would have been mortally offended if he'd added a single piece of decoration. There was nothing in the room, save for a desk, a handful of chairs, a projector and a handful of portraits, showing the last nine Presidents of the Solar Union. Allen wondered, with a trace of resentment, just how they would have handled the Tokomak, if the threat had come to fruition in their time. They'd known it might happen...

...But Allen was the one on the spot when the gods finally noticed the human race.

"The fleet is in position," Mongo assured him. "We should be ready to give them one hell of a nasty surprise."

"I know, Admiral," Allen said. "But will it be nasty enough?"

On Earth, he'd felt...a *depression* sapping his strength, sapping the wills of his countrymen to stand up for their country. It had been nothing he could have placed his finger on; a sense, perhaps, that resistance was not only futile, but *wrong*. Or, perhaps, a sense that one simply couldn't fight City Hall, that even winning one battle would be a pointless victory. The government would have its revenge. And all the hotheads who had talked of gunning down federal agents or shooting the bureaucrats... it had come to nothing.

There had been no challenges, he'd thought, no frontiers to cross. No dreams for the young, no hope of anything, apart from a 9-5 job if they were lucky. No wonder America and the West had become dependent on antidepressants, he'd thought at the time. They had been taught to dream and yet their dreams were ruthlessly squashed.

But the Solar Union had lacked that depression, he knew. The children of the Solar Union were untouched by the shadows of the past. They could build a society without the hang-ups that had damaged the United States to the point the country started to come apart at the seams. It was the hope of the future, the rebirth of the human dream...assuming, of course, they survived the coming war.

He shook his head. There was no time to get pensive about the future.

"We will certainly give them a few surprises," Mongo assured him. "One way or the other, their complacency will end soon."

"I got a complaint from Earth," Allen said. "They're demanding that we exclude them from the Declaration of War."

Mongo snorted. Allen knew how he felt. It wasn't funny, not really, but there was definitely a certain *something* about it. The Galactics barely noticed Sol as a political entity in its own right. They certainly didn't draw any distinction between the Solar Union and Earth, let alone America, France, Germany and Russia. He had a feeling that trying to explain political divisions on a tiny planet on the edge of explored space to the Tokomak would be a waste of time. They would probably only demand to know why humanity hadn't united itself under one rule yet.

They would probably have expected Steve Stuart to make himself ruler of the world, he thought. *The idea of a separate state would have stunned them.*

He looked up at Mongo. Fame – true lasting fame – was rare in the Solar Union, but the Stuart Family were definitely famous. What would Steve Stuart make of the Solar Union as it was now? Or, for that matter, what would he make of the war? Would he come up with something new or...

"You're thinking about my brother," Mongo said. "I could tell by the look on your face."

Allen scowled at him, schooling his face into impassivity. "What would your brother make of this?"

"George Washington kept slaves," Mongo said.

Allen blinked. "That makes no sense," he protested.

"Steve used to say it, every so often," Mongo said. "He would come back home, without fanfare, and reporters would gather round him, ready to write down everything he said as if it were pearls of wisdom from a prophet. And he would always remind them that George Washington kept slaves."

"I don't see the point," Allen said.

"Steve's point was that Washington, who was effectively deified by America, was only a man," Mongo said. "He was a good military leader, a great politician and a true patriot, but he was only a man. Some of his acts, like keeping slaves or burning Indian townships, make him out to be a far darker character than the saint we were taught to revere. He was just a man, without all the answers, let alone a modern sense of values. Steve wouldn't be able to come here, sit down at your desk and hand out answers like glasses of beer at Oktoberfest."

Mongo shrugged. "Don't look to me for your answers, I think he meant," he added, after a moment. "Find them for yourself."

Allen smiled. "Thank you for that clarification," he said, dryly. "But I'm not sure it was particularly helpful."

"Neither is being spoon-fed the answers – right or wrong," Mongo countered. "And *that* was something Steve knew better than to do, even before he became our Founding Father."

— —

"THE FLEET IS ready to depart?"

"Yes, Your Excellency," the Admiral said. "We have a direct course set for Earth."

Neola clicked her fingers. "And the new training programs?"

"They have been problematic," the Admiral admitted. "The crews are not used to them."

"Then tell them to *get* used to them," Neola snapped. She would have preferred to wait longer, to get her ships and crews ready for the coming fight, but time wasn't on her side, not when word was already spreading through the empire. The Old Ones would hear about it soon and relieve her of command. "The humans are unlikely to play by the rules."

The Admiral bowed, then retreated, leaving her in the CIC.

"The new exercises are having a devastating effect on morale," He'cht observed, from the shadows. "Your crews are not prepared for scenarios that aren't scripted right down to the last detail."

"So I have heard," Neola said. The Admiral had complained loudly. So had every commanding officer of every ship, without exception. Complaints about the new regime were probably also winging their way up the gravity points too. "But can we beat the humans?"

"It depends," He'cht said. "Do you have more firepower than the humans? Probably. Do you have more flexibility than the humans? Probably not. You will just have to hope that you have enough firepower to make their flexibility immaterial."

Neola sighed, bitterly.

One hour later, the fleet dropped into FTL and started the crawl towards Earth.

THIRTY-TWO

The Japanese Government finally passed the long-awaited law forcing all Japanese women to have at least four children before reaching the age of thirty. This law, which is intended to replenish the ethnic Japanese population (which has been in decline for the last seventy years) has been hotly opposed by protesters both in and out of Japan. However, with the Conservative Government in firm control, it is unlikely the act will not be enforced. It is as yet unclear what penalties will be assigned to women who fail to comply with the law.

—Solar News Network, Year 53

"Captain," Yolanda said. "We will return to normal space in five minutes."

"Take us out as planned," Captain Singh ordered, calmly. "And give me a full tactical report the moment we come out of FTL."

"Aye, sir," Yolanda said. It had been a long flight, with rumours spreading that the Tokomak had ignored Hades and launched an immediate attack on Earth instead. She had no idea what the squadron would have done if it had returned home to find a devastated solar system, but she doubted it would have been pretty. "We will return to normal space in one minute."

She counted down the remaining seconds until the squadron slipped back into normal space, then plunged her mind into the sensor nodes. The inky darkness of FTL was suddenly replaced by stars…and icons representing unknown starships. IFF signals started to come in seconds later, identifying them as the Solar Union Navy. There were over four hundred starships waiting for them.

"Captain," she said. "The entire Solar Navy is here."

"Shoot the Admiral a tactical download," the Captain ordered. "Everything from the moment we arrived at Hades to now."

"Aye, Captain," Commander Gregory said.

Yolanda barely heard him. She was staring at the starships, a multitude of human and alien designs. Most of them were converted freighters or Galactic warships that had fallen into human hands, but a small number were identical to *Freedom*. Humanity's own design of warship, elegant and yet practical…she felt a lump in her throat as she looked at the fleet, finally understanding why the Tokomak viewed her people as a threat. Fifty years after gaining access to alien technology, the human race had put together a formidable force, enough to tip the balance in the endless Proxy War.

"There's a private message from the Admiral for you, Captain," Commander Gregory said, softly. "You're ordered to read it in private."

"You have the bridge," Captain Singh said. "I'll be in my ready room."

Beyond the warships, there were a number of surprises. Some objects weren't broadcasting an IFF, their purposes unknown; others were automated weapons platforms, a design copied from the Galactics years ago and endlessly refined. It looked as though someone was planning an ambush, but how could they be sure where their enemy would appear? Anyone with the right technology could detect a starship in flight, yet they couldn't predict the exact emergence point. How could they?

"We have picket ships out several light years in all directions," Commander Gregory said, once the Captain had left the bridge. Clearly, she'd accessed a tactical download from the fleet datanet. "We will know when they are coming and will move position, if necessary, to intercept."

Yolanda frowned. A glance at the navigation subroutine told her they were placed along a least-time course from Varnar to Earth, but it still didn't explain how they were going to intercept the Tokomak. The Galactics were unlikely to drop out of FTL long enough to engage the human ships, if only because they wouldn't know they were there. There was no point in mock-threatening the Varnar worlds if the threat wasn't visible. It made no sense.

Think outside the box, she told herself. *What does the Admiral have in mind?*

"You will also review the tactical planning files," Commander Gregory added, "then start drilling. By the time they arrive, we need to be one united fleet."

"Yes, Commander," the bridge crew said.

Yolanda smiled. Commander Gregory might be a hard-ass when it came to running endless drills, but her heart was in the right place – and besides, she was entirely correct. Hard training, easy mission; easy training, hard mission. Better to get all the mistakes out of the way before lives were actually placed at risk…

She sighed, then accessed the tactical files and frowned. They all seemed to believe that the aliens would appear right in front of the human fleet. But why?

— —

"I SUPPOSE," NEOLA said, "that you have an explanation for this?"

She glowered at the holographic images, wishing she could reach through the datanet and strangle the commanding officers in person. They hadn't listened to her, even though she'd taken the precaution of having the fleet fly in close enough formation to allow them to drill together, even in FTL. And the latest set of simulated exercises had been an embarrassing disaster, worse than any of them thought. They didn't know – yet – that the enemy commander had been a Varnar, not any of her Tokomak subordinates.

"I told you to use your brains," she said. "I told you not to use predictable formations and flight paths. I told you to actually *think* before you acted. And what did you do? You followed the same old routines, time and time again, until the enemy smashed your ships into rubble!"

"Your Excellency," one of the commanders said, "these tactics have been laid down since the dawn of empire..."

"Yes, they have," Neola said. "And the universe has changed since then! Didn't you realise that Tactical Pattern ZZ-Alpha was leading you into a trap? The Admirals who devised it didn't have to reckon with long-range energy weapons, did they? You practically impaled yourselves on their weapons because you didn't bother to think!"

She took a long rasping breath. "And you *then* fell back on an entirely predictable defensive formation," she thundered. "And you didn't even change it when you realised the enemy was taking *advantage* of your lack of thought!"

"This is the way things have been done since time out of mind," one of the older commanders insisted. He hated her for being younger than him and yet his superior, Neola knew. It was understandable, in a way, but not after Hades. "These tactics served our forefathers well."

"Yes, they did," Neola said. "And charging while throwing spears *also* served our forefathers well, until they ran into machine guns and got killed. The universe has changed since the days we built the empire! We need to adapt or be slaughtered."

She clenched her fists in irritation. It was hard for her, so very hard, to adapt to the new universe. Every conservative bone in her body called for her to stay with the old ways, the routines she'd been taught since she was a child. There was no grounds for change, they insisted; the old ways were more than good enough. Hadn't they built an entire empire? But the universe was different now and they had to adapt too...

The humans had obtained Galactic technology, somehow. *That* was certain. The last time the Varnar had looked at them, they had been barely capable of flight. A fast rate of expansion, particularly as they'd been riding horses when the Tokomak had logged their world in the database, but not fast enough to propel them to spaceflight by now. Or so she hoped. If the humans really had developed spaceflight and FTL without help, in four hundred years, the Tokomak were doomed. They had barely been able to adapt to changes wrought by far slower Galactics. A race that progressed at breakneck speed would outstrip the empire before the empire knew there was a threat…

There had been races that had advanced fast, she knew. They'd tended to destroy themselves before they ever got into deep space. But there were rumours that some had been exterminated by her superiors, just in case…

She made a note of the thought for later contemplation, then glowered at her subordinates.

"You will run the exercise again," she said. "And this time you will use your brains. Or I will dig out the old regulations and put them back to use."

They blanched. The *really* old regulations, dating back all the way to the pointless wars before FTL had been invented, gave her the power of life and death over her subordinates. If she wanted, she could flog, maim or even kill them…and no one would be able to complain, no matter how barbaric it seemed. She was the supreme commander, after all, and the regulations had never been revised or removed from the book. Given how conservative her race actually was, it was no surprise.

"Go," she ordered.

The images blinked out of existence, to be replaced with the final image from the simulated battle. A dozen battleships had been destroyed, along with thirty smaller ships…it would have been an embarrassing defeat, in real life. Instead, it was a learning experience – she hoped. Coming up with new tactics on the fly wasn't something her crews did.

"That could have gone better," she said.

"It could have gone worse," the Varnar countered. He'd been lurking in the shadows at the rear of her cabin, knowing that he couldn't be seen by the officers. They would have protested his involvement. "At least they listened to you."

Neola clenched her teeth. The fleet was four days from Earth and hadn't shown many signs of improvement. Morale was in the pits, at least partly because she'd ordered the crews to remain on alert, even though they were in FTL and thus immune to the universe. Normally, the crew would take FTL as a chance to relax and burnish the internal decoration; now, they were standing watches, running simulations of their own and practicing repair work. It had chilled her to the bone, after the first drill, to realise just how poorly prepared they were for a real battle. But the crew hadn't come to agree with her.

"They listened because I threatened them," Neola said. Other races had it easy. To them, a six hundred year old officer was worthy of respect. But to the Tokomak, she was little more than a child. "What's going to happen when we encounter the humans?"

"You'll take heavy losses," He'cht said. The Varnar seemed unbothered by the thought. "I don't think your crews are prepared for damage control duties, so the damage will swiftly mount up and eventually doom your ships. You have to hope you have enough firepower to absorb the losses and keep going."

He paused. "You should have accepted our offer of additional crewmen," he added. "They would have made your ships stronger, more able to fight."

Neola would have accepted, if regulations had allowed it. But she couldn't have, which was something of a blessing. At least the Varnar wouldn't get a close look at just how unprepared her ships were for war, after all. They were sitting on top of the gravity point leading further into the empire, allowing them to pose a real threat if they changed sides. There was no point in giving them ideas.

She contemplated He'cht, coldly. As useful as he was, he could not be allowed to go home after serving as her aide. He had simply seen too much.

"Four days," she mused. "Four days to get the fleet ready for battle."

The plan was simple enough. Drop out of FTL near Earth and advance on the planet, firing long-range missiles as they approached. There would be no attempt to occupy the planet, not after the humans had proved themselves so dangerous. Instead, Earth would be destroyed, her population exterminated. In the meantime, the fast little human ships would have no choice; they would have to come to her and fight, or watch helplessly as their homeworld died.

And without their homeworld, she thought, *the rest of their population will dwindle and die.*

"You will need to run more simulations," He'cht said, softly. "Because the humans are many things, but they are not cowards. And they will know you are coming."

MARTIN WIPED SWEAT from his brow as he exited the simulation and nodded to Lieutenant Robbins, who looked as tired as he felt. Days of endless simulations, of running through every possible contingency plan they could imagine, had left a toll on them all. If they hadn't been heavily augmented, he had a feeling they would have collapsed by now.

"Good work, everyone," Robbins said. Her voice was alarmingly quiet, nothing like any of the Drill Instructors. But then, she had more than earned their respect. "You could have moved quicker in the latter half of the exercise, but you've done well."

Martin nodded. The computer hacking protocols had failed – according to the random chance written into parts of the simulation – and the Marines had had to fall out of the ship, leaving a nuclear warhead behind. It wasn't a tactic he would have cared to try, if there had been any alternative, but there had been none.

"BRUTE should have moved faster," he said. "We could have had the ship if they hadn't had the wit to separate the infected datacore from their datanet."

"I moved as fast as possible," the AI's voice said, stiffly. "The simulation was simply not devised to give me a chance to subvert the ship before it was too late."

"We cannot expect to simply take over every ship," Robbins said, firmly. "The Galactics may not have AIs, but they do understand the dangers of hacking software and other electronic weapons. Their precautions may work better in combat than in the simulations."

"Their datacores are cranky and old," BRUTE added. "Some of them crumble at an AIs mere touch."

Martin looked up towards the ceiling, where he imagined BRUTE to be. "Why? Why don't they use AIs themselves?"

"They may have had a bad experience with AIs in the past," BRUTE said, "and thus designed their systems to completely preclude the possibility of spontaneously generating an AI of their own. Or they may simply be masters of bad or no maintenance. The computer cores on the captured starships should have been replaced regularly and weren't. Even with Galactic-level tolerance engineered into the design, they were on the verge of collapse even before we captured them."

"Poor bastards," Robbins muttered.

Martin found himself caught between agreeing with her and being irked at her attitude. He knew just how much starships depended on computers, how absolutely impossible it was to use FTL drives without computers monitoring the gravity flux and compensating for any shifts if necessary. Navigating home, too, would be difficult without the computers. But, on the other hand, anything that wrecked a Tokomak starship before it had a chance to engage the human fleet was a good thing. The Tokomak were throwing overwhelming force at Earth. If they lost a few ships because of their poor maintenance...well, that was their problem, wasn't it? *He* certainly wasn't going to complain.

"Dismissed," Robbins said. "Report back here in six hours if the alert doesn't sound before then."

The Marines saluted, then walked out the door. Martin headed out of Marine Country and up through the network of corridors towards Officer Country, wondering when – precisely – *Freedom* had become home. He knew everyone on the ship, from the Captain himself to the lowliest crewman, without having to resort to his implants. And it was...*safe*. There was no need to constantly watch his back, at least when he wasn't exercising and drilling with the other Marines. The ship was home in a way the ghetto never could have been.

He tapped on Yolanda's hatch and smiled as it opened, then stepped inside. Yolanda was lying on her bunk, while her roommate was absent.

"Simone has been dating a girl in engineering," Yolanda explained, as she sat up. "So we agreed we'd vacate the cabin in a couple of hours for them to have their fun."

"Oh," Martin said. He started to pull off his shirt, then grinned. "We'd better be quick, then."

"You're always quick," Yolanda said, sticking out her tongue.

"It's the implants," Martin said, as he removed his trousers. "Whoever would have thought the most common use for implants was *sex*?"

Yolanda smirked. "The same people who took cameras and used them to take naughty photos, the same people who used camcorders to make naughty movies, the same people who used the internet to share pornography with everyone..."

"Oh, shut up," Martin said. He climbed onto the bunk, then began to unbutton her shirt, revealing her breasts. "Sex is a natural part of human existence."

Yolanda kissed his lips, then pulled him towards her.

Afterwards, they held each other tightly, knowing that time was running out. Martin looked down at her and wondered, absently, just how they fitted together. Yolanda wasn't the kind of girl he'd expected to have a relationship with...and he would have bet half of his salary that he wasn't the kind of boy she'd planned to date. But the thought of abandoning her was unthinkable.

"Yes," Yolanda mused. "Those implants do come in handy, don't they?"

Martin elbowed her. "Are you feeling all right?"

"I feel better now," Yolanda said. "And it helps, being completely separate from my past life. And thank you too, for being different."

"You're different too," Martin said, although he understood. Stereotypes were far too prevalent on Earth, if only because there was no shortage of idiots who tried to live up – or down – to them. "And thank you."

He kissed her, then checked his implants for the time. They didn't really have time for another round before they had to vacate the quarters…and there was nowhere else to go for some privacy. The Captain had been less than happy to discover a pair of crewmen making out in one of the intership tubes, a few weeks ago…

Moments later, the alarms sounded.

"Shit," Yolanda said, springing to her feet. "They're nearly here!"

THIRTY-THREE

War graves in Arlington Cemetery were desecrated yesterday by what is believed to be a Jihadist Group. Arabic graffiti was painted over the tombstones, while several graves were uprooted and the various war memorials were defaced. The President attempted to downplay the incident at a press conference, but widespread public anger may force him to take a different path.

—Solar News Network, Year 53

"They're due in one hour," Commander Gregory said, as Yolanda hurried onto the bridge and hastened towards her console. "You don't need to run."

Yolanda flushed and hastily sat down, wishing she could die of embarrassment. Her nanotech would clean her up, she knew, but it was nothing like as good as a proper shower, perhaps one shared with Martin...she pushed the thought aside and brought up the status display, cursing her timing. If the enemy had waited for just one more hour...

She plunged her mind into the sensors and shuddered, inwardly, as she saw the sheer scale of the enemy fleet. There were so many gravimetric signatures approaching the Sol System – and the Solar Navy – that they were blurring together, making it impossible to determine precisely how many there were. Perhaps their obsession with perfect formations had a point after all, she reasoned; random flight paths and positions would make it much harder to compensate for so many starships in FTL so close together at the same time.

"There are at least three hundred signatures," she said, out loud. "But I can't be sure."

"It may make no difference, Lieutenant," Commander Gregory said. "Just relax and wait."

Yolanda couldn't do either. How could the human fleet be planning an ambush? There was no way to engage starships in FTL, as far as she knew. They might as well be on the other side of the galaxy for all the Tokomak would see of them. But she had to assume that Admiral Stuart knew what he was doing…gritting her teeth, she forced herself to continue to parse out the gravimetric signatures, trying to isolate as many separate starships as possible.

The minutes ticked away slowly, leaving her feeling more and more frustrated with every breath. It just didn't make sense…angrily, she called on her implants, dampening her feelings as much as possible. But even with her emotions under control, her thoughts still chased themselves round and round in circles. There was no way they could ambush the enemy fleet, was there?

"Signal from the flag," Lieutenant Elves said. "We are to move to a new position."

"Make it so," Captain Singh ordered.

Yolanda rolled her eyes – that joke had been old long before her mother had been born – but obeyed. The human fleet was now spread out in a giant arc, surrounding the least-time course from Varnar to Earth. But it still made absolutely no sense…she worried at the thought as the captured freighters were moved forward, dumping their cargo of long-range missiles into space. Even if the Varnar attacked the human fleet, the moment they saw the missiles they would drop back into FTL and retreat. They couldn't be pinned in place, exposed to incoming fire…could they?

She stared down at the display, studying the handful of unmarked units. What *were* they?

The seconds ticked down to zero. On the display, the Tokomak fleet drew closer, travelling at many times the speed of light. It was impossible for her to grasp just how far apart the fleets actually were, not when it seemed she could reach out and touch them. And then...

She blinked as waves of gravity – artificial gravity – started to pervade space. Understanding followed, moments later. No one, not even the Galactics, could go into FTL close to a large planetary mass. Now, human technicians had created an artificial gravity well, right in front of the Tokomak fleet. And they were about to run right into it...

IT WAS SHEER luck that Neola was in the CIC when the entire starship shook violently, then crashed back into normal space. Standard procedure was to spend time in FTL burnishing the inner hull or simply relaxing, not running endless drills. If she hadn't been trying to set a good example, if she hadn't insisted that full watches be online at all times, the human ambush might have wrecked her entire fleet before she had a chance to react.

Even so, comprehending what had happened pushed her to the limit.

She had known the humans would detect her incoming fleet. There was simply no way to mask a single gravimetric signature, let alone a giant haze of gravimetric distortion generated by hundreds of starships flying in close formation. But she had never imagined anyone using an artificial gravity field to yank an entire fleet out of FTL. She cursed under her breath as the datanet rapidly updated, warning her that nearly seventy battleships had crashed back to normal space so violently that their drives were permanently offline. A light year from Sol, the closest star, they would take at least four years to reach somewhere safe...

"Your Excellency," the Admiral said. "We are surrounded by human starships. They are demanding our surrender."

Neola fought down panic. Some of her ships couldn't escape? So what? The humans wouldn't be able to escape either, not as long as they kept the artificial gravity field in place…and they would have to, unless they wished her remaining FTL-capable ships to continue the advance on Earth. They were prisoners of their own success…

She studied the display, thoughtfully, allowing cold logic to banish panic. There were over four hundred ships facing her, but most of them weren't warships. Indeed, most of them were converted freighters. And most of the *warships* were ancient designs. There was no need to panic, not really. The humans might pack a punch, but she still had the advantage.

"Advance forward to firing range," she ordered, coolly. Maybe some of her commanders would take the humans seriously, now. "And chart out their gravity field."

"The humans are opening fire," the Admiral said. "They're launching missiles at us."

For a moment, Neola couldn't grasp what she was seeing. Everyone *knew* that missiles – long-range missiles – were useless in ship-to-ship engagements. If the humans wanted to waste their firepower, who was she to stop them? And yet, she knew they were up to something…

It struck her in a moment of blinding horror. The long-range missiles weren't wasted, not when her fleet couldn't escape into FTL. They were about to be ripped apart…unless she reacted quickly. None of their scenarios had envisaged being locked out of FTL; at worst, she'd always known she would be able to escape. But she'd been wrong.

"Bring up the point defence," she ordered. For once, the routine formations they'd practiced would work in their favour. "And launch our own long-range missiles back at them."

The Admiral swing around. "Your Excellency?"

"If we're locked out of FTL, so are they," Neola snapped. She cursed her superiors under her breath. Perhaps this entire disaster could have been averted if they'd encouraged the youngsters to develop an imagination. "And we can hit them too."

Moments later, her battleships started to spew missiles into space.

She watched, coldly and dispassionately, as the gravity field was slowly charted out in front of her. A planetary gravity field was easy to track; it was a sphere, surrounding the planetary mass. There were rarely any fluctuations in its strength that made life interesting for starships trying to cut their travel times to the bare minimum. But the artificial gravity field looked hazy and imprecise, as if it had multiple sources...

"Locate the generators," she ordered. Blowing apart an entire planet to escape the gravity field was excessive, even by Tokomak standards, but she could locate the gravity generators and destroy them. "Once you have located them, destroy them."

She watched, helplessly, as the waves of missiles descended on her ships. Most of them were clearly of Tokomak origin, taken – she assumed – from Hades. The Varnar had been right, she understood now, to point out that the entire plan had been badly flawed. It had rested on the key assumption that the human race would be mesmerised by the sheer level of firepower arrayed against them and when that had been proven false, so had the plan. The Tokomak had provided their enemies with the weapons to use against them.

Hundreds of missiles were swatted out of existence, but hundreds more made it through. She cursed her own oversight even as she mentally praised her gunnery crews, who had improved a hundredfold in the weeks they'd spent drilling, after watching the Battle of Hades and how quickly a formerly-invincible squadron had been torn apart. But there were just too many missiles...she gritted her teeth as they started to slam into shields, weakening some and shattering others. Far too many shield generators were too old and outdated to stand up to sudden blows.

"The enemy fleet is taking losses," the Admiral reported. "But they're continuing the attack."

— —

MONGO HADN'T BEEN enthusiastic about the idea of hurling the Tokomak missiles right back at their designers. There hadn't been time to take the warheads apart and make sure they didn't have any backdoors, which would have allowed the Tokomak the chance to turn them off before it was too late. But he had to admit that the idea had worked surprisingly well, even though the Tokomak had promptly copied his idea and started to return fire. Some of his older ships had already been destroyed by their missiles.

"Launch the hammers," he ordered. "And then follow up with the ECM drones."

The gravity field shifted, suddenly. "Report!"

"They took out one of the Zahn Generators," Commander Wilson snapped. "They're actively searching for others."

"Of course they are," Mongo said.

He smirked, then mentally tipped his hat to the Tokomak commander. A human commander would have started to hunt for the gravity generators at once...and, by their very nature, they were impossible to hide. But, caught by surprise, he was moderately impressed the Tokomak commander had caught on so rapidly. It wasn't something she would have known to expect.

But she should have, he reflected. The Tokomak had practically *invented* gravity-related technology, even though they hadn't taken it to its logical extreme. But then, some of the ideas human science-fiction had devised had proven surprisingly practical, when twinned with alien technology. If the idea for boosting the sun's gravity field ever proved workable, they could ensure that no alien ship could ever approach Earth without being forced to leave FTL a long way before its prime targets.

He dismissed the thought as the Hammers plunged towards their targets, wondering absently what the Tokomak made of them. They would be easily detectable, but – by their very nature – hellishly hard to destroy. If he'd had a few thousand of them, the battle would be over by now, yet there were only a handful on hand.

A few more years, he thought, *and we would have utterly destroyed the fleet without taking a single casualty*.

The Hammers approached their targets...and drew fire. He watched with grim amusement as energy weapons flared out...and vanished. Moments later, the Hammers smashed home, crashing right *through* the enemy shields and into their hulls. Several of them kept plunging onwards, others were caught and destroyed as their targets exploded. The survivors altered course and started to hunt for new targets.

And they could have built Hammers for themselves, if they'd thought of the concept, he thought. *Instead, they let themselves ossify and decline.*

NEOLA WATCHED IN disbelief as twelve battleships died a fiery death, four of their killers escaping onwards, then turning around to seek new targets. It was impossible...she forced herself to put her emotions aside and reason it out logically. What was she actually seeing?

"Microscopic black holes," one of her officers said. "They actually generated a self-sustaining gravity well."

It made sense, Neola realised, coldly. The humans had produced a black hole generator and loaded it on a missile. Instead of a drive, the missile had plunged towards the black hole...but as the black hole was always a set distance from the missile, it had effectively pulled itself onwards and onwards. And it had swallowed everything in its path, from energy weapons fire to hull material. The concept was far from impossible. It was merely something the Tokomak had never bothered to develop for themselves.

Because we saw ourselves as invincible, she thought, coldly. What would happen to the Tokomak Empire, which was dependent on its vast fleet of warships, if someone produced a relatively cheap weapon that could smash a battleship without breaking a sweat? *And black hole missiles would have altered the balance of power against us.*

"Continue firing," she ordered. "And take us right towards them. We have to close the range."

She tapped her console, issuing updates. There were ways to deal with the black hole missiles that didn't involve panic, as long as they were used carefully. Her crews might be shocked, but at least they weren't coming apart. She silently thanked her foresight in ordering endless drills, then turned her attention to the battle. Sooner or later, the humans would run out of tricks. All she had to do was hold her fleet together until then. And then she could jump back into FTL and continue the advance on Earth.

— —

YOLANDA GRITTED HER teeth as the Tokomak advanced, clearly trying to either force the humans into a close-range engagement or escape the artificial gravity wells. Either one would offer them a chance to turn the battle around, even though they were taking a beating. The endless stream of updates, processed and analysed by the AIs, suggested that a number of Tokomak ships had actually lost their FTL drives. If so, they could remain in place and harass the human ships while their compatriots attacked Sol.

Freedom shuddered as an antimatter missile detonated far too close to her shields. Yolanda altered course randomly, as Commander Gregory picked off another two missiles that would have otherwise have posed a threat. Thankfully, the combination of ECM and sensor decoys was making it harder for the Tokomak to target their weapons, or the humans would be in considerably more trouble. Even so, the losses were starting to mount…and they were running out of stolen missiles.

"Orders from the flag," Commander Gregory said. "We are to advance and harass the enemy."

"Take us into the fire," Captain Singh ordered. "Random course changes, remember."

Yolanda smiled, then plunged her mind back into the computer datanet until the ship was practically an extension of her own body. *Freedom* seemed to brace herself, like a man waiting to bungee jump off a cliff, and then lunged forward at her command, weapons flaring with deadly light. She twisted her flight path and lanced between two lumbering battleships, Commander Gregory launching torpedoes with wild abandon. One of the battleships exploded, the other stumbled to one side, but kept firing. Yolanda threw *Freedom* into a madcap series of evasive manoeuvres, then yanked the ship to one side as the enemy fire suddenly sharpened up.

Either they'd replaced the gunnery crews or they'd allowed their electronic servants to take over targeting...it hardly mattered. She whooped – not out loud, she hoped – and spun the ship close to her next target, dodging blast after blast of incoming fire. The enemy ship was even hurling long-range missiles towards *Freedom*, at alarmingly short range.

"Keep us as close to them as possible," Captain Singh ordered. "But not too close."

Yolanda frowned. *Lightning* had already died, simply from accidentally ramming one of the giant battleships, destroying both ships in a single blast. The Tokomak could keep trading battleships for cruisers and still come out ahead, even if...*Freedom* shook violently as a phased energy beam struck her shields, sending her spinning through space. Yolanda regained control and swung the ship into a different series of patterns, before the enemy could capitalise on their success and hammer her shields into nothingness.

"Aye, sir," she said.

Commander Gregory kept firing, beams of energy raking the hulls of additional battleships as they lumbered onwards, trying to ignore the deadly gnats shooting at them. It wasn't a bad tactic, Yolanda had to admit; they couldn't hope to catch the human cruisers if they tried, so they were attempting to escape the gravity field. And the humans had to close in and enter weapons range if they wanted to kill the aliens...

"New targets," Captain Singh said. "Alter course and engage."

Yolanda fought to control the ship. It was easier said than done, particularly as the Tokomak were altering their formation to allow more of their ships a shot at the gnats. They were actually making it harder for her to enter close range...she swung *Freedom* around, then powered her way right towards the enemy formation. There would be a moment, she was sure, when they wouldn't dare fire on her because of the risk of hitting other ships.

You shouldn't have devised such a tight formation, she thought, as she flew past the enemy vessels. *It's not tight enough to stop me and too tight to let you fight back effectively...*

"Approaching new targets now, sir," she said. Alerts flared up in front of her mind. "They're locking weapons on us."

"Launch the Marines as soon as we reach the closest point of approach," Captain Singh ordered. "And then pull us away from them."

Martin, Yolanda thought. She had never wanted to pray, not since realising that the mercy and tolerance of her stepmother's religion wasn't extended to mixed-race children. *Please God, let him come through this alive.*

And then she dragged her attention back to the battle.

THIRTY-FOUR

Scotland Yard today refused to disclose murder rates for London for the third year running, citing ethnic and religious concerns. However, Tory Buckminster, the exiled leader of the British National Party, claimed that the murder rates were produced by ethnic cleansing, carried out by immigrant communities against outsiders. The victims, according to sources within the Metropolitan Police, tend to bear out this assertion.

—Solar News Network, Year 53

Neola watched, feeling cold anticipation burning through her mind, as the gravity field slowly started to fade out of existence. They'd taken losses, heavy losses, but most of the fleet was still intact. Irritatingly, the humans seemed to have devised a way to separate the FTL-capable ships from the stranded ships, but it hardly mattered. She still had enough firepower to reduce Earth to rubble.

If I don't have enough missiles left, she thought, as another human starship died in fire, *I can simply bombard the planet with asteroids until the population is dead and gone.*

"The human ships are converging," the Admiral warned. "They're closing in on our formation."

"Order the crippled ships to cover us," Neola ordered. There was no point in ordering them to fall back, not now. Recovering the ships and their crews would depend on victory – and nothing else. "And continue firing until we reach the edge of the gravity field."

She watched, with cold amusement, as another ex-Galactic warship died. The stars themselves knew just how many hands the ship had passed through before the humans purchased – or captured, or stole – it, but they'd modified the ship extensively. There was no way to avoid the simple fact that humans were supremely disruptive, even when limited to Galactic-level technology. Whatever her personal thoughts on the matter, there was no alternative. The humans had to go.

"Only two more generators to go," another officer added. "Their gravity field is fading fast."

Neola nodded, impatiently.

"Your Excellency," a third officer said. "They're launching...*something*...at us."

"Show me," Neola ordered. What now? She was on the verge of escaping the trap, of heading to Earth with thirty battleships, all reasonably undamaged. Had the humans produced something new? "What are they?"

"I don't know," the officer admitted. "They're coming towards us on attack vector."

— —

MARTIN FELT SICK. The giant alien starship looming over him was unimaginably large, so huge he couldn't even *begin* to grasp just how immense it was. His implants provided statistics, informing him that the ships was five kilometres long, its hull studded with weapons and sensor blisters. It was so huge that, the closer he got, the more it swallowed up the rest of the universe. And they were supposed to *attack* it?

"Combat interlink online," Lieutenant Robbins said. "Prepare for shield disruption."

Martin closed his eyes as energy flickered over his suit. The shield disruptor, they'd been told, would work...but only at very short range. There was no point in fitting it to a missile, the designers had said, yet they hadn't had any problem fitting it to a Marine Combat Suit. He opened his eyes again, just in time to see the enemy hull falling towards him at terrifying speed. His suit automatically compensated, saving him from smashing himself into a pulp; he touched down on the enemy hull and looked around. There was something oddly impressive about the decorations carved into the metal, even though hardly anyone would ever see them. The Tokomak were clearly more than a little anal.

He smirked, then flinched as darkness suddenly descended over the hull. When he looked up, all he saw was an inky omnipresent darkness, so dark it seemed to capture the eyes. He cursed, then looked back down at the darkened hull. The Tokomak had made it back into FTL, going somewhere...he'd bet they were headed towards Earth. It was the only thing they could do, after the damage they'd taken. They *had* to win or their reputation would be forever destroyed.

"There's a hatch over there," Robbins called. "Follow me."

Martin obeyed, linking his mind into the rest of the suits. There were fifty-seven heavily-armed Marines on the hull, ready to break into the ship and try to take control. But there should have been two hundred... he wanted to check to see if the remainder had been diverted, or if their shield disruptors had failed, but he forced himself not to look. There was nothing to be gained from checking, not now.

He followed Robbins to the hatch, then watched as she blew it open. The outer airlock wasn't that strong, he noted; the inner airlock was broken. It should have sealed itself automatically, but instead it just hung open. Atmosphere started to blow out of the hull moments later, rushing past the Marines and out into the nothingness of FTL. Martin wondered, absently, just what would happen to the ship if it lost power suddenly, then followed Robbins into the hull. According to the plans they'd recovered from the first ship, they were less than a kilometre from the command core.

"They'll know we're here," Robbins said, as the remainder of the Marines flooded into the ship. Captain Lockland either hadn't made it or had been diverted to another ship. "We have no time to lose."

Martin nodded, then found a convenient datanode. The alien tech was standard, without any flourishes; he inserted a hacking node, then waited. If they were lucky, they could assert control of the ship without having to fight their way through small armies of aliens…

— —

"THE SHIP HAS been boarded!"

Neola would have been shocked, but she was too tired to feel real emotion. No one had dared to board a Tokomak ship since…she shook her head, unable to remember when – if – it had last happened. Certainly, it hadn't happened by force for thousands of years. The treacherous officer who had surrendered at Hades had allowed his ship to be boarded, instead of losing control to a landing party.

"Isolate that section," she ordered. She should have brought a small army with her, she saw now, as well as just the ships. But it was hard enough to convince enough young Tokomak to join the Navy, let alone the groundpounders. They simply didn't have the manpower to keep the ceremonial regiments up to strength. "And then…and then arm the crew. Get them to keep the section sealed off."

"Your Excellency," the Admiral said. "None of the crew have weapons training…"

"I imagine that was skipped too," Neola scowled.

She swore a silent oath to herself. If she made it back alive, with Earth in radioactive ruins, she would make sure things changed. There would be no more polishing the decks until they gleamed, no more carefully scripted exercises, no more scrapping of basic training while concentrating in ceremonials. And if the Old Ones complained, she would force them to see just how badly out of touch they were with the galaxy. They had to understand that the universe was changing and, even if the humans died, nothing would ever be the same again.

"Then give them weapons and hope for the best," she ordered. "And shut down all, but essential systems. We don't want them to subvert our computers."

"That's impossible," the Admiral said, hotly.

Neola met his eyes, glaring him into submission. "Would you bet your life on it?"

She pressed on before he could answer. "Shut down all, but essential systems," she repeated, angrily. "They've shown us too many unpleasant surprises for us to take them lightly."

Four hours to Earth, she thought, as her subordinates scurried to do her bidding. *Their fleet will give chase, of course, but unless their stardrives are faster we will get to Earth first. And then we can bombard their world into submission…or destroy it completely, leaving the rest of their race to die.*

"NO JOY, LIEUTENANT," Martin reported. "Their system is secure. The RI believes it will take at least seven hours to crack the locked datacores."

He cursed under his breath. BRUTE had far more processing power than a mere RI, along with the spark of intuition that came with being an intelligent entity in its own right. But BRUTE was cut off from them by the FTL drive. There was no way they could reconnect before the ship arrived at Earth.

"Then we take the ship by force," Robbins said.

She started to issue orders, quickly and decisively. The Marines abandoned the airlock – there was no point in leaving a rearguard, as they would either win or lose – and advanced forward into the ship. No resistance greeted them, which made the Marines nervous. Chatter slowed to a halt as they moved from compartment to compartment, scattering nanotech drones ahead of them. The ship might feel hauntingly empty, but they were sure the enemy was waiting for them somewhere.

Martin couldn't help thinking of the last time they'd boarded a Tokomak ship as he looked at the decor, but this ship's commander was even more obsessive about decorating his vessel. Strange pieces of artwork were scattered everywhere, in line with an aesthetic that was very definitely alien. Some of the pieces were understandable, others might as well have been alien pornography for all he knew. The paintings, hanging from the bulkheads or lying on the deck, shaken loose by the bombardment the ship had taken, were just as eerie. He wondered if they had some deep meaning to the Tokomak, or if the ship's commander was nothing more than a collector for the sake of collecting. There was no way to know.

"The nanotech drones have run into killer clouds," Corporal Henderson reported. "We don't have any sensor access past the next compartment."

"Which means the enemy are probably setting up their ambush there," Robbins said. "Douglas, Williams, Patel; you're on point. Go right through them."

Martin nodded, then slipped up the corridor. The lights were flickering and flaring, although he wasn't sure if the ship was losing power or if the aliens were trying to disconcert their unwanted guests. Either made sense...he glanced at the internal display, checking on the progress of the hack, but the RI hadn't managed to get any further into the system. He sighed to himself, then hefted his assault rifle and selected the grenade launcher. The killer cloud was right ahead of them...

A chill ran down his spine as alerts flared up in front of his eyes. Nanomachines were so tiny that they could slip between atoms; the thought of an entire cloud of invisible machines waiting to devour him was terrifying. His suit was protected, as was his body, but he'd been warned more than once that no defence was perfect. He wanted to close his eyes again; instead, he forced himself to walk forward. The alerts faded moments later...allowing his suit's sensors to pick up the sound of heavy breathing directly ahead of them. There were at least a dozen Tokomak waiting for them.

It wasn't a bad spot for an ambush, he realised, if a little amateurish. The passageway was thin enough to force the Marines to walk one by one, straight into the teeth of enemy fire. It would have worked too, he told himself, as he lifted the grenade launcher and fired four HE grenades into the ambush, bracing himself for the shock. There was a colossal explosion as all four grenades detonated; he forced himself to run forward, weapon aimed and ready to engage any enemy targets. Most of the Tokomak were dead or stunned; he killed the remainder, then moved on to secure the edge of the corridor. A line of Tokomak appeared out of nowhere, carrying a handful of weapons, and charged right at him.

"Like shooting fish in a barrel," Williams said. "They're not even *bothering* to think about their tactics!"

"Or they're expending expendable crewmen to force us to waste ammunition," Robbins said, coldly. The remainder of the Marines came up behind Martin, then fanned out. "We can't use their weapons, remember?"

Martin nodded. The Tokomak were remarkably careless with their starships, but much less so with their personal weapons. It was a mystery why they were prepared to install ID software on their weapons, rather than their starships, yet in the end the reasons didn't matter. All that mattered was that Robbins was right. They couldn't count on using anything they captured from the ship's crew.

"Then we press on," Robbins said. "And hurry."

"THE MARINES BOARDED before the enemy ships went into FTL, sir," Commander Grant said, softly. "Most of them will make it through..."

"Take us into FTL," Mongo ordered. There was no doubt where the enemy were going. The only real question was if they would understand where the Solar Union was based...or if they would go directly for Earth, on the assumption that it was the centre of human civilisation. "Take us back to Earth."

"Aye, sir," Grant said. "What about the remaining enemy ships?"

Mongo glanced at the display. Seventy battlecruisers remained, their FTL drives nothing more than useless wreckage. The technicians had predicted, in all seriousness, that *all* of the fleet would be crippled, but Mongo hadn't counted on it. If they'd been right...he shook his head, dismissing the what-might-have-been, and then focussed his mind on the problem facing him.

"Inform them that we will be back to accept their surrender," Mongo said. "Or they can start trying to limp back home, if they like."

He doubted they would do anything, apart from surrender. Even assuming the ships held together, it would take them hundreds of years to reach the nearest friendly star. By then, the war would be long over and the galaxy forever changed. They could head for Earth, he assumed, but it would be at least four years before they arrived. There would be plenty of time to prepare a proper welcome.

"FTL online, sir," Grant said.

"Take us to Earth," Mongo ordered, quietly.

— —

YOLANDA BARELY HAD a moment to comprehend that the enemy ships had vanished before Captain Singh started spitting orders. The squadron disengaged from the remaining Tokomak ships, which were still firing, and retreated rapidly. There was no need to hammer the stranded ships still further.

Martin was on the enemy ship, she thought. Thirty battleships had vanished into FTL, leaving their comrades behind. *Is he still alive?*

"We're picking up orders from the flag," Commander Gregory said. "We are to set course for Earth, effective immediately."

"Then take us to Earth," Captain Singh ordered. "Best possible speed."

But, Yolanda asked herself, *will we get there before the Tokomak?*

— —

"THEY'RE ADVANCING THROUGH all the barricades," the Admiral said. "But we are slowing them down."

Neola nodded. The internal security system had been a low priority for refit – after all, if the thought of internal trouble was unthinkable, there had been no point in maintaining the system – but enough of it had survived poor maintenance and the battle to make life difficult for the humans. But the humans were still pressing onwards, making a beeline for the command core. They would be threatening her in her very place of power soon enough.

But not in time to save their world, she thought, vindictively. *We will be there in time to bombard their world into ashes.*

"MR. PRESIDENT?"

Allen looked up from his desk. "Yes, Colonel?"

"Deep Space Tracking Stations have reported a number of drive signatures heading to Sol," Colonel Peterson said. "They're almost certainly battleships, judging by their power curves."

Allen sucked in a breath. "The ambush failed?"

"It looks more like the ambush partly succeeded," Peterson reported. "The reports we received from Varnar stated that there would be two hundred battleships in the fleet, but the sensor readings we're getting suggest there are considerably fewer ships advancing towards us."

"But they're still advancing towards us," Allen said. Given the disparity in firepower between the Solar Union and the Tokomak, it was quite possible that the entire Solar Navy had been wiped out. "Send the emergency alert, Colonel. The entire community is to go dark."

"Aye, sir," Peterson said.

He nodded and withdrew from the room, leaving Allen alone.

There was no way to know, Allen reflected, if the Tokomak knew that the Solar Union was almost completely separate from Earth. They would occupy or destroy humanity's homeworld and then...would they search for the asteroids? It seemed implausible that they would miss the asteroid settlements, yet the Galactics were firmly fixated on worlds. No other advanced race used asteroid settlements as extensively as humanity.

Would Earth's death be mourned? It was a grim thought; Mother Earth had given birth to humanity, after all. But the remaining societies on humanity's homeworld were mad, barbaric or both. Their death would not be mourned. And maybe, if the Tokomak thought they'd won and withdrew, it would be for the best. But billions of humans would die…

But if we emit a single betraying pulse, he thought, *they'll know where to find us*.

Had it been a mistake to reject the ultimatum? There was no way to know, save the certainty that humanity would be enslaved or destroyed if they surrendered. It was better to live as free men, rather than slaves, he'd thought. And the public had agreed…but what if the alternative to servitude was death? No, not just death, extermination. Was it better for the human race to live in slavery rather than be wiped out?

He sighed, then smiled darkly. The Tokomak didn't know – would never know – just how many colony ships had been launched into the darkness of unexplored space, each one with a Galactic-level tech base. One or more of them would establish a successful colony, then come back to Earth for revenge. Given fifty years of development, the Tokomak wouldn't stand a chance…

And if none of those colonies succeeds, he thought, *at least our example will show the other Galactics that the masters of the universe are far from invincible.*

THIRTY-FIVE

A number of teachers were reported murdered after their bodies were discovered in an isolated warehouse in Chicago. While police have declined to speculate on the motive, several PTA representatives have informed the media that the teachers were the target of three successive attempts to have them removed from their jobs, which were barred by the Teacher's Union.

—Solar News Network, Year 53

"We are approaching Earth's gravity well," the Admiral reported. "Preparing to drop out of FTL."

Neola nodded, impatiently. The human boarders were making their remorseless way towards the command core, no matter what she put in their way. Part of her mind started to devise contingency plans; the remainder focused on the job at hand. Their homeworld might be heavily defended – she had to assume it was – but it was still vulnerable. It simply couldn't run.

"Good," she said. "Take us out of FTL as near as you can to the gravity well."

A low groan ran through the ship as the much-abused FTL drive powered down, returning them to normal space. Neola would have been amused, under other circumstances, at how the only ships that had escaped the ambush were the ones whose commanding officers had taken her instructions seriously. The commanders who hadn't listened to her and continuing painting their hulls were the commanders who remained stranded, in deep space. Perhaps she would leave them there indefinitely, just to teach them a lesson. Or perhaps she wouldn't bother to save them at all. Let them save themselves, if they could.

"The human homeworld," the Admiral said, quietly.

Neola's eyes narrowed. "Are you sure we headed to the right system?"

Earth was a blue-green world, like so many others in the galaxy. It would have been a surprise if it *hadn't* developed higher life forms, given the sheer stubbornness of life, once it was brought into existence. The humanoid form was common throughout the galaxy, particularly on Earth-like worlds. It represented the simplest solution to the problem posed by evolution.

But Earth looked…undeveloped. There was no network of battlestations, no clouds of orbital weapons platforms, no swarms of starships boiling towards the intruding fleet, intent on obliterating Neola and her ships before they could threaten Earth. All her sensors could detect were a few hundred satellites, all achingly primitive. There were very few hints of Galactic-level technology, at least on the planet's surface. Was she looking at a deliberately low-tech world?

"The navigation computer confirms this is Earth," the Admiral said. He essayed a short laugh. "The stars are definitely in the right place."

Neola glanced down at her console, checking for herself. It had been centuries since the Tokomak had noted the worthless world and its primitive inhabitants…if the humans hadn't received help, they wouldn't have been in a position to threaten anyone. There was no mistake, no glitch in the navigational systems. They were advancing on the homeworld of the human race.

Were the humans hiding their defences, for some reason, or were there *no* defences? It looked absurd, but if the humans had thrown all their resources into building the fleet that had devastated her formation, perhaps they hadn't had the chance to build fixed defences too. Or…perhaps they were simply focused on attacking, like many primitive races, and didn't consider the advantages of a sturdy defence against attack. Or...

There were no shipyards. Indeed, apart from clear signs of terraforming on two rocky worlds, there were few signs the humans had managed to move beyond their atmosphere...something that puzzled her. Even as primitive as the humans were, they should have done much more...and they *had* built a war fleet. The Coalition wouldn't have needed to play games if they had the same technology, let alone use humans as mercenaries. Her allies would have been destroyed years ago, if the Coalition had human-grade weapons.

She pushed the thought aside as the blue-green world came closer. Whatever game the humans were playing, the majority of their race would die today. And then the Tokomak would relentlessly hunt down the hidden bases and colonies...there were quite a few unexplored stars near Earth, systems deemed of no interest to anyone. The humans had probably built their bases there.

"Lock weapons on population centres," she ordered. It was a small mercy, but one she would offer to worthy foes. "Prepare to fire."

"Yes, Your Excellency," the Admiral said. "Missiles locked on target."

— —

"WE'RE RETURNED TO normal space," Robbins said. "They must have reached Earth."

Martin cursed under his breath as he ducked a spray of plasma fire. The Tokomak were definitely not *trained* soldiers, but they were displaying a surprising amount of initiative in slowing down the Marines. So far, they'd done everything from sneaky ambushes to outright charges, throwing automated cleaning machines at the humans to soak up their fire. He couldn't help wondering if they were running into different commanders with each airlock, as they were using different tactics, or if the Tokomak were deliberately trying to confuse them.

"Get through the next airlock," Robbins added. "We have to get to the command core."

"Try and link to someone outside," Hendrix observed, as they punched through the next airlock and into a long bland corridor. It was ideal ambush territory, so the Marines launched a spread of grenades ahead of them, clearing the Tokomak out of their path. "The Solar Union might be able to send support."

Red lights flared up in Martin's HUD as another force of Tokomak charged forward, spearheaded by yet another set of cleaning machines. The machines were supposed to be harmless, just like the automated units he'd seen on some of the asteroid settlements he'd visited, but they could do real damage if they had a chance. This time, one of them carried a crude flamethrower, which poured fire towards the Marines. It wasn't hot enough to burn the suit, Martin noted with some relief, but it played merry hell with the sensors.

He targeted the lead machine and fired. It exploded into a sheet of fire as whatever it was using to power the flamethrower exploded, knocking several of the other machines over and onto the deck. Exposed, the following Tokomak threw themselves to the deck, then opened fire, handheld plasma weapons throwing bursts of deadly green light at their enemies. Their reactions were faster than Martin had expected, but he had no doubt they'd learned from the experiences of the first Tokomak to engage the human intruders. Making oneself a target was just asking to be shot.

"Grenades," Roger yelled. "Duck!"

He launched a set of grenades over the wreckage and into the enemy mass. The explosions shook the deck, blowing holes in material that was probably worth more than their collective salaries for the year. Martin sprang forward, noting the remains of the Tokomak with disgust, then reached the end of the corridor and hurled a grenade through. The suit picked up alien screams as the remainder of the Marines joined him, then crashed through into the next section. A handful of dead or wounded Tokomak stared up at him, accusation clearly visible on their alien faces. The Marines disposed of them and moved onwards.

Martin felt sick, just for a moment, before his implants compensated. The Tokomak were monsters, intending to destroy Earth – and, as bad as Earth had become, it was still the homeworld of the human race. And yet, part of him felt guilty for gunning down helpless opponents, even though he knew the living ones wouldn't be helpless for long. They couldn't afford to show mercy, not now.

"No direct link to enemy command system," his suit informed him.

Of course not, he thought, sourly. *That would be easy.*

He ducked as a flash of brilliant white light shot over his head, then fired a stream of plasma pulses back towards the shooter. His suit compensated automatically for the flash of white light as a plasma containment system exploded, sending gouts of white fire rushing out in all directions. It was hot enough to melt parts of the bulkhead, the hidden layers of super-strong composite material that made up the inner structure of the starship. He found himself feeling an odd flash of sympathy for whoever had been wielding the weapon, hoping they had died instantly. Plasma burns were no joke.

"Shit," Roger said. "The LT!"

Martin swore as a new alert flared up in his HUD. Deliberately or otherwise, the Tokomak had killed Lieutenant Robbins. She'd seemed too mean to die. Martin hadn't thought there was *anything* that could kill her, after watching how she handled Marines who were larger and stronger than her. There were women in the ghetto who would have killed for her strength, skill and ability to command respect. She couldn't be dead.

But she was.

He swallowed as the combat net checked through the surviving Marines, then presented him with the bad news. *He* was in command now.

"Keep moving," he ordered, cursing as he fell back. He couldn't take point any longer, not when he was meant to be in command. They'd certainly swapped operational command in exercises often enough for him to know what he should do. But he didn't like it, not even slightly.

It smacked of retreat in the face of the enemy. "And don't let up for a moment!"

The command net opened in front of him, for all the good it did. As far as it was concerned, the remaining Marines were *all* the surviving human military units in the vicinity. There was no link to anyone outside the ship, no hint that there might be help on the way…hell, there was no hint they were even anywhere near Earth. It was quite possible the Tokomak ship had simply suffered a drive failure and had been ejected back into normal space, somewhere in the middle of the interstellar wasteland.

And if that was the case, he told himself, *surely they would have tried to talk.*

He couldn't see the Tokomak continuing the fight when it was pointless. They weren't cowards, but they were pragmatic. There was simply no point in waging war if they were stuck in interstellar space, light years from help. No, the Tokomak had reached their destination and were preparing to attack. It was the only possibility that made sense.

"Keep moving," he repeated, as he checked the map. They weren't *far* from the command deck, but they were running into more and more barricades and ambushes. "We have got to take this ship out before it's too late."

— —

YOLANDA BRACED HERSELF as *Freedom* returned to normal space. Earth appeared in her awareness, followed by Luna and the network of primitive satellites surrounding Earth, most of them nothing more than scrap metal. The Solar Union had supplied a handful of communications satellites, she recalled from her studies, which supported the datanet and handled all of Earth's telecommunications. Everything else…had just been allowed to decay into nothingness. Earth was the old world, collapsing under its own weight, while the Solar Union was the future.

She grimaced as the Tokomak battleships came into view. They were a sorry sight; twenty-eight of them, plunging towards Earth. There should have been thirty, she reminded herself, but the remaining two failed to materialise. Had they lost their FTL during the trip to Earth, she wondered, or had the enemy tripped the self-destruct rather than allow the Marines to take control? There was no way to know.

"They're entering weapons range of Earth," Commander Gregory said.

It was worse than that, Yolanda knew. The Solar Treaty had prohibited the Solar Union from emplacing weapons in orbit around Earth, as if it would cause delays in responding to any provocation from a nation-state on the homeworld. There was nothing stopping the Tokomak from launching ballistic weapons towards Earth...or simply ramming their battleships into the biosphere. At the speeds they were travelling, the impact would be far worse than an asteroid, exterminating the entire planet.

But the human race will live on, she thought, savagely. *We'll be back for you bastards.*

"Close to engagement range," Captain Singh ordered. "And open fire as soon as you can."

"Aye, sir," Commander Gregory said.

— —

"THE HUMAN FLEET has arrived," the Admiral said.

Neola looked at the display, then bit down a vile word. The human fleet had been much reduced by the battle – she hadn't left them completely unscathed, then – but there were enough survivors to obliterate her remaining ships. And only a handful of her vessels could even hope to escape, if they fled back into FTL. Several of the survivors needed urgent repairs before they dared enter FTL...

But it didn't matter. Earth was at their mercy. And she dared show none.

"Prepare to fire," she ordered. She'd held fire long enough to ensure the human defences, if there were any, would be unable to stop *all* of her missiles. Now, there was no longer any point in further delay. "Fire..."

An explosion cut off her words.

THE TOKOMAK SEEMED to consider themselves aristocrats, Martin had noted, as they fought their way through the ship, but their officers were clearly considered royalty. Their quarters were staggeringly luxurious by their own standards, completely decadent by human standards; the Marines had even encountered a handful of enemy officers who were clearly skiving off the battle, even though human soldiers were rampaging through their ships. If they'd been trained by Marine Corps Drill Instructors...he bit off the happy thought about what would happen to anyone who turned up to Roll Call drunk as a lord, then followed the point men into the next section.

"Push through," he snapped, as the Tokomak rallied. They seemed to be using all kinds of furniture to make barricades, something that made him smile. It was odd to think he had anything in common with the Tokomak, but if *he'd* had to work for officers who surrounded themselves with so much luxury, he would have been glad of the opportunity to smash their expensive furniture too. "Don't give them a moment to recover."

There was a deafening series of explosions, then the resistance slackened suddenly. This time, the enemy had nowhere to run. The Marines advanced rapidly, throwing their remaining grenades ahead of them to clear the way, then finally reached the hatch leading into the command core. It was gaudy, decorated with what looked like a coat of arms covered with an entire page of strange alien writing, but it was unmistakable. And large enough to allow the Marines to walk through, two abreast. It was clear, Martin noted as the Marines fixed charges to the hatch, that the designers had never anticipated anyone actually boarding and storming one of their battleships.

"Now," he ordered.

The charges detonated. Martin watched as the hatch fell inwards, pieces of debris falling into the massive compartment, then followed the point men into the command core. It was far larger than he'd expected, crammed with Tokomak and holographic displays – and was that a Varnar in the corner, standing there like a naughty child? The Tokomak looked shocked, utterly shocked, to see the humans. Hadn't they *known* their craft was being boarded?

"Stand away from the consoles," Martin ordered, in Galactic Standard. It was unlikely that any of the Tokomak had bothered to learn English, or any other language. They might not even have loaded translation modules into their implants. "Do not attempt to draw a weapon or do anything to resist."

The Tokomak obeyed, one by one. It was hard to tell which of them was in charge – they all wore gaudy uniforms, covered in yellow and black stripes that indicated high rank – but they obeyed. His implants informed him, helpfully, that a third of the Tokomak were female, although it was hard to see how anyone could tell the difference. They all looked alike to him.

"Good," he said. "Which one of you is in command?"

— —

NEOLA WATCHED THE humans, too tired to be shocked that they had forced their way into the command core. It was...it was blasphemy. The only aliens allowed in the command core were subject races, people who knew where they stood. But the humans had forced their way onto the ship...

Her mind raced, accessing her implants and issuing a final set of orders, as she rose to her feet and faced the humans. It was impossible to see their faces, hidden in their crude suits, but she imagined them cowering before her might. The Tokomak might have been embarrassed by the battle – and it would be years before the repercussions died away – yet they were still the Tokomak, still the founders of the largest interstellar empire known to exist. And what were the upstart humans to them?

"I am," she said.

The teleport field claimed her a moment later. She allowed herself a smile as the command core dissolved into light, leaving the humans behind...

— —

MARTIN SWORE AS the Tokomak teleported out. Her command crew stared, some shocked, some fearful, as he took a step forward, then stopped himself. The teleport had taken the one person he'd wanted to capture and sent her...where?

"Extend the jamming field," he ordered, angrily. He'd be in deep shit for not anticipating the possibility. "And then secure the ship and prisoners."

The Tokomak offered no resistance as they were searched, bound and placed by the side of the compartment as the humans hacked into the command network. Inside the command core, it was easy to gain access and take control of the ship, then signal to the human fleet. A prize crew was already on the way.

He scowled as he saw the Varnar. The images he'd seen in the simulations had given him the creeps...and, in person, they were much worse. They resembled the little grey aliens of humanity's nightmares...and, given that they were the first to use humans as unwilling soldiers, it was generally believed that was no coincidence.

"I believe we should talk," the Varnar said. "I have much to tell you."

"My superiors will want to see you," Martin replied. "Until then, behave."

THIRTY-SIX

Riots swept the globe today after it was disclosed that an alien power had attempted to attack and destroy Earth. Solar Union facilities came under attack from rioting crowds; thankfully, the guards were on the alert and managed to repel the attackers with minimum losses. Other local governments were also targeted, raising the threat of election defeats or outright civil war.

—Solar News Network, Year 53

"So they managed to get a handful of ships out of the system?"

"Yes, sir," Yolanda said. "They managed to escape into FTL."

She looked down at her console, watching as shuttlecraft approached the stricken Tokomak ships. Their desperate rush at Earth had been averted, barely. The updates from the Marines stated that they had come within seconds of launching missiles at Earth. If there had been a delay...

Her thoughts mocked her. She'd often wished her stepmother and stepsiblings dead, but the thought of them actually dying...it was horrific. And the rest of the human population...there were nine billion people on Earth, according to the official estimate. The thought of the entire population dying was completely unimaginable. It was a number so high as to be completely beyond comprehension. She could barely grasp the names and faces of the crew of her ship, let alone the enormity of Earth's population. And yet they would all have died.

And Martin may have died, she thought. It was clear the Marines had taken staggering casualties before the Tokomak lost control of their ships. *What if he's gone too?*

"Track them as long as you can," Captain Singh ordered. "They may be trying to sneak back through the edge of the Sol System."

Yolanda doubted the Tokomak would think of it – without FTL, it would take months, if not years, to sneak back into attack range – but she did as she was told, using the order as a distraction from her churning thoughts. A request popped up in her display and she looked at it, then forwarded it to Commander Gregory. Fleet Command wanted a complete download from every starship in the fleet before they started to repair and rearm their ships.

"Take us to the shipyard," Captain Singh ordered. "Best possible speed."

"Aye, sir," Yolanda said.

She plunged her mind back into the command network and swung the starship around. There was so much debris in the vicinity, perhaps from Tokomak starships that had shattered when they'd crashed back into normal space, that she wanted to put a considerable distance between the ship and the debris before she risked taking *Freedom* into FTL. Behind her, she was suddenly aware of Captain Singh walking across the bridge and staring up at the main display.

"There's nothing more melancholy than a battle lost," the Captain said to himself, "except a battle won."

"That isn't the right quote," Commander Gregory pointed out. "And we did win. Think how *they* must be feeling!"

Yolanda concealed her mixture of amusement and horror with an effort. *She* would never have dared to correct the Captain, certainly not so lightly. But she also understood the Captain's thought. The battle was over, the crews of the surrendered ships were being moved to POW camps...and the Solar Union had to clear up the mess.

But we still won, she told herself, firmly. *We won*!"

— —

IT WAS LUCKY, Martin reflected, that the Tokomak were so stunned by their defeat. Otherwise, they could have caused real trouble. There were over five thousand Tokomak to a battleship, most of whom had survived the battle, the invasion or simple systems failures caused by the unexpected war. If they had managed to get organised, they might have tried something that would have gotten most of them killed. Instead, they just walked into the shuttlecraft for the first leg of their journey to the POW camps, without a single complaint.

"Corporal Douglas," a voice said. "This is Greeley. Do you have the Varnar prisoner secure?"

"Yes, sir," Martin said, nervously. Major-General Greeley was the CO of the 4th Marine Division, several dozen steps up the hierarchy from Martin and his comrades. Martin had only met him once, back when he'd graduated from Boot Camp. "We separated him from the Tokomak and placed him in a private compartment, under guard."

"Good work," Greeley said. "There's a shuttle on the way from the spooks. When it arrives, you are to transfer your prisoner to the shuttle, then accompany him. I want you escorted by at least four other Marines from your platoon."

"Yes, sir," Martin said.

He frowned, biting down a yawn. The instructions puzzled him. He was tired and sweaty and wanted nothing more than bed, but he wasn't tired enough to let an unarmed alien prisoner get the better of him. But maybe no one was meant to know they'd taken a Varnar POW. There had been few prisoners in the Proxy War and most of them had been traded back, after a few months in Coalition POW camps. A new prisoner might raise the prospect of learning something new, instead of merely being returned to his people after a short delay...

Or maybe it was the fact he was on a Tokomak ship, Martin thought, as he summoned two additional Marines. *He must know what they had in mind.*

As soon as the Marines had relieved him, he walked down to the compartment and nodded to the Marine on guard duty. It was annoying to have to expend three Marines, all of them in powered combat armour, guarding a single prisoner, but his orders had left no room for misinterpretation. Stepping inside, he saw the other two Marines watching the Varnar, who was standing in the centre of the compartment like a living statue. Up close, they were *definitely* creepy, he thought. They made no movement that wasn't planned. There wasn't a single involuntary motion in their muscles.

"You will come with us," Martin said. He linked into the command network and issued orders, clearing a line from the compartment to the makeshift shuttlebay that would allow them to move the Varnar through the hull without being seen. "My people wish to speak with you."

The Varnar moved in quicksilver flashes, jerky motions that nagged at Martin's mind, as if he was recalling something very old. Merely watching the alien was disconcerting; he rubbed his rifle, calculating just how quickly the alien could actually move. Fast enough to be a real problem, he decided, if they were enhanced too. But a powered combat suit could still rip the alien's head off before the alien even realised he was under attack.

He motioned for the Varnar to climb into the shuttle, then followed, cursing the obvious lack of any restraints. Prisoners were meant to be treated gently, but firmly; he would have felt safer if the Varnar was cuffed and shackled. But there was no equipment to do either...he forced himself, instead, to keep a sharp eye on the Varnar as the shuttle closed its airlock, then drifted away from the battleship's hull. Again, the Varnar sat perfectly still. There was no hint of unwanted movement in its posture.

A human would be asking questions by now, Martin calculated. The dreaded Conduct After Capture course had warned him that some people responded better to captivity than others – and that there was a wide range of precedents for how POWs were treated. *But the Varnar is saying nothing.*

He used his implants to write a quick message for Yolanda – there was no one else outside the Marines who would give a damn if he lived or died – and then returned his attention to the alien. The Varnar showed no hint he knew or cared if he was being watched or not; he merely sat there, waiting. But waiting for what?

The sooner this duty is over, Martin thought, *the better.*

THE SECURITY OFFICERS had thrown a fit at the mere thought of allowing Mongo to actually meet the Varnar, face-to-face. After a long argument, they had finally consented to allow Mongo to use a holographic projection to meet with the alien, which would guarantee his safety if the alien turned out to be hostile. The alien didn't have any weapons or weapons implants, according to the scans, but they'd been fooled before. Everyone knew the Varnar had a reputation for being sneaky.

He closed his eyes, then opened them as the compartment – not exactly a cell, but locked and isolated from the rest of the compound – shimmered into existence around him. There were two chairs, including one designed for a child-sized alien, but the Varnar hadn't sat down. Instead, he was standing beside the desk, looking rather like a junior officer reporting to his senior. Mongo pushed that impression aside as he walked the projection around the room, then sat down behind the desk. The Varnar didn't move, merely blinked once.

Mongo eyed the Varnar with ill-concealed distaste, then used his implants to present a blank, neutral facade to the alien. It was unlikely the alien could read human emotions, any more than humans could read alien emotions from their expressions and gestures, but there was no point in taking chances. Besides, the Varnar had been fighting human mercenaries for over fifty years, ever since Kevin had made the first deal with the Coalition. It was quite possible that they had been making a special study of humans since then.

And they took humans to use as cyborgs, he reminded himself. *Is that why you think they may know us better than you want to admit?*

"I am Admiral Stuart," he said, shortly. "You stated your wish to see someone high in the human military. You will not meet anyone higher than myself."

The Varnar cocked his head, as if it could read the truth of that statement. There was no *proof* their strange semi-hive mentalities could read human thoughts, but there were no shortage of people who believed it. Mongo himself rather doubted it. If the Varnar could read minds, they wouldn't have been fought to a standstill in the Proxy War.

"I am Admiral He'cht," the Varnar stated. "My people would like to ally with yours."

Mongo had to bite down a laugh. "You want to *ally* with us?"

"That is correct," the Varnar said. "We have a mutual enemy."

"The Tokomak, I assume," Mongo said.

"That is correct," the Varnar repeated. "We do not enjoy their dominion over us, or their decision to take direct control of this sector for themselves. And now we know they can be beaten."

"You could have acted sooner, if you'd wished," Mongo said. He understood why the Varnar might have hesitated, if they truly hated the Tokomak as much as their representative implied, yet it smacked of changing sides after the war was already won. "Instead, you allowed them to attack Earth."

"One does not *allow* the Tokomak to do anything," the Varnar stated. "It was not within our power to stop them."

"It was," Mongo said. "If we fought them to a standstill, Admiral, what could your far greater fleet have done?"

"We did not *know* it was within our power to stop them," the Varnar said, coolly. "And we have other issues apart from the masters of the universe."

He looked up, inky dark eyes boring into Mongo's face. "My superiors have empowered me to make an offer to you," he added. "We hope you will accept."

Mongo frowned. "You *anticipated* being captured?"

"All possibilities must be prepared for," the Varnar said. "Even those we deem unlikely."

"True," Mongo agreed, keeping his voice flat. "And you had a contingency plan for being captured."

He smiled, rather thinly. The Varnar made even the Solar Union's logistics officers look sloppy, in the way they prepared everything before launching the operation, right down to the last little detail. Maybe they'd picked the habit up from the Tokomak, he considered. Their masters certainly operated along the same lines.

"That is correct," the alien said. "We will ally with you. We will drive the Tokomak though the gravity point and out of the sector. Absent control over the gravity points, it will take them a considerable number of years to mount a counter-offensive, by which time we will be ready for them. In exchange for this, we want an end to the Proxy War. You will convince the Coalition to end the fighting on terms."

Mongo considered it. The whole idea looked reasonable, to him; he had no illusions about the true intention of the Proxy War. And, it seemed, the Varnar had none either. But he knew the Coalition would want more than vague promises of peace.

"We can try," he said. "What would you offer them?"

"Worlds we held prior to the war would remain ours," the Varnar said. "Their worlds would remain theirs. Border worlds would be allowed to become independent, under their own governments. And there would be peace."

"Peace," Mongo repeated.

"If the war goes on, there will be disaster," the Varnar warned. "We will have no choice, but to side with the Tokomak and plan the destruction of many worlds."

Mongo winced. The Tokomak, whatever else they had done, had kept a lid on interstellar war, banning the use of weapons of mass destruction against inhabited worlds. But they'd shown their willingness to break their own rules, when they considered it necessary, and no one else would ever respect them, ever again. Push the Varnar to the point of defeat, the Varnar were saying, and they'd make damn sure they took their enemies down with them.

"I will bring your suggestions to the President," he said. "Right now, I can promise nothing else."

— —

MARTIN HAD EXPECTED to return to *Freedom* immediately, but it was not to be. Instead of a shuttle flight back to his ship, there was a long debriefing session with the SIA's analysts and then a quicker session with several senior Marines. The only mercy was that no one seemed to be blaming him for the enemy commander's escape; it had clearly been planned in advance, the senior officers said, and everyone else tended to agree. By the time he finally caught a shuttle flight back to *Freedom*, the others having been released much sooner, he felt too exhausted to care about anything or anyone.

"Wake up," a voice called. "Please!"

Martin jerked awake. He was on the shuttle...he'd fallen asleep on the shuttle, even if the seats were pretty damn uncomfortable. They still beat the bunks he'd had to use in Boot Camp, or the times he'd had to catch his sleep in the suit, or on the ground...coming to think of it, where had he put his suit? If he'd lost it, he would be in deep shit.

"Your baggage is already out the hatch," the pilot said, impatiently. "I have to get back to the asteroid."

"Thank you," Martin muttered, as he staggered to his feet. "I'll give you a tip as soon as I get my salary."

"Don't worry about it," the pilot said. He sounded almost as tired as Martin felt. "Just go."

The hatch closed as soon as Martin had stepped through, something that made him start giggling inanely. No doubt the pilot had wanted to be rid of his snoring passenger too...not that Martin could really blame him. He stank to high heaven.

"Martin," Yolanda called. "Welcome home!"

He smiled, despite his tiredness. "I don't think you want to hug me right now," he said, before she could wrap her arms around him. "I smell."

"And to think I thought the smell was an experiment with chemical warfare," Yolanda said, mischievously. She wrinkled her nose, theatrically. "What do you want to do?"

Martin rolled his eyes. The Solar Union had no laws against chemical warfare, mainly because nanotech rendered most chemical warfare weapons useless. His Drill Instructors had also pointed out that refusing to use a subset of weapons, on principle, wasn't always the best of ideas.

"Get into the decontamination chamber and get fumigated," he said, pushing the thought aside. It brought back memories of Boot Camp, when they'd been shown just how inhuman man could be to man. He glanced at the case containing his suit, then carefully picked it up and manhandled it down the corridor. "Or at least have a very long shower."

"We're going to Varnar," Yolanda said, as she started to follow him. "As soon as we've reloaded, I mean. There won't be any chance for shore leave."

"I wish I could say I was surprised," Martin said, remembering the Varnar he'd captured on the Tokomak battleship. The senior officers had gone over the capture again and again, wanting to extract every last detail. They'd even fixated on where the Varnar had been standing at the moment the command core had been breached. "There's nowhere else to go."

He reached the shower chamber and opened the door, then stepped inside. It was empty, thankfully; he had a feeling that most of the crew was trying to sleep, now the battle was over and done. Yolanda followed him inside before he could close the door, something he wouldn't have thought possible of the shy girl he'd met, years ago. They had both grown and matured since leaving Earth behind.

"Let me have a moment to wash the grime from my body," he said, hastily. His uniform was badly stained; he dropped it in the basket so he could pick it up and clean it later. Marines didn't get maid service, something the Drill Instructors had pointed out with great glee. "And then we can spend time together."

"Of course," Yolanda said. She started to strip off her uniform, then waited for him to finish washing himself. "But don't take too long."

Afterwards, Martin held her tightly and tried not to think about the men he'd seen die.

THIRTY-SEVEN

Reports of a genetically-engineered disease loose in South Africa surfaced today, following the defection of a famous doctor who was apparently under a gag order issued by the government. According to him, the disease specifically targets mixed-race children, but is likely to mutate and strike more generally within months. The South African Government has issued an official denial, which no one believes.

If these reports are accurate, it represents the fifth attempt to use racially-targeted disease as a means of ethnic cleansing in the past decade.

—Solar News Network, Year 53

"We have returned to Varnar, Your Excellency."

Neola nodded, then glared at the young officer who had been sent to give her the message. He sputtered, then scurried away, no doubt to moan to his fellows that the Viceroy had been mean to him, like the child he was…she stood, trying hard to push away the anger and horror that had dominated her mind for the past two weeks. There was no time to waste. Even if the Varnar didn't know about the defeat – and it was quite possible they knew already – they would know soon enough. And then…

She paced through the decorated corridors until she reached the command core, where the battleship's commander was viewing the main display. He was surprisingly young for his post, which probably explained why he'd managed to keep his ship intact while the remainder of the fleet had been battered to pieces. His crew had actually taken the orders to carry out unscripted exercises to heart.

"Captain," she said.

"Your Excellency," Captain Drew said. There was no trace of disrespect in his tone, unsurprisingly. If she'd died at Earth, he would have been the senior surviving officer, the only person left to take the blame. "We have arrived at Varnar."

"I know," Neola said. She looked up at the display. The handful of Tokomak ships that had remained behind, mainly cruisers and freighters, were still intact. Behind them, the Varnar ships didn't look as though they were planning to open fire. "Raise one of the cruisers and send them a *complete* copy of our records, then order her commander to proceed straight through the gravity point and back home."

"Yes, Your Excellency," Captain Drew said. He didn't argue, for which she was grateful. An older officer might well have objected to sending a message back to the Old Ones when the fleet was in disarray, but he was too young to notice the danger. "And the Varnar?"

"Inform them that we will be holding a planning session in two hours," Neola ordered. The last thing she wanted to do was show weakness. They would see her at her best, planning the defence of the gravity point, which would also remind them of the thousands of battleships still in commission. "And that we will discuss the full situation then."

She took her seat and studied the display, silently calculating vectors in her head. What would the humans do, now they had scored a great victory? Attack Varnar and engage the Varnar themselves, as well as the remains of her fleet? Unite the Coalition against the Tokomak as well as the Varnar? Or remain in their star system, licking their wounds? Their technology was advanced, hellishly so, but not enough to compensate for the losses they'd taken in the battle. She had had plenty of time to consider all the angles, including her own mistakes. The humans might be strong, in one way, but they simply lacked the raw numbers they needed for success.

Or so she told herself, she admitted in the privacy of her own head, because the alternative was too terrible to contemplate.

LIFE ON VARNAR, Kevin had discovered, was both exciting and boring at the same time. It felt rather like working in the CIA station in Yemen or Somalia, where there were few laws and yet a certain kind of order. The Varnar had opened up their homeworld to all kinds of aliens, including a number who had brought criminal connections with them. Making new contacts, some immediately useful while others held promise for the future, was something that never really went out of style.

But it was also tedious, at times. There was no true risk, not when the Varnar were turning a blind eye to his activities. He had thought he needed to stay below their radar, particularly as Earth was still involved in the Proxy War, and yet...they were making it easy for him. They hadn't even twitched when he'd purchased information on the planet's defence net, something that bothered him more than he cared to admit. Either the information was fake and it was part of an elaborate con, which was quite possible, or they were desperate. He wasn't sure which answer he feared more. Being conned would be irritating – and it happened in the intelligence world, no matter how many precautions one took – but desperate people made desperate and foolish mistakes. Who knew which way the Varnar would jump, if the shit hit the fan?

He was sitting in his makeshift office, skimming through the planetary datanet, when a message from Sally popped up in his implants. It was nothing more than a simple, curt, COME AT ONCE. Kevin disengaged from the datanet, made a brief report to the rest of his team, then started the long walk to Sally's apartment. She had warned him, after the first meeting, not to try to visit Mr. Ando's office again. There was too much risk of someone noticing in a way that couldn't be concealed.

Sally was waiting for him when he arrived, a grim expression on her unlined face.

"There have been developments," she said. "You may have heard already?"

Kevin shook his head, then took the seat she indicated.

"There has been a great battle," Sally said. "And the Tokomak lost."

"Good," Kevin said. Given the odds, a Tokomak victory would have resulted in the destruction of the Solar System. He would have had no choice, but to seek what revenge he could, even if it was ultimately unsatisfying. "What happened?"

"There aren't many details, yet," Sally said, flatly. "All we really know is that two hundred Tokomak battleships set out on a mission of genocide; five returned, all damaged to a greater or lesser extent. More might come limping in over the next few days..."

Kevin found himself smiling, openly. "How many ships did they lose?"

"We don't know for sure," Sally reminded him, "but if they'd won they would be crowing about it to everyone who would listen. I think it's fairly self-evident they lost the battle, and perhaps the war."

"There will be a message from Earth soon," Kevin said. He was sure of it. "Where does this leave...*us*?"

"Right now, there's a feeler out to some of our friends," Sally said. "But it might be some time before they can reply. The Viceroy apparently survived and has summoned the High Command to her ship."

There was nothing else to do, so Kevin sat on the sofa, drank a mug of tea and reviewed the rumours flying through the datanet. The Varnar were doing what they could to limit speculation, he noted, but even endless censorship and thread deletions couldn't prevent rumours from spreading. No one could avoid seeing the battleships, after all, or calculating that if seven had returned, one hundred and ninety-three had been lost. By now, word would be spreading through the sector. Given a couple of weeks, thanks to the gravity points, half the galaxy would know. There was no putting the genie back in the bottle.

Sally sat at her desk, reading through endless files. Kevin half-wondered if he should invite her to bed, then dismissed the thought before he could make a complete fool of himself. It was easy to tell that Sally was ambivalent about her involvement with human spies, even though she *was* human. If he ever wrote a book about his adventures, Kevin privately resolved, that detail would be left out. There was no shortage of idiots who would accuse her of secretly being a traitor to humanity, simply for doubting what she was doing.

Not everyone puts the good of humanity ahead of themselves, he thought, *particularly when their career or life is at stake.*

Two hours later, with boredom howling at the corner of Kevin's mind, Sally received a message.

"We have to go down to the Pan-Gal," she said, as she rose to her feet. "And you have to accompany me."

Kevin nodded. If it was a trap, he'd find out soon enough; if it wasn't, he didn't want to waste the opportunity by declining the meeting. He watched Sally as she pulled on a coat, then led the way through the door and down a flight of stairs that had clearly been designed for the Varnar, rather than anyone larger. At the bottom, a small automated cab was already waiting for them, completely unmarked. Kevin took a seat next to Sally and watched, without surprise, as the cab rose into the air and headed for the Pan-Gal. The towering complex was just as he remembered it, only louder. There was an aroma of fear in the air that surprised him...

Or maybe it shouldn't, he told himself, tartly. *Everyone who visits the Pan-Gal is well connected. They probably know about the battle and defeat by now.*

Sally jumped out of the cab as soon as it landed on the roof and led him down a sloping shaft into the heart of the building. They passed a line of gambling halls, where racial differences were forgotten in the glow of the urge to make money, and cafes where races were effectively segregated, if only because one race's food was another race's stomach ache. Kevin had grown up on a ranch, where he'd seen meat taken from the cow and cooked into something edible, but he still had to look away when an alien that resembled a giant pile of sludge lifted a crab-like creature and dropped it into his (or her?) waiting jaws.

"It's rather like being a preteen here," Sally muttered, as they stopped outside a pair of unmarked doors. "I feel young every time I come."

Kevin lifted his eyebrows. "Why?"

"There's nothing here, but polite interaction," Sally said.

"Evidently, your preteen years were tamer than mine," Kevin countered. Having Steve and Mongo for older brothers had given him an outlook on the world that was very different from many of his fellow trainees at Langley, nearly eighty years ago. "I don't think anyone would have said my brothers and I were *polite*."

Sally shook her head. "That's not what I meant," she said. "It's just..."

She shook her head. "When you turn into a teenager, sex starts rearing its head," she explained.

"In more ways than one," Kevin said, dryly.

Sally glowered at him, then went on. "You start evaluating all of your relationships in terms of sex," she explained. "Even when you're an adult, you keep doing it; you look at someone and you think they're sexy, or not sexy. You feel affection, which might not be returned; they feel affection, which you don't return."

"You grew up in the Solar Union," Kevin said. His father had been quite liberal, for his time, but he still remembered the day he'd bawled Steve out for making love to a girl without intending to marry her. Or the rumours that had floated around the district after two girls were found in a compromising position. "Where anything goes."

"Yeah," Sally said. "And sometimes it was a little too much.

"But here? There's no sex, but there's little real social interaction either."

Kevin understood. If humans could be so different as to face insurmountable differences in everything from culture to sexual mores, how much harder would it be to form a real relationship with an alien? There would be very little in common, while features common to one would be horrendously offensive to the other. Sally was truly alone in many ways, even though she did have some relationships with her co-workers. None of them could ever form a close friendship with her.

The hatch opened, revealing a small conference room. Four Varnar – the same ones he'd met earlier, Kevin assumed – were standing behind the table; two chairs, both designed for human rears, were placed prominently in front. It was a gesture of respect, Kevin realised, as well as an unspoken promise. The Varnar would respect humanity as long as humanity extended them the same courtesy.

"There have been developments," the lead Varner said, without preamble. They rarely bothered with anything humans would regard as social graces. "The Tokomak fleet was beaten. Soundly beaten."

"So I have heard," Kevin said, carefully. It was never a wise idea to let one side think they knew more than you, even if they did. "I assume there is a reason for this meeting?"

"We wish to discuss cooperation," the Varnar stated. "One of us has attempted to reach your people, but may not have succeeded. If he has been killed, your people will not have heard the message."

Kevin frowned. The messenger must have been with the Tokomak fleet, he realised slowly, or he could have just parked his ship on the edge of the Sol System and tried to raise the Solar Union. He wouldn't have been greeted with a hail of fire if he hadn't posed an immediate and obvious threat. Shooting first and asking questions later was rarely a good idea in interstellar relationships.

"I have not heard anything from my superiors," he said, smoothly. Given the time between the return of the fleet and the meeting, they wouldn't expect anything more. Human starships weren't significantly faster in FTL than Galactic ships. "However, I believe they would seek your cooperation, if you were prepared to offer it."

Sally prompted him helpfully as he negotiated quickly and efficiently. The Varnar didn't bargain, not as humans did; they rarely demanded much in the expectation of having to settle for little. They seemed happy to accept the end of the war, on terms. It was better, he hoped, than continuing the Proxy War indefinitely. If nothing else, the Coalition didn't need the Tokomak supplying the Varnar with warships and weapons until the sheer mass of supplies burned the Coalition beyond hope of recovery.

"Very well," the Varnar said, finally. The voice was largely toneless, but Kevin thought he detected a hint of anticipation in the alien's words. "When the time comes, we will switch sides."

With that, the meeting came to an end.

Once the Varnar were gone, Kevin allowed Sally to take him back to the apartment, but encoded a message for the team before he did anything else. There would be an opportunity to slip a message back to Earth soon enough, he knew, and then Earth would know what was brewing on Varnar. They could take advantage of it...

...And put an end to the war before it was too late.

— —

THE VARNAR WERE up to something. Neola was sure of it. Oh, they said all the right things and mouthed all the right platitudes, as if nothing was wrong with the universe, but they were up to something. Perhaps it was just paranoid, but after everything that had happened, she felt as though she had a right to be paranoid. But then, so did they.

Her terminal chimed. "Your Excellency," Captain Drew said, "the reinforcements have arrived."

Neola sent a silent command to the display, activating the holographic display. The gravity point was invisible to the naked eye, of course, but the stream of battleships materialising from a star system five hundred light years away were not. One hundred battleships, reinforcements she had demanded as soon as she'd realised the situation wasn't anything like she'd been told, ready to deal out death to the enemies of the empire.

They wouldn't be properly maintained, of course, she knew. But they wouldn't actually have to leave Varnar for weeks, if not months. By then, she would have the crews knocked into shape, with threats, rewards and the certain knowledge that failing to tend to their jobs – their proper jobs – would result in another disaster.

"Order the fleet to rendezvous with us," she said. "I will host the commanding officers in the lounge, once they have read the new standing orders. Tell them…tell them that they can make all the complaints they want and send them all the way to the homeworld if they wish, but they will carry out the standing orders. Anyone who balks will be executed."

"Yes, Your Excellency," Captain Drew said. If he doubted her words – or the wisdom of making enemies of so many officers – he allowed no trace of it in his voice. "It will be done."

They'd hate her, of course, Neola knew. For thousands of years, all the Navy had known was ceremonial formations and displays, each one perfectly calculated to show the grandeur and unstoppable might of the Tokomak. The commanding officers had lavished their wealth in ensuring that their ships showed off *their* power and resourcefulness. They had never really considered that they might have to fight. The thought of being told to ditch everything that had won them their spurs…

They'd be horrified. She had no doubt they would complain, long and loud, to their superiors – and demand her immediate relief from command. But they would do as they were told or they would die, either at her hands, if she dragged up very old regulations, or at the hands of the human race…

She allowed herself to smile, coldly, for the first time since she'd fled Earth. The humans thought they'd won. They thought there was nothing left to do, but mop up the remains of her fleet and the Varnar. But they were wrong.

It wasn't over yet.

THIRTY-EIGHT

The New Mexico State Government convened today to discuss the prospect of separating ties from the United States and declaring itself either part of Mexico or the independent state of Aztecan. In a statement issued yesterday, the Mexican Government declared that it would be happy to accept the return of territory stolen by the Gringos in the Mexican-American War. The White House has refused to comment, but given the demographics of the Southern United States, New Mexico may be merely the first state to go.

—Solar News Network, Year 53

"We have returned to normal space, sir," Yolanda said. "I am picking up IFF signs from human and Coalition warships."

"Good," Captain Singh said. "Transmit our IFF to them, then hold us steady."

"Yes, sir," Yolanda said.

She frowned as she did as she was told. The RV point was only five light years from Varnar, theoretically out of sensor range. She'd wondered why the higher-ups hadn't decided to assemble the fleet elsewhere, but she didn't know who she could ask. The orders had been passed down from Admiral Stuart himself, right from the very top. No doubt he had his reasons.

The fleet was huge, larger than she'd expected. Two hundred human warships, mostly converted Galactic starships, were aligned with over a thousand Coalition warships, many of them larger than anything under human command. She honestly didn't understand why the Coalition needed human help at all, until she remembered that the Varnar deployed much the same number of starships. The Proxy War had been balanced so perfectly that it could have gone on for centuries without either side gaining a decisive advantage.

And none of the battleships she saw through *Freedom's* sensors were anything like as large as the Tokomak ships. The Tokomak, it seemed, had mistaken size for power and forbidden anyone to build their own five kilometre-long starships. It wouldn't have been a bad gambit, she told herself, if weapons and training had remained static. But the Coalition had far more experience than the Tokomak, as well as human ingenuity. Given a few more years, those colossal battleships might be smashed as easily as clay targets on the shooting range.

"We're picking up orders from the flag," Commander Gregory said. "The fleet is to enter FTL in ten minutes. Destination; Varnar."

Yolanda sucked in her breath, feeling tension rising on the bridge. Varnar wouldn't just make or break the war, it would either ensure the victory of the Coalition or the ultimate success of the Tokomak. It was a gamble, all the more so as no one knew if the Tokomak had reinforcements on the way, but one that had to be taken. The Tokomak couldn't be allowed to fall back and prepare for a long war. Given the sheer preponderance of firepower on their side, it might well prove disastrous.

"Course laid in, sir," she said. "They'll see us coming."

"Unfortunately," Commander Gregory said, dryly. Her voice became contemplative. "The designated endpoint is surprisingly close to the gravity point."

"They probably want to bar the Tokomak from calling for help," Captain Singh speculated, cheerfully. "Commander. Is my ship ready for combat?"

"Yes, sir," Commander Gregory said. "Your ship is fully ready for command."

Yolanda smiled. The flight time between Earth and Varnar hadn't been wasted. Every last millimetre of the ship had been checked and rechecked for damage, then the crew had trained constantly until they could practically fight the battle in their sleep. The Tokomak might have realised the importance of training and experience after their catastrophic defeat, but they didn't have time to match the human ships. Or, for that matter, the Coalition.

But they might let the Varnar take the lead, she thought. *And that would be dangerous for us.*

"Signal from the flag," Commander Gregory said. "It's time to go."

"Take us into FTL," Captain Singh ordered.

"Aye, sir," Yolanda said. *Freedom* shivered slightly as she slipped into FTL, her drives compensating effortlessly for the presence of so many other starships nearby. "We're on the way."

— —

"YOUR EXCELLENCY," THE sensor officer reported. "We have picked up incoming signatures."

Neola leaned forward as brilliant red icons appeared on the display, advancing remorselessly towards Varnar. They were flying in close formation, making it impossible for her sensors to pick out individual starships, but there were definitely over a thousand warships inbound on her position. There was no way to determine the owners, not directly, yet she knew they had to include Coalition warships. If the humans had enjoyed so many ships, her force would have been utterly wiped out before it reached Earth.

"Bring the fleet to alert, then move our formations forward," she ordered. The Varnar might have more experience, but they didn't have something to prove. Besides, they could guard their homeworld, while *she* needed to guard the gravity point. "And inform the commanding officers that I expect them to do as they're told, rather than arguing over The Book."

"Yes, Your Excellency," Captain Drew said.

Neola smiled, rather coldly. Her staff had intercepted messages from her subordinate officers to her superiors, each one demanding her immediate removal from command. The reasons were many and varied, but they all boiled down to one simple fact. She just wasn't acting as a Tokomak should. Even after viewing the records of the battle, half of them still thought she was exaggerating the danger posed by the human race. Didn't they realise that a far larger force had been smashed midway to Earth?

But they see that as part of a trick, she thought. The gravity field that had yanked her ships out of FTL had been a nasty surprise, but it had inflicted a considerable amount of damage as well. Her subordinates wanted to believe that it had merely been a trick, because it was easier to accept a trick than the humans having any sort of qualitative advantage. *And so they are still inclined to dismiss the humans.*

Idly, she speculated on where the humans would choose to emerge. She'd tried discussing the concept of building her own gravity net with the Varnar, but they'd seemed adamant it would take at least ten years to build a similar device. By then, no doubt the humans would have thought of something new. She shook her head, then tapped the display with one long finger. Her subordinates might have opposed her in writing, but they weren't trying to defy her in the middle of a battle. Their formations were moving forward with commendable speed.

She turned her attention back to the main display as the human ships entered the system and advanced, still in FTL, towards the gravity point. It made sense, she told herself, even though the humans didn't realise just how strongly she'd been reinforced. Cut the Varnar off from the Tokomak...the Varnar would either have to retake the gravity point, whatever the cost, or accept eventual defeat. They wouldn't even be able to uncover their homeworld at all, not even to prevent the loss of other worlds...

"The human fleet is dropping out of FTL," the sensor officer stated. There was a long pause as the display started to update. "They're using some form of jamming, Your Excellency. It's hard to pick out individual ships."

Neola cursed. Trust the humans to come up with something new. The display was fuzzy, as though the sensor probes were reporting nothing, but gibberish. At one point, there seemed to be a million starships facing them; at another, less than a hundred. It would be hard – impossibly hard – to use any long-range missiles on the human fleet. But it would have been pointless anyway. This time, there was no gravity net.

"Prepare to engage," she ordered. The humans were still diving towards the gravity point, but her advance formations would get there first. And then the humans would have to come to them. "And order the Varnar to cover our backs."

"Yes, Your Excellency," Captain Drew said.

Neola forced herself to relax as the two fleets converged, sheer power allowing her sensors to burn through some of the layers of jamming. She'd been right, she noted; the Coalition had provided many of the warships facing her now. They didn't seem to have quite the flexibility of the cruisers the humans had built for themselves, but they did have more training and actual experience than any of her officers. And they were clearly prepared to make a stand against the Tokomak. They would die, of course, along with anyone else who dared question Tokomak power, but it was still disappointing.

"Raise them," she ordered. "Inform them that we will accept surrender."

There was a long pause. "No response, Your Excellency," the communications officer said. "They didn't even send an acknowledgement."

"Noted," Neola said. "Prepare to engage."

— —

MONGO SCOWLED AS he saw the Tokomak fleet – bare and exposed before his sensors – and cursed under his breath. He had never assumed that the Tokomak wouldn't get reinforcements, but he hadn't expected another hundred battleships and assorted escort vessels. It said unpleasant things about the Tokomak ability to mobilise their fleet rapidly, if necessary. A cursory glance at the sensor console told him that the Tokomak had even managed to improve their training procedures. Much of their equipment was primitive, by Coalition standards, but they were using it very well.

And just because someone is using primitive technology, he reminded himself, *doesn't make him either stupid or useless.*

Their formation was better too, he noted; they'd spread their ships out enough to allow them to fire freely, without limiting their ability to cover each other if necessary. It was still a crude formation, but better than their previous work. And, if their technology had been better, it would have made their victory certain. As long as they held the gravity point, they could keep feeding new starships into the sector and eventually bury everyone – even the Varnar – under the sheer weight of reinforcements.

"Inform all starships," he ordered. "They are to fire at will. I say again, fire at will."

YOLANDA BRACED HERSELF, then plunged her mind back into the computer network as the two fleets converged with terrifying speed. The Tokomak opened fire as soon as the humans came into range, scattering their fire madly through space; the Coalition, more disciplined, held their fire until they came into effective range, then opened fire themselves. And then the two fleets were joined...Yolanda hung on for dear life as she flipped the starship through a maze of evasive manoeuvres while Commander Gregory bombarded the Tokomak battleships with her weapons. One Tokomak battleship exploded in front of her, forcing her into another series of evasive patterns before a piece of debris struck them; moments later, she fell into formation with two other cruisers and raged towards a second battleship.

"Break left and right," she ordered, as the enemy ship fired towards them. There were just too many targets for the enemy to cope with; they tried to split their fire, too late. Human torpedoes slammed home, blowing the enemy ship into another ball of expanding plasma. "And then follow me."

She flew between two enemy battleships, then spun on a dime and raced back towards the closest ship, daring it to fire on her. *Freedom* shuddered as the enemy scored a direct hit, then Commander Gregory slammed four torpedoes into the enemy's hull. No one was trying to conserve torpedoes now. Moments later, it too was gone. Yolanda spared a thought for the ship's crew, dead before they had a chance to reach the lifepods, and then turned her attention back to the battle.

It was even, much more even than she'd dared fear. The Tokomak had taken losses, but they were inflicting them too. A number of Coalition and human ships had died, weakening their respective forces far more than the losses they'd inflicted on their enemies. It didn't seem fair, part of her mind whined as she evaded another burst of enemy fire; they could obliterate this enemy force, or one far larger, and *still* lose the war. But they couldn't avoid fighting either…

A missile cruiser – an adapted Galactic freighter – moved past her, spitting out missiles towards the Tokomak formation. They posed no threat to the enemy, Yolanda knew, but they would give her some cover. She flipped *Freedom* around, then followed the missiles as they lunged towards the Tokomak ship. By the time the missiles were all picked off, *Freedom* was in attack position and firing savagely. The Tokomak ship flipped out of formation, then lost power. Commander Gregory teleported a nuke into its suddenly-unsecure interior; Yolanda watched, as dispassionately as she could, as the ship exploded into a gout of fire.

Sooner or later, someone will figure out a way to beat teleport jamming, she thought. It was, after all, an obvious way to take out a starship. *And when they do, the universe will change once again.*

Freedom groaned again as two enemy blasts struck her shields, knocking her out of formation and right towards a third enemy cruiser, which lunged forward. Yolanda hastily evaded a deliberate attempt to ram her ship, then put some distance between herself and the suicidal crew. Everyone agreed the Tokomak were brave, if only because they had no real concept of defeat, but no one had suggested they were mad. But then, trading *Freedom* for one of their escort ships would be highly advantageous – to the enemy. They could replace their losses far faster than humanity, the Coalition and the Varnar combined.

"The Marines are ready to deploy," Captain Singh said. "Find them an ideal target."

"Yes, sir," Yolanda said. Five enemy battleships were heading towards the human formation, firing rapidly enough they were bound to hit *something*, even if their targeting was piss-poor. "I think I have one right here."

"Then take us right through their formation," Captain Singh said. "And launch ECM drones at the same time."

"Aye, sir," Commander Gregory said.

Yolanda thought, briefly, of Martin, then did as she was told.

— —

MARTIN HAD TO call on his implants to avoid panic as soon as he launched himself into space, even though he'd done the operation in simulators often enough to know what he was doing. There were just so *many* warships nearby, each one capable of swatting him like a bug if it bothered to notice the fire team. Four Marines simply didn't register on their sensors, not when the ECM drones were hitting them with sensor ghosts and other illusions. But if they happened to score a lucky hit…

He remained calm as the Tokomak warship rose up in front of him, a giant gleaming cylinder, glowing with light. Energy flickered and flared around them as they passed through its shields, then fell to the hull. As soon as they were on the surface, he led the charge to the airlock and forced it open, allowing the atmosphere to drain out. This time, he couldn't help noticing the enemy had clearly fixed their airlocks. This time, the outflow was surprisingly low. They'd clearly learned *something* from the last battle.

Quickly, he picked up the nuke – so small, for something so destructive – and shoved it into the hull, then banged the airlock closed. There was no time to waste; they launched themselves off the hull, heading right for the enemy shields. This time, they might not make it through before it was too late…

The nuke detonated. Below him, the enemy craft shuddered and lost power. Explosions flared out along her hull, although large parts of her remained intact. She'd been designed to cope with weapons a little bit stronger than nukes, Martin reminded himself; the briefing officers had even suggested that antimatter would have worked better, if there had been enough to go round. But it hardly mattered. The Tokomak ship would need years of work in a shipyard before she was back in fighting trim, if they bothered to waste the effort. Personally, he would have sent her to the yard for scrapping.

"The shuttle is on the way," Wilson said. "She'll take us to the next target."

Martin nodded, relieved. The naked eye couldn't see much, apart from flashes of light, but his suit was happily filling in the details. There were hundreds of starships, fighting and dying, all around him. He forced himself to look away, then focused on the databursts from the Marines. Two of the assault teams had been wiped out completely, probably through a lucky shot; a third had made it to their target, then detonated the nuke ahead of time, damaging the ship, but not knocking it out of the fight.

"So we go do it again," he said. The shuttle came into view, a tiny boxy craft, covered with stealth coating that should have made it invisible. "And again and again, until they wise up."

A streak of light flashed through space and struck the shuttle, which exploded. Martin gaped, then hastily pushed himself away from where the craft had been. He hadn't even seen the enemy ship that had fired the fatal shot! But it had clearly seen *something*…maybe they'd mistaken the shuttle for an ECM drone or maybe it had been a lucky shot…it didn't matter, not really. All that mattered was that they were stranded in the middle of a battlefield.

"Contact Fleet Command," he ordered. If the enemy were looking for shuttles now, it was unlikely a second craft would be sent to rescue them. No ship would risk lowering its teleport shields long enough to snatch them up, not when the enemy would be watching and waiting for such a moment of weakness. "Inform them of our status and request pickup."

He closed his eyes for a long moment, then accessed the suit's sensors once again. If nothing else, he could watch the battle...and pray that someone remained alive long enough to pick them up, once the battle was done.

THIRTY-NINE

A privately-funded college was today surrounded by protesters demanding the immediate restoration of a lecturer who was suspended, two weeks ago, for turning his lectures into political seminars. In a statement issued after the protests began, the College President noted that none of the protestors actually studied at the college and opinion among the student body was largely in favour of the suspension. However, the lecturer has lodged a claim of political discrimination with the state anti-discrimination body...

—Solar News Network, Year 53

It was hard, very hard, to tell which side was actually winning.

The Human-Coalition Alliance was inflicting more losses, Mongo was sure, but the Tokomak simply had more ships and firepower. They could afford to trade ten-for-one indefinitely, if they liked, knowing they could just keep reinforcements flowing down the chain from their homeworld. In the meantime, humanity would have to replace its losses through new construction and there was no way that could match the deployment of older, but still functional starships.

And then there were the Varnar...

Their starships were hanging back, avoiding involvement on either side. Mongo couldn't tell if they were hedging their bets or if they were waiting for the right moment to stab the Tokomak in the back. Were they hoping the Tokomak would weaken their rivals first, before they attacked, in the hopes of winning the entire sector? Humanity was far from the only race to notice just how weak the Tokomak actually were...

He shook his head, then keyed a switch. "Inform our Varnar friend that the time has come," he ordered. On the display, a human starship blew a Tokomak battleship apart, only to be swatted out of space by a hail of fire from another battleship. "They need to take a side now or be forever under the Tokomak thumb."

SHE WAS WINNING.

It was slow, very slow, and painful, yet she was winning. The enemy might have been hurting her fleet – that was unarguable – but she simply had more starships than they did and the promise of far more reinforcements to come. One by one, the advanced starships were being swatted out of space, smashed to pieces by her firepower. And the enemy formation was starting to come apart.

Although they might have designed it that way, she thought. The Tokomak had envisaged space battles as slow and stately, while the humans had devised battle tactics that relied on speed and decisiveness. They treated their cruisers as if they were expendable gunboats, each one darting *through* her formations and daring her ships to fire, knowing the risk of hitting their fellows. *Can I truly count on it?*

But the Coalition fought normally, she saw, and it was slowly losing. She knew it was humiliating to see her ships perform so badly against their enemies, but she was slowly winning. Even if her fleet was wiped out, the Coalition wouldn't recover in time before her reinforcements arrived, bent on revenge. The Proxy War would come to an end as her people imposed direct rule on the troublesome sector.

She leaned forward, then smiled. "Advance the fleet forward," she ordered. "Force them to engage us at close range."

It was clear the humans hadn't shared their tactics with their allies. The Coalition ships were as slow and stately as her own – and smaller, too. Their datanets were better and their weapons more advanced, but they couldn't match the sheer number of weapons crammed into her battleships. A close-range duel favoured her, even though the enemy had more experience and advanced technology. And, without the Coalition, the humans would be unable to stand up to their enemies.

Or maybe the Coalition didn't see the value in their proposed techniques, she thought. *They wouldn't want to risk throwing out The Book when The Book helped us win an empire…*

"Your Excellency," the sensor officer snapped. "The Varnar are targeting us!"

Neola looked up, shocked. She'd suspected betrayal, but not in the middle of a battle.

"Raise them," she snapped. "Demand to know what they're doing…"

"The Varnar have opened fire," the sensor officer reported. "And they're hacking into our datanet!"

"Lock them out," Neola thundered. She'd had no choice, but to allow them to link into the datanet, despite the risk. Now…it had turned into a disaster. The Varnar didn't have override authority, in theory, yet they had the access they needed to hack into the main systems and insert viruses. "Crash and reform the datanet, if necessary."

She turned her head towards the display. The Varnar were hammering the rear of her formation, which had been caught completely by surprise. Demands for orders were popping up in front of her, even as the Varnar pushed their sudden advantage. And she honestly didn't know what to do.

"Lock missiles on the planet and fire," she snapped. Most of the missiles, perhaps all of them, would be taken out by the defenders, but it would give them something else to think about than merely hammering the rear of her fleet. "And then converge all of our ships on the gravity point."

"Yes, Your Excellency," Captain Drew said.

Neola forced herself to think as her subordinates struggled to obey her orders. She'd been winning…now, she was losing, thanks to the Varnar. She wanted to turn on them, to obliterate them for daring to take a stand, but they'd timed it perfectly. If she tried to attack their homeworld, she would be obliterated by the combined fleet; if she turned on their ships to the exclusion of all else, she would be destroyed by the Coalition. There was no option, but retreat.

"And all ships are to put the Varnar on top of their targeting lists," she added. There would be time for ruthless extermination later; right now, she would settle for whatever revenge she could get. "Their ships are to be smashed."

THE GRAVITY POINT was an odd twist in the fabric of space-time; invisible, unsurprisingly, to the naked eye, but all too clear to the starship's sensors. Yolanda yanked *Freedom* around the gravity point and took her back towards the battle, just in time to see that the situation had changed completely. The Varnar had opened fire…on the Tokomak. And the Tokomak seemed to be ignoring everyone else, in favour of trying to slaughter the Varnar.

"Interesting," Captain Singh said. Missiles were roaring towards Varnar itself, aimed right at the planet's surface. "And positively encouraging."

He paused. "Take us towards the Tokomak," he added. "Right into their midst."

The Tokomak seemed confused, Yolanda noted, as she obeyed. She pulled the ship through a series of sweeping evasive tricks, but hardly any of the Tokomak ships bothered to fire on her, even though they knew human ships were deadly. And their datanet was fragmenting. Instead of every ship working in unison, they all seemed to have fallen back on their own resources.

"Fire," Captain Singh ordered.

Yolanda smiled as Commander Gregory opened fire. The Tokomak fired back, but their shots were badly aimed. Two of them even grazed their own ships in their confusion, while the human ships opened fire with missiles of their own. They should have been useless, Yolanda knew, but the Tokomak were too confused to take effective countermeasures.

Behind her, the remainder of the Human-Coalition fleet surged forward, targeting the gravity point. The Tokomak twisted and turned, but they were caught between two fires; they couldn't turn to deal with one of them without being taken out by the other. Yolanda would have felt sorry for them, if she hadn't known they'd tried to bombard Earth into radioactive ashes. Some of their ships were already breaking formation and trying to escape...

And then waves of twisted gravity shimmered through space. It wasn't enough to cause damage, but it was enough to prevent a starship from dropping into FTL. One wave struck the gravity point, disrupting its stability; two starships which attempted to pass through it shattered into debris, which was tossed through space with terrific force. The Tokomak were trapped.

"We have them, Captain," Commander Gregory reported.

"Then keep firing until they see sense and surrender," Captain Singh ordered. "The battle isn't over yet."

NEOLA FELT COLD ice trickling down the back of her spine as she saw the shift in the gravity point. The Tokomak had always assumed the gravity points were fixed, utterly immutable...but then, they hadn't been stupid enough to experiment on them. If they'd somehow shut down a single gravity point, or the whole network, it would have destroyed their empire. And they had discouraged advanced gravity research, out of fear that someone might manage to do just that...

...And the humans, it seemed, had made that fear *real*.

She studied the display for a long moment and realised the battle was lost. The Varnar had tipped the balance in favour of the Human-Coalition Alliance, while the humans had trapped her ships thousands of light years from home. There was no hope of escape, or of inflicting enough losses to make up for the sheer scale of the defeat. The Tokomak Empire was in very real trouble. Once word of *this* defeat reached restive subject races, it wouldn't be long before they too started to rebel.

And her crews, the handful of officers and crewmen who had experience of actually *fighting* would be lost. It could not be allowed.

"Raise the enemy flagship," she ordered. "Tell them we wish to surrender, on terms."

There was a long pause. Then messages started blinking up in her display, not from the humans, but from the other ships in the fleet. None of their commanders seemed willing to believe she would countenance a surrender, no matter what else happened. The Tokomak didn't surrender to lesser races…except they had, during the earlier battle.

"I'm picking up a message from the human commander," the communications officer said. "They're willing to accept surrender, but they want us to cease fire at once and hold position."

"Do so," Neola ordered.

She keyed her console, opening a channel to the other ships, as she searched frantically for words. The Tokomak didn't surrender. Everyone knew they took surrenders, but never surrendered. Except they did.

"This is a direct order from the flag," she said, finally. "There is to be no argument, no debate. The battle is lost. You are ordered to surrender, if we can get suitable terms, and obey all orders from the humans in line with those terms. I take full responsibility for ordering the surrender.

"Hold your fire, but keep your shields and jammers up until we come to terms," she added, keeping her voice even. The defeat would echo through the empire, until its very foundations were badly shaken. "Do not engage the enemy any further without my specific authorisation."

She closed the channel before anyone could respond, then looked over at the communications officer. "Tell the humans that we would like to surrender in line with standard protocols," she said. "And add that I suggest they hurry."

— —

MONGO FROWNED AS the enemy fire came to an end.

"Inform them that they will be taken into POW camps and treated in line with the standard protocols of the Proxy War," he said. "But we want their computer datacores intact."

He settled back in his chair as the message was sent, thinking hard. He wasn't blind to some of the implications. It was rare for anyone of significant importance to be captured, which was why prisoner trading took place on a regular basis, but the Tokomak simply didn't have many experienced officers and crewmen. Returning the captured Tokomak would only make them more dangerous, even if they agreed the returnees wouldn't be allowed to go back to war. Their other trainees would be able to learn from the ones who had fought and survived.

"They are willing to accept your terms," the communications officer said.

"Then tell them to drop shields and jammers," Mongo ordered. He was surprised; he had expected more of an argument, or perhaps a demand that their surrender be to a specific race in the hopes of causing trouble for the alliance. "The Marines will be on their way shortly to accept their surrender."

Maybe we beat hell out of them, he thought. It was something he'd seen before, on the battlefields of Earth. A side that believed itself to have been thoroughly defeated, like France in 1940 or the United States in Vietnam, was often unable to summon the willpower to fight back effectively, even though it might not have actually *lost*. The Tokomak might have reached a stage where they had been psychologically defeated, to the point where physical resistance was impossible.

"They have confirmed their surrender," the communications officer said.

"Raise the Varnar," Mongo ordered. Shipping the prisoners to Earth or a Coalition world would be a logistical nightmare. "Ask them to prepare POW camps for a few hundred thousand prisoners."

He sighed. Now the battle had come to an end, it was far too possible that the war between the Coalition and the Varnar would reignite, even though it would be suicide. Surely, both sides would realise the advantages in cooperating? Or would they seek to declare their independence from one another to the point they would refuse to work together, even if they needed to help one another.

A problem for the diplomats, he thought. Interstellar diplomacy was complex, far more than fighting a battle. If humans could get offended over the merest of things, aliens were far worse. *Hopefully, it's one I won't have to solve.*

— —

"THIS COULD BE worse," Wilson said.

"Thank you," Martin said, dryly. The interior of the Tokomak ship was giving him flashbacks to the desperate struggle near Earth. "And *how* could it be worse?"

"We could still be drifting in space," Wilson pointed out. "Or we could be the last survivors of the battle."

"Shut up," Martin said. "And keep a sharp eye on the bastards."

He gritted his teeth. They'd been teleported to the nearest cruiser as soon as the battle had come to an end, then sent to the Tokomak flagship to assume control. So far, there hadn't been any resistance, but he wasn't feeling hopeful. The way the Tokomak were looking at him and his crew, it felt as though they were going to do something stupid any second now.

They've been masters of the universe so long, he thought, *that they can't abide the thought of their own defeat*.

They reached the command core without incident, much to his relief. A handful of Tokomak stood in the centre of the compartment, their personal weapons lying on the deck. Their faces were twisted with some unreadable emotion, but they seemed to have themselves under control. Martin motioned for them to step to one side, then hacked into the nearest console and linked through to their command datacores. As ordered, they remained intact and open, just waiting for the spooks to go to work.

"You will be taken from this place to a POW camp, where your needs will be met," he informed them. It struck him, suddenly, that their leader was familiar; he'd seen her vanishing into a teleport field, weeks ago. Now, there was no way out. "And you will be returned to your people once we have a definite peace treaty."

The Tokomak offered no resistance as they were shepherded through the corridors and out to the airlocks, where the Varnar shuttles were already waiting. It wouldn't be easy to set up so many POW camps on such short notice, Martin knew, assuming his experiences in the Sol System were any guide. But at least it would give the Varnar something to do and keep them from causing trouble, as well as making it impossible for them to backslide. The Tokomak wouldn't forgive in a hurry.

He pushed the thought to one side as the spooks arrived and started to copy the datacores into their systems, before the ship was even completely emptied of her crew. The spooks didn't seem to give a shit about the risks, so Martin settled for keeping a wary eye on them as the remaining Tokomak were herded down to the airlocks and sent to Varnar. It was nearly four hours before the ship was finally empty, by which time the situation outside the hull had settled down...

"You can go back to the ship in twenty minutes," Captain Lockland ordered. "You have some relief on the way, from the Varnar. They want a handful of these ships for themselves."

"Understood," Martin said. There hadn't been *that* many Solar Marines attached to the fleet, if only because no one expected the Tokomak to allow themselves to be boarded and stormed again. But then, they hadn't had time to scream for groundpounders as well as starships before the final battle began. "We'll teleport back as soon as they arrive."

— —

"It wasn't the final battle," Yolanda said, later. "There's a much larger empire out there, even if we are sitting on top of the gravity point. They could keep coming at us until they win."

"Maybe they've been beaten too badly to think about it," Martin said. "Or...

His voice trailed off. He'd seen too many fights in the ghetto to fail to miss the obvious. The Tokomak here might know they had been beaten, but their distant masters would be completely untouched by the fighting. It wouldn't be quite *real* to them. They would try to learn from the experience, but they wouldn't surrender. Instead, they'd just keep sending their people to die until they either won the war – or lost completely.

"Enjoy the peace while it lasts," he said. Maybe the diplomats would come to some agreement with the Tokomak. But their pride and reputation had been so badly dented that they would have no choice, but to either continue the war or accept the loss of their empire when their subjects rebelled. "It's all we can do, really."

FORTY

Reports are just coming in of a military coup in Washington, DC. Soldiers from the 3rd Infantry Division have seized the White House, the Pentagon and other buildings of political, military and historical importance, while Marines have sealed the city and have been conducting house-to-house searches for certain people. Local radio and television channels have been broadcasting messages warning people to stay indoors and informing them that a Government of National Salvation will be assuming control shortly…

…As yet, there has been no word from the President. However, there are reports of violent protests and riots in a dozen cities, with community leaders screaming their outrage into the datanet. Many of the riots have started to take on the air of ethnic cleansing, as they are primarily directed against other ethnic and religious groups. Churches, mosques and synagogues have been destroyed, forcing their occupants to flee. Armed vigilantes are patrolling hundreds of communities, despite strict gun control laws…

—Solar News Network, Year 53

"And you think the peace treaty will hold?"

Kevin smiled. After spending two weeks meditating while the Coalition and the Varnar haggled, it was almost a relief to face the War

Cabinet. They might order his immediate sacking, certainly for exceeding his orders to some degree, but they wouldn't restart a war that would weaken the sector to the point the Tokomak could just come back and take over without a fight.

"I believe both sides understand they need to cooperate," he said, calmly. "They will not be entirely *happy* about the terms, but they have little choice. The Tokomak will be back, sooner or later."

The President nodded. "And our own role in this?"

"They do want to trade technology with us," Kevin said. "But I don't think we can maintain a monopoly on everything for much longer, in any case. We have shown too many people what is possible and knowing what can be done is half the battle. Trading will probably help us to garner extra political influence – and warships, of course. We're going to need them in the future.

"And as for joining the expanded Coalition…well, it's time we committed ourselves," he added. "*Someone* has to sit between the two sides, if nothing else."

"That will have to be discussed in the Senate," Bute said.

"I can't see them all being happy about it," Marie added. "We chose not to join formally for a reason, Director."

"I know," Kevin said. "But the Proxy War is now over, thanks to us. We owe it to ourselves to both stand against the Tokomak and try to keep the Coalition together."

He sighed. So far, all attempts to raise the Tokomak Government and come to a permanent agreement had failed. It wouldn't be long, he suspected, before the Tokomak Government attempted to launch yet another attack on the sector, probably through the gravity point at Varnar. The disrupter had worked once, but it wouldn't work indefinitely. Besides, sooner or later, the Tokomak would find a way to reverse its effects.

And after that? God alone knew what would happen.

"We keep working with our allies, we keep developing our own technology and we keep focusing on ultimate victory," he added. "We have a talent for helping people of different races to work together, after all. I think we should use it."

"The Senate will debate the issue," the President said. "And much else."

Kevin nodded. The Council had bent the rules as far as they would go – and *that* couldn't go unpunished. In a week or two, the Senate would assemble to pass judgement on the Councillors, including the President. It was quite possible that they would all find themselves unemployed, shortly afterwards. They hadn't exactly *abused* their positions, which would have guaranteed a jail term, but they had certainly bent the letter of the law. The Senate might not approve.

Steve would have approved of them standing in judgement, he thought, ruefully. *He always thought the politicians should be held accountable by the people.*

"So," Bute said. "We now have the issue of a coup in the United States."

"It isn't our concern," Marie snapped. "We stay out of politics on Earth for a reason."

Kevin smiled, then rose. The coup bothered him on an emotional level – if it succeeded, it meant the end of America; if it failed, it *also* meant the end of America – but it really wasn't his concern. His home was the Solar Union now…absently, he wondered how Mongo would take the news. He had always been less…flexible where patriotism was concerned.

"With your permission," he said, "I will return to my duties. There is much work to be done."

"And the prospect of losing your job," the President noted. "Good luck, Director."

Kevin nodded and walked through the hatch, past a pair of armed Marines. Outside, Sally was waiting for him, sitting on a bench.

"I hope that didn't take as long as you feared," Kevin said. The asteroid's garden was lovely, even though it was utterly untamed. He was tempted to just walk with her for hours and forget the universe. "I'm sorry about bringing you back here."

"I wasn't wanted back on Varnar," Sally said. "Not after..."

"I'm sorry," Kevin said. Mr. Ando had politely, but firmly, released Sally from her duties after the war had come to an end. "But I do have a job offer for you, if you want it."

Sally's lips thinned. "Spying?"

"Helping the diplomats," Kevin said. "Earth is probably going to be hosting more talks over the next few months. You're already experienced in dealing with aliens, you have quite a few contacts of your own and... well, you'd be good at the job. Or you can try to find a job elsewhere. There are no shortage of corporations planning to do business with aliens who would find you very useful."

"I'll think about it," Sally said. "But thank you."

"You're welcome," Kevin said. "And, for what it's worth, you more than earned that medal."

Sally snorted, then rose and started to walk through the garden.

After a moment, Kevin followed her.

"I'M BEING ASSIGNED to *Formidable*," Martin said, awkwardly. They sat together in their hotel room, on shore leave. "And yourself?"

"*Thor*," Yolanda said. "I've been promised a fast track to Commander if I do well, but apparently I need some more seasoning before they can give me the rank."

"They told me I might be promoted to Lieutenant myself, depending on the new recruits," Martin said. "Apparently, someone filmed our adventures in space and sent the records to the datanet. *Everyone* wants to be a Marine."

"You might be getting new recruits from Earth too," Yolanda reminded him. "Have you seen the news?"

"They're saying it's the beginning of the end," Martin said. "A coup in Washington, tanks on the streets in the South, race riots in a hundred cities...it's good we got out, I think.

He shivered. If he'd still been on Earth, he would probably have joined one of the black mobs driving everyone else out of the area. And if he'd been born white or brown, he would have joined one of *their* mobs and practiced ethnic cleansing on their behalf instead. His life would have come to an end, perhaps, when the government sent in the tanks… or perhaps it would have been destroyed in an orgy of rape and looting. And, in the end, what would it have gained anyone? His life in the Solar Union was so much more fulfilling.

"Yeah," Yolanda said. He wondered if she was thinking about her father and stepmother. "It could have been worse."

Martin hesitated. He'd never really talked to a girl before moving to the Solar Union, not really. The ghetto didn't encourage long relationships, if only because a person could get more benefits from the system by remaining single. Besides, it wasn't a manly thing to do, he'd been told. Fuck them and leave them…maybe, if he survived his teenage years, then he could consider a relationship. It had honestly never occurred to him just how destructive many of the patterns were until he was seeing them from the outside.

"If I wait for you," he said, "will you wait for me?"

"I would love to," Yolanda said. "But can we?"

They'd been lucky, Martin knew. They'd started as friends and then become lovers. And they'd been assigned to the same ship…

But that had finally come to an end. Who knew when they would see each other again?

Robbins was right, he thought. *This is the moment of decision.*

He swallowed, then pushed forward. "If you find someone else, while you're on your ship and I'm on mine, I won't mind," he said. "And we can try again after we finish our terms…"

"I don't think you want to finish your term," Yolanda said. "You've found a *meaning* in the Marine Corps."

Martin nodded. She was right. There were no shortage of jobs for retired Marines, but he didn't *want* to retire.

"And yourself?" He asked, dreading the answer. "Do you want to stay in for life?"

"I don't know," Yolanda admitted. "I'm twenty-two. I have hundreds of years ahead of me."

"I know," Martin said. Yolanda could stay in the navy for fifty years, then buy her own starship and go trading among the stars, or simply find something else to do with her time, if she wished. "I may change my mind too, after a hundred years of being shot at."

Yolanda smiled. "You might," she agreed.

"Then we will see," Martin said. He leaned forward to kiss her. "And, whatever happens, I will always be your friend."

— —

THEY HAD LET her go.

Neola didn't understand why the humans had simply let her go. She had agreed, of course, to carry their messages of peace to the Old Ones, but any Tokomak could have done that! And she was the one who had surrendered an entire fleet to its enemies. It was unlikely the Old Ones would want anything to do with her, after that failure. They were much more likely to hurl her out the airlock bodily rather than risk her defeatism contaminating the younger generations.

But it wasn't defeatism, not really,

The humans were strong, and innovative, and very determined to win. And so, in their way, were both powers in the Proxy War. But their alliance didn't have the towering resources of the Tokomak, let alone the colossal advantage in manpower and scientific understanding. The younger generations could be forced into preparing for war, the older teachings could be swept aside and the scientists, who had thought they knew all there was to know about the universe, reenergised by evidence of human discoveries.

She would go home and she would *make* the Old Ones listen. Or she would remove them from power, whatever the cost. They would come to understand just how dangerous the humans were…and just how badly their reputation had been shattered by their defeats. The Reserve would be activated, new spacers would be trained and then the Tokomak would go back to war, having rediscovered their own vigour. Next time, it would be a different story.

Neola sat in her cabin and waited. It was only a few months from Varnar to the Homeworld, after which she could get to work. The Old Ones would listen or the entire empire would be destroyed. She would *make* them listen. Her race had conquered an empire before, crushing all opposition with ease. They could do it again.

Next time, she promised herself, it would be different.

The End

AFTERWORD

In 2003, I attended a talk on Islamophobia – in particular, it's historical background. The speaker, who demonstrated an impressive grasp of the sweep of history, asserted that the Western World had been waging war on Islam ever since its foundation and put forward a historical pattern that seemed to support that argument. Leaving aside the flaws with that approach, there was still one major problem.

It was utter nonsense.

As I saw it, and said at the time, no one in modern Britain really gives a damn about what happened between King Richard and Saladin. Most people think of King Richard as nothing more than a background character in the tale of Robin Hood, the lionhearted king who left his wicked brother on the throne while he went off to fight in the Holy Land. They don't really draw a connection between the Muslim armies of Saladin (a fascinating character in his own right) and the terrorist scum who slaughter everyone who doesn't agree with their ideology 100%. Very few could tell the difference between the Four Caliphs who followed the Prophet, let alone the origin of the Sunni-Shia Split. It was simply immaterial to them, while 9/11, bomb attacks in Britain, raving madmen in the streets and waves of blatantly uncivilised barbarities were all too material.

In short, modern-day Islamophobia was fed by acts committed by Muslims today.

The average British citizen doesn't have a decent grasp of history. Personally, I find that somewhat regrettable. There have been quite a few darker moments in British history – Bloody Mary, Charles and Cromwell, King John – but there have also been moments we can and should be proud of, if we knew they existed. Most of our historical education is biased or overly simplistic. I've had teachers who taught about the glories of an independent Scotland and others who refused to discuss the British Empire out of fear it might offend the students of Indian or Pakistani descent in the class. And, of course, there are no shortages of lessons from history that really should be remembered today.

But this does have one advantage. We don't let past history overshadow our future.

Let me put this in perspective. We fought two wars with the Germans, last century, that were among the bloodiest in human history. The Germans committed unspeakable acts in the name of National Socialism. But, right now, we don't hold those crimes against their modern-day descendents. We draw a line between the shockingly evil Germans of the past and the Germans who live today. And we do the same for our other historical enemies. How many people know – really know – that we fought two wars with the United States?

In one sense, at least, history is over. The winners won, the losers lost – and it is over. And everyone involved is dead.

This is true of other nations too. Most of the politicians – Israeli, Arab, Palestinian, American, French, British – who played a role in the foundation of Israel are dead. The holocaust? Pretty much everyone responsible is dead. Japanese war crimes? Pretty much everyone responsible is dead. The Armenian Genocide? Pretty much everyone responsible is dead.

What other historical injustices are there? American slavery and the Confederate States of America? There isn't a single person alive who fought on either side of the American Civil War. The Indian Wars? Ditto. The Highland Clearances? Ditto. The oldest living human being in existence is a mere 116 years old. How responsible are they for crimes that took place before their birth?

The West generally chooses not to dwell on history. And that isn't always a bad idea.

Yes, the Germans committed horrific war crimes. But persecuting the current generation of Germans for what their ancestors did is counterproductive. At best, it will lead to sullen resentment; at worst, it will lead to another war. (Blaming the Germans for everything worked out *so* well in 1919.) Nor does it do much good to nag the Turks over the Armenian Genocide. The guilty are dead and their descendents are innocent of their crimes.

But, as Dale Cozort points out in his essay, *The Power of Get Over It*, there are parts of the world where history casts a long shadow over the landscape. They tend to be among the worst places to live. As Dale says, people dwelling on ancient injustices and using them as excuses to fight tear their own societies apart. Anyone with half a brain gets out, leaving the remainder to fight, suffer and die.

That is not to say that we should forget history. Merely, perhaps, that we should not allow it to drive us.

— —

BUT THAT ISN'T the easiest thing to do, is it?

It's easy to say to someone in Palestine (or Israel, for that matter) that they should let go of the past. But how can they? For Israel, history shows that their enemies are determined to destroy them and any show of weakness will only invite attack; for Palestine, history shows that Israel will keep them crushed and weak, while their Arab neighbours prefer to use them as rallying cries rather than treat them as equals. Indeed, history ensures that neither side can actually win, or even escape. The conflict is seemingly endless because there are factors preventing either side from scoring a decisive victory.

Nor are they the only people in the Middle East affected by the curse of history. Much of the current crisis in Iraq could fairly be termed the result of *ignoring* history – and the underlying realities of the Middle East.

As I have noted before, Iraq was divided between three different sects; Sunni, Shia and Kurd. The Sunnis were on top, under Saddam, and thus supported his rule, because they knew that if they fell from power, their enemies would want revenge. In the wake of the American Invasion of 2003, they were proved right…which forced them to turn to the Jihadists for support. Even when the United States managed to crush the jihadists and build new power structures, Iraq remained poor because the Shia were reluctant to share power and money. Unsurprisingly, the Sunni – feeling themselves marginalised – allowed the ISIS to return to Iraq.

Could this have been prevented? Yes, it could have been, but only if history was acknowledged, then deliberately overridden. Power could have been shared out in a balancing act that supported all three factions, making it impossible (or at least much harder) for sloth, apathy and downright hatred to shatter the peace. This would have required, however, constant engagement from the United States, which simply wasn't forthcoming.

— —

BUT EVEN THAT leads to another problem that must be faced.

I referred to 'Sunni,' 'Shia' and 'Kurd' as groups. This does not allow for any recognition of them as *individuals*. The idea that someone can be born of a mixed marriage – and thus have a fair claim to being 'Sunni-Shia' – is not recognised within this structure. There were no shortage of mixed marriages within Iraq, but any children born to such unions would have problems defining which group they actually belonged to. (A problem that also appeared in Ireland and every other multi-ethnic society.) Nor are these the only groups, the only ways o drawing lines between one group of humans and another.

Consider. Christians. Muslims. Jews.

That's three groups right there. But…Christians (Protestant, Catholic). Muslims (Sunni, Shia). Jews (Orthodox, Reform). How many groups do we have now?

And that's only based on religion. What about race? White, Black, Brown, Yellow…? Sexuality? Straight, Gay, Bi, Mono…?

To cut short a long list of potential examples, just how many ways are there to separate humanity into subgroups?

This is a very dangerous trend. *People are not numbers.* How can you lump together people into one group, based on outward appearance, religion or sexuality? I would not care to be judged by some of the worst examples of my kind. But that is precisely what the so-called Social Justice Warriors do.

— —

LIKE SO MANY other political concepts, particularly those relating to political correctness, 'Social Justice' and 'Social Justice Warrior' are slippery. Any attempt to define them runs into problems; there are, as always, exceptions to every rule (which ironically undermines their core position.) As I see it, 'Social Justice' refers to 'justice' for groups, while 'Social Justice Warrior' refers to those who fight for 'justice' for groups. (Or, given that most of them are active on the internet, rant and rave for 'justice' for groups.)

This is problematic for many different reasons, but the most important one, in my opinion, is that it erases the individual in favour of the group. It is more important, according to the Social Justice Warriors, to belong to a group, rather than stand as an individual. What this means, in practice, is that you will be *judged* by your group, rather than your own merits.

The ideal of the West is that of individual rights and responsibilities, with all equal before the law. Little details such as age, gender, race, religion and suchlike are held to be unimportant; all are equal before the law. The idea put forward by Social Justice Warriors, encouraged by radicals from all sorts of factions, is that the rights of *groups* come before the rights of *individuals*. As such – for example – black men in America can be determined to belong to their own group, as do American white men. Homosexuals are another such group; a gay man will not be regarded as an individual, but as part of the Gay Community. Naturally, Islam is considered one such group, even though (as I have noted above) Islam is *not* one unified entity.

This gets more complicated when you add in the concept of automatic victims and victimisers. By belonging to a designated 'victim' group, a person or group of persons is given a free pass by Social Justice Warriors. Alternatively, if a person should belong to a 'victimiser' group, he is savagely attacked by 'intellectuals.' On a national scale, Israel is always treated as the guilty party by the liberal media, rather than any attempt to provide a balanced view. (For example, rocket attacks from the West Bank or Gaza are ignored, while the eventual Israeli response receives massive condemnation.) On a more local scale, the shooting of Trayvon Martin by George Zimmerman rapidly turned into a media circus, with the prosecutors ignoring all of the evidence that didn't fit their approved story – Martin was shot because he was black (and therefore a designated victim) and his killer was white (a designated victimiser.)

(Just to complicate matters, George Zimmerman was actually Hispanic. Under other circumstances, he could easily have been a 'victim' rather than a 'victimiser.')

If this is bad enough, consider this. The Social Justice Warriors consider you (and everyone else) to be bound to their groups. Not unlike the ancient idea of social immobility (where if you were born a serf, you stayed a serf until the day you died) the Social Justice Warriors argue that you cannot escape your race, religion, sexuality or anything else that can be used to draw a line between one group of humans and another. It is your task to *support* your group, because you are nothing without it.

And where this turns actively poisonous is when the Social Justice Warriors attack those who dare to *leave*, because this calls their entire ethos into question. Thus, in the wake of the last set of midterm US elections, we have been treated to shocking displays of racial attacks mounted against newly-elected black politicians who dared to call themselves republicans. 'Race Traitor' is among the kindest charge hurled at them. And this was done, mostly, by Social Justice Warriors.

Why?

The average Social Justice Warrior rarely thinks of anyone as an individual, not when said individual can be considered part of a group. It does not suit their narrative to have individuals from such groups setting out on their own...or calling the narrative into question. If blacks are oppressed across America, one might ask, how did a black man become a Republican Senator? Was he ever truly 'one of us.'?

— —

THIS IS CORROSIVE to society in so many different ways. Social Justice Warriors, with the best of intentions, may insist that police departments reflect the racial make-up of their communities. BUT...this raises dangerous questions about the competence of the police force. Did a certain officer get his badge because he earned it...or because the department had to meet some affirmative action target? Imagine yourself an officer in that police station. Can you trust your fellow officer when you suspect he got the job without the right qualifications? Or, if you *were* that officer, how would you feel knowing that your fellows distrusted you?

It gets worse. Cries of 'racism,' 'sexism,' and all other forms of discrimination have only made it harder for anyone to see *real* racism, assuming it exists. 'Racism' has become an easy stick to use to beat someone, with the net result that the worth of the word has declined sharply. Indeed, it has pervaded our society to the point where the so-called 'racist' must prove his innocence, rather than the accuser prove his guilt. But how do you prove a negative?

These days, I never believe *any* charges of racism until I am given substantial proof, simply because it is far too easy to say the word.

And so, with the best possible motives, the Social Justice Warriors have corroded the foundations of our society.

— —

No one would deny that grave crimes have been committed throughout history. The oppressors of one century may well be the oppressed of the next. But constantly digging up crimes and using them as justifications for other crimes only keeps those conflicts going, over and over and over again. It would be nice, perhaps, to build a society on the other side of the moon, where the sole condition for entry is that you leave the past behind.

But perhaps that is only dreaming. Perhaps we have so much history behind us that it overshadows our future.

Christopher G. Nuttall
Edinburgh, 2014